A Book Of

ORGANISATIONAL BEHAVIOUR

For
MBA (Semester - I)
Choice Based Credit System and Grading System
MPM (Semester I) and PGDBM (Semester I)
As Per New Revised Syllabus
Effective from June 2016

Sunil Lalla
B.A., M.B.A., M.M.M., D.P.L. (Diploma in Taxation Laws)

Dr Praveen Prasad
M.Com., Ph.D. and D.H.E. (Diploma in Higher Education)

NIRALI PRAKASHAN
ADVANCEMENT OF KNOWLEDGE

N2955

Organisational Behaviour - MBA, MPM and P.G.D.B.M. (Sem. - I)

First Edition : July 2016

© : Authors

Published By :
NIRALI PRAKASHAN
Abhyudaya Pragati, 1312, Shivaji Nagar,
Off J.M. Road, PUNE – 411005
Tel - (020) 25512336/37/39, Fax - (020) 25511379
Email : niralipune@pragationline.com

☞ DISTRIBUTION CENTRES

PUNE
Nirali Prakashan : 119, Budhwar Peth, Jogeshwari Mandir Lane, Pune 411002, Maharashtra
Tel : (020) 2445 2044, 66022708, Fax : (020) 2445 1538
Email : bookorder@pragationline.com, niralilocal@pragationline.com
Nirali Prakashan : S. No. 28/27, Dhyari, Near Pari Company, Pune 411041
Tel : (020) 24690204 Fax : (020) 24690316
Email : dhyari@pragationline.com, bookorder@pragationline.com

MUMBAI
Nirali Prakashan : 385, S.V.P. Road, Rasdhara Co-op. Hsg. Society Ltd.,
Girgaum, Mumbai 400004, Maharashtra
Tel : (022) 2385 6339 / 2386 9976, Fax : (022) 2386 9976
Email : niralimumbai@pragationline.com

☞ DISTRIBUTION BRANCHES

JALGAON
Nirali Prakashan : 34, V. V. Golani Market, Navi Peth, Jalgaon 425001,
Maharashtra, Tel : (0257) 222 0395, Mob : 94234 91860

KOLHAPUR
Nirali Prakashan : New Mahadvar Road, Kedar Plaza, 1st Floor Opp. IDBI Bank
Kolhapur 416 012, Maharashtra. Mob : 9850046155

NAGPUR
Pratibha Book Distributors : Above Maratha Mandir, Shop No. 3, First Floor,
Rani Jhanshi Square, Sitabuldi, Nagpur 440012, Maharashtra
Tel : (0712) 254 7129

DELHI
Nirali Prakashan : 4593/21, Basement, Aggarwal Lane 15, Ansari Road, Daryaganj
Near Times of India Building, New Delhi 110002
Mob : 08505972553

BENGALURU
Pragati Book House : House No. 1, Sanjeevappa Lane, Avenue Road Cross,
Opp. Rice Church, Bengaluru – 560002.
Tel : (080) 64513344, 64513355,Mob : 9880582331, 9845021552
Email:bharatsavla@yahoo.com

CHENNAI
Pragati Books : 9/1, Montieth Road, Behind Taas Mahal, Egmore,
Chennai 600008 Tamil Nadu, Tel : (044) 6518 3535,
Mob : 94440 01782 / 98450 21552 / 98805 82331,
Email : bharatsavla@yahoo.com

niralipune@pragationline.com | www.pragationline.com

Also find us on ⓕ www.facebook.com/niralibooks

Preface ...

Dear Students,

Welcome to the all new Organisational Behaviour text book. Organisational Behaviour as we will all study are actions and attitudes of individuals and groups toward one another and toward the organisation as a whole, and its effect on the organisation's functioning and performance.

It is important to remember that business is about people. From the smallest enterprise to the largest corporation, organisations are created and designed by people to fulfil human objectives. Organisational Behaviour (OB) seeks to understand how we can best do this. The subject OB aims to provide a **better understanding of human behaviour in organisations.**

It introduces the concepts and theories of behaviour in organisations that have been formulated. In general, it examines diversity, ethics, and authority, power and conflict, and the issues and stresses that arise from them. In particular, it examines the individual attitudes, personalities, perceptions and motivations, and the group dynamics of teamwork, communication and leadership, all within the context of restructuring, change and development.

This book is designed to be student friendly with several new features keeping up with current trends, relevant research and changes made in the Syllabus 2016.

The hallmark features comprise a clear writing style, cutting edge content and compelling pedagogy.

The key changes in the text book are:

1. **Case Studies:** Each chapter contains one relevant case study, which helps to clarify concepts and to answer application-based questions with examination point of view.

2. **Multiple Choice Questions (MCQs):** These MCQ's will help in reinforcing the learning and will help in solving the new online MCQ's examination.

3. **Key Points Highlighted:** All through the chapters key points are highlighted and boxed for easy revision at a glance.

4. **Activities:** Activities at the end of each chapter will help you to connect theory with the real world.

5. **Questions for Discussion:** These questions have been added to test the ability of student's understanding of the concepts and theories discussed in the chapters.

Your suggestions for improvements in the text will be highly appreciated.

Authors

Acknowledgements

Organisational Behaviour is one of our most favourite subjects. We are truly grateful to Nirali Prakashan for giving us an opportunity to write a book on this. We sincerely thank Shri Dineshbhai Furia and Shri Jignesh Furia, the publishers, for making this happen. We consider this as a privilege.

We thank Mrs. Nirja Sharma and Mr. Prasad Chintakindi for the care with which they have studied the script and their attention to each and every detail.

We would also like to thank Mr. Malik Shaikh, Mrs. Anjali Muley and Miss Neha Banswadekar who have painstakingly attended to all the details to make this book appear good.

We are also grateful to all the staff members of Nirali Prakashan, who were involved in the publication of this book.

Authors

Syllabus ...

With effect from June 2016

For MBA

1. Fundamentals of OB (7 + 2)

Definition, Scope and Importance of OB, Relationship between OB and the individual, Evolution of OB, Theoretical Framework (Cognitive, Behaviouristic and Social Cognitive), Limitations of OB.

2. Individual Process and Behaviour (8 + 2)

2.1 Personality and Attitude: Definition Personality, importance of personality in Performance, The Myers-Briggs Type Indicator and The Big Five personality model, Significant personality traits suitable to the workplace (personality and job — fit theory), Personality Tests and their practical applications, Johari Window Definition Attitude Importance of attitude in an organization, Right Attitude, Components of attitude, Relationship between behavior and attitude, Developing Emotional intelligence at the workplace, Job attitude, Barriers to changing attitudes

2.2 Perception: Meaning and concept of perception, Factors influencing perception, Selective perception, Attribution theory, Perceptual process, Social perception (stereotyping and halo effect).

2.3 Motivation: Definition and Concept of Motive and Motivation, The Content Theories of Motivation (Maslow's Need Hierarchy and Herzberg's Two Factor model Theory), The Process Theories (Vroom's expectancy Theory and Porter Lawler model), Contemporary Theories-Equity Theory of Work Motivation

3. Interpersonal Processes And Behavior, Team and Leadership Development
(8 + 2)

3.1 Foundations of Group Behavior: The Meaning of Group and Group behavior and Group Dynamics, Types of Groups, The Five -Stage Model of Group Development

3.2 Managing Teams: Why Work Teams, Work Teams in Organization, Developing Work Teams, Team Effectiveness and Team Building

3.3 Leadership: Concept of Leadership, Styles of Leadership, Trait Approach, Contingency Leadership Approach, Contemporary leadership, Meaning and significance of contemporary leadership, Concept of transformational leadership, Contemporary issues in leadership, Contemporary theories of leadership, Success stories of today's Global and Indian leaders.

4. Organization System (5 + 2)

4.1 Organizational Culture: Meaning and Definition of Organizational Culture, Creating and Sustaining Organizational Culture, Types of Culture (Strong vs. Weak Culture, Soft vs. Hard Culture and formal vs. Informal Culture) , Creating Positive Organizational Culture, Concept of Workplace Spirituality.

4.2 Stress Management: Work stress: Meaning of stress, Stressors, Sources of Stress, Types of stress, Burnout. Stress Management — Individual and Organizational Strategies

5. Managing Change (7 + 2)

5.1 Organizational Change: Meaning, definition and Nature of Organizational Change, Types of Organizational change, Forces that acts as stimulants to change.

5.2 Implementing Organizational Change: How to overcome the Resistance to Change, Approaches to managing Organizational Change, Kurt Lewin's - Three step model, Seven Stage model of Change and Kotter's Eight-Step plan for Implementing Change, Leading the Change Process, Facilitating Change, Dealing with Individual and Group Resistance, Intervention Strategies for Facilitating Organizational Change, Methods of Implementing Organizational Change, Developing a Learning Organization

***

1. Fundamentals of OB

Understanding OB: Definition, scope and importance of OB, Relationship between OB and the individual, Evolution of OB, Theoretical framework (Cognitive, behaviourist and social cognitive), Limitations of OB.

Dynamics of People and OB: Disciplines that contribute to the field of OB (psychology, social psychology, sociology, anthropology), Relationship with the function in an organisation, Behavioural approach top management.

Models of OB: How, to-develop models of OB (understanding dependent and independent, variables), Decision-making model, Robin's OB model, Feudal, Autocratic, Supportive, Collegial and Custodian models, Human value model and contingency model.

OB and organisational, performance: What are organisations, perspectives of organisational Effectiveness - organisational earning perspective, stake holder perspective, high performance work practices perspective. Task Performance, organisational citizenship, counter productive work Behaviours Meaning and importance, Setting goals for organisational performance, Role of people in organisational performance.

2. Individual Process and Behaviour

(a) Ability: Meaning and significance of matching right abilities to the right job, Intellectual and physical abilities and the effects of disabilities.

(b) Learning: Definition of learning and significance of continuous learning in an organisation, Theories of learning, Action learning, Learning from individuals and learning from the environment.

(c) Attitude: Importance of attitude in an organisation, Right Attitude, Components of attitude, Relationship between behaviour and attitude, Developing Emotional intelligence at the workplace, Job attitude, Barriers to changing attitudes.

(d) Personality and values: Definition and importance of Personality for performance, The Myers-Briggs Type Indicator and The Big Five personality model, Significant personality traits suitable to the workplace (personality and job – fit theory), Personality Tests and their practical applications.

(e) Perception: Meaning and concept of perception, Factors influencing perception, Selective perception, Attribution theory, Perceptual process, Social perception (stereotyping and halo effect).

(f) Motivation: Definition and Concept of Motive and Motivation The Content Theories of Motivation (Masrow's Nee Hierarchy and Herzberg's Two Factor model Theory), 'The Process Theories (Vroom's expectancy Theory and 'Porter Lawler model), Contemporary Theories- Equity Theory of Work Motivation.

(g) Emotional Intelligence: Emotions in the work Place, Emotions, Attitudes and Behaviour; Emotional Intelligence Concepts of Employee Engagement, Empowerment.

3. Interpersonal Processes and Behaviour, Team and Leadership Development

(a) Foundations of Group Behaviour: The Meaning of Group and Group behaviour and Group Dynamics, Types of Groups, The Five-Stage Model of Group Development.

(b) Managing Teams: Why Work Teams, Work Teams in Organisation, Developing Work Teams, Team Effectiveness and Team Building.

(c) **Managing Conflict:** Meaning of Conflict, Types of Conflicts (Intergroup Conflict, Intra-Individual Conflict and Interpersonal Conflict), Johari Window, Overcoming Conflict.

(d) **Leadership:** Concept of Leadership, Styles of Leadership, Trait Approach, Contingency Leadership Approach, Contemporary leadership, Meaning and significance of contemporary leadership, Concept of transformational leadership, Contemporary issues in leadership, Contemporary theories of leadership, Success stories of today's Global and Indian leaders.

4. Organisation System

(a) **Foundations of Organisation Structure:** Concept of Organisation and Organisational Structure, Basic elements in designing OS.

(b) **Organisational Culture:** Meaning and Definition of Organisational Culture, Creating and Sustaining Organisational Culture, Types of Culture (Strong vs. Weak Culture, Soft vs. Hard Culture and formal vs. Informal Culture) Creating Positive Organisational Culture, Concept of Workplace Spirituality.

5. Managing Change

(a) **Organisational Change:** Meaning, Definition and Nature of Organisational Change, Types of Organisational change, Forces that acts as stimulants to change.

(b) **Implementing Organisational Change:** How to overcome the Resistance to Change, Approaches to managing Organisational Change, Kurt Lewin's - Three step model, Seven Stage model of Change and Kotter's Eight-Step=plan for Implementing Change, Leading the Change Process, Facilitating Change, Dealing with Individual Group Resistance, Intervention Strategies for Facilitating Organisational Change, Methods of Implementing Organisational Change, Developing a Learning Organisational.

For PGDBM

1. Fundamentals of OB

Definition, Scope and Importance of OB, Relationship between OB and the individual, Evolution of OB, Theoretical Framework (Cognitive, Behaviouristic and Social Cognitive), Limitations of OB.

2. Individual Process and Behaviour

2.1 Attitude: Importance of attitude in an organisation, Right Attitude, Components of attitude, Relationship between behaviour and attitude, Developing Emotional intelligence at the workplace, Job attitude, Barriers to changing attitudes.

2.2 Personality and Values: Definition and importance of Personality for performance, The Myers-Briggs Type Indicator and The Big Five personality model, Significant Personality

Traits suitable to the Workplace (Personality and Job — fit Theory), Personality Tests and their Practical Applications.

  2.3 Perception: Meaning and concept of perception, Factors influencing perception, Selective perception, Attribution theory, Perceptual process, Social perception (stereotyping and halo effect).

  2.4 Motivation: Definition and Concept of Motive and Motivation, The Content Theories of Motivation (Maslow's Need Hierarchy and Herzberg's Two Factor Model Theory), The Process Theories (Vroom's Expectancy Theory and Porter Lawler model), Contemporary Theories - Equity Theory of Work Motivation

3. Interpersonal Processes and Behaviour, Team and Leadership Development

  3.1 Foundations of Group Behaviour: The Meaning of Group and Group Behaviour and Group Dynamics, Types of Groups, The Five-Stage Model of Group Development.

  3.2 Managing Teams: Why Work Teams, Work Teams in Organisation, Developing Work Teams, Team Effectiveness and Team Building.

  3.3 Leadership: Concept of Leadership, Styles of Leadership, Trait Approach, Contingency Leadership Approach, Contemporary Leadership, Meaning and Significance of Contemporary Leadership, Concept of Transformational Leadership, Contemporary Issues in leadership, Contemporary Theories of Leadership, Success Stories of Today's Global and Indian Leaders.

4. Organisation System

Organisational Culture: Meaning and Definition of Organisational Culture, Creating and Sustaining Organisational Culture, Types of Culture (Strong vs. Weak Culture, Soft vs. Hard Culture and formal vs. Informal Culture), Creating Positive Organisational Culture, Concept of Workplace Spirituality.

5. Managing Change

  5.1 Organisational Change: Meaning, Definition and Nature of Organisational Change, Types of Organisational change, Forces that acts as stimulants to change.

  5.2 Implementing Organisational Change: How to overcome the Resistance to Change, Approaches to managing Organisational Change, Kurt Lewin's Three Step Model, Seven Stage model of Change and Kotter's Eight-Step plan for Implementing Change, Leading the Change Process, Facilitating Change, Dealing with Individual and Group Resistance, Intervention Strategies for Facilitating Organisational Change, Methods of Implementing Organisational Change, Developing a Learning Organisation.

***

Contents ...

***

Chapter **1**...

Fundamentals of OB

Contents ...

- Points to Remember
- Case Study
- Questions for Discussion
- Multiple Choice Questions (MCQ's)
- Activity
- Questions from Previous Pune University Examinations
- Web Links/Further Readings

Learning Objectives

After studying this chapter, you should be able to:

1. Define organisational behaviour (OB)
2. Explain the value of the systematic study of OB
3. List the major challenges and opportunities for managers to use OB concepts
4. Identify the contributions made by major behavioural science disciplines to OB
5. Describe why managers require a knowledge of OB
6. Explain the need for a contingency approach to the study of OB

Introduction

"We need to ....celebrate all these fantastic people we've hired, unlock their ability to contribute." **Anonymous Microsoft Employee**

The *"Great Places to Work For"* lists and ranks organisations according to the positive and happy perceptions and experiences of the employees, whose findings are collated by an anonymous survey of the employees. The objective of this organisation and survey is to identify the parameters that make employees in an organisation positive, motivated, and passionate about their work.

Some of the common parameters identified are as follows:

- Employee empowerment and freedom to work independently.
- Opportunities for training and development.
- Identifying high performers or 'hi pot' as they are called, and extending to them development opportunities.
- Engaging employees by involving them in designing the policies, guidelines, major purpose or strategy, dreams for the organisation.
- Treating employees like members of the organisation family and celebrating birthdays, anniversaries, picnics, spots and hobbies.

- Working towards a holistic development of employees by having gymnasiums at work.
- Well designed work places, multi cuisine cafeterias.
- Chauffer driven pick up and drops for the employees and so on.

All the above examples, indicate that now a days a lot of stress is being put on employee behaviour and well being within the organisation. It is because it has been established that their behaviour in an organisation matters. The field of **Organisation Behaviour** deals with this study that is human behaviour in organisations.

The study of people at work is generally referred to as the study of organisational behaviour. This chapter will start by defining the term organisational behaviour and briefly reviewing its origins. Organisational behaviour is the systematic study of the actions and attitudes that people exhibit within organisations.

Each person regularly uses intuition or "gut feelings" in trying to explain phenomena. For example, a friend catches a cold and we're quick to remind him that he "didn't take his vitamins" or the boss was angry with his subordinates, means he was in a bad mood. The field of organisational behaviour seeks to replace intuitive explanations such as this example with systematic study. The objective, of course, is to draw more accurate conclusions (Wilson 1994).

1.1 Understanding OB

1.1.1 Definition

Formally defined, Organisational Behaviour is the multidisciplinary field that seeks knowledge of behaviour in organisational settings by systematically studying individual, group and organisational processes. This knowledge is used both by scientists interested in understanding human behaviour and managers interested in enhancing individual well being.

According to **Larry Cummings**, *"Towards Organisational Behaviour"* Academy of Management Review, January 1978, Organisation Behaviour is the study of human behaviour in organisational settings, of the interface between human behaviour, and of the organisation itself.

So, organisations influences and is influenced by the individuals. There is a huge linkage among the human behaviour in organisational settings - the individual, - organisation interface, the organisation and the environment surrounding the organisation. In order to improve the organisational functioning and the quality of life of people working in organisations, managers depend heavily on knowledge derived from OB research.

Some of the questions asked by the researchers in order to understand the aspects of organisational behaviour are:

1. How can goals be set in order to enhance people's performance?
2. How can jobs be designed in order to motivate employees' feelings of satisfaction?
3. What should the organisations do in order to reduce stress?
4. What should the leaders do in order to enhance the effectiveness of the teams?

Organisational Behaviour focuses at three levels – Individuals, Groups and Organisations.

All these answers can be provided through a study of Organisation Behaviour (OB). OB focuses at three levels – Individuals, Groups and Organisations. The field of OB recognises that all three levels of analysis must be considered to understand the complex dynamics of organisations i.e. individuals, groups and organisations.

1.1.2 Scope and Importance of OB

Organisational behaviour is a field of study that investigates the impact that individuals, groups and structures have on behaviour within an organisation for the purpose of applying such knowledge towards improving an organisation's effectiveness.

It is an interdisciplinary field that includes sociology, psychology, communication, and management; and it complements the academic studies of organisational theory (which is focused on organisational and intra-organisational topics) and human resource studies (which are more applied and business-oriented). It may also be referred to as organisational studies or organisational science. The field has its roots in industrial and organisational psychology.

Organisational studies encompass the study of organisations from multiple viewpoints, methods, and levels of analysis. For instance, one textbook divides these multiple viewpoints into three perspectives: modern, symbolic, and postmodern.

Another traditional distinction, present especially in American academia, is between the study of "micro" organisational behaviour – which refers to individual and group dynamics in an organisational setting – and "macro" strategic management and organisational theory which studies whole organisations and industries, how they adapt, and the strategies, structures and contingencies that guide them.

To this distinction, some scholars have added an interest in *"meso"* scale structures - power, culture, and the networks of individuals and i.e. units in organisations – and "field" level analysis which study how whole populations of organisations interact.

Whenever people interact in organisations, many factors come into play. Modern organisational studies attempt to understand and model these factors. Like all modernist social sciences, organisational studies seek to control, predict, and explain.

One of the main goals of organisational theorists is, according to Simms (1994), "to revitalise organisational theory and develop a better conceptualisation of organisational life.

An organisational theorist should carefully consider levels assumptions being made in theory and be concerned with helping managers and administrators.

The importance and scope of Organisational Behaviour and their study is growing rapidly due to changing cultural, ethical and business environment of Organisation.

A manager should concentrate on employee's nature, reaction and response to different situations in the organisation which are becoming an important part in today's scenario.

People, Environment, Technology and structure - are the main four elements of organisational behaviour.

Organisational Behaviour helps to understand different activities and actions of people in organisation. It also helps to motivate them. People, Environment, Technology and Structure are the main four elements of organisational behaviour. Simply stated, the scope of this mix is the scope of Organisational Behaviour.

The scope of organisational behaviour is as under:

- Elements of organisational behaviour.
- Impact of personality on performance.
- Motivation of employees.
- Leadership.
- Structure of teams and groups.
- Perception.
- Development of the soft Skills.
- Organisational Structures: Their Study and Development.
- Improvement/Enhancement of Individual and Organisational development.
- Individual behaviour, Group behaviour, Power And Politics, Attitude and Learning.
- Perception.
- Organisation Design.
- Job Design.
- Culture and Environment Factors.
- Management of Change, Conflict and Stress.
- Organisational Development.
- Study of Emotions.
- Transactional Analysis.

This is the scope of Organisational Behaviour. In the current scenario Organisational Behaviour i.e. understanding and modifying the behaviour of employees in organisation to benefit the organisation is becoming a crucial area of action for organisation management.

Organisational Behaviour provides direction to Organisations. OB helps to understand and predict organisational life. It also helps to understand nature and activities of people in an organisation. It helps to motivate employees and to maintain interrelations within the organisation.

The importance of organisational behaviour is as under:

1. Helps to improve skills (ability of employees and use of knowledge to become more efficient).
2. It also an important part to improve marketing process by understanding consumer (buying) behaviour.
3. OB helps to understand basis of motivation and different ways to motivate employees properly.
4. Understanding of personnel/employee nature is important to manage them properly.
5. The scientific study of behaviour helps to understand and predict organisational events.
6. Helps to increase efficiency and effectiveness of organisation
7. It helps to create healthy, ethical and smooth environment in organisation.
8. Improves managers as well as employees work skill.

Ultimately OB helps to increase efficiency and productivity i.e. profit of organisation.

What does organisational behaviour study?

The study of organisational behaviour includes actions (or behaviours) and attitudes. The behaviours that get the bulk of attention in organisational behaviour are three, which have proven to be very important determinants of employee performance. They are productivity, absenteeism, and turnover (Wilson 1994). The importance of productivity is obvious.

Managers are constantly concerned with the quantity and quality of the work their employees perform. However, absence and turnover are particularly a cause for concern because of the adverse effect these may have on an employee's productivity. In terms of absence, it's hard for an employee to be productive if he or she isn't at work.

High rates of employee turnover increase costs and tend to place less experienced people into jobs (Daniels 1994). In organisations in India, especially in the IT sector, attrition levels are rising. Much of this can be traced to the behaviour of employees at all levels in the organisation.

Organisational behaviour is also concerned with employee job satisfaction, which is an attitude.

There are three reasons why managers should be concerned with their employees' job satisfaction:

First, there is a link between satisfaction and productivity.

Second, satisfaction appears to be negatively related to absenteeism and turnover.

Third, managers have a humanistic responsibility to provide their employees with jobs that are challenging and rewarding (Daniels 1994).

The second part of organisational behaviour's definition that needs to be explained is "organisation". For our purposes organisational behaviour is specifically concerned with work-related behaviour-and that takes place in organisations. *An organisation is a formal structure of planned coordination, involving two or more people, in order to achieve a common goal (Daniels 1994).*

1.1.3 Dynamics of People and OB

Contributing Disciplines

(A) Individual Level

At the individual level of analysis, organisational behaviour involves the study of learning, perception, creativity, motivation, personality, turnover, task performance, cooperative behaviour, deviant behaviour, ethics, and cognition. At this level of analysis, organisational behaviour draws heavily upon Psychology, Engineering, and Medicine.

Fields of study: Learning, motivation, personality, emotions, perception, training, leadership effectiveness, job satisfaction, individual decision making, performance appraisal, attitude measurement, employee selection, work design, work stress.

(B) Group Level

At the group level of analysis, organisational behaviour involves the study of group dynamics, intra- and intergroup conflict and cohesion, leadership, power, norms, interpersonal communication, networks, and roles. At this level of analysis, organisational behaviour draws upon the sociological and socio-psychological sciences.

Sociology: The study of people in relation to their fellow human beings.

Fields of study: Group dynamics, work teams, communication, power, conflict, inter-group behaviour.

Social Psychology: An area within psychology that blends concepts from psychology and sociology and that focuses on the influence of people on one another.

Fields of study: Behavioural change, attitude change, communication, group processes, group decision making.

Anthropology: The study of societies to learn about human beings and their activities.

Fields of study: Comparative values, comparative attitudes, cross-cultural analysis.

Political Science: The study of the behaviour of individuals and groups within a political environment.

Fields of study: Conflict, inter-organisational politics, power-conflict, intra-organisational politics, power.

(C) Organisational System Level

At the organisation level of analysis, organisational behaviour involves the study of topics such as organisational culture, organisational structure, cultural diversity, inter-organisational cooperation and conflict, change, technology, and external environmental forces. At this level of analysis, organisational behaviour draws upon Sociology, Anthropology and Political Science.

Sociology: Formal organisation theory, organisational technology, organisational change, organisational culture.

Political science: Conflict, intra-organisational politics, power.

Anthropology: Organisational culture, organisational environment.

Relationship with the Functions in an Organisation

Organisational Behaviour is a field of study that investigates the impact that individuals, groups and structure have on behaviour within organisations, for the purpose of applying such knowledge toward improving an organisation's effectiveness. An organisation is comprised of individuals who make up organisational behaviour. From top management down to the employee, organisational behaviour takes shape. The effectiveness of the organisation largely depends on the structure of the organisation, and how well the individuals or groups behave within the structure.

Organisational behaviour is important to all management functions, roles and skills.

Since organisations are built up of levels - individual, group and an organisational system as a whole, it is important for managers to understand human behaviour in order to meet the organisation's overall goals.

Managements function is to plan, organise, lead and control. Management roles can be interpersonal, informational or decisional. Management skills can be technical, human or conceptual. In order to be effective, the behavioural science disciplines of psychology, sociology, social psychology, anthropology and political science all contribute to the means of applying OB concepts.

Managers are able to develop an understanding of what motivates employees to learn, train and perform optimally as individuals through the use of OB concepts. Managers realise that there are many dynamics behind working within a group and the importance of group behaviours and communicating is the key link to empowering and controlling conflicts within a group.

Overall, in order for managers to be successful and effective they must utilise and develop the use of OB concepts that will enhance not only their own abilities but also those of their employees.

Importance of Organisational Behaviour

The concept of Organisational Behaviour (OB) is vital to any organisation because its main purpose is to improve the effectiveness /performance of the organisation by studying the people within it.

Behavioural Approach to Management

Edward Tolman has made significant contributions to this approach. Behaviouristic framework focuses on observable behaviours. Ivan Pavlov and John B. Watson were the pioneers of the behaviouristic theory. They explained human behaviour on the basis of the connection between stimulus and response.

The social learning approach incorporates the concepts and principles of both the cognitive and behaviouristic frameworks. In this approach, behaviour is explained as a continuous reciprocal interaction between cognitive, behavioural and environmental determinants.

The behavioural school of management emphasised what the classical theorists ignored – the human element. While classical theorists viewed the organisation from a production point of view, the behavioural theorists viewed it from the individual's point of view.

The behavioural approach to management emphasised individual attitudes and behaviours and group processes, and recognised the significance of behavioural processes in the workplace. The table below gives an overview of the key contributions to management theory by the behavioural management school of thought.

Contributions of Behavioural Thinkers to Management Thought

Name	Period	Contribution
Mary Parker Follet	1868-1933	Emphasised group influence and advocated the concept of 'power sharing' and integration
Elton Mayo	1880-1949	Laid the foundation for the Human Relations Movement; recognised the influence of group and workplace culture on job performance
Abraham Maslow	1908-1970	Advocated that humans are essentially motivated by a hierarchy of needs
Douglas McGregor	1906-1964	Differentiated employees and managers into Theory X and Theory Y personalities
Chris Argyris	-	Classified organisations based on the employees' set of values

Organisational Behaviour and Corporate Culture

The terms "corporate culture" and "organisational behaviour" are sometimes used interchangeably, but in reality, there are differences between the two. Corporate culture encompasses the shared values, attitudes, standards, and beliefs and other characteristics that define an organisation's operating philosophy. Organisational behaviour, meanwhile, can be understood in some ways as the academic study of corporate culture and its various elements, as well as other important components of behaviour such as organisation structure and organisation processes.

Organisational behaviour, said Gibson, Ivancevich, and Donnelly, is "the field of study that draws on theory, methods, and principles from various disciplines to learn about individual perceptions, values, learning capacities, and actions while working in groups and within the total organisation; analysing the external environment's effect on the organisation and its human resources, missions, objectives, and strategies.

Effective managers know what to look for in terms of structure, process, and culture and how to understand what they find. Therefore, managers must develop diagnostic skills; they must be trained to identify conditions symptomatic of a problem requiring further attention. Problem indicators include declining profits, declining quantity or quality of work, increases in absenteeism or tardiness, and negative employee attitudes. Each of these problems is an issue of organisational behaviour."

1.1.4 Features of OB

The following are the Features of OB:

1. OB is multidisciplinary in nature

The field is multidisciplinary in nature. It draws heavily from a variety of social science disciplines.

The study of OB considers the orientation of psychology, to understand the human mind and so, behaviour and sociology, to understand the role of an individual in an organisation, as a member of the organisation group, its diversity of ideas, culture, food, language, its ideas, and values.

2. OB attempts to improve organisational effectiveness and the quality of life at work

In earlier times, the people as employees in companies were assumed and considered to be lazy who disliked work, and if given the choice would not like to work. Such a theory was propounded by a researcher called McGregor and this theory was called Theory X.

Today if you ask officials, they are very optimistic of the people in an organisation as employees and believe that if they are given the right opportunities and are adequately trained, then people as employees love to work and enjoy the challenges that work provides.

The approach that assumes that people are not inherently lazy is called Theory Y, and it assumes that people have a psychological need to be recognised and enjoy a high self esteem by seeking to achieve good performances and so, enjoy a higher social status in society. The theory Y perspective prevails within the field of Organisational Behaviour today.

3. OB recognises the dynamic nature of organisations

OB scientists recognise that organisations are not static, but dynamic and ever changing. They recognise that organisations are open systems, i.e. self sustaining systems that are constantly in the process of processing input into output.

For example, as a human resources function, organisations take skilled manpower from society, train them and make them capable of creating products and services that the organisation specialises in. These are further sold back in the society and community. When people buy these products or services, in turn organisational employees make more and the cycle continues.

4. OB assumes that there is no one best approach

What is the best leadership style to be adopted? What motivates people to bring out the best in them? Should important decisions be made by groups or individuals? There is no one best answer for all these points.

This means that OB uses a Contingency Approach = An orientation that recognises that behaviour in work settings is the complex result of many interacting factors.

1.1.5 Relationship between OB and the Individual

OB is concerned with the study of what people do in an organisation and how that behaviour affects the performance of the organisation.

It therefore emphasises behaviour as related to concerns such as jobs, work, absenteeism, employment turnover, productivity, human performance, and management.

OB includes core topics of motivation, leadership behaviour and power, interpersonal communication, group structure and processes, learning, attitude development and perception, change processes, conflict, work design, and work stress.

Growing Importance of Interpersonal Skills

- Organisations need to develop their manager's interpersonal skills in order to get and retain high performing employees.
- Wages and fringe benefits are no longer an employees' first priorities.
- Quality of the employees' job and the supportiveness of their work environments are far more important for employees.
- A manager with good interpersonal skills is likely to make the workplace more pleasant for the employees.
- In today's increasingly competitive and demanding workplace, manager's need to have good people skills apart from technical skills.

1.1.6 Evolution of OB

Historical Development of OB

In the early days, people worked from dawn until dusk under intolerable conditions of disease, filth, danger and scarcity of resources.

During the period of Industrial Revolution (1800) **Robert Owen**, a young factory owner first emphasised the human needs of employees. He refused to employ young children. He taught his workers cleanliness, and improved their working conditions. He was called 'The Heal Father' of personnel administration.

Andrew Ure published his work "The Philosophy of Manufactures in 1935". In this work he recognised the value of the human factor in manufacturing. He facilitated the provision of tea, medical treatment, sickness payments and ventilation to workers.

Fredrick W. Taylor is called the father of scientific management. His work led to improved recognition and productivity for industrial workers.

In 1914 **William Gilbreth** published his work "The Psychology of Management" which gave emphasis to the human side of work.

In 1920's and 1930's **Mayo** studied human behaviour at work at Harvard University. The study was conducted at the Western Electric Company, Hawthorne Plant. This study showed that the worker is not a simple tool but a complex personality interacting in a group situation. Mayo is recognised as the father of 'human relations.'

In the 1940's and 1950's major research projects were developed in the University of Michigan, and Ohio State University. An age of human relations had begun. In 1957 **Douglas McGregor** presented Theory X and Theory Y, in which alternative assumptions about employees were formulated. According to these theories management's personnel practices, decision making, operating practices, and even the organisational design flow form assumptions about human behaviour.

Theory 'X' assumes that most people dislike work and will try to avoid work, so that the management is forced to coerce, control and threaten employees to obtain satisfactory performance. Theory 'Y' assumes that employees will exercise self-direction and self-control if the management provides an appropriate environment. Thus, historical background supports that OB is a maturing field, which has a bright future.

1.1.7 Theoretical Framework (Cognitive, Behaviourist and Social Cognitive)

Organisational behaviour is the study and application of knowledge about how people as individuals and as groups act within organisations. It can be defined as the understanding, prediction and management of human behaviour in organisations. OB is related to other disciplines like Organisations Theory, Organisation Development and Personnel/Human Resources Management.

Managers need certain skills and competencies to successfully achieve their goals. The most significant management skills are the technical, human and conceptual skills.

Henry Mintzberg classified management roles depending on the extent of interpersonal relationships, the transfer of information and decision-making involved in the job. Managers need certain skills and competencies to successfully achieve their goals. The most significant management skills are the technical, human and conceptual skills.

People develop generalisations by observing, sensing, asking and listening to various people around them. They use these generalisations to explain or predict the behaviour of others.

A systematic approach to the study of behaviour will bring to light important facts and relationships that provide the basis for more accurate understanding, prediction and control of behaviour.

It is important to know how a person perceives a situation to predict his behaviour. There are differences as well as consistencies that can be seen in people's behaviour.

An overall model of organisational behaviour can be developed on the basis of three theoretical frameworks. They are:

- Cognitive
- Behaviouristic, and
- Social learning

The cognitive approach gives more credit to people than the other approaches and is based on the expectancy, demand and incentive concepts.

Cognitive Theories

- **Expectancy Theory:**

  It describes internal processes of choice among different behaviours

- **Equity Theory:**

  It describes how and why people react when they feel unfairly treated

- **Goal Setting Theory:**

  It focuses on how to set goals for people to reach

A group, made up of different individuals and multiple relationships among those individuals, is even more complex. In the fact of this overwhelming complexity, organisational behaviour must be managed.

Ultimately the work of organisations gets done through the behaviour of people, individually or collectively, on their own or in collaboration with technology. Thus, central to the management task is the management of organisational behaviour.

"To do this, there must be the capacity to *understand* the patterns of behaviour at individual, group, and organisation levels, to *predict* what behaviour responses will be elicited by different managerial actions, and finally to use this understanding and prediction to achieve *control.*"

Organisational behaviour scientists study four primary areas of behavioural science:

- Individual behaviour
- Group behaviour
- Organisational structure, and
- Organisational processes.

They investigate many facets of these areas like personality and perception, attitudes and job satisfaction, group dynamics, politics and the role of leadership in the organisation, job design, the impact of stress on work, decision-making processes, the communications chain, and company cultures and climates.

They use a variety of techniques and approaches to evaluate each of these elements and its impact on individuals, groups, and organisational efficiency and effectiveness.

In their work, *Organisations: Behaviour, Structure, Processes,* Gibson, Ivancevich, and Donnelly stated, "The behaviour sciences, have provided the basic framework and principles for the field of organisation behaviour."

Each behavioural science discipline provides a slightly different focus, analytical framework, and a theme for helping managers, answer questions about themselves, non-managers, and environmental forces."

In regard to individuals and groups, researchers try to determine why people behave the way they do. They have developed a variety of models designed to explain individuals' behaviour. They investigate the factors that influence personality development, including genetic, situational, environmental, cultural, and social factors.

Researchers also examine various personality types and their impact on business and other organisations. One of the primary tools utilised by organisational behaviour researchers in these and other areas of study is the job satisfaction study.

These tools are used not only to measure job satisfaction in such tangible areas as pay, benefits, promotional opportunities, and working conditions, but also to gauge how individual and group behaviour patterns influence corporate culture, both positively and negatively.

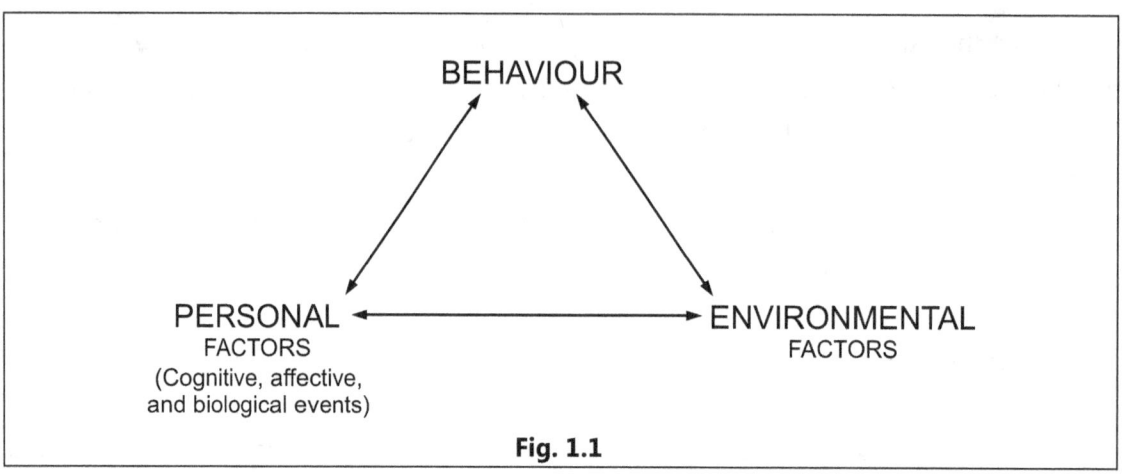

Fig. 1.1

Social Cognitive

Social cognitive theory, used in psychology, education, and communication, points that portions of an individual's knowledge acquisition can be directly related to observing others within the context of social interactions, experiences, and outside media influences.

In other words, people do not learn new behaviours solely by trying them and either succeeding or failing, but rather, the survival of humanity is dependent upon the replication of the actions of others.

Depending on whether people are rewarded or punished for their behaviour and the outcome of the behaviour, that behaviour may be modelled. Further, media provide models for a vast array of people in many different environmental settings.

Social cognitive theory is a learning theory based on the ideas that people learn by watching what others do and will not do, these processes are central to understanding personality.

While social cognitists agree that there is a fair amount of influence on development generated by learned behaviour displayed in the environment in which one grows up, they believe that the individual person (and therefore cognition) is just as important in determining moral development.

People learn by observing others; the environment, behaviour, and cognition all counting as the chief factors in influencing development.

People learn by observing others, with the environment, behaviour, and cognition

These three factors are not static or independent elements; rather, they influence each other in a process of triadic reciprocal determinism. For example, each behaviour witnessed can change a person's way of thinking (cognition).

Similarly, the environment one is raised in may influence later behaviours, just as a father's mindset (also cognition) will determine the environment in which his children are raised.

It is important to note that learning can occur without a change in behaviour. According to J.E. Ormrod's general principles of social learning, while a visible change in behaviour is the most common proof of learning, it is not absolutely necessary.

Social learning theorists say that because people can learn through observation alone, their learning may not necessarily be shown in their performance.

Social cognitive theory is applied today in many different areas. Mass media, public health, education, and marketing are just a very few. An example of this is the use of celebrities to endorse and introduce any number of products to certain demographics.

1.1.8 Limitations of Organisational Behaviour

Some of the limitations of Organisational Behaviour are:

- Organisational behaviour cannot abolish conflict and frustration but can reduce them. It is a way to improve but not an absolute answer to problems.

- It is only one of the many systems operating within a large social system.

- People who lack system understanding may develop a 'behavioural basis', which gives them a narrow view point, i.e., a tunnel vision that emphasises on satisfying employee experiences while overlooking the broader system of an organisation in relation to all its public.

- The law of diminishing returns also operates in the case of organisational behaviour. It states, that at some point increase of a desirable practice starts to produce declining returns and sometimes, negative returns.

- The concept implies that for any situation there is an optimum amount of a desirable practice. When that point is exceeded, there is a decline in returns. For example, too much security may lead to less employee initiative and growth. This relationship shows that organisational effectiveness is achieved not by maximising one human variable but by working all system variables together in a balanced way.

- A significant concern about organisational behaviour is that its knowledge and techniques could be used to manipulate people without regard for human welfare. People who lack ethical values could use people in unethical ways.

Although organisational behaviour does have limitations, these limitations should not blind us to the tremendous potential that O. B. can contribute to the advancement of civilisation. It has provided and will provide much improvement in the human environment.

By building a better climate for people, organisational behaviour will release their creative potential to help solve major social problems. In this way organisational behaviour may contribute to social improvements that stretch far beyond the confines of any one organisation. A better climate may help some person a major breakthrough in solar energy, health, or education.

Improved organisational behaviour is not easy to apply. But the opportunities are there. It should produce a higher quality of life in which there is improved harmony within each person, among people, and among the organisations of the future.

1.2 Models of OB

The four models of OB are:

1. The Autocratic Model,
2. The Custodial Model,
3. The Supportive Model and
4. The Collegial Model.

The autocratic model is based on power. It works well especially in times of an organisational crisis.

The custodial model of OB takes into consideration the security needs of employees. A custodial environment gives a psychological reassurance of economic rewards and benefits.

The supportive model of OB seeks to create supportive work environment and motivate employees to perform well on their job.

In the collegial model, the management nurtures a feeling of partnership with its employees, and makes the employees feel themselves as an asset to the organisation.

Overview

1. A model is an abstraction of reality, a simplified representation of some real-world phenomenon.
2. There are three levels of analysis in OB:
    *   Individual
    *   Group
    *   Organisational Systems Level
3. The three basic levels are analogous to building blocks; each level is constructed upon the previous level.
4. Group concepts grow out of the foundation laid in the individual section; we overlay structural constraints on the individual and group in order to arrive at organisational behaviour.

Basic OB Model

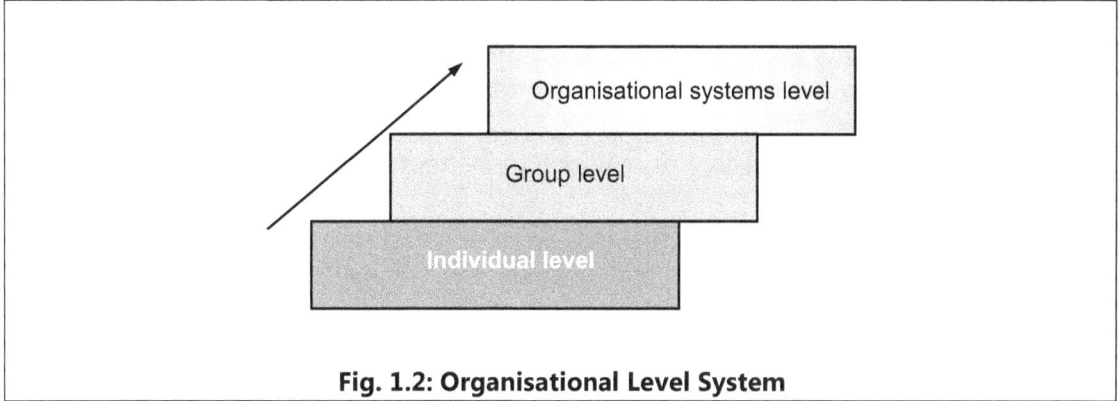

Fig. 1.2: Organisational Level System

I. The Dependent Variables

1. Dependent variables are the key factors that you want to explain or predict and that are affected by some other factor.

2. Primary dependent variables in OB:

   - Productivity

   - Absenteeism

   - Turnover

   - Job satisfaction

   - A fifth variable – organisational citizenship – has been added to this list

Productivity

1. It is achieving goals by transferring inputs to outputs at the lowest cost. This must be done both effectively and efficiency.

2. An organisation is effective when it successfully meets the needs of its clientele or customers.

   Example: When sales or market share goals are met, productivity also depends on achieving those goals efficiently.

3. An organisation is efficient when it can do so at a low cost.

   Popular measures of efficiency include: ROI, profit per dollar of sales, and output per hour of labour.

4. Productivity is a major concern of OB: What factors influence the effectiveness and efficiency of individuals, groups and the company?

Absenteeism
1. Absenteeism is the failure to report to work.
2. A one-day absence by a clerical worker can cost a U.S. employer up to $100 in reduced efficiency and increased supervisory workload.
3. The workflow is disrupted and often important decisions must be delayed.
4. All absences are not bad. For instance, illness, fatigue, or excess stress can decrease an employee's productivity – it may well be better to not report to work rather than perform poorly.

Turnover
1. Turnover is the voluntary and involuntary permanent withdrawal from an organisation.
2. A high turnover rate results in increased recruiting, selection, and training costs.
3. All organisations have some turnover and the "right" people leaving – under-performing employees – thereby creating opportunity for promotions, and adding new/fresh ideas, and replacing marginal employees with higher skilled workers.
4. Turnover often involves the loss of people the organisation does not want to lose.

Job satisfaction
1. Job satisfaction is "the difference between the amount of rewards workers receive and the amount they believe they should receive."
2. Unlike the previous three variables, job satisfaction represents an attitude rather than a behaviour.
3. It became a primary dependent variable for two reasons:
   - Demonstrated relationship to performance factors
   - The value preferences held by many OB researchers
4. Managers have believed for years that satisfied employees are more productive, however:
   - Much evidence questions that assumed causal relationship
   - It can be argued that advanced societies should be concerned not just with the quantity of life, but also with the quality of life
   - Ethically, organisations have a responsibility to provide employees with jobs that are challenging and intrinsically rewarding.

Organisational citizenship
1. Organisational citizenship is a discretionary behaviour that is not a part of an employee's formal job requirements, but that nevertheless promotes the effective functioning of the organisation.
2. Desired citizenship behaviours include:
   - Constructive statements about work group and organisation
   - Helping others on their team
   - Volunteering for extra job activities
   - Avoiding unnecessary conflicts

- Showing care for organisational property
- Respecting rules and regulations
- Tolerating occasional work-related impositions

II. The Independent Variables

1. Organisational behaviour is best understood when viewed essentially as a set of increasingly complex building blocks: individual, group, and organisational system.
2. The base, or first level, of our model lies in understanding individual behaviour.
3. Individual-level variables:
   - People enter organisations with certain characteristics that will influence their behaviour at work.
   - The more obvious of these are personal or biographical characteristics such as age, gender, and marital status; personality characteristics; an inherent emotional framework; values and attitudes; and basic ability levels.
   - There is little management can do to alter them, yet they have a very real impact on employee behaviour.
4. There are four other individual-level variables that have been shown to affect employee behaviour:
   - Perception
   - Individual decision making
   - Learning
   - Motivation
5. The middle level of our model lies in understanding behaviour of groups.
6. Group-level variables:
   - The behaviour of people in groups is more than the sum total of all the individuals acting in their own way.
   - People behave differently in groups than they do when alone.
   - People in groups are influenced by:
     (a) Acceptable standards of behaviour by the group
     (b) Degree of attractiveness to each other
     (c) Communication patterns
     (d) Leadership and power
     (e) Levels of conflict
7. The top level of our model lies in understanding organisations system level variables
8. Organisational behaviour reaches its highest level of sophistication when we add formal structure.
9. The design of the formal organisation, work processes, and jobs; the organisation's human resource policies and practices, and the internal culture, all have an impact.

Models of Organisational Behaviour

The science of organisational behaviour uses models, which are abstract constructs, intended to represent reality.

According to **Schermerhorn, Hunt, and Osborn**, models are used to analyse the independent variables, or causes, of situations and to determine possible dependent variables, or results.

1.2.1 Decision Making Model

Definition: Decision making is a conscious process of making choices among one or more alternatives with the intention of moving toward some desired state of affairs.

Rational Choice Decision Process

The rational planning model is the process of realising a problem, establishing and evaluating planning criteria, creating alternatives, implementing alternatives, and monitoring progress of the alternatives. It is used in designing neighbourhoods, cities, and regions.

The rational planning model is central in the development of modern urban planning and transportation planning. The very similar rational decision-making model, as it is called in organisational behaviour, is a process for making logically sound decisions.

This multi-step model aims to be logical and follow the orderly path from problem identification to solution.

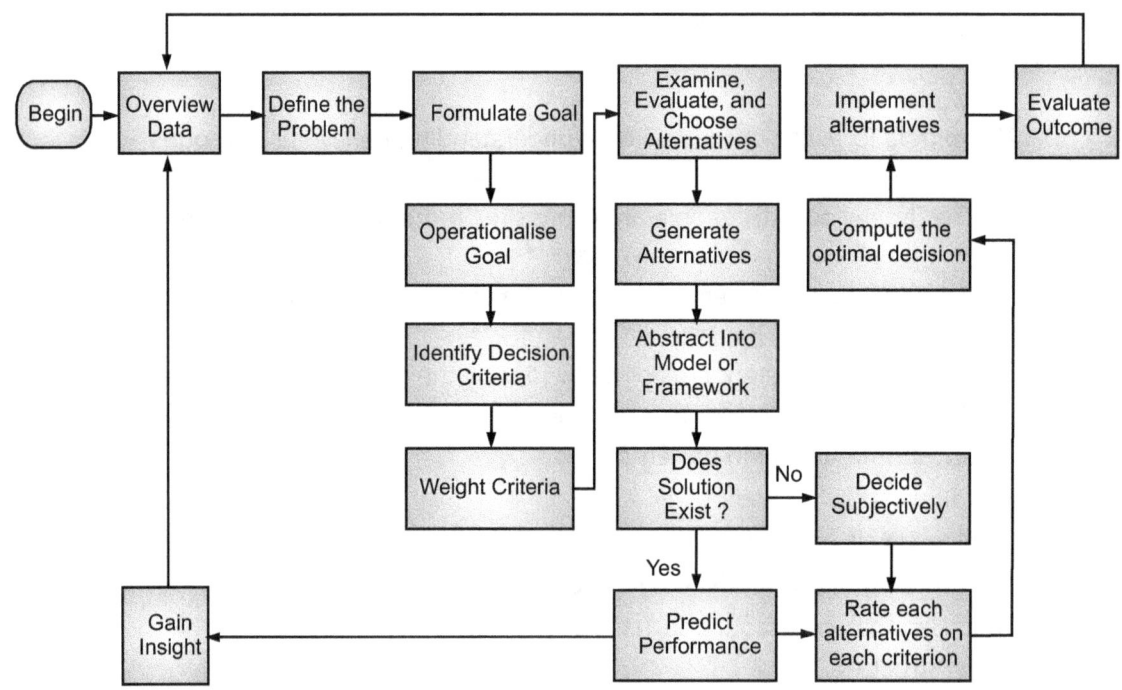

Fig. 1.3

Rational decision-making or planning follows a series of steps detailed below:
(a) Verify, define, and detail the problem

Verifying, defining and detailing the problem (problem definition, goal definition, information gathering).

This step includes recognising the problem, defining an initial solution, and starting primary analysis. Examples of this are creative devising, creative ideas, inspirations, breakthroughs, and brainstorms.

The very first step which is normally overlooked by the top level management is defining the exact problem. Though we think that the problem identification is obvious, many times it is not. The rational decision making model is a group-based decision making process.

If the problem is not identified properly then we may face a problem as each and every member of the group might have a different definition of the problem. Hence, it is very important that the definition of the problem is the same among all group members. Only then is it possible for the group members to find alternate sources or problem solving in an effective manner.

(b) Generate all possible solutions

This step encloses two to three final solutions to the problem and preliminary implementation to the site. In planning, examples of this are Planned Units of Development and downtown revitalizations.

This activity is best done in groups, as different people may contribute different ideas or alternative solutions to the problem. Without alternative solutions, there is a chance of arriving at a non-optimal or a rational decision. For exploring the alternatives it is necessary to gather information. Technology may help with gathering this information.

(c) Generate objective assessment criteria

Evaluative criteria are measurements to determine success and failure of alternatives. This step contains secondary and final analysis along with secondary solutions to the problem. Examples of this are site suitability and site sensitivity analysis.

After going thoroughly through the process of defining the problem, exploring for all the possible alternatives for that problem and gathering information this step says evaluate the information and the possible options to anticipate the consequences of each and every possible alternative that is thought of.

At this point, optional criteria for measuring the success or failure of the decision taken, needs to be considered.

(d) Choose the best solution generated

This step comprises a final solution and secondary implementation to the site. At this point the process has developed into different strategies of how to apply the solutions to the site.

Based on the criteria of assessment and the analysis done in previous steps, choose the best solution generated.

These four steps form the core of the Rational Decision Making Model.

(e) Implement the preferred alternative

This step includes final implementation to the site and preliminary monitoring of the outcome and results of the site. This step is the building/renovations part of the process.

(f) Monitor and evaluate outcomes and results

This step contains the secondary and final monitoring of the outcomes and results of the site. This step takes place over a long period of time.

(g) Feedback

Modify the decisions and actions taken based on the evaluation.

1. Planner defines the problem (not goal).
2. Planner considers several alternatives and analyses each.
3. Preliminary choices of the alternative for best fit considering feedback and impact of the client group.
4. Planner designs and implements course of action in the form of an experiment.
5. Evaluation of effects of the course of action. Did it alleviate the problem? Any feedback from course of action?
6. On the basis of the feedback should the project or course of action be continued, changed, etc. If effective institutionalise the course of action.

1.2.2 Robbins and Judge Model

According to Robbins and Judge, models present a simplified view of reality to identify quantifiable observations and predict likely outcomes. This discipline seeks to understand scientific causes rather than relying upon generalised notions unsupported by analysis. The goal of organisational behaviour is to modify and guide conduct to support organisational goals.

Managers with Social Science Skills

Managers who gain a better understanding of how individuals fit into the organisational culture are better able to maximise productivity. Gaining this understanding requires the use of cross disciplinary tools.

Robbins and Judge suggest that organisational behaviour uses applied social sciences including

- Psychology
- Social Psychology
- Sociology and
- Anthropology

to form the foundation of this discipline.

How the Social Sciences Work Together

Psychology analyses individual behaviour and social psychology blends elements of psychology and sociology to further study how groups of individuals interact with the organisation. Sociology studies group behaviour and how it affects organisational structure. Anthropology analyses the cultural and environmental triggers that affect group behaviour and its subsequent effect on the organisation.

Types of Organisational Culture

Identifying types of behaviour provides a useful description of an organisation's culture, including traditions, mores, and group dynamics. Organisations come in strong and weak cultures. When employees are motivated and aligned with corporate goals, they reinforce the organisation's strengths; without shared goals, a weak culture can fail.

According to Schermerhorn, Hunt, and Osborn, in the field of organisational behaviour, three broad categories of organisational culture are,

- Constructive
- Passive/Defensive, and
- Aggressive/Defensive.

Constructive Cultures

Constructive cultures offer employees a positive environment, which supports achievement, close affiliations, and respect for diversity. This nurturing effect encourages employees to fully participate, to share responsibility, and to inspire creativity. Constructive behaviour supports strong organisational cultures. Employee involvement, when supported by management, encourages and inspires individual employees to share corporate goals.

Defensive Cultures

Unlike the constructive culture, both defensive cultures have negative consequences. In a passive/defensive culture workers seek to protect their status within the company. Workers avoid challenges because potential failure bears unacceptable risk to individual status. Greater dependence on maintaining the status quo stifles innovation. In the aggressive/defensive culture, excessive forcefulness can lead to conflict among staff members and with outside parties. Relationships are oppositional and employees seek to acquire and retain power rather than to work together to achieve shared goals.

Communication and Management Functions

A significant part of a manager's job requires good interpersonal skills to build working relationships within the organisation. Human skills include the ability to communicate and empathise with other people.

If a manager can understand the motivation of subordinates, he or she can engage in persuasive conversation, moderate disputes, and resolve conflicts. Using effective communication is part of the leadership function of management and can be used to organise and coordinate the actions of individuals into an efficient group effort.

1.2.3 Feudal Model

The feudal model treated employees as inferior elements in an organisation. The employees should be treated sternly. People's desires and values were not considered for management purposes. It was very well known as Theory X where in actions, policies, procedures were considered superior to human beings. Carrot (money) and stick (threat of retrenchment) approach was used for motivation. It concentrated on formal organisation and ignored social and human values.

1.2.4 Autocratic Model

The basis of this model is power with a managerial orientation of authority. The employees in turn are oriented towards obedience and dependence on the boss. The employee need that is met is subsistence. The performance result is minimal.

In this model disobedient employees are penalised. This model depends on power. Managerial orientation is formal in this type of environment. Authority is delegated by the right to command over people. Management believes that it knows what is best; it also assumes that employees have to be directed, persuaded and pushed into performance. Management does the thinking and employees obey the orders. This model leads to tight control of employees at work. As a result of this environment employees become dependent on their authority, but they do not respect them.

A majority of employees give minimum performance, and receive minimum wages. However there are some employees who give higher performance because of internal motivation.

The major drawback of this model is its high human costs but it does get moderate results. The major advantage of this model is that it is a successful way to accomplish work. The Autocratic model is more useful when there are no well-known alternatives or when there is an organisational crisis.

Employees' feelings of insecurity, frustrations and aggressions towards authorities are the outcome of the autocratic model. As employees are not able to express these feelings directly towards their boss, they express these negative emotions in their families and community. Thus, relationships among community members get disturbed.

In order to improve an employees' quality of work, his needs for satisfaction and security should be fulfilled. During 1890's and 1900's many organisations began welfare programs called 'Paternalism'.

1.2.5 Custodial Model

The basis of this model is economic resource with a managerial orientation of money. The employees in turn are oriented towards security and benefits and dependence on the organisation. The employee need that is met is security. The performance result is passive co-operation.

After the 1930's employers started applying the custodial model. This custodial approach leads to employee's dependency on the organisation, rather than on the boss. Employees depend on organisations for their security and welfare.

Success of this approach depends on economic resources. Managerial orientation is towards money to pay wages and benefits. Satisfaction of security needs is an important motivating factor for work and is looked after by the employer, for example, the provision of child-care centers at the work place.

Employees working with this approach become psychologically preoccupied with their economic rewards and benefits. Because of such rewards they are well maintained, happy and contented. However the problem of motivation and co-operation still remains.

The major drawback of this model is that most employees do not utilize their full capacities, or do not get motivated to increase their capacity.

The major advantage of this model is that it leads to security and satisfaction of workers.

A series of studies at the University of Michigan on the other hand showed that "the happy employee is not necessarily the most productive employee", and thus began the search for a better model of OB by academicians.

1.2.6 Supportive Model

The basis of this model is leadership with a managerial orientation of support. The employees in turn are oriented towards job performance and participation. The employee need that is met is recognition. The performance result is awakened drives.

This model does not depend on power or money, but depends on leadership. In this approach, it is assumed that workers are not passive and resistant to organisational needs by nature, but they are made so by an inadequately supportive climate at work. Through effective leadership, management provides a favorable climate for the employees' capabilities to grow and improve. Thus, in the supportive model, managements approach is to support the employee's job performance. This approach leads to employees feeling of participation and task involvement in the organisation. A "We" feeling is created. Employees are more strongly motivated than by earlier models because their status and recognition needs are met. The Management helps employees to solve their problems and accomplish their work.

The Supportive model works well with both employees and managers. A Survey conducted in the USA reported that 90% of middle managers in United States agreed with the supportive model.

The supportive models tends to be more effective in developed countries rather than in developing nations, because this model awakens employee drives towards a wide array of needs and their current needs and social conditions are quite different.

1.2.7 Collegial Model

The basis of this model is partnership with a managerial orientation of teamwork. The employees in turn are oriented towards responsible behaviour and self-discipline. The employee need that is met is self-actualisation. The performance result is moderate enthusiasm.

The collegial model is an extension of the supportive model. The term collegial relates to a body of persons having a common purpose.

This model depends on the management building a feeling of partnership with employees. As a result of which employees feel needed and useful. Managers are seen as joint contributors rather than as bosses. The collegial model tends to be more useful, with unprogrammed work and an intellectual environment. This model was less used on assembly lines because of a rigid work environment.

There are different ways of creating positive feelings among employees, for example, providing common transport or canteen facilities to managers and other employees. Some organisations provide common parking spaces for executives and others, while some organisations arrange picnics or get-together programs for their staff in which managers also take an active part.

Managerial orientation is towards teamwork, a sense of responsibility is created among employees. They work hard because they feel strongly that it is their duty. They feel that it is obligatory to uphold quality standards that will bring credit to their jobs and company.

Outcome of the collegial approach is cultivation of self-discipline among employees. In this kind of environment employees have feelings of fulfillment and self-actualization. These are positive feelings which create enthusiasm in performance.

The following table summarises these four models.

Models of Organisational Behaviour

	Autocratic	Custodial	Supportive	Collegial	System
Basis of Model	Power	Economic Resources	Leadership	Partnership	Trust, community meaning
	Authority	Money	Support	Team work	Caring compassion
	Obedience	Security and Benefit	Job performance	Responsible behaviour	Psychological ownership
	Dependence on Boss	Dependence on organisation	Participation	Self-discipline	Self-motivation
	Subsistence	Security	Status and recognition	Self-actualisation	Wide range
	Minimum	Basic co-operation	Awakened drive	Moderate corporation	Commitment to organisational rules

1.2.8 System Model

An emerging model of organisational behaviour is the system model. It is the result of a strong search for higher meaning at work by many of today employees. They want more than a pay-check and job security from their job.

In this, the model helps for gowning sense of community amongst co-workers.

Under the system model managers try to convey to each other that:

- You are an important part of your whole system.
- We sincerely care about of you.
- We want to join together to achieve a better product or service local community and society at large.

To accomplish this, managers must increasingly demonstrate a sense of caring and compassion, being sensitive to the needs of a diverse workforce with rapidly changing needs and complex personal and family needs.

In response, many employees embrace the goal of organisational effectiveness, and reorganise the mutuality of company-employee obligations in a system viewpoint. They experience a sense of psychological ownership for the organisation and its product and services.

They go beyond the self-discipline of the collegial approach until they reach a state of self-motivation, in which they take responsibility for their own goals and actions. As a result, the employee needs that are met are wide-ranging but often include the highest-order needs (e.g., social, status, esteem, autonomy, and self actualisation).

Because it provides employees an opportunity to meet these needs through their work as their work as well as understand the organisation's perspectives, this new model can engender employees' passion and commitment to organisational goals. They are inspired; they feel important; they believe in the usefulness and viability of their system for the common good.

1.2.9 Human Value Model

An organisation should appreciate human values of employees rather than economic values. People work in the organisation not only for fulfilling the economic needs but they devote time therefore getting satisfaction and fulfilling their social and psychological needs. They bother for human dignity. It is briefly known as SOBC model.

The organisation behaviour model (S, O, B, C) has incorporated the best aspects from the three frameworks of human behaviour. In this model, the letters S, O, B, C represent situation, organism, behaviour and consequences, respectively.

In modern times, managers confront many challenges and opportunities. The greatest challenges among all of them are the result of environmental changes occurring due to globalisation, information technology, total quality, and diversity and ethics.

THE S-O-B-C MODEL

This model is used to identify the major variables in OB and to show how they relate to one another. The letters S - O - B - C stands for Stimulus – Organism – Behaviour – Consequences respectively. The framework of this model is based on social learning.

OB model says that internal cognitions (O) lead to behaviour (B). The S-B-C model emphasizes the need to identify observable contingencies (S and C) for the prediction and control of behaviour (B). S - O - B - C is the expanded model which recognizes the interactive nature of the environment (S and C) the person's cognitions (O) and the behaviour itself (B) in the determining behaviour. According to this model causes for behaviour, the behaviour itself and the effects of the behaviour can be observable or non-observable.

S - O - B - C model does not abandon the emphasis on behaviour, it merely expands the group of variables to include cognitive mediating processes and observable (covert) and non-observable (overt) behaviours.

The following figure graphically shows the S - O - B - C model.

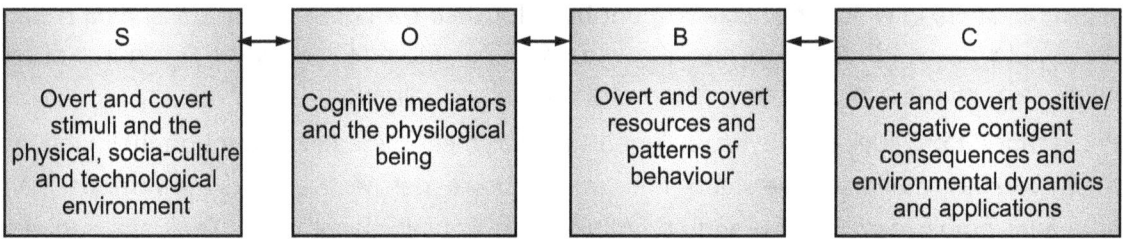

Fig. 1.4: S-O-B-C Model

Source : Adapted from Fred. Luthans, "Organisational Behaviour",
4th Edition. McGraw Hill Book Company, P. 23.

Thus S - O - B - C model is an eclectic model taken from both cognitive and behaviourist approaches, but it is based mainly on the new social learning approach. This model can perhaps best meet the goals of organisational behaviour. The S - O portion deals with understanding and the B - C portion deals with prediction and control. If the organisational situation is substituted for S, the organisational participant is substituted for O and the dynamics and applications are put into C, the model can serve as a conceptual framework for the study of OB.

People differ from each other in their needs and values

OB models help managers to face these challenges and take appropriate actions.

People differ from each other in their needs and values. Group effort eases their task of achieving organisational goals effectively. Human relations can be defined as motivating people in organisations to work as a team.

Although human relationships have existed from quite some time in the past, the study of human relations has developed only recently.

Social sciences like sociology, psychology, anthropology, economics and political science have contributed to the development of OB and human relations.

Human relations and OB play a significant role in the development of the skills of employees and the improvement of organisational performance.

Various studies and theories in the field of organisational behaviour have given new insights into the behaviour of people at work. The most important studies are the Hawthorne studies, Theory X and Theory Y, and Theory Z. The Hawthorne Studies, conducted by Elton Mayo at the Western Electric Company, was the first systematic study that recognised the significance of informal groups in the workplace and its impact on productivity.

The conclusion drawn from these studies was that it was security and recognition, not just good physical working conditions that bring a drastic improvement in productivity. Moreover, informal groups operating within the work settings exert strong control over work habits of individual workers.

Douglas McGregor formulated two theories called Theory X and Theory Y. In these theories, he has made two contrasting sets of assumptions about individuals at work - negative and positive. Theory X assumes that people are lazy and have an inherent dislike for work, so they have to be forced to work in order to get the desired results.

On the contrary, Theory Y believes that work comes naturally to people and they would be more dedicated if they understood and believed in the goals of the organisation. William Ouchi proposed Theory Z as an integrative model of organisational behaviour. This theory blends the positive aspects of Japanese and American styles of management and stresses on building a close and trusting work environment.

1.2.10 Contingency Approach to Organisational Behaviour

The contingency approach to management is based on the idea that there is no one best way to manage and that to be effective, planning, organising, leading, and controlling must be tailored to the particular circumstances faced by an organisation. Managers have always asked questions such as "What is the right thing to do? Should we have a mechanistic or an organic structure? A functional or divisional structure? Wide or narrow spans of management? Tall or flat organisational structures? Simple or complex control and coordination mechanisms? Should we be centralised or decentralised? Should we use task or people oriented leadership styles? What motivational approaches and incentive programs should we use?" The contingency approach to management (also called the situational approach) assumes that there is no universal answer to such questions because organisations, people, and situations vary and change over time. Thus, the right thing to do depends on a complex variety of critical environmental and internal contingencies.

This approach has been widely used in recent years to integrate management theory with the increasing complexity of organisations.

According to this theory, there is no one best way to manage all situations. In other words, there is no one best way to manage the response "It depends" holds good for several management situations.

The contingency approach was developed by managers, consultants, and researchers who tried to apply the concepts of the major schools of management thought to real-life situations.

Managers, who follow this approach, make business decisions or adopt a particular management style only after carefully considering all situational factors.

Contingency theory is a class of behavioural theory that claims that there is no best way to organise a corporation, to lead a company, or to make decisions. Instead, the optimal course of action is contingent (dependent) upon the internal and external situations.

According to the contingency approach, "The task of managers is to identify which technique will, in a particular situation, under particular circumstances, and at a particular time, best contribute to the attainment of management goals"

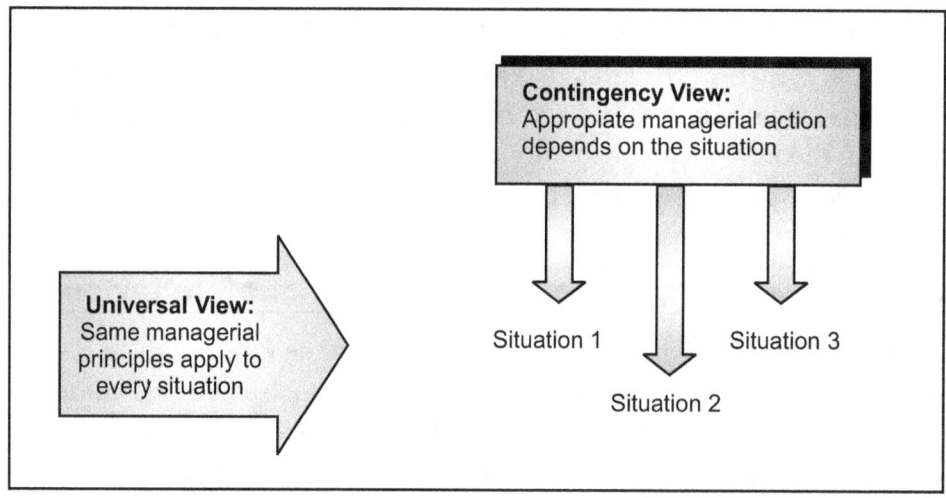

Fig. 1.5

The contingency approach refers to situational factors that are variables which moderate the relationship between the independent and dependent variables.

There are four key dependent variables (productivity, absenteeism, turnover, and job satisfaction) and a large number of independent variables (for example, motivation, leadership, work processes), organised by level of analysis, that research indicates have varying effects. Because of the large number of variables, the study of OB is complex and requires a systematic approach within organisations as we seek to predict the behaviour of people at work.

Contingency Perspective and Leadership

Dissatisfaction with trait-based theories of leadership effectiveness led to the development of contingency leadership theories. Fred Fiedler, in the 1960s and 1970s, was an early pioneer in this area. Various aspects of the situation have been identified as impacting the effectiveness of different leadership styles. For example, Fiedler suggests that the degree to which subordinates like or trust the leader, the degree to which the task is structured, and the formal authority possessed by the leader are key determinants of the leadership situation. Task-oriented or relationship oriented leadership should would each work if they fit the characteristics of the situation.

Other contingency leadership theories were developed as well. However, empirical research has been mixed as to the validity of these theories.

1.3 OB and Organisational Performance

Organisational behaviour is the application of knowledge about how people, individuals, and groups act in organisations, in order to achieve the highest performance and dominant results.

The goal of nearly every organisation is to motivate those involved towards a unified vision. By identifying the major individual variables that influence work behaviour, an organisation can offer an atmosphere that provides mandatory components for success. All organisations experience the direct relationship between job satisfaction, and performance. In order to maximize the performance of those within a system it is important to develop an optimal interpersonal chemistry.

1.3.1 What are Organisations?

An organisation is a social unit of people that is structured and managed to meet a need or to pursue collective goals. All organisations have a management structure that determines relationships between the different activities and the members, and subdivides and assigns roles, responsibilities, and authority to carry out different tasks. Organisations are open systems, they affect and are affected by their environment.

1.3.2 Perspectives of Organisational Effectiveness

Organisational effectiveness is the concept of how effective an organisation is in achieving the outcomes the organisation intends to produce. It can also be defined as the efficiency with which an association is able to meet its objectives. The main measure of organisational effectiveness for a business will generally be expressed in terms of how well its net profitability compares with its target profitability. Additional measures might include growth data and the results of customer satisfaction surveys.

Organisational effectiveness is critical to success in any economy. In order to achieve increased and sustainable business results, organisations need to execute strategy and engage employees. To create organisational effectiveness, business leaders need to focus on aligning and engaging their people, the people management systems, and the structure and capabilities (including organisational culture) to the strategy. Put simply, it results in higher financial performance, higher customer satisfaction, and higher employee retention. An organisation that can sustain such alignment will achieve increased business results.

An effective organisation is one that excels, is one that continually strives to identify and focus on factors critical to its customers and improves its processes in order to provide the highest-quality product or service possible.

Elton Mayo is known as the founder of the Human Relations Movement and with his research showing the importance of groups in affecting the behaviour of individuals at work. Mayo says that organisational effectiveness is a function of productivity that results from employee satisfaction.

There are many ways to measure the effectiveness of an organisation, which include different criteria such as productivity, profits, growth, turnover, stability and cohesion. Rational perspectives focus on the achievement of previously set goals and on output variables such as quality, productivity and efficiency. Natural system perspectives focus on the support goals of the organisation such as employee satisfaction, morale and interpersonal skills. Open system perspectives focus on the exchanges with the environment; this includes information processing, profitability, flexibility and adaptability.

Effectiveness criteria also can be divided, depending on the goals set in time perspective, to short- term (up to one year), as well as medium and long-term. The short-term achievements that show an organisation is effective include effectiveness in accomplishing its purposes; efficiency in the acquisition and use of scarce resources; and being a source of satisfaction to its owners, employees, clients and the society.

In achieving medium-term criteria, an effective organisation must be adaptive to new opportunities and hurdles, as well as being capable of developing the abilities of its members and itself.

Longer term criteria (approximately five years) require that the effective organisation should be capable of surviving in a world of uncertainties.

There are five main approaches in measuring organisational effectiveness, which include goal approach, internal process approach, system resource approach, constituencies approach and internal processes approach.

The goal approach measures the effectiveness of the ability of an organisation to excel at one or more output goals. This is the most common effectiveness measurement approach. According to the goal approach, an organisation is effective when it accomplishes its stated goals. This approach is most often applied when the set goals are clear, time bound and measurable. A hurdle to applying such an approach is that the goals can be difficult for defining and measuring, as organisations are not immune to ambiguity and measurement error.

According to the internal process approach effectiveness is the ability to excel at internal efficiency, coordination, motivation and employee satisfaction. This approach measures effort rather than the achieved effect. This type of efficiency measurement is an assessment of conformity of a given objective that can be decoupled from output performance.

The system resource approach defines effectiveness as the ability to acquire scarce and valued resources from the environment. It is preferred when there exists a clear connection between inputs and outputs.

Constituency approach measures the effectiveness of the ability to satisfy multiple strategic constituencies both within and outside the organisation. This approach is very useful for organisations that depend highly on response to demands. Criteria depends on the constituency group. For owners the typical criteria would be the return on investment and profit growth, while for employees the criteria are compenzation, other benefits and job satisfaction. For clients the main criteria are satisfaction with the price, quality and service. Suppliers focus on payments and future sales, while creditors pay attention to credit payments.

According to the domain approach effectiveness is the ability to excel in one or more among several domains as selected by senior managers.

1.3.3 Task Performance

Task performance means employee behaviours that are directly involved in the transformation of organisational resources into the goods or services that the organisation produces.

Organisational behaviour refers to the way that people, either as individuals or in groups, behave within the context of an organisation. Psychological theories, meanwhile, seek to explain the reasons people behave as they do.

The intersection of organisational behaviour and psychological theory provides insight into why people act as they do in the context of work. Such insight can help leaders create environments conducive to better performance. Specific psychological theories have different relationships with organisational behaviours.

Motivation

Motivation in employees allows them to sustain effort in a particular direction for some period of time. Naturally, management wants motivated employees. But, motivated by what and to what end? Psychological theory often attempts to explain motivation through evaluating people's needs.

In Maslow's' theory, for instance, needs are ordered from those of basic survival to metaphysical fulfilment. The lowest unmet need, according to theory, is the one driving an individual's behaviour. Meshing the motivations of employees with a company's needs can help leaders achieve goals.

Reciprocity

Social exchange theory refers to cooperative, reciprocal behaviour that emerges when a person is the recipient of some benefit. A relationship begins when a benefactor bestows something upon another and the recipient, in turn, returns the favour by becoming the benefactor. As the exchange of benefits continues, the relationship grows, built on a sense of mutual obligation and an implied contract.

In terms of organisational behaviour, social exchange theories predict that those in leadership roles can gather employee backing for company agendas if those employees are treated favourably. If an organisation breaks its contract by not keeping benefits up, employees may feel released from their contract with the employer at the cost of loyalty and effort on the company's behalf.

Positivity

The advent of the 21st century saw the development of a new way of approaching organisational behaviour. Instead of trying to eliminate the negative, current psychological theory looks at accentuating the positive.

This new study falls under the positive psychology movement. Phrases such as "positive organisational behaviour" or "positive organisational psychology" are used when positive psychology is applied to organisational behaviour. Applied that way, it looks at the positive psychological capital of an organisation -- in other words, this new theoretical approach emphasises what's right and figures out where it comes from so an organisation can propagate more of the same.

Confidence, hope, resiliency and optimism - these are the important positive psychological traits that lay behind constructive activity and organisational behaviour. This capital can belong to individuals, groups, leaders and to the organisation itself.

Group Belonging

Social identity theory refers to the identity a person feels as a member of a group. A sense of group belonging can be a powerful force in an organisation because people tend to favour others who are of their group as an extension of self.

This can be damaging if the social identity is, for instance, based on race or gender. On the other hand, social identity can create a sense of camaraderie among members of a work team and give it a competitive edge.

1.3.4 Organisational Citizenship Behaviour (OCB)

Organisational citizenship behaviour (OCB) has undergone subtle definitional revisions since the term was coined in the late 1980s, but the construct remains the same at its core. OCB refers to anything that employees choose to do, spontaneously and of their own accord, which often lies outside of their specified contractual obligations. In other words, it is discretionary. OCB may not always be directly and formally recognised or rewarded by the company, through salary increments or promotions for example, though of course OCB may be reflected in favourable supervisor and co-worker ratings, or better performance appraisals. In this way it can facilitate future reward gain indirectly. Finally, and critically, OCB must 'promote the effective functioning of the organisation' (Organ, 1988, p. 4).

OCB has been shown to have a positive impact on employee performance and wellbeing, and this in turn has noticeable flow-on effects on the organisation. The effects on employee performance are threefold. Firstly, workers who engage in OCB tend to receive better performance ratings by their managers (Podsakoff et al., 2009). This could be because employees who engage in OCB are simply liked more and perceived more favourably (this has become known as the 'halo effect'), or it may be due to more work-related reasons such as the manager's belief that OCB plays a significant role in the organisation's overall success, or perception of OCB as a form of employee commitment due to its voluntary nature (Organ et al., 2006). Regardless of the reason, the second effect is that a better performance rating is linked to gaining rewards (Podsakoff et al., 2009) – such as pay increments, bonuses, promotions or work-related benefits. Thirdly, because these employees have better performance ratings and receive greater rewards, when the company is downsizing e.g. during an economic recession, these employees will have a lower chance of being made redundant.

OCB is linked to lower rates of employee turnover and absenteeism, but on the organisational level increased productivity, efficiency and customer satisfaction, as well as reduced costs, have also been observed (Podsakoff et al, 2009).

Why does OCB seem to have such compelling effects on the individual and the success of an organisation? Organ et al. (2006) has offered the following suggestions. OCB can:

- enhance productivity (helping new co-workers; helping colleagues meet deadlines)
- free up resources (autonomous, cooperative employees give managers more time to clear their work; helpful behaviour facilitates cohesiveness (as part of group maintenance behaviour).
- attract and retain good employees (through creating and maintaining a friendly, supportive working environment and a sense of belonging)
- create social capital (better communication and stronger networks facilitate accurate information transfer and improve efficiency)

1.3.5 Counter Productive Work Behaviour

Within organisations today counterproductive behaviour at work is a huge issue which can have severe consequences. At least 30% of all businesses are believed to fail due to counterproductive work behaviours. All it takes is one employee engaging in serious counterproductive work behaviour to have detrimental effects on an organisation. For instance, the actions of one person led to the collapse of ENRON.

Due to the large potential losses to an organisation from counterproductive behaviour, it is important that counterproductive behaviours in the workplace are not over looked. Steps need to be taken to reduce the risk of potential loss due to counterproductive behaviours occurring within the workplace.

Definition

Counterproductive work behaviour is any intentional unacceptable behaviour that has the potential to have negative consequences to an organisation and the staff members within that organisation. These behaviours include acts such as theft, calling in sick when you're not sick, fraud, sexual harassment, violence, drug and alcohol use, and inappropriate use of the internet.

Counterproductive behaviours can range in severity from minor offences such as stealing a pen to serious offences such as embezzling millions from an organisation.4 They can occur at either the interpersonal level or at an organisational level. Counterproductive behaviours at the interpersonal level are behaviours that affect the employees within the organisation and include acts such as favouritism, gossip, and harassment. At the organisational level are behaviours directed towards the organisation, these include behaviours such as absenteeism and misuse of the employer's assets.

Key factors identified as associated with counterproductive work behaviour are:

- Personality – especially conscientiousness;
- Psychological contract breach;
- Leadership styles such as authoritative and laisser-faire;

- Unfair reward allocation;

- Individual competition; and

- Unfair interpersonal treatment.

Suggested ways to reduce counterproductive work behaviours include:

- Personality based integrity tests;

- Clearly articulated contract;

- Fair, unbiased reward systems;

- Clear zero tolerance organisational policy endorsed by management that defines unacceptable behaviour and the penalties for those behaviours, and provides a channel for communicating issues.

It is important to reduce counterproductive work behaviours to improve the well-being of organisations and employees. By using personality based integrity testing, implementing organisational policies that actively discourage counterproductive behaviours, implementing reward systems that insure fairness, and finally, clearly articulating employer and employee obligations organisations can reduce, and hopefully eliminate, counterproductive work behaviours.

1.3.6 Setting Goals for Organisational Performance

An organisation is effective to the degree to which it achieves its goals. An effective organisation will make sure that there is a spirit of cooperation and sense of commitment and satisfaction within the sphere of its influence.

The Top Three Business Benefits of Clearly Setting and Aligning Organisational Goals:

1. Increased Operating Margins

Employees who clearly understand their individual goals-and how they relate to those of their company, naturally become more engaged with their work. Once employees see how they can make a direct contribution to their company's success, they begin to focus on finding ways to work smarter and more efficiently. This boost in employee productivity will naturally lead to increased operating margins and profitability for the company.

To achieve these results, the company must put a performance management process in place that:

- Increases employee engagement with "SMART" goals.
- Provides visibility up, down and across reporting levels.
- Creates shared accountability between employees by "cascading" goals from one employee to another when relevant.
- Communicates expectations clearly during every phase of goal completion.

2. Quicker Execution of Company Strategy

Tighter goal alignment and goal visibility allows for quicker execution of company strategy by enabling the management team to allocate labour resources across various projects more effectively.

By exposing redundant business initiatives, it also increases overall efficiency by ensuring employees are not duplicating the efforts of others. Plus, goal alignment strengthens the leadership at the company by allowing managers to:

*   Understand more clearly all responsibilities associated with specific goals.
*   Eliminate redundancies across job titles.
*   Focus their staffs on the most pertinent goals of the company.

3. Reduced Employee Turnover

The business value of having employees engaged in their work cannot be overestimated. As proof, a recent Gallup poll showed that companies with large numbers of dissatisfied workers experience greater absenteeism and lower productivity-as well as a 51% higher employee turnover rate.

Fortunately, clear goal alignment can remedy this situation by helping to create greater employee ownership in a company's ultimate success. Goal alignment also lets you establish a true pay-for-performance culture at the company by providing the foundation for closely linking reward systems with both individual and team performance.

1.3.7 Role of People in Organisational Performance

The management of people at work is an integral part of the management process. To understand the critical importance of people in the organisation is to recognise that the human element and the organisation are synonymous.

A well-managed organisation usually sees an average worker as the root source of quality and productivity gains. Such organisations do not look to capital investment, but to employees, as the fundamental source of improvement.

The success of performance management practices in any organisation depend upon the commitment and involvement of the different stakeholders like top management, line managers, employees and the HR specialists.

Role of Top Managers in Performance Management

The top managers play a lead in the entire process by setting trends for the lower rung and acting as role models for the employees. Their responsibility is to design policies which ensure an efficient management of performance in an organisation and to define and act upon the core values relating to performance.

Top management plays a vital role in convincing the line managers that performance management can be instrumental in the achievement of business goals and thus ensure that they take this aspect seriously in their work front for maximising employee satisfaction and productivity.

Top managers are expected to develop a high performance culture in an organisation by ensuring the following:

- By communicating the organisation's mission and values to its customers and employees.
- By clearly defining the work expectations and communicating to everyone for ensuring success in the achievement of business goals and facilitating an overall performance improvement.
- By keeping the employees informed about their progress towards the achievement of goals and suggesting corrective actions for non-achievement of performance.
- By establishing a shared belief amongst the employees regarding the importance of continuous improvement in performance.

A remarkable example is Infosys Technology Ltd., an international IT company and a world leader. The chairman Mr. Narayan Murthy has been dedicated and committed towards an efficient management of performance of the employees for developing a vast talent pool in the organisation.

He considered his employees as the most powerful wealth responsible for driving the success and the future of his organisation. He introduced the best reward systems in the industry for retaining the existing talent and the attracting the best from the industry. He encouraged an open communication and provided them with an opportunity to interact with the management and share ideas in meetings. He established a Leadership Institute in Mysore for grooming the future leaders for successfully tackling the challenges of the changing markets.

Similarly, the management of United Parcel Service of America (UPS), selects only those people who fit into their organisational culture for efficiently managing their performance and projecting a positive image before the customers.

Role of Line Managers in Performance Management

The line managers or the front line management play a very crucial role in implementing and enacting the HR policies. Hence, it is very important for the management to ensure that the line managers possess a right attitude towards the performance management approaches and equally possess the right competencies for executing it.

The line managers mostly consider the performance management process as a mere bureaucratic chore and hence they consider it as a sheer waste of time. Some managers lack the required skills for reviewing the performance of the employees, providing feedback and identifying objectives along with them.

These limitations can be overcome by adopting the following remedies:

- By providing leadership from the top.
- By communicating to the line managers the importance of performance management in driving successful results and how it is a part of their responsibility.
- By maintaining simplicity in the overall process of performance management.
- By reducing the pressure from the line managers by making the process an ongoing one instead of an annual review.
- By involving the line managers in the design and development of the performance management processes by representing them in pilot studies.

Role of Employees in Performance Management

The employees have a vital role to play in the performance management cycle as the entire process revolves around them.

They play an active part in formulating performance agreements along with their line managers and participate in 360 degree assessment schemes. They discuss their roles and the competencies required and define objectives in conjunction with their superiors. Hence, the employees should be trained in all these activities.

Role of HR in Performance Management

The HR department today is a strategic partner and plays a vital role in pursuing a particular strategy. For facing the challenges of a globalised world, Indian organisations have reformed their HRM strategies for managing employee performance by considering part time work, outsourcing and temporary workers.

HR no longer today plays the role of a rubber stamp department, rather is a performance enabler by closely working with the management and all the major functional departments of an organisation.

Companies like Maruti Udyog Ltd. and Mahindra and Mahindra, revamped their entire organisational set up and were able to create performance efficiency due to the efforts of the HR department.

The Future of Organisational Behaviour

The international economy has taken on added importance in organisational behaviour circles in recent years, as international companies have special requirements and dynamics to contend with.

Researchers currently are studying such things as communications between and among foreign business operations, cultural differences and their impact on individuals, language difficulties, motivation techniques in different cultures, as well as the differences in leadership and decision-making practices from country to country.

Today, organisational behaviour scientists are dealing with a wide range of problems confronting the business world. For instance, they continue to study downsizing, career development in the global economy, social issues such as substance abuse and changes in family composition, and the global economy. They are trying to determine just what effects such factors are having on the workplace and what can be done to alleviate associated problems.

Points to Remember

- *Managers need certain skills and competencies to successfully achieve their goals. The most significant management skills are the technical, human and conceptual skills.*
- *People learn by observing others, with the environment, behaviour, and cognition all as the chief factors in influencing development.*
- *Organisational behaviour is important to all management function, roles and skills.*
- *Organisations are built up of levels - individual, group and an organisational system as a whole, it is important for managers to understand human behaviour in order to meet the organisations overall goals.*
- *People differ from each other in their needs and values. Group effort eases their task of achieving organisational goals effectively. Human relations can be defined as motivating people in organisations to work as a team.*
- *Organisational effectiveness is the concept of how effective an organisation is in achieving the outcomes the organisation intends to produce. It can also be defined as the efficiency with which an association is able to meet its objectives.*
- *OCB refers to anything that employees choose to do, spontaneously and of their own accord, which often lies outside of their specified contractual obligations.*
- *Counterproductive work behaviour is any intentional unacceptable behaviour that has the potential to have negative consequences to an organisation and the staff members within that organisation.*
- *The management of people at work is an integral part of the management process. To understand the critical importance of people in the organisation is to recognise that the human element and the organisation are synonymous.*

Case Study

Vikram had just finished his first week at Ozone Enterprises and decided to drive upstate to a small lakefront lodge for some fishing and relaxation. Vikram had worked for the previous ten years for the Wills Company, but Wills had been through some hard times of late and had recently shut down several of its operating groups, including Vikram's, to cut costs. Fortunately, Vikram's experience and recommendations had made finding another position fairly easy. As he drove the interstate, he reflected on the past ten years and the apparent situation at Ozone.

At Wills, things had been great. Vikram had been part of the team from day one. The job had met his personal goals and expectations perfectly, and Vikram believed he had grown greatly as a person. His work was appreciated and recognised; he had received three promotions and many more pay increases.

Vikram had also liked the company itself. The firm was decentralised, allowing its managers considerable autonomy and freedom. The corporate Culture was easygoing. Communication was open. It seemed that everyone knew what was going on at all times, and if you didn't know about something, it was easy to find out.

The people had been another plus. Vikram and three other managers went to lunch often and played golf every Saturday. They got along well both personally and professionally and truly worked together as a team. Their boss had been very supportive, giving them the help they needed but also staying out of the way and letting them work.

When word about the shutdown came down, Vikram was devastated. He was sure that nothing could replace Wills. After the final closing was announced, he spent only a few weeks looking around before he found a comparable position at Ozone Enterprises.

As Vikram drove, he reflected that "comparable" probably was the wrong word. Indeed, Ozone and Wills were about as different as you could get. Top managers at Ozone apparently didn't worry too much about who did a good job and who didn't. They seemed to promote and reward people based on how long they had been there and how well they played the never-ending political games.

May be this stemmed from the organisation itself, Vikram pondered. Ozone was a bigger organisation than Wills and was structured much more bureaucratically. It seemed that no one was allowed to make any sort of decision without getting three signatures from higher up. Those signatures, though, were hard to get. All the top managers usually were too busy to see anyone, and interoffice memos apparently had very low priority.

Vikram also had had some problems fitting in. His peers treated him with polite indifference. He sensed that a couple of them resented that he, an outsider, had been brought right in at their level after they had had to work themselves up the ladder. On Tuesday he had asked two colleagues about playing golf. They had politely declined, saying that they did not play often. But later in the week, he had overheard them making arrangements to play that very Saturday.

It was at that point that Vikram had decided to go fishing. As he steered his car off the interstate to get gas, he wondered if perhaps he had made a mistake in accepting the Ozone offer without finding out more about what he was getting into.

Case Questions

Q. 1 What advice can you give Vikram? How would this advice be supported or tempered by behavioural concepts and processes?

Q. 2 Is it possible to find an "ideal" place to work? Explain.

Questions for Discussion

1. Define *organisational behaviour.*
2. "Behaviour is generally predictable, so there is no need to formally study OB." Do you agree or disagree with this statement? Why?
3. What does it mean to say that OB takes a contingency approach in its analysis of behaviour?
4. What are the three levels of analysis in OB model? Are they related? If so, how?
5. What are some of the challenges and opportunities that managers face in today's workplace?
6. Write short notes on:
   (i) The SOBC Model
   (ii) Organisational effectiveness
   (iii) Task performance
   (iv) Organisational citizenship
   (v) Counterproductive Work behaviour

Multiple Choice Questions (MCQ's)

Qs. 1-10
State whether True or False:

1. Managers need certain skills and competencies to successfully achieve their goals.
2. The management skills like technical, human and conceptual skills are insignificant.
3. People do not learn by observing others.
4. Organisational behaviour is important to all management function, roles and skills.
5. It is not important for managers to understand human behaviour in order to meet the organisations overall goals.
6. People do not differ from each other in their needs and values.
7. Group effort eases the task of achieving organisational goals effectively.
8. Good human relations can de-motivate people in organisations to work as a team.
9. Organisational Behaviour is the multidisciplinary field that seeks knowledge of behaviour in organisational settings by systematically studying individual, group and organisational processes.
10. Organisational behaviour is a field of study that investigates the impact that individuals, groups and structures have on behaviour in an organisations.

Qs. 11-20 Fill in the Blanks:

11. OB is an interdisciplinary field that includes ……
12. Manager should concentrate on employee's …… to different situations of organisation which are becoming an important part in today's scenario.

13. In the current scenario Organisational Behaviour i.e. behaviour of ...... in an organisation is becoming the main thing for the organisations' management.
14. OB helps to increase ...... and productivity i.e. profit for the organisation.
15. The behaviours that get the bulk of attention in organisational behaviour are three, which have proven to be very important determinants of employee performance. They are ...... and turnover
16. OB attempts to improve organisational effectiveness and the ...... at work.
17. Organisations need to develop their manager's ...... skills in order to get and keep high performing employees.
18. ...... is the study and application of knowledge about how people as individuals and as groups act within organisations.
19. An overall model of organisational behaviour can be developed on the basis of three theoretical frameworks. They are:
21. Organisational behaviour cannot abolish ...... and ...... but can only reduce them. It is a way to improve but not an absolute answer to problems.

Ans. To MCQs:

1. True
2. False
3. False
4. True
5. False
6. False
7. True
8. False
9. True
10. True
11. Sociology, psychology, communication, and management;
12. Nature, reaction and response
13. Employees
14. Efficiency
15. Productivity, absenteeism
16. Quality of life
17. Interpersonal
18. Organisational behaviour
19. Cognitive, behaviouristic and social learning
20. Conflict and frustration

Activity

Consider a group situation in which you have worked. To what extent did the group rely on the technical skills of the group members vs. their interpersonal skills? Which skills seemed most important in helping the group function well?

QUESTIONS FROM PREVIOUS PUNE UNIVERSITY EXAMINATIONS

1. Elaborate the S-O-B-C Model of Organisation Behaviour with Examples.

    [M.B.A. April 2007]

2. Write Short Note on:

    (a) Elements of Organisational Behaviour.   **[M.B.A. Dec. 2007]**

3. What is Organisational Behaviour? Describe the Fundamental Concepts of Organisational Behaviour?   **[P.G.D.B.M. April 2007]**

4. Define organisational behaviour. Discuss its importance and scope.

    [MBA April 2009, 2010]

5. Explain supportive model of OB.   **[PGDBM April 2009]**

6. Explain in detail any two models of OB.   **[MBA April 2011]**

7. What is SOBC? Explain each concept with suitable illustrations.   **[MBA April 2012]**

8. Define OB. Explain the scope, importance and fundamental concepts of OB.

    [MBA Dec. 2012]

Web Links/Further Readings:

*   H. Mintzberg, *"The Nature of Managerial Work"*, (Prentice Hall, 1973).
*   F. Luthans, *"Successful, Effective Managers"*, (Academy of Management Executives, May 1998).
*   DW Organ, *"Organisational Citizenship Behaviour: The Good Soldier Syndrome"* (Lexiton Books 1988).
*   Stephen P. Robbins, Timothy Judge, Seema Sanghi *"Organisational Behaviour"*, 13th Edition.

Chapter **2**...

Individual Process and Behaviour

Contents ...

Learning Objectives

After studying this chapter you should be able to:

1.   Contrast the two types of ability.

2.   Define intellectual ability and relate its relevance to O.B.

3.   Define learning and outline the three major theories of learning.

4.   Contrast the three components of an attitude.

5. Summarise the relationship between attitude and behaviour.

6. Compare and contrast the major job attitudes.

7. Define job satisfaction.

8. Summarise the main causes of employee satisfaction.

9. Define personality, evaluate it and explain the factors that determine an individual's personality.

10. Describe the Myers-Briggs Type Indicator personality framework and assess its strengths and weaknesses.

11. Identify the key traits in the Big Five Personality Model.

12. Demonstrate how the Big Five Traits predict behaviour at work.

13. Define perception and explain the factors that influence it.

14. Explain attribution theory and list the three determinants of attribution.

15. Identify the shortcuts individuals use in making judgements about others.

16. Describe the three key elements of Motivation.

17. Identify four early theories of motivation and evaluate their applicability today.

18. Demonstrate how organisational justice is a refinement of equity theory.

19. Apply the key tenets of expectancy theory to motivating employees.

20. Contrast the evidence for and against the existence of emotional intelligence.

2.1 Ability

Meaning, Significance of matching right abilities to the right job, Intellectual and physical abilities and the effects of disabilities

2.1.1 Introduction

Regardless of how motivated you are, it's unlikely that you can play cricket as well as Sachin or play chess as well as Viswanathan Anand. However, this does not mean that some individuals are inferior to others. Everyone has strengths and weaknesses in terms of ability that makes him or her relatively superior or inferior to others in performing certain tasks or activities.

We are all not created equal. Individuals differ in ability and biographical characteristics. These differences affect employee performance and satisfaction.

2.1.2 Definition

Ability: *Ability may be defined as an acquired or natural capacity or talent that enables an individual to perform a particular job or task successfully.*

It may be an Aptitude, Intelligence or a Skill.

- An **Aptitude** implies an inherent capacity for learning, understanding or performing a task.
- An **Aptitude** implies an inherent capacity for learning, understanding or performing a task.
- **Intelligence** is the capacity to acquire and apply knowledge to perform a task.
- A **Skill** stresses an ability acquired or developed through experience.

> *Aptitude, Intelligence and Skill possessed by an individual is the product of certain original tendencies and the training received by the person.*

2.1.3 Significance of Matching Right Abilities to the Right Job

Ability is the capacity to perform various tasks. As discussed, people differ greatly with respect to their abilities. Skills are defined as the dexterity at performing specific tasks which have been acquired through training or experience. People also differ greatly with respect to their skills.

Skills and abilities should match the job requirements. Job seekers must therefore take the time to consider how their skills fit into the company and match the requirements of the job.

2.1.4 Ability-Job Fit

Ability-job fit is said to be high if there is a proper match between employee's abilities and the abilities required for the job that employees should perform. If employees do not possess the ability required for the job, they are likely to fail.

Sometimes an employee has an ability which far exceeds the requirement of the job. In such situations also the Ability-job fit is not right. If an employee's ability exceeds the ability required by the job he may not be satisfied with the job.

2.1.5 Intellectual and Physical Abilities

An individual ability is essentially made up of two factors:

(1) Intellectual ability
(2) Physical ability

(1) Intellectual Ability

Ability to perform mental activities is known as intellectual ability. Intellectual abilities have got seven dimensions.

1. **Number aptitude:** It is an ability to do speedy and accurate arithmetic.
2. **Verbal comprehension:** It is the ability to understand what is read and heard and the relationship of words to each other.
3. **Perceptual speed:** It is the ability to identify visual similarities and differences quickly and accurately.

4. **Inductive reasoning:** It is the ability to identify a logical sequence in a problem and then solve the problem.

5. **Deductive reasoning:** It is the ability to see logic and assesses the implication of an argument.

6. **Special visualisation:** It is the ability to imagine how an object would look like if its position in space was changed.

7. **Memory:** It is the ability to retain and recall past experience.

(2) Physical Ability

These abilities are required for successfully doing less skilled and more standardised jobs. Physical abilities are required to do tasks that demand stamina, strength and similar characteristics.

The Nine different Physical Abilities

1. **Dynamic strength:** Ability to exert muscular force continuously over time.
2. **Trunk strength:** Ability to exert muscular using trunk muscles.
3. **Static strength:** Ability to exert force against external objects.
4. **Explosive strength:** Ability to expand a maximum of energy in one or a series of explosive acts.
5. **Extent flexibility**: Ability to move the trunk and back muscles as far as possible.
6. **Dynamic flexibility**: Ability to make rapid, repeated flexing movements.
7. **Body co-ordination**: Ability to co-ordinate the simultaneous actions of different parts of the body.
8. **Balance:** Ability to maintain equilibrium despite forces pulling off balance.
9. **Stamina:** Ability to continue maximum effort requiring prolonged efforts overtime.

> *Disabilities require a number of adjustments: physically, emotionally and psychologically.*

2.1.6 The Effects of Disabilities

Disability brings about profound changes to lifestyle and attitudes. Acquiring a disability through illness or accident affects not only the person with the disability but family and friends as well. Disabilities require a number of adjustments; physically, emotionally and psychologically.

Disabled persons have equal rights and deserve equal status with all other employees.

Community

Disabilities affect how a person is viewed by his community, his family and his friends. A disability may make others uncertain of how to approach or interact with the disabled person. Friendships and other relationships may be a casualty for a person already struggling with learning how to live with his new limitations. This is especially true if the person with the disability remains angry and pushes others away instead of allowing them to assist and "be there" for him. Another more positive effect of a disability, especially one from illness or accident, is when it pulls a community together in support.

Work Place

The effects disabled employees have on the workplace are varied. Small business owners should not discourage the hiring of physically and mentally challenged workers in their establishments, but rather work with disabled employees to utilise their talents.

Points to Remember

Ability is the capacity to perform various tasks. People differ greatly with respect to their abilities.

Ability-job fit is said to be high if there is a proper match between employee's abilities and the abilities required of the job that employees should perform.

An individual ability is essentially made up of two factors:

(1) Intellectual ability

(2) Physical ability

2.2 Learning

Definition of learning, significance of continuous learning in an organisation, Theories of learning, Action learning, Learning from individuals and learning from the environment.

2.2.1 Introduction

You must have seen people in the process of learning and you must have also seen people behave in a particular way as a result of the learning. We can infer that learning has taken place if an individual behaves, reacts, and responds as a result of experience in a manner different from the way he formerly behaved. To explain and predict behaviour, we need to understand how people learn, so that we can apply the theories of learning for shaping employee behaviours. This section defines learning and presents the popular theories of learning. All complex behaviour is learned.

2.2.2 Definition

Learning: *Learning is acquiring new, or modifying existing knowledge, behaviours, skills, values, or preferences and may involve synthesising different types of information.*

> *Learning: Any relatively permanent change in behaviour that occurs as a result of experience.*

Learning itself cannot be measured, but its results can be. Learning is any relatively permanent change in behaviour that occurs as a result of experience.

2.2.3 Significance of Continuous Learning in an Organisation

It should be noted that, for organisations wishing to remain relevant and thrive, learning better and faster is critically important.

Learning is the key to success—some would even say survival—in today's organisations. At the organisational level, continuous learning is increasingly important for the success of the organisation because of changing economic conditions.

Given the current business environment, organisations must be able to learn continuously in order to deal with these changes and, in the end, to survive. Knowledge should be continuously enriched through both internal and external learning. For this to happen, it is necessary to support and energise organisation, people, knowledge, and technology for learning.

2.2.4 Theories of Learning

Behaviourist Theories

Consider learning as the association of stimulus and response (S-R) connection and the response and stimulus (R-S) connection.

Classical Conditioning

A type of conditioning in which an individual responds to some stimulus that would not ordinarily produce such a response.

Examples of Classical Conditioning

Individual	Stimulus	Response
	Watches favourite tennis player winning a tournament	Jumps with joy
	Touches a hot vessel	Moves away
	Hears good music	Hums and rocks gently
	Steps on a nail	Jumps and screams in pain

Operant Conditioning

A type of conditioning in which desired voluntary behaviour leads to a reward or prevents punishment.

Examples of Operant Conditioning

Individual	Response	Stimulus
	Browses the internet	Obtains desired information
	Carries a credit card	Finds it convenient to shop
	Pays loan installments promptly	Attracts no penalty
	Achieves sales target	Obtains incentives and gifts
	Uses power carefully	Saves money

Cognitive Theories

Cognitive theory consists of a relationship between cognitive environment cues and expectation. Learning is considered as developing a pattern of behaviour from bits of knowledge about and cognition of the environment. This learning is termed as S-S (Stimulus-Stimulus) Learning.

Social-learning Theory

People can learn through observation and direct experience.

2.2.5 Action Learning

Action Learning is the approach that links the world of learning with the world of action through a reflective process within small cooperative learning groups known as 'action learning sets'. The 'sets' meet regularly to work on individual members' real-life issues with the aim of learning with and from each other. The 'father' of Action Learning, Reg Revans, has said that there can be no learning without action and no (sober and deliberate) action without learning.

2.2.6 Learning from Individuals and Groups

Much of what we have learned comes from watching our parents, teachers, peers, motion pictures and television performers, bosses, and so forth - people whom we consider as our role models. Individuals can learn by observing what happens to other people and just by being told about something as well as through direct experiences.

Points to Remember

Learning: Any relatively permanent change in behaviour that occurs as a result of experience. At the organisational level, continuous learning is increasingly important to the success of the organisation because of changing economic conditions.

Theories of learning are:

- **Behaviourist theories:** Considers learning as the association of stimulus and response (S-R) connection and the response and stimulus (R-S) connection.
- **Classical conditioning:** A type of conditioning in which an individual responds to some stimulus that would not ordinarily produce such a response.

- **Operant conditioning:** A type of conditioning in which desired voluntary behaviour leads to a reward or prevents punishment.
- **Cognitive theories:** It consists of a relationship between cognitive environment cues and expectation. Learning is considered as developing a pattern of behaviour from bits of knowledge about and cognition of the environment. This learning is termed as S- S (Stimulus-Stimulus) Learning.
- **Social-learning theory:** People can learn through observation and direct experience.

Action Learning is the approach that links the world of learning with the world of action through a reflective process within small cooperative learning groups known as 'action learning sets'.

2.3 Attitude

Importance of attitude in an organisation, Right Attitude, Components of attitude, Relationship between behaviour and attitude, Developing Emotional intelligence at the workplace, Job attitude, Barriers to changing attitudes.

2.3.1 Introduction

When someone says "I like your dress," she is expressing her attitude towards your dress.

Attitudes are evaluative statements about objects, people, or events. These statements may be either favourable or unfavourable.

Many organisations are concerned with the attitudes of their employees, as attitudes are linked to behaviour. Employees' satisfaction or dissatisfaction with their jobs affects the workplace. Attitudes are complex, to understand them better; we need to break them up into their fundamentally properties or components.

2.3.2 Definition

Attitude: *Attitude can be defined as, "a complex mental state involving beliefs and feelings and values and dispositions to act in certain ways."*

For example, if someone says that "I like my Job". This statement expresses his attitude towards his Job.

2.3.3 Components of Attitude

The definition of attitude indicates that they have three components: cognitive, affective, and behaviour. Sometimes, our cognitions may influence our feelings, which may, in turn, influence our behavioural tendencies. However, it is important to recognise that different people with the same beliefs may develop different feelings, and that different people with the same feelings may develop different behavioural intentions. Also, we will see there may even be cases, in which our beliefs which will be influenced by our feelings, or even by our actual behaviours.

There are three components of attitude:
- Cognitive component
- Affective component
- Behavioural Component

(1) Cognitive Component

It refers to that part of attitude which is related in general know how of a person. For example, He says,"smoking is injurious to health". Such type of idea of a person is called cognitive component of attitude.

The cognitive component of attitudes is our cognitions or beliefs about the facts pertaining to the attitude object. For example, we may believe that salespersons in our firm receive high pay or that our firm is the oldest in the industry. These beliefs may be correct or incorrect.

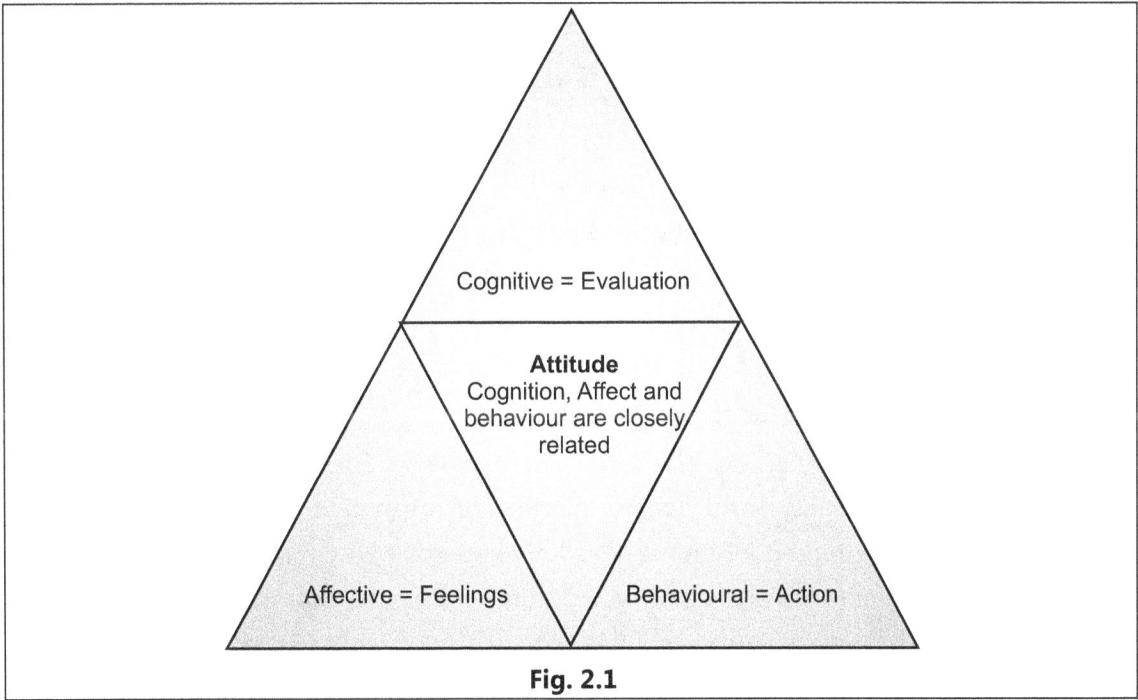

Fig. 2.1

There are three components of attitude:
- Cognitive component
- Affective component
- Behavioural Component

(2) Affective Component

The second component, the affective component is made up of our feelings toward the attitude object. It involves evaluation and emotion. For instance, we may think favourably or unfavourably about another employee or think a particular rule is good or bad.

This part of attitude is related to the statement which affects another person. For example, in an organisation a personal report is given to the general manager, in the report he points out that the sale staff is not performing their due responsibilities.

(3) Behavioural Component

The third component, the behavioural tendency component is the way we intend to behave toward the attitude object. We may, for example, intend to tell off the boss or ask for a raise or outperform a co-worker.

It's generally agreed that attitudes form only one determinant of behaviour. They represent predispositions to behave in particular ways, but how we actually act in a particular situation will depend on the immediate consequences of our behaviour, how we think others will evaluate our actions, and habitual ways of behaving in those kinds of situations.

2.3.4 How Attitude Influences Behaviour

It's generally agreed that attitudes form only one determinant of behaviour. They represent predispositions to behave in particular ways, but how we actually act in a particular situation will depend on the immediate consequences of our behaviour, how we think others will evaluate our actions, and habitual ways of behaving in those kinds of situations. In addition, there may be specific situational factors influencing behaviour. Sometimes we experience a conflict of attitudes, and behaviour may represent a compromise between them.

Compatibility between Attitudes and Behaviour

The same attitude may be expressed in a variety of ways. For example, having a positive attitude towards a Political Party doesn't necessarily mean that you actually become a member, or that you attend public meetings. But if you don't vote for this Political Party in a general election, people may question your attitude. In other words, an attitude should predict behaviour to some extent, even if this is extremely limited and specific.

> *Every single instance of behaviour involves four specific elements:*
> 1. *A specific action.*
> 2. *Performed with respect to a given target.*
> 3. *In a given context.*
> 4. *At a given point in/of time.*

Attitudes can predict behaviour, provided that both are assessed at the same level of generality. There needs to be a high degree of compatibility (or correspondence) between them.

Attitudes can predict behaviour if you ask the right questions.

According to the principle of compatibility, measures of attitude and behaviour are compatible to the extent that the target, action, context and time element are assessed at identical levels of generality or specificity.

For example, a person's attitude towards a 'healthy lifestyle' only specifies the target, leaving the other three unspecified. A behavioural measure that would be compatible with this global attitude would have to aggregate a wide range of health behaviour across different contexts and times.

The Strength of Attitudes

Most modern theories agree that attitudes are represented in memory, and that an attitude's accessibility can exert a strong influence on behaviour. By definition, strong attitudes exert more influence over behaviour, because they can be automatically activated. One factor that seems to be important is direct experience.

> *The components of an organisation's attitude include strategy, posture and culture.*

Successful organisations like Apple, Coca-Cola, the Red Cross and Rits-Carlton all have a distinct attitude. For example, Apple leads its competitors in designing innovative products. Winning attitudes do not emerge by chance. Leaders aligning their organisation's strategy, posture and culture create them.

2.3.5 Developing Emotional Intelligence at the Workplace

When you are emotionally aware, you become free to grow personally and professionally. You learn to take everything in and separate the good from the bad. Accepting the good and being unaffected by the bad.

> *An emotionally intelligent individual is not offended by the judgments of others.*

An emotionally intelligent individual is not offended by the judgments of others. They can see past them as they try to find the benefit, if any, that they can use to grow and improve. If there isn't any benefit, they have the ability to move on, unaffected.

Benefits of Emotional Intelligence

Emotional Intelligence allows you to develop social skills that help you build constructive relationships. You learn to communicate with respect at the forefront of every discussion and make others feel at ease: it's not about you, make it about them.

Your opinion matters to others. You become an unbiased authority, someone that can be trusted; someone that eases the insecurities of others. This is why successful leaders are known to exhibit a high degree of emotional intelligence. It is a skill that gets people to follow you.

A Job Attitude

A **job attitude** is a set of evaluations of one's job that constitute one's feelings toward, beliefs about, and attachment to one's job.

Employees evaluate their advancement opportunities by observing their job, their occupation, and their employer. A job attitude is a set of evaluations of one's job that constitute one's feelings toward, beliefs about, and attachment to one's job.

Overall job attitude can be conceptualised in two ways:

- Either as affective job satisfaction that constitutes a general or global subjective feeling about a job, or
- As a composite of objective cognitive assessments of specific job facets, such as pay, conditions, opportunities and other aspects of a particular job.

2.3.6 Types of Job Attitudes

Global Job Attitudes

Global job attitudes are attitudes developed towards a job through the organisation, working environment, affective disposition, aggregate measures of job characteristics and the social environment. They depend on the broad totality of work conditions. In fact, job attitudes are also closely associated with more global measures of life satisfaction. Scales such as "Faces" enable researchers to interpret overall satisfaction with work. The Job in General scale focuses on the cognitive perspective (rather than applied) of the effects of job attitudes. A variety of job attributes are associated with different levels of satisfaction within global job attitudes.

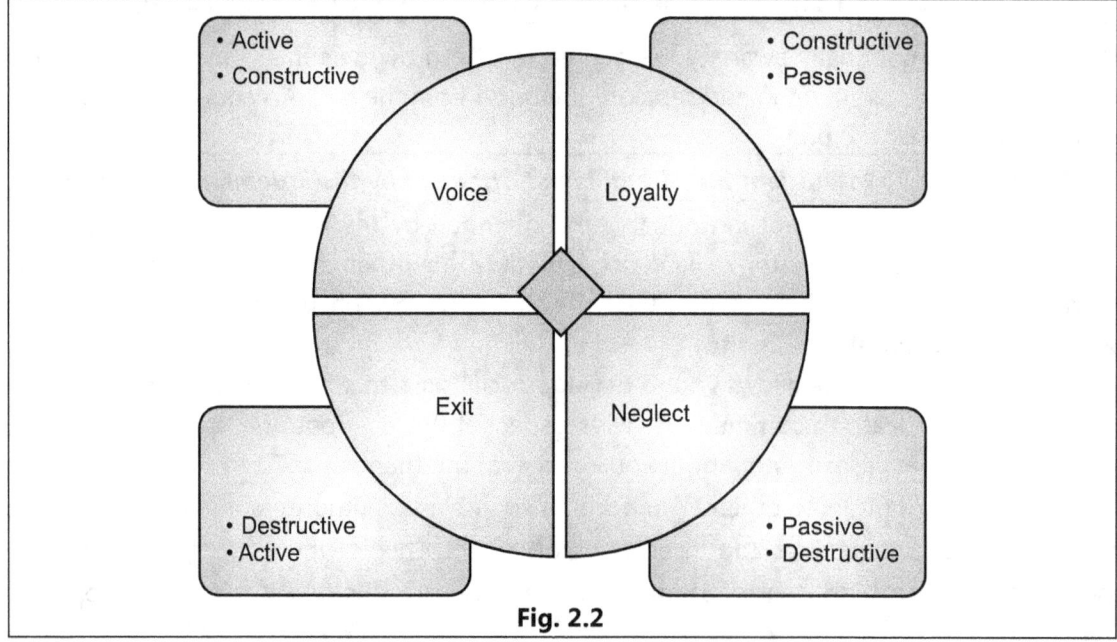

Fig. 2.2

Other Types of Job Attitudes

These are as follows:

Job Involvement: Identifying with one's job and actively participating in it, and considering performance, important to self-worth.

Organisational Commitment: Identifying with a particular organisation and its goals, and wishing to maintain membership in the organisation.

Perceived Organisational Support (POS): The degree to which employees feel the organisation cares about their well-being.

Employee Engagement: An individual's involvement with, satisfaction with, and enthusiasm for the organisation.

2.3.7 Barriers to Changing Attitudes

Employees' attitudes can be changed and sometimes it is in the best interests of managements to try to do so. For example, if employees believe that their employer does not look after their welfare, the management should try to change their attitude and help develop a more positive attitude in them. However, the process of changing the attitude is not always easy. There are some barriers which have to be overcome if one strives to change somebody's attitude. There are two major categories of barriers that come in the way of changing attitudes:

1. **Prior commitment** when people feel a commitment towards a particular course of action that has already been agreed upon and thus it becomes difficult for them to change or accept the new ways of functioning.

2. **Insufficient information** also acts as a major barrier to change attitudes. Sometimes people simply see any reason to change their attitude due to unavailability of adequate information.

Points to Remember

Attitude is a complex mental state involving beliefs and feelings and values and dispositions to act in certain ways.

There are three components of attitude.

*   Cognitive component
*   Affective component
*   Behavioural component

The components of an organisation's attitude include strategy, posture and culture. An emotionally intelligent individual is not offended by the judgments of others. They can see past them as they try to find the benefit, if any, that they can use to grow and improve.

A job attitude is a set of evaluations of one's job that constitute one's feelings toward, beliefs about, and attachment to one's job.

2.4 Personality and Values

Definition and importance of Personality for performance, The Myers-Briggs Type Indicator and The Big Five personality model, Significant personality traits suitable to the workplace (personality and job – fit theory), Personality tests and their practical applications.

2.4.1 Introduction

Our personalities shape our behaviours. If we want to understand the behaviour of someone in the organisation, it helps to know something about their personality. When psychologists talk about personality, they don't mean that a person has charm, a positive attitude toward life, a smiling face, nor is a contestant in a beauty pageant. They mean a dynamic concept describing the growth and development of a person's whole psychological system.

Personality looks at the aggregate whole, rather than looking at parts of a person. The aggregate whole is greater than the sum of the parts.

Some people are loud and aggressive, while some others are quiet and passive. Certain personality types of people are better adapted than others for certain jobs.

2.4.2 Definition

A brief definition of personality would be that personality is made up of the characteristic set of thoughts, feelings, and behaviours that make a person unique.

In addition to this, personality arises from within the individual and remains fairly consistent throughout life.

2.4.3 The Five Factor Model of Personality

The Big Five Personality Model

1. **Openness to experience** – ranks the individual as inventive/ curious, appreciative of a variety of experiences versus being more consistent and cautious.
2. **Conscientiousness** – compares tendencies towards efficient/organised versus easy-going/careless. A tendency to show self discipline and aim for achievement; planned rather than spontaneous behaviour
3. **Extraversion** – looks at predispositions towards being outgoing and energetic versus solitary and reserved.
4. **Agreeableness** – Ones tendency to be friendly/compassionate and cooperative rather than cold/unkind, suspicious or antagonistic towards others.
5. **Neuroticism** – compares nervousness and sensitivity (a tendency to experience unpleasant emotions like anger, anxiety or depression easily) versus someone who is more secure and confident.

By and large these traits are considered fixed and unchanging across time. Of these, conscientiousness is the trait most often affiliated with performance as it considers ones tendency towards self discipline and their drive for achievement against outside expectations and measures. Conscientious individuals are considered thorough, reliable, organised, industrious, and self-controlled, among other traits.

Conscientiousness is not without its limitations; however, namely that it relies on factor analysis of associated adjectives and in so doing eliminates those adjectives with few synonyms (and antonyms) from consideration. Another confound is that research has shown that the relative importance of the above qualities will likely vary depending on the type of achievement under consideration. Indeed it has been suggested, for example, that self-control, one's ability to resist temptation, is a poor predictor of very high level achievement, whereas achievement orientation was shown to better predict job proficiency and educational success than did dependability.

2.4.4 The Myers-Briggs Type Indicator (MBTI)

MBTI assessment is a psychometric questionnaire designed to measure psychological preferences in how people perceive the world and make decisions.

Fundamental to the Myers-Briggs Type Indicator is the theory of psychological type as originally developed by Carl Jung xiii. Jung proposed the existence of two dichotomous pairs of cognitive functions:

The "rational" (judging) functions: thinking and feeling

The "irrational" (perceiving) functions: sensation and intuition

Four Dichotomies

Extraversion (E)	(I) Introversion
Sensing (S)	(N) Intuition
Thinking (T)	(F) Feeling
Judging (J)	(P) Perception

Note that the terms used for each dichotomy have specific technical meanings relating to the MBTI which differ from their everyday usage. For example, people who prefer judgement over perception are not necessarily more judgmental or less perceptive. Nor does the MBTI instrument measure aptitude; it simply indicates preference for one over another.

Someone reporting a high score for extraversion over introversion cannot be correctly described as more extraverted: they simply have a clear preference.

Point scores on each of the dichotomies can vary considerably from person to person, even among those with the same type. However, Isabel Myers considered the direction of the preference (for example, E vs. I) to be more important than the degree of the preference (for example, very clear vs. slight). The expression of a person's psychological type is more than the sum of the four individual preferences. The preferences interact through type dynamics and type development.

Attitudes: Extraversion/Introversion (E/I)

Myers-Briggs literature uses the terms extraversion and introversion as Jung first used them. Extraversion means "outward-turning" and introversion means "inward-turning".These specific definitions vary somewhat from the popular usage of the words.

The preferences for extraversion and introversion are often called "attitudes". Briggs and Myers recognised that each of the cognitive functions can operate in the external world of behaviour, action, people, and things ("extraverted attitude") or the internal world of ideas and reflection ("introverted attitude"). The MBTI assessment sorts for an overall preference for one or the other.

People who prefer extraversion draw energy from action: they tend to act, then reflect, then act further. If they are inactive, their motivation tends to decline. To rebuild their energy, extraverts need breaks from time spent in reflection. Conversely, those who prefer introversion "expend" energy through action: they prefer to reflect, then act, then reflect again. To rebuild their energy, introverts need quiet time alone, away from activity.

The extravert's flow is directed outward toward people and objects, and the introvert's is directed inward toward concepts and ideas. Contrasting characteristics between extraverts and introverts include the following:

- Extraverts are "action" oriented, while introverts are "thought" oriented.
- Extraverts seek "breadth" of knowledge and influence, while introverts seek "depth" of knowledge and influence.
- Extraverts often prefer more "frequent" interaction, while introverts prefer more "substantial" interaction.
- Extraverts recharge and get their energy from spending time with people, while introverts recharge and get their energy from spending time alone.
- Functions: sensing/intuition (S/N) and thinking/feeling (T/F)

Jung Identified Two Pairs of Psychological Functions

The two perceiving functions, sensing and intuition. The two judging functions, thinking and feeling.

According to the Myers-Briggs typology model, each person uses one of these four functions more dominantly and proficiently than the other three; however, all four functions are used at different times depending on the circumstances.

Sensing and intuition are the information-gathering (perceiving) functions. They describe how new information is understood and interpreted. Individuals who prefer sensing are more likely to trust information that is in the present, tangible, and concrete: that is, information that can be understood by the five senses. They tend to distrust hunches, which seem to come "out of nowhere". They prefer to look for details and facts. For them, the meaning is in the data. On the other hand, those who prefer intuition tend to trust information that is more abstract or theoretical, that can be associated with other information (either remembered or discovered by seeking a wider context or pattern). They may be more interested in future possibilities. For them, the meaning is in the underlying theory and principles which are manifested in the data.

Thinking and feeling are the decision-making (judging) functions. The thinking and feeling functions are both used to make rational decisions, based on the data received from their information-gathering functions (sensing or intuition). Those who prefer thinking tend to decide things from a more detached standpoint, measuring the decision by what seems reasonable, logical, causal, consistent, and matching a given set of rules. Those who prefer feeling tend to come to decisions by associating or empathising with the situation, looking at it 'from the inside' and weighing the situation to achieve, on balance, the greatest harmony, consensus and fit, considering the needs of the people involved. Thinkers usually have trouble interacting with people who are inconsistent or illogical, and tend to give very direct feedback to others. They are concerned with the truth and view it as more important than being tactful.

As noted already, people who prefer thinking do not necessarily, in the everyday sense, "think better" than their feeling counterparts; the opposite preference is considered an equally rational way of coming to decisions (and, in any case, the MBTI assessment is a measure of preference, not ability). Similarly, those who prefer feeling do not necessarily have "better" emotional reactions than their thinking counterparts.

Dominant Function

According to Myers and Briggs, people use all four cognitive functions. However, one function is generally used in a more conscious and confident way. This dominant function is supported by the secondary (auxiliary) function, and to a lesser degree the tertiary (third) function. The fourth and least conscious function is always the opposite of the dominant function. Myers called this inferior function the shadow.

The four functions operate in conjunction with the attitudes (extraversion and introversion). Each function is used in either an extraverted or introverted way. A person whose dominant function is extraverted intuition, for example, uses intuition very differently from someone whose dominant function is introverted intuition.

Lifestyle

Judging/Perception (J/P)

Myers and Briggs added another dimension to Jung's typological model by identifying that people also have a preference for using either the judging function (thinking or feeling) or their perceiving function (sensing or intuition) when relating to the outside world (extraversion).

Myers and Briggs held that types with a preference for judging show the world their preferred judging function (thinking or feeling). So TJ types tend to appear to the world as logical, and FJ types as empathetic. According to Myers, judging types like to "have matters settled".

Those types who prefer perception show the world their preferred perceiving function (sensing or intuition). So SP (Sensing-Perceiving) types tend to appear to the world as concrete and NP(Intuitive-Perceiving) types as abstract. According to Myers, perceptive types prefer to "keep decisions open".

For extraverts, the J or P indicates their dominant function; for introverts, the J or P indicates their auxiliary function. Introverts tend to show their dominant function outwardly only in matters "important to their inner worlds".

2.4.5 Significant Personality Traits Suitable to the Workplace (Personality and Job-fit Theory)

Significant Personality Traits Suitable to the Workplace

Some psychologists and researchers agree that personality and job performance might be relevant in certain occupations, but the connection could be less important in other jobs. Studies looked at the relationship between agreeableness, conscientiousness, openness to experience, self-esteem, and emotional stability to determine if the two were related. The results showed high correlations in some areas, but found cognitive ability — memory, adaptability, thinking ahead, focus, etc. — often represented a more important factor.

Research reveals, A person with the personality trait of agreeableness might not represent the best candidate for a supervisor's job,. His or her personality and job performance might clash if agreeableness makes it hard to delegate tasks and enforce company regulations regarding attendance and productivity. A supervisor who lacks this trait, however, might make unreasonable demands on employees and lose their respect.

Job performance in sales or marketing might be linked to extroversion. An extrovert commonly becomes energised around other people, especially in social situations. These social skills might provide job performance indicators when hiring candidates in these professions. Conversely, if a job requires solitary work, cognitive abilities might be more important for getting the job done.

Personality and Job – Fit Theory

The Personality–Job fit theory postulates that a person's personality traits will reveal insight as to adaptability within an organisation. The degree of confluence between a person and the organisation is expressed as their Person-Organisation (P-O) fit. This is also referred to as a person–environment fit. A common measure of the P-O fit is workplace efficacy; the rate at which workers are able to complete tasks. These tasks are mitigated by workplace environs. For example, a worker who works more efficiently as an individual than in a team will have a higher P-O fit for a workplace that stresses individual tasks (such as accountancy). By matching the right personality with the right company workers can achieve a better synergy and avoid pitfalls such as high turnover and low job satisfaction. Employees are more likely to stay committed to organisations if the fit is 'good'.

Significant Personality Traits suitable to the Workplace

In practice, P-O fit would be used to gauge integration with organisational competencies. The individual is assessed on these competencies, which reveals efficacy, motivation, influence, and co-worker respect. Competencies can be assessed using various tools like psychological tests, competency based interview, situational analysis, etc.

If an individual displays a high P-O fit, we can say that the individual would most likely be able to adjust to the company environment and work culture, and would be able to perform at an optimum level.

2.4.6 Personality Tests and their Practical Applications

(1) Personality Tests

A personality test is a questionnaire or other standardised instrument designed to reveal aspects of an individual's character or psychological makeup. The first personality tests were developed in 1920's and were intended to ease the process of personnel selection, particularly in the armed forces.

Since those early efforts, a wide variety of personality tests have been developed, notably the Myers Briggs Type Indicator (MBTI), the MMPI, and a number of tests based on the Five Factor Model of Personality.

(2) Practical Applications of Personality Tests

Personality and aptitude tests (psychometrics) are helpful for managing people and for understanding yourself. You should also consider using personality and aptitude tests if you are recruiting or developing people.

(3) Values

Values provide understanding of the attitudes, motivation, and behaviours of individuals and cultures. They Influence our perception of the world around us and represent interpretations of "right" and "wrong." Values imply that some behaviours or outcomes are preferred over others.

(4) Definition

Definition of Values: Mode of conduct or end-state that is personally or socially preferable (i.e., what is right and good).

Personality

A brief definition would be that personality is made up of the characteristic set of thoughts, feelings, and behaviours that make a person unique. In addition to this, personality arises from within the individual and remains fairly consistent throughout life.

2.5 Perception

Meaning and Concept of Perception, Factors influencing Perception, Selective Perception, Attribution Theory, Perceptual Process, Social Perception (Stereotyping and Halo Effect).

2.5.1 Introduction

The world as it is perceived, is the world that is, behaviourally important. People's behaviour is based on their perception of what reality is, not on reality itself.

What we perceive can be substantially different from objective reality. For example, employees at Google may view it as a great place to work - excellent benefits, favourable working conditions, interesting job assignments, good pay, understanding and responsible management – but it is very unusual to find such agreement amongst all employees.

2.5.2 Meaning and Concept of Perception

Perception is the organisation, identification, and interpretation of sensory information in order to represent and understand the environment.

All perception involves signals in the nervous system, which in turn result from physical stimulation of the sense organs. For example, vision involves light striking the retinas of the eyes, smell is mediated by odour molecules and hearing involves pressure waves.

> *Perception is the organisation, identification, and interpretation of sensory information in order to represent and understand the environment.*

Perception is not the passive receipt of these signals, but can be shaped by learning, memory, and expectation. Perception involves these "top-down" effects as well as the "bottom-up" process of processing sensory input. The "bottom-up" processing is basically low-level information that's used to build up higher-level information (i.e. - shapes for object recognition).

The "top-down" processing refers to a person's concept and expectations (knowledge) that influence perception. Perception depends on complex functions of the nervous system, but subjectively seems mostly effortless because this processing happens outside conscious awareness

Perception is a process by which individuals organise and interpret their sensory perceives in order to give meaning to their environment.

2.5.3 Factors Influencing Perception

A. **Factors in the perceiver**
   *   Attitudes
   *   Motives
   *   Interests
   *   Experience
   *   Expectations

B. **Factors in the situation**
   *   Time
   *   Work setting
   *   Social setting

C. **Factors in the target**
   *   Novelty
   *   Motion
   *   Sounds
   *   Size
   *   Background
   *   Proximity
   *   Similarity

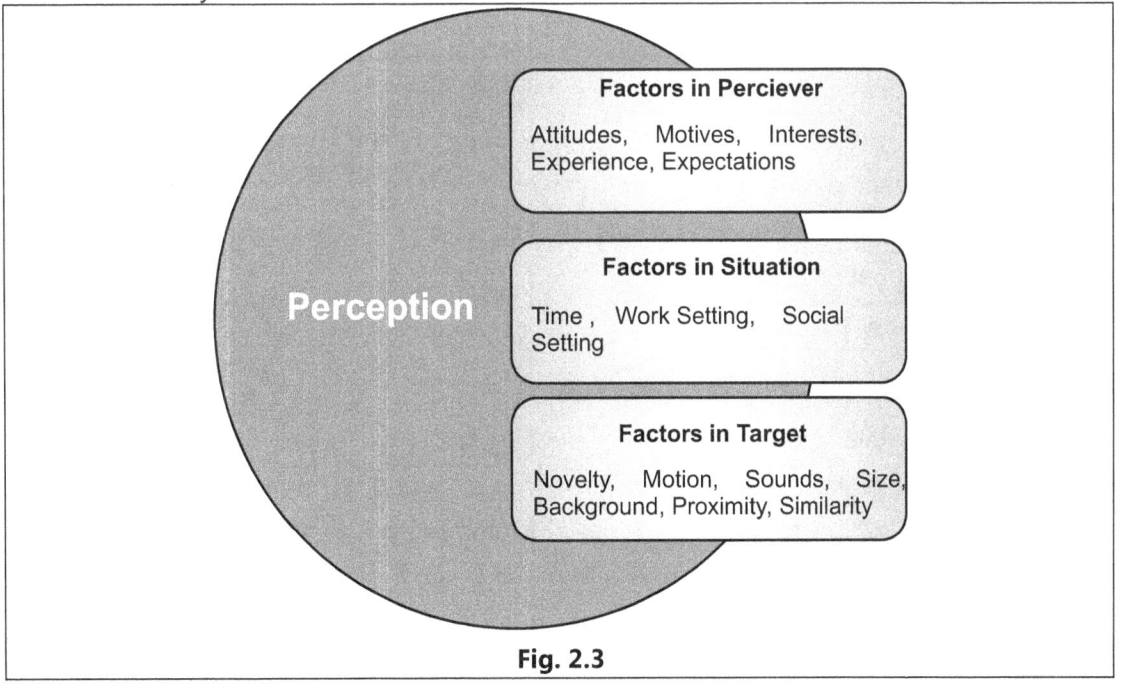

Fig. 2.3

When an individual looks at a target and attempts to interpret what he or she sees, that interpretation is heavily influenced by the personal characteristics of the individual perceiver. Personal characteristics that affect perception includes a person's attitudes, personality, motives, interest, past experiences, and expectations. For instance if you expect police officers to be authoritative, young people to be lasy, or individuals holding office to be unscrupulous, you may peeve them as such regardless of their cultural traits.

Characteristics of the target being observed affect what is perceived. Loud people are more likely to be noticed in a group than quiet ones. So, are extremely attractive or unattractive individuals. Because targets are not looked at in isolation, the relationship of a target to its background also influences perception, as does our tendency to group close things and similar things together. For instance, women people of colour or members of any other group that has clearly distinguishable characteristics in terms of features or colour are often perceived as alike in other, unrelated characteristics as well. A shrill voice is never perceived to be one of authority.

❖ Practice some vocal exercises to lower the pitch of your voice. Here is one to start: Sing – but do it an octave lower on all your favourite songs. Practice this regularly and after a period of time, your voice will lower. People will perceive you as nervous and unsure if you talk too fast. Also, be careful not to slow down to the point where people feel tempted to finish your sentences.

The context in which we see objects or events is also important. The time at which an object or event is seen can influence attention, as can location, light, heat, or any number of situational factors. For example, at a nightclub on Saturday night, you may not notice a 22 year old female dressed to the nines. Yet that same woman so attired for your Monday morning management class would certainly catch your attention (and that of the rest of the class). Neither the perceiver nor the target changed between Saturday night and Monday morning, but the situation is different.

2.5.4 Selective Perception

Selective perception is the process by which individuals perceive what they want to in media messages while ignoring opposing viewpoints. It is a broad term to identify the behaviour all people exhibit to tend to "see things" based on their particular frame of reference. It also describes how we categorise and interpret sensory information in a way that favours one category or interpretation over another. In other words selective perception is a form of bias because we interpret information in a way that is congruent with our existing values and beliefs. Psychologists believe this process occurs automatically.

A psychological cognitive bias related to how a person's expectations or the degree to which something stands out can affect observations. Selective perception can be used by a business to target its marketing campaigns to influence and appeal to desirable potential customers for its product or service.

2.5.5 Attribution Theory

This theory basically looks at how people make sense of their world; what cause and effect inferences they make about the behaviours of others and of themselves. **Heider** states that there is a strong need in individuals to understand transient events by attributing them to the actor's disposition or to stable characteristics of the environment.

The purpose behind making attributions is to achieve *cognitive control* over one's environment by explaining and understanding the causes behind behaviours and environmental occurrences.

Making attributions gives order and predictability to our lives; helps us to cope. Imagine what it would be like if you felt that you had no control over the world.

When you make attributions you analyse the situation by making inferences (going beyond the information given) about the dispositions of others and yourself as well as inferences about the environment and how it may be causing a person to behave.

Two basic kinds of attributions made:
• **INTERNAL - dispositional** • **EXTERNAL - situational**

The attribution theory is a theory developed by psychologist, Frits Heider that describes the processes by which individuals explain the causes of their behaviour and events. A form of attribution theory developed by psychologist, Bernard Weiner describes an individual's beliefs about how the causes of success or failure affect their emotions and motivations. Bernard Weiner's theory can be defined into two perspectives: intrapersonal or interpersonal. The intrapersonal perspective includes self-directed thoughts and emotions that are attributed to the self. The interpersonal perspective includes beliefs about the responsibility of others and other directed affects of emotions; the individual would place the blame on another individual.

Individuals formulate explanatory attributions to understand the events they experience and to seek reasons for their failures. When individuals seek positive feedback from their failures, they use the feedback as motivation to show improved performances.

For example, using the intrapersonal perspective, a student who failed a test may attribute their failure for not studying enough and would use their emotion of shame or embarrassment as motivation to study harder for the next test. A student who blames their test failure on the teacher would be using the interpersonal perspective, and would use their feeling of disappointment as motivation to rely on a different study source other than the teacher for the next test.

Attribution theory identifies attributions made by people as the basis of their motivation. It explains the relationship between personal perception and interpersonal behaviour.

Assumptions

1. They try to provide a logical explanation to all that is happening.
2. They attribute actions of individuals to internal or external causes.
3. These theories propose that individuals follow a fairly logical approach in making attributions.

> *Attribution theory tries to answer the "why" aspect of motivation and behaviour.*

Locus of Control Attributions

- Those employees who believe that there is an internal control for all outcomes feel that they have the power to change or influence the outcomes by means of their ability, skill and efforts.
- Those who believe that external factors control all outcomes, factors like luck, chance, etc. are responsible for influencing outcomes.
- Employees with an internal locus of control are usually happier in their jobs, occupy managerial positions, and prefer the participatory style of management as compared with employees with an external locus of control.
- Managers with an internal locus of control are, in general, better performers, considerate towards their subordinates, are not over-stressed, and follow a strategic approach.
- However, some studies show that managers with an external locus of control are perceived to take more initiative and be more considerate.
- Besides having important implications for managerial behaviour and performance, attribution theory helps in explaining goal-setting behaviour, leadership behaviour and employee performance.
- The process of attribution plays an important role in the formation of coalitions within organisations. Members have been found to have strong internal attributions, such as ability and desire, whereas non-members have a perceived external locus of control.
- Other attributions: Bad luck attributions: when people blame their failures to external causes like bad luck, fate etc. it helps reduce the pain and disappointment associated with failure.
- When people attribute their success to internal factors, their expectations of success in the future tend to be higher.

Co-variation Model of Attribution

Co-variation principle states that people attribute behaviour to the factors that are present when a behaviour occurs and absent when it does not. Thus, the theory assumes that people make causal attributions in a rational, logical fashion, and that they assign the cause of an action to the factor that co-varies most closely with that action. Harold Kelley's co-variation model of Attribution looks to three main types of information from which to make an attribution decision about an individual's behaviour. The first is *consensus information*, or information on how other people in the same situation and with the same stimulus behave. The second is *distinctive information*, or how the individual responds to different stimuli. The third is *consistency information*, or how frequent the individual's behaviour can be observed with similar stimulus but varied situations. From these three sources of information observers make attribution decisions on the individual's behaviour as either internal or external.

Three-dimensional Model of Attribution

Bernard Weine proposed that individuals have initial affective responses to the potential consequences of the intrinsic or extrinsic motives of the actor, which in turn influence future behaviour. That is, a person's own perceptions or attributions as to why they succeeded or failed at an activity determine the amount of effort the person will engage in activities in the future. Weiner suggests that individuals exert their attribution search and cognitively evaluate casual properties on the behaviours they experience. When attributions lead to positive affect and high expectancy of future success, such attributions should result in greater willingness to approach to similar achievement tasks in the future than those attributions that produce negative affect and low expectancy of future success. Eventually, such affective and cognitive assessment influences future behaviour when individuals encounter similar situations.

Weiner's achievement attribution has three categories:

1. Stable theory (stable and unstable).
2. Locus of control (internal and external).
3. Controllability (controllable or uncontrollable).

Stability influences individuals' expectancy about their future; control is related with individuals' persistence on mission; causality influences emotional responses to the outcome of task.

2.5.6 Perceptual Process

The perceptual process is a sequence of steps that begins with the environment and leads to our perception of a stimulus and an action in response to the stimulus. This process is continual, but you do not spend a great deal of time thinking about the actual process that occurs when you perceive the many stimuli that surround you at any given moment.

The process of transforming the light that falls on your retinas into an actual visual image happens unconsciously and automatically. The subtle changes in pressure against your skin that allow you to feel object occur without a single thought.

The Steps in the Perceptual Process

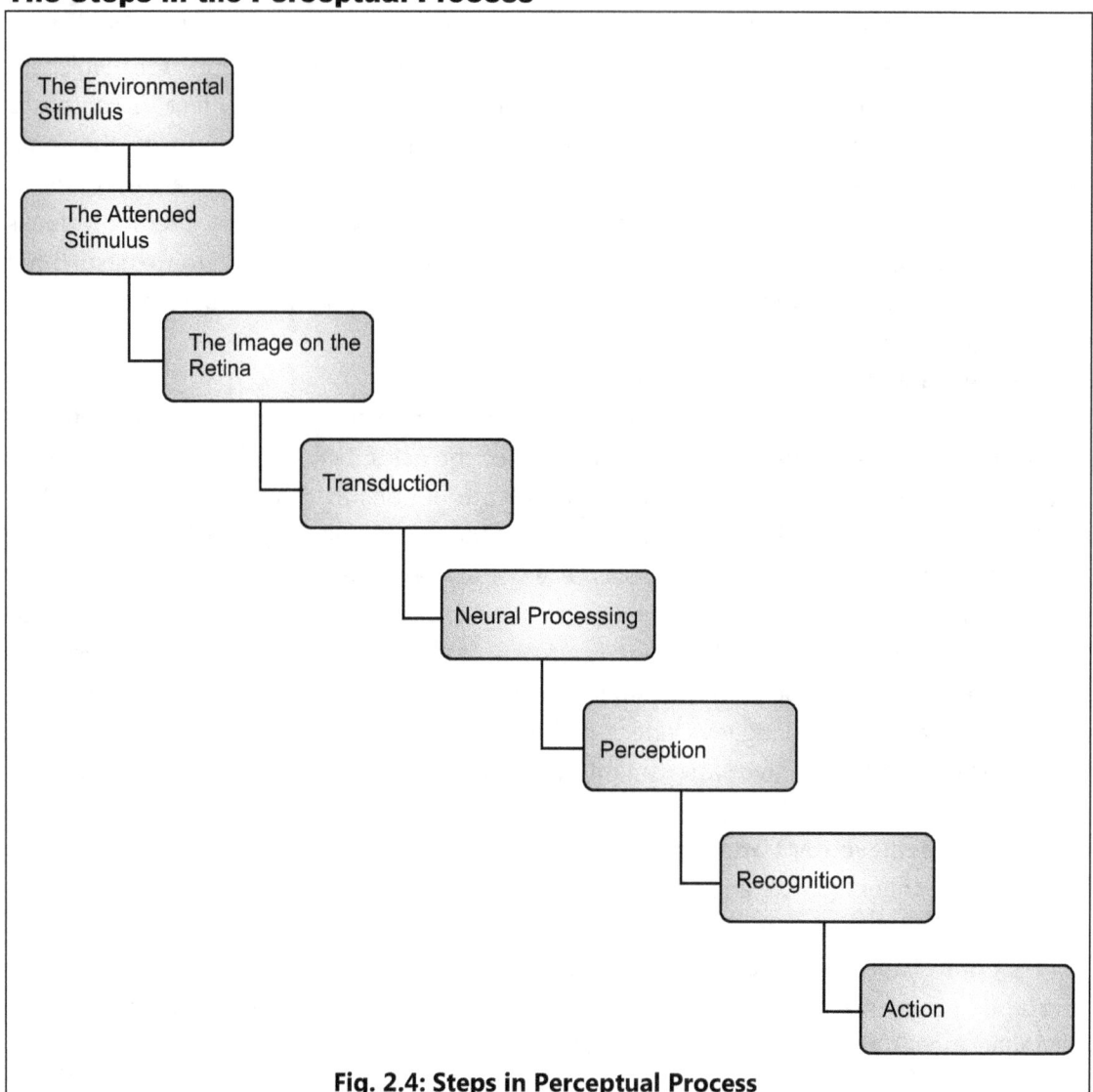

Fig. 2.4: Steps in Perceptual Process

Frequently used shortcuts in judging others

- **Selective Perception:** People selectively interpret what they see on the basis of their interests, background, experience, and attitudes.
- **Halo effect:** Drawing a general impression about an individual on the basis of a single characteristic. E.g. intelligence, sociability, or appearance.

- **Contrast effects:** Evaluation of a person's characteristics that are affected by comparisons with other people recently encountered who rank higher or lower on the same characteristics.
- **Projection:** Attributing one's own characteristics to other people.
- **Stereotyping:** Judging someone on the basis of one's perception of the group to which that person belongs. E.g. "women want relocate for a promotion"; "men aren't interested in child care"; overweight people lack discipline."

Points to Remember

Perception is the organisation, identification, and interpretation of sensory information in order to represent and understand the environment. All perception involves signals in the nervous system, which in turn result from physical stimulation of the sense organs. For example, vision involves light striking the retinas of the eyes, smell is mediated by odor molecules and hearing involves pressure waves.

Selective perception is the process by which individuals perceive what they want to in media messages while ignoring opposing viewpoints.

Attribution Theory:

Two basic kinds of attributions made: INTERNAL and EXTERNAL

INTERNAL - dispositional

EXTERNAL - situational

2.6 Motivation

2.6.1 Introduction

A majority of employees working in organisations today have no enthusiasm for their work. Motivation is an important issue today. It is therefore the most frequently researched topic in OB. What motivates people to excel? Is there anything organisations can do to encourage their employees? The theories of motivation attempt to answer these questions.

2.6.2 Definition and Concept of Motive and Motivation

- *Motive: An emotion, desire, physiological need, or similar impulse that acts as an incitement to action.*
  Motivation is the result of an interaction between an individual and a situation. The level of motivation varies both between individuals and within individuals at different times.
- *Motivation: is a psychological feature that arouses an organism to act towards a desired goal and elicits, controls, and sustains certain goal directed behaviours.*
  It can be considered a driving force; a psychological one that compels or reinforces an action toward a desired goal. For example, hunger is a motivation that elicits a desire to eat.

Motivation has been shown to have roots in physiological, behavioural, cognitive, and social areas.

Motivation may be rooted in a basic impulse to optimise well-being, minimise physical pain and maximise pleasure. It can also originate from specific physical needs such as eating, sleeping or resting, and sex.

Types of Motives

> *Motive: An emotion, desire, physiological need, or similar impulse that acts as an incitement to action.*

Primary Motives

- When a motive is not learned and it is physiologically based.
- The most common primary motives are hunger, thirst, sleep, sex, avoidance of pain and maternal concern.
- Although primary motives take precedence over the other kinds of motives in some theories of motivation, secondary motives do dominate over the primary motives in certain situations.

Secondary Motives

- Learned secondary motives play a very important role in understanding motivation in a complex and economically advanced society.
- Some important secondary motives are power, achievement and affiliation. Security and status motives are also important secondary motives.

General Motives

- General motives include those which are neither purely primary nor purely secondary, but rather in between.
- These motives are not learned, but also not based on physiological needs.
- General motives also called "stimulus motives," stimulate tension within an individual.
- The motives of curiosity, manipulation, and motive to remain active and to display affection are examples of general motives.
- Curiosity, Manipulation, Motive to Remain Active: These result in innovations and better ways of doing things.
- The Affection Motive: Love is part primary and part secondary motive. Therefore to avoid confusion it is included as a General Motive.

> *Motivation is an inner drive to behave or act in a certain manner.*

Motivation is an inner drive to behave or act in a certain manner. It's the difference between waking up before dawn to pound the pavement and lasing around the house all day. These inner conditions such as wishes, desires, goals, activate to move in a particular direction in behaviour.

In summary, motivation can be defined as the purpose for, or psychological cause of, an action.

2.6.3 Maslow's Hierarchy of Needs

Content theory of human motivation includes both Abraham Maslow's hierarchy of needs and Hersberg's two-factor theory. Maslow's theory is one of the most widely discussed theories of motivation.

The American motivation psychologist Abraham H. Maslow developed the hierarchy of needs consisting of five hierarchic classes. According to Maslow, people are motivated by unsatisfied needs. The needs, listed from basic (lowest-earliest) to most complex (highest-latest) are as follows:

1. Physiology (hunger, thirst, sleep, etc.)
2. Safety/Security/Shelter/Health
3. Belongingness/Love/Friendship
4. Self-esteem/Recognition/Achievement
5. Self actualisation

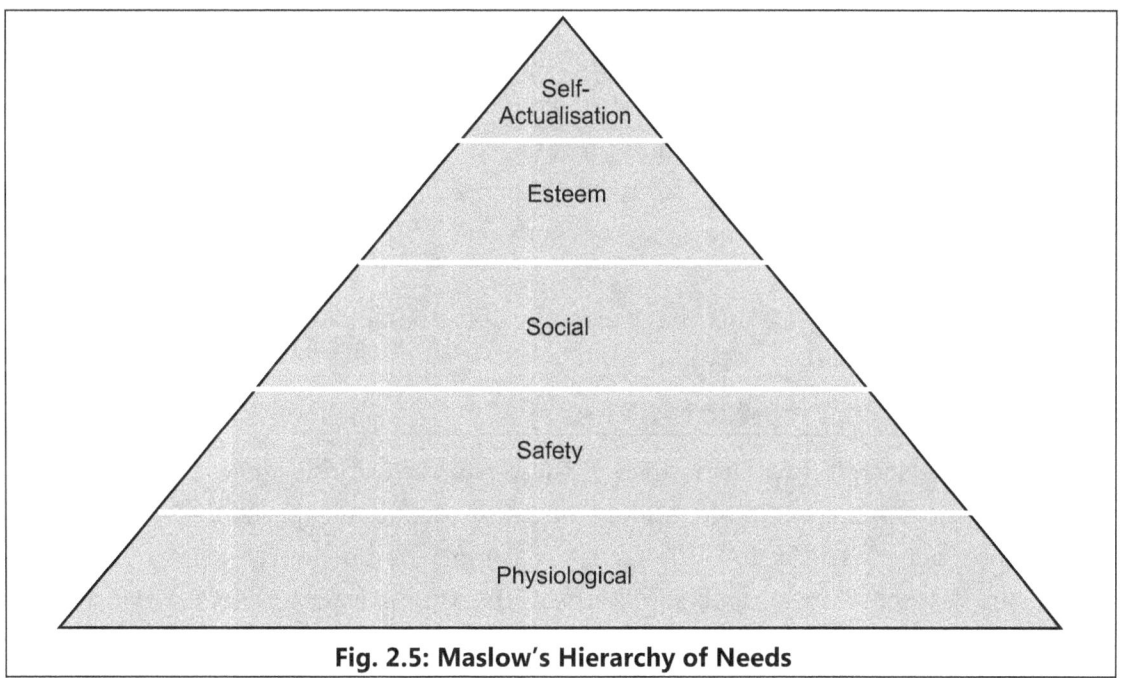

Fig. 2.5: Maslow's Hierarchy of Needs

Maslow's Hierarchy of Needs

The basic requirements build upon the first step in the pyramid: physiology. If there are deficits on this level, all behaviour will be oriented to satisfy this deficit. Essentially, if you have not slept or eaten adequately, you won't be interested in your self-esteem desires.

Subsequently we have the second level, which awakens a need for security. After securing those two levels, the motives shift to the social sphere, the third level. Psychological requirements comprise the fourth level, while the top of the hierarchy consists of self-realisation and self-actualisation.

> *Motivation is the processes that account for an individual's intensity, direction, and persistence of effort toward attaining a goal.*

Hierarchy of Needs Theory: Within every individual there exists a hierarchy of five needs:

- **Physiological:** Hunger, thirst, shelter, sex, and other bodily needs.
- **Safety:** Security and protection from physical and emotional harm.
- **Social:** Affection, belongingness, acceptance, and friendship.
- **Esteem:** Internal esteem factors such as self-respect, autonomy, and achievement; and external factors such as status, recognition, and attention.
- **Self-actualisation:** The drive to become what one is capable of becoming: includes growth, achieving one's potential, and self-fulfillment.

> *As each need is substantially satisfied, the next need becomes dominant.*

Maslow's Hierarchy of Needs theory can be summarised as follows:

Human beings have wants and desires which influence their behaviour. Only unsatisfied needs influence behaviour, satisfied needs do not.

Needs are arranged in order of importance to human life, from the basic to the complex.

The person advances to the next level of needs only after the lower level need is at least minimally satisfied.

The further the progress up the hierarchy, the more individuality, humanness and psychological health a person will show.

2.6.4 Herzberg's Two-factor Theory

Frederick Hersberg's two-factor theory, a.k.a. intrinsic/extrinsic motivation, concludes that certain factors in the workplace result in job satisfaction, but if absent, they don't lead to dissatisfaction but no satisfaction. The factors that motivate people can change over their lifetime, but "respect for me as a person" is one of the top motivating factors at any stage of life.

- Proposed by psychologist Frederick Hersberg.
- Also known as motivation-hygiene theory: Intrinsic factors are related to job satisfaction, while extrinsic factors are associated with dissatisfaction.
- Intrinsic factors, such as advancement, recognition, responsibility, and achievement seem to be related to job satisfaction. Employees who felt good about their work

tended to attribute these factors to their own selves. On the other hand, dissatisfied respondents tended to cite extrinsic factors, such as, pay, company policies, and working conditions.

*   Hersberg felt that the opposite of satisfaction is not dissatisfaction. Removing dissatisfying characteristics from the job does not necessarily make the job satisfying.

> *Hersberg felt that the opposite of satisfaction is not dissatisfaction.*

He distinguished between:

Motivators: (e.g. challenging work, recognition, responsibility) which give positive satisfaction, and Hygiene factors: (e.g. status, job security, salary and fringe benefits) that do not motivate if present, but, if absent, result in de-motivation.

The name Hygiene factors is used because, like hygiene, the presence will not make you healthier, but absence can cause health deterioration.

The theory is sometimes called the "Motivator-Hygiene Theory" and/or "The Dual Structure Theory."

Hersberg's theory has found application in such occupational fields as information systems and in studies of user satisfaction.

Contrasting views of Satisfaction and Dissatisfaction

*   **Traditional view:** Satisfaction and Dissatisfaction are opposite to each other.
*   **Hersberg's view:** Motivators lead to satisfaction or to No satisfaction.
*   **Hygiene factors:** Factors – such as company policy and administration, supervision, and salary – that, when adequate in a job, placate workers. When these factors are adequate, people will not be dissatisfied.
*   If we want to motivate people on their jobs, Hersberg suggested emphasising factors associated with the work itself or to outcomes directly derived from it, such as promotional opportunities, opportunities for personal growth, recognition, responsibility, and achievement i.e. characteristics that people find intrinsically rewarding.

2.6.5 Process Theory

Process theory is a commonly used form of scientific research study in which events or occurrences are said to be the result of certain input states leading to a certain outcome (output) state, following a set process.

Process theory holds that if an outcome is to be duplicated, so too must the process which originally created it, and that there are certain constant necessary conditions for the outcome to be reached. When the phrase is used in connection with human motivation, process theory attempts to explain the mechanism by which human needs changes. Some of the theories that fall in this category are expectancy theory, equity theory, and goal setting.

In management research, process theory provides an explanation for 'how' something happens and a variance theory explains 'why'.

2.6.6 Vroom Expectancy Theory

Like the needs-goal theory, motivation strength is determined by the perceived value of the result of performing a behaviour and the perceived probability that the behaviour performed will cause the result to materialise.

> *People tend to perform the behaviours that maximise their rewards over the long term.*

As both of these factors increase, so does motivation strength, or the desire to perform the behaviour. People tend to perform the behaviours that maximise their rewards over the long term.

- An employee will be motivated to exert a high level of effort when he or she believes that effort will lead to a good performance appraisal; that a good appraisal will lead to organisational rewards such as a bonus, a salary increase, or a promotion; and that the rewards will satisfy the employee's personal goals.

The theory, therefore, focuses on three relationships:

- **Effort-performance relationship:** The probability perceived by the individual that exerting a given amount of effort will lead to performance.
- **Performance-reward relationship:** The degree to which the individual believes that performing at a particular level will lead to attainment of a desired outcome.
- **Rewards-personal goals relationship:** The degree to which organisational rewards satisfy an individual's personal goals or needs and the attractiveness of those potential rewards for the individual.

2.6.7 Porter-Lawler Theory

The Porter-Lawler Theory accepts the premises that felt needs cause human behaviour and that the effort expended to accomplish a task is determined by the perceived value of rewards that will result from finishing the task and the probability that those rewards will materialise. The model holds that performance in an organisation is dependent on three factors:

1. An employee should have the desire to perform, i.e. he must feel motivated to accomplish the task.
2. Motivation alone cannot ensure successful performance of a task. The employee should have the abilities and skills required to successfully perform the task.
3. The employee should have a clear perception of his role in the organisation and an accurate knowledge of the job requirements. This will enable him to focus his efforts on accomplishing the assigned tasks.

Important Variables in the Model

- **Effort:** This denotes the amount of energy expended by an individual to perform a specific task. Motivation is the force that drives an individual to make an effort to perform a certain task.
- **Performance:** Making an effort does not deliver effective performance on its own. Performance also depends on his abilities and skills and the way he perceives his role in accomplishing the task.
- **Rewards:** May be intrinsic or extrinsic in nature. Intrinsic rewards are less likely to be affected by disturbing or negative thoughts and influences of others. While for extrinsic rewards, it is difficult to establish a relationship between rewards and performance.
- **Satisfaction:** Depends upon whether the actual reward offered fall short of, match or exceed what the individual perceives as an equitable level of reward.

2.6.8 Contemporary Theories

Equity Theory

Equity theory looks at an individual's perceived fairness of an employment situation and finds that perceived inequalities can lead to changes in behaviour. When individuals believe that they have been treated unfairly in comparison with their co-workers, they will react in one of four ways:

> *Equity theory looks at an individual's perceived fairness of an employment situation and finds that perceived inequalities can lead to changes in behaviour.*

1. Changing their work inputs to better match the rewards they are receiving.
2. Ask for a raise or take legal action.
3. Change their perception of the situation.
4. Quit.

- Individuals compare their job inputs and outcomes with those of others and then respond to eliminate any inequities.
- If we perceive our outcome-input ratio to be equal to that of the relevant others with whom we compare ourselves, a state of equity is said to exist. We perceive our situation as fair—that justice prevails.
- When we see the ratio as unequal, we experience equity tension.
- When we see ourselves as under-rewarded, the tension creates anger; when over-rewarded, the tension creates guilt. This negative state provides the motivation to do something to correct it.

Important Variables in Equity Theory

The referent chosen is an important variable in equity theory.

1. **Self-inside:** An employee's experiences in a different position inside his or her current organisation.
2. **Self-outside:** An employee's experiences in a situation or position outside his or her current organisation.
3. **Other-inside:** Another individual or group of individuals inside the employee's organisation.
4. **Other-outside:** Another individual or group of individuals outside the employee's organisation.

Employee's Choices when Inequity is Perceived

1. Change their inputs i.e. don't exert as much effort.
2. Change their outcomes i.e. if paid on piece-rate basis, they can increase their quantity of units produced.
3. Distort perceptions of self i.e. "I now realise that I work a lot harder than others."
4. Distort perceptions of others i.e. "his job isn't as desirable as I previously thought it was."
5. Choose a different referent i.e. make comparison with someone who isn't as well of.
6. Leave the field i.e. quit the job.

Propositions Relating to Inequitable Pay

1. Given payment by time, over-rewarded employees will produce more than will equitably paid employees.
2. Given payment by quantity of production, over-rewarded employees will produce fewer, but higher-quality, units than will equitably paid employees.
3. Given payment by time, under-rewarded employees will produce less or poorer quality of output.
4. Given payment by quantity, under-rewarded employees will produce a large number of low-quality units in comparison with equitably paid employees.
   - **Distributive justice:** Perceived fairness of the amount and allocation of rewards among individuals.
   - **Procedural justice:** The perceived fairness of the process used to determine the distribution of the rewards. These are particularly relevant to OCB (Organisational Citisenship Behaviour).

Points to Remember

Motivation: It is a psychological feature that arouses an organism to act towards a desired goal and elicits, controls, and sustains certain goal directed behaviours. It can be considered a driving force; a psychological one that compels or reinforces an action toward a desired goal.

Motivation has been shown to have roots in physiological, behavioural, cognitive, and social areas. Motivation may be rooted in a basic impulse to optimise well-being, minimise physical pain and maximise pleasure. It can also originate from specific physical needs such as eating, sleeping or resting, and sex.

Abraham H. Maslow developed the hierarchy of needs consisting of five hierarchic classes:

1. Physiology (hunger, thirst, sleep, etc.)
2. Safety/Security/Shelter/Health
3. Belongingness/Love/Friendship
4. Self-esteem/Recognition/Achievement
5. Self actualisation

Frederick Hersberg's two-factor theory, a.k.a. intrinsic/extrinsic motivation, concludes that certain factors in the workplace result in job satisfaction, but if absent, they don't lead to dissatisfaction but no satisfaction.

Vroom Expectancy Theory: Like the needs-goal theory, motivation strength is determined by the perceived value of the result of performing a behaviour and the perceived probability that the behaviour performed will cause the result to materialise. As both of these factors increase, so does motivation strength, or the desire to perform the behaviour. People tend to perform the behaviours that maximise their rewards over the long term.

The Porter-Lawler Theory accepts the premises that felt needs cause human behaviour and that the effort expended to accomplish a task is determined by the perceived value of rewards that will result from finishing the task and the probability that those rewards will materialise.

Equity theory looks at an individual's perceived fairness of an employment situation and finds that perceived inequalities can lead to changes in behaviour.

Expectancy Theory: People tend to perform the behaviours that maximise their rewards over the long term.

2.7 Emotional Intelligence

2.7.1 Emotions in the Workplace

Businesses are nowadays structured in a way that almost everyone has some level of decision making ability. Whether the decisions are big or small, they have a direct impact on how successful, efficient and effective individuals are on the job. Till now, it was assumed that successful people are basically very smart and hard-working. It has been found that there is some correlation between Intelligence Quotient (IQ) and success. But, on the other hand, it is also true that some people with high IQ have failed in a job, while some with average intelligence have performed exceptionally well.

New studies and research suggest that emotional intelligence, measured by Emotional Intelligence Quotient (EQ), is a better predictor of success than the traditional measures of IQ. Emotional intelligence is the foundation of sound decision making, which is at the core of consistent high performance. It is not about being soft, emotional and nice, in fact, it is the ability to sense, understand and effectively apply the power and acumen of emotions to facilitate high levels of collaboration and productivity.

Employers treat EQ seriously these days and this is why there is a lot of focus on workplace happiness and congeniality. In the business environment, EQ is important because it helps you leverage your awareness of emotions for effectiveness in the workplace.

Emotional Intelligence Quotient is defined as a set of competencies demonstrating the ability one has to recognise his or her behaviours, moods, and impulses, and to manage them best according to the situation. Typically, "emotional intelligence" is considered to involve emotional empathy; attention to, and discrimination of one's emotions; accurate recognition of one's own and others' moods; mood management or control over emotions; response with appropriate (adaptive) emotions and behaviours in various life situations (especially to stress and difficult situations); and balancing of honest expression of emotions against courtesy, consideration, and respect (i.e., possession of good social skills and communication skills).

2.7.2 Emotions, Attitudes and Behaviour

Emotions are physiological, behavioural, and psychological episodes experienced toward and object, person, or event that create a state of readiness.

Behaviour is determined by two processes: cognitive and emotional process. In a cognitive process, we include logical reasoning before we behave some ways. This process is conquered by attitudes. Attitudes are the cluster of beliefs, assessed feelings, and behavioral intentions toward a person, object, or event. Attitudes are judgements, whereas emotions are experiences. Attitudes consist of three main processes:

- **Beliefs:** Belief is something we believe to be true. For example, I believe that wage cutting increases cost efficiency. Beliefs are based on past experience and other forms of learning.
- **Feelings:** Feelings represent how we perceive something.
- **Behavioural intentions:** This includes the motivation to engage in a particular behaviour.

Emotions shape an individual's belief about the value of a job, a company, or a team. Emotions also affect behaviours at work. Research shows that individuals within your own inner circle are better able to recognise and understand your emotions.

So, what is the connection between emotions, attitudes, and behaviours at work? This connection may be explained using a theory named *Affective Events Theory (AET)*. Researchers Howard Weiss and Russell Cropansano studied the effect of six major kinds of emotions in the workplace: anger, fear, joy, love, sadness, and surprise. Their theory argues that specific events on the job cause different kinds of people to feel different emotions. These emotions, in turn, inspire actions that can benefit or impede others at work.

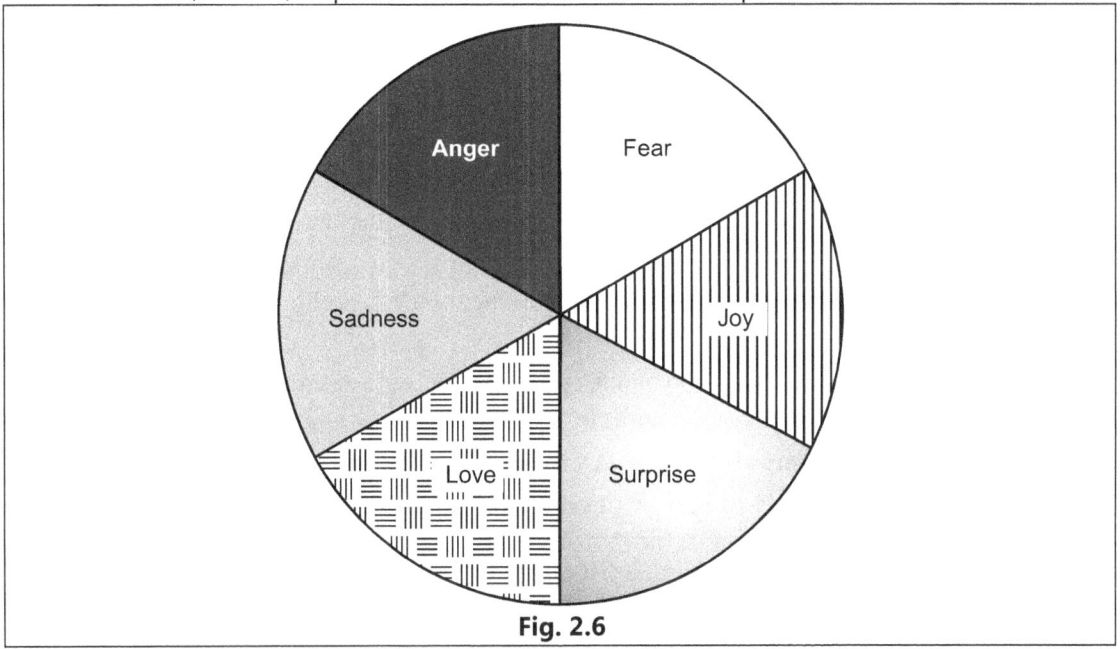

Fig. 2.6

According to Affective Events Theory, six emotions are affected by events at work.

For example, imagine that a coworker unexpectedly delivers your morning coffee to your desk. As a result of this pleasant, if unexpected experience, you may feel happy and surprised. If that coworker is your boss, you might feel proud as well. Studies have found that the positive feelings resulting from work experience may inspire you to do something you hadn't planned to do before. For instance, you might volunteer to help a colleague on a project you weren't planning to work on before. Your action would be an *affect-driven behavior*. Alternatively, if you were unfairly reprimanded by your manager, the negative emotions you experience may cause you to withdraw from work or to act mean toward a coworker. Over time, these tiny moments of emotion on the job can influence a person's job satisfaction. Although company perks and promotions can contribute to a person's happiness at work, satisfaction is not simply a result of this kind of "outside-in" reward system. Job satisfaction in the AET model comes from the inside-in—from the combination of an individual's personality, small emotional experiences at work over time, beliefs, and affect-driven behaviours.

Jobs that are high in negative emotion can lead to frustration and burnout—an ongoing negative emotional state resulting from dissatisfaction. Depression, anxiety, anger, physical illness, increased drug and alcohol use, and insomnia can result from frustration and burnout, with frustration being somewhat more active and burnout more passive. The effects of both conditions can impact coworkers, customers, and clients as anger boils over and is expressed in one's interactions with others.

2.7.3 Emotional Intelligence

Emotional Intelligence can be defined as an actual intelligence: the mental ability to reason about emotions and the capacity to think better by using emotions. It can also be defined as a set of abilities that help us respond to the world around us appropriately.

In brief, the growing interest in emotional intelligence stems from a slow-but-steady recognition that the people who inhabit office spaces are, in fact, human beings.

A person who is emotionally intelligent can recognise and understand his or her own reactions to workplace events, while also recognising, understanding and appreciating the responses of others.

For too long, emotions have been unwelcome at work. However it is also a fact that as humans we cannot make any decision without letting our emotions be involved.

Emotional Intelligence Competencies that Correlate to Workplace Success

The following outlines a set of five emotional intelligence competencies that have proven to contribute more to workplace achievement than technical skills, cognitive ability, and standard personality traits combined.

Social Competencies—Competencies that Determine How We Handle Relationships

Intuition and Empathy: Our awareness of others' feelings, needs, and concerns. This competency is important in the workplace for the following reasons:

- Understanding others: an intuitive sense of others' feelings and perspectives, and showing an active interest in their concerns and interests
- Customer service orientation: the ability to anticipate, recognise, and meet customers' needs
- People development: ability to sense what others need in order to grow, develop, and master their strengths
- Leveraging diversity: cultivating opportunities through diverse people

Political Acumen and Social Skills: Our adeptness at inducing desirable responses in others. This competency is important in the workplace for the following reasons:

- **Influencing:** Using effective tactics and techniques for persuasion and desired results.
- **Communication:** Sending clear and convincing messages that are understood by others.

- **Leadership:** Inspiring and guiding groups of people.
- **Change catalyst:** Initiating and/or managing change in the workplace.
- **Conflict resolution:** Negotiating and resolving disagreements with people.
- **Building bonds:** Nurturing instrumental relationships for business success.
- **Collaboration and cooperation:** Working with coworkers and business partners toward shared goals.
- **Team capabilities:** Creating group synergy in pursuing collective goals.

Personal Competencies - Competencies that Determine How We Manage Ourselves.

Self Awareness: Knowing one's internal states, preferences, resources, and intuitions. This competency is important in the workplace for the following reasons:

- **Emotional awareness:** Recognising one's emotions and their effects and impact on those around us.
- **Accurate self-assessment:** Knowing one's strengths and limits.
- **Self-confidence:** Sureness about one's self-worth and capabilities.

Self Regulation: Managing one's internal states, impulses, and resources. This competency is important in the workplace for the following reasons:

- **Self-control:** Managing disruptive emotions and impulses.
- **Trustworthiness:** Maintaining standards of honesty and integrity.
- **Conscientiousness:** Taking responsibility and being accountable for personal performance.
- **Adaptability:** Flexibility in handling change.
- **Innovation:** Being comfortable with an openness to novel ideas, approaches, and new information.

Self Expectations and Motivation: Emotional tendencies that guide or facilitate reaching goals. This competency is important in the workplace for the following reasons:

- **Achievement drive:** Striving to improve or meet a standard of excellence we impose on ourselves.
- **Commitment:** Aligning with the goals of the group or organisation.
- **Initiative:** Readiness to act on opportunities without having to be told.
- **Optimism:** Persistence in pursuing goals despite obstacles and setbacks.

2.7.4 Concept of Employee Engagement

Employee engagement is a workplace approach designed to ensure that employees are committed to their organisation's goals and values, motivated to contribute to organisational success, and are able at the same time to enhance their own sense of well-being.

> *"This is about how we create the conditions in which employees offer more of their capability and potential."*   **– David Macleod**

There are differences between attitude, behaviour and outcomes in terms of engagement. An employee might feel pride and loyalty (attitude); be a great advocate of their company to clients, or go the extra mile to finish a piece of work (behaviour). Outcomes may include lower accident rates, higher productivity, fewer conflicts, more innovation, lower numbers leaving and reduced sickness rates. But all three – attitudes, behaviours and outcomes – are part of the engagement story. There is a virtuous circle when the pre-conditions of engagement are met when these three aspects of engagement trigger and reinforce one another.

Engaged organisations have strong and authentic values, with clear evidence of trust and fairness based on mutual respect, where two way promises and commitments – between employers and staff – are understood, and are fulfilled. Although improved performance and productivity is at the heart of engagement, it cannot be achieved by a mechanistic approach which tries to extract discretionary effort by manipulating employees' commitment and emotions. Employees see through such attempts very quickly; they lead instead to cynicism and disillusionment. By contrast, engaged employees freely and willingly give discretionary effort, not as an 'add on', but as an integral part of their daily activity at work.

In particular, engagement is two way: organisations must work to engage the employee, who in turn has a choice about the level of engagement to offer the employer. Each reinforces the other.

An engaged employee experiences a blend of job satisfaction, organisational commitment, job involvement and feelings of empowerment. It is a concept that is greater than the sum of its parts. Despite there being some debate about the precise meaning of employee engagement there are three things we know about it: it is measurable; it can be correlated with performance; and it varies from poor to great. Most importantly employers can do a great deal to impact on people's level of engagement. That is what makes it so important, as a tool for business success.

The construct, employee engagement emanates from two concepts that have won academic recognition and have been the subjects of empirical research *Commitment and Organisational Citisen Behaviour (OCB) (Robinson, Perryman and Hayday, 2004; Rafferty et al., 2005).* Employee engagement has similarities to and overlaps with the above two concepts.

Robinson et al. (2004) state that neither commitment nor OCB reflect sufficiently two aspects of engagement-its two-way nature, and the extent to which engaged employees are expected to have an element of business awareness, even though it appears that engagement overlaps with the two concepts. *Rafferty et al (2005)* also distinguish employee engagement and the two prior concepts- Commitment and OCB, on the ground that engagement clearly demonstrates that it is a two-way mutual process between the employee and the organisation.

Definition of Employee Engagement

To date, there is no single and generally accepted definition for the term employee engagement. This is evident if one looks at the definitions forwarded for the term by three well-known research organisations in human resource area, let alone individual researchers. Below are the definitions:

Perrin's Global Workforce Study (2003) uses the definition "employees" willingness and ability to help their company succeed, largely by providing discretionary effort on a sustainable basis. According to the study, engagement is affected by many factors which involve both emotional and rational factors relating to work and the overall work experience.

Gallup organisation defines employee engagement "as the involvement with and enthusiasm for work. Gallup as cited by Dernovsek (2008) likens employee engagement to a positive employees emotional attachment and employees' commitment".

Robinson et al. (2004) define employee engagement as "a positive attitude held by the employee towards the organisation and its value. An engaged employee is aware of business context, and works with colleagues to improve performance within the job for the benefit of the organisation. The organisation must work to develop and nurture engagement, which requires a two-way relationship between employer and employee".

This verdict and definition forwarded by *Institute of Employment Studies* gives a clear insight that employee engagement is the result of two-way relationship between employer and employee pointing out that there are things to be done by both sides.

Furthermore, *Fernandes (2007)* shows the distinction between job satisfaction, the well-known construct in management, and engagement contending that employee satisfaction is not the same as employee engagement and since managers can not rely on employee satisfaction to help retain the best and the brightest, employee engagement becomes a critical concept. Other researchers take job satisfaction as a part of engagement, but it can merely reflect a superficial, transactional relationship that is only as good as the organisation's last round of perks and bonuses; Engagement is about passion and commitment the willingness to invest oneself and expand one's discretionary effort to help the employer succeed, which is beyond simple satisfaction with the employment arrangement or basic loyalty to the employer *(Blessing White, 2008; Erickson, 2005; Macey and Schnieder, 2008)*. Therefore, the full engagement equation is obtained by aligning maximum job satisfaction and maximum job contribution.

Stephen Young, the executive director of Towers Perrin, also distinguishes between job satisfaction and engagement contending that only engagement (not satisfaction) is the strongest predictor of organisational performance (Human Resources, 2007).

Recent researches also indicate that Employee commitment and OCB are important parts and predictors of employee engagement in that commitment is conceptualised as positive attachment and willingness to exert energy for success of the organisation, feeling proud of being a member of that organisation and identifying oneself with it and OCB is a behaviour observed within the work context that demonstrates itself through taking innovative initiatives proactively seeking opportunities to contribute one's best and going extra mile beyond employment contract. However, these constructs constitute the bigger construct employee engagement and they can not independently act as a replacement for engagement *(Macey and Schneider, 2008; Robinson et al, 2004)*.

2.7.5 Employee Empowerment

Employee empowerment is a strategy and philosophy that enables employees to make decisions about their jobs. Employee empowerment helps employees own their work and take responsibility for their results. Employee empowerment helps employees serve customers at the level of the organisation where the customer interface exists.

"Employee empowerment" is a term that is used to express the ways in which non-managerial staff members can make decisions without consulting their bosses or managers. These decisions can be small or large, depending upon the degree of power with which the company wishes to invest employees. Employee empowerment can begin with training and converting a whole company to an empowerment model. Conversely, it might merely mean giving employees the ability to make some decisions on their own.

For employee empowerment to work successfully, the management team must be truly committed to allowing employees to make decisions. Managers might want to define the scope of decisions that their employees can make. Building decision making teams is often one of the models used in employee empowerment, because it allows for managers and workers to contribute ideas toward directing the company.

Important Definitions

➢ **Important Definitions:**
- *Ability* may be defined as an acquired or natural capacity or talent that enables an individual to perform a particular job or task successfully.
- *Learning* is acquiring new, or modifying existing, knowledge, behaviours, skills, values, or preferences and may involve synthesising different types of information.
- *Attitude* can be defined as, "a complex mental state involving beliefs and feelings and values and dispositions to act in certain ways."
- *Personality* is made up of the characteristic set of thoughts, feelings, and behaviours that make a person unique. In addition to this, personality arises from within the individual and remains fairly consistent throughout life.

- **Values** are the mode of conduct or end-state that is personally or socially preferable (i.e., what is right and good).
- **Motive:** An emotion, desire, physiological need, or similar impulse that acts as an incitement to action.
- **Motivation:** is a psychological feature that arouses an organism to act towards a desired goal and elicits, controls, and sustains certain goal directed behaviours. It can be considered a driving force; a psychological one that compels or reinforces an action toward a desired goal. For example, hunger is a motivation that elicits a desire to eat.

Points to Remember

- An **Aptitude** implies an inherent capacity for learning, understanding or performing a task.
- **Intellectual and physical abilities:** An individual ability is essentially made up of two factors:
  (1) Intellectual ability
  (2) Physical ability
  Disabilities require a number of adjustments: physically, emotionally and psychologically.
  Learning: Any relatively permanent change in behaviour that occurs as a result of experience.
  Learning is the key to success—some would even say survival—in today's organisations.
- **There are three components of attitude:**
  - Cognitive component
  - Affective component
  - Behavioural Component
- **Every single instance of behaviour involves four specific elements:**
  1. A specific action
  2. Performed with respect to a given target
  3. In a given context
  4. At a given point in time.
  The components of an organisation's attitude include strategy, posture and culture.
  An emotionally intelligent individual is not offended by the judgments of others.
- **A job attitude** is a set of evaluations of one's job that constitute one's feelings toward, beliefs about, and attachment to one's job.
  Personality arises from within the individual and remains fairly consistent throughout life.
- **Two basic kinds of attributions made: INTERNAL and EXTERNAL**
  INTERNAL - Dispositional
  EXTERNAL - Situational
- Perception is the organisation, identification, and interpretation of sensory information in order to represent and understand the environment.

- Attribution theory tries to answer the "why" aspect of motivation and behaviour.
- **Motive:** An emotion, desire, physiological need, or similar impulse that acts as an incitement to action.
  Motivation is an inner drive to behave or act in a certain manner.
  As each need is substantially satisfied, the next need becomes dominant.
- Hersberg felt that the opposite of satisfaction is not dissatisfaction.
- People tend to perform the behaviours that maximise their rewards over the long term.
- Equity theory looks at an individual's perceived fairness of an employment situation and finds that perceived inequalities can lead to changes in behaviour.

Questions for Discussion

1. Describe and Contrast the two types of ability.
2. Define intellectual ability.
3. Define learning and list the three major theories of learning.
4. Differentiate the three components of an attitude.
5. Explain the relationship between attitude and behavior.
6. Differentiate the major job attitudes.
7. Enumerate job satisfaction and show how it can be measured.
8. Summarise the main causes of employee satisfaction.
9. Define personality, describe how it is measured.
10. Describe the Myers-Briggs Type Indicator personality framework.
11. Enumerate the key traits in the Big Five personality model?
12. Describe how the Big Five traits predict behaviour at work?
13. Define perception and explain the factors that influence it.
14. Explain attribution theory.
15. Identify the shortcuts individuals use in making judgments about others.
16. List the three key elements of Motivation.
17. Evaluate the applicability of early theories of motivation today.
18. Define organisational justice.
19. Enumerate the key tenets of expectancy theory.
20. Contrast the evidence for and against the existence of emotional intelligence.

Multiple Choice Questions (MCQ's)

➤ **Qs. Nos. 1 to 10: State whether True or False:**
1. Everyone has strengths and weaknesses in terms of ability that makes him or her relatively superior or inferior to others in performing certain tasks or activities.
2. We do not need to understand how people learn, if we want to explain and predict behaviour.
3. Employees' satisfaction or dissatisfaction with their jobs affects the workplace.
4. If we want to understand the behaviour of someone in the organisation, it does not help to know something about his/her personality.

5. People's behaviour is based on their perception of what reality is, not on reality itself.
6. The level of motivation does not vary both between individuals and within individuals at different times.
7. Intelligence is the capacity to acquire and apply knowledge to perform a task.
8. Aptitude, Intelligence and Skill possessed by an individual is not the product of certain original tendencies and the training received by the person.
9. Ability-job fit is said to be high if there is a proper match between employee's abilities and the abilities required of the job that employees should perform.
10. Learning is not any relatively permanent change in behaviour that occurs as a result of experience.

> ➤ **Qs. Nos. 11 to 20: Fill in the Blanks:**

11. A type of conditioning in which an individual responds to some stimulus that would not ordinarily produce such a response is known as ....
12. A type of conditioning in which desired voluntary behaviour leads to a reward or prevents punishment is known as ....
13. ...... theory states that people can learn through observation and direct experience.
14. ...... is the self-perceptions of how well a person can cope with situations as they arise.
15. Given the current business environment, organisations must be able to learn ...... in order to deal with changes and, in the end, to survive.
16. ...... is a complex mental state involving beliefs and feelings and values and dispositions to act in certain ways.
17. ...... is made up of the characteristic set of thoughts, feelings, and behaviours that make a person unique.
18. ...... is a psychometric questionnaire designed to measure psychological preferences in how people perceive the world and make decisions.
19. ...... is the organisation, identification, and interpretation of sensory information in order to represent and understand the environment.
20. ...... is an inner drive to behave or act in a certain manner.

Answers to MCQs:

1. True.
2. False.
3. True.
4. False.
5. True.
6. False.
7. True.
8. False.
9. True.
10. False.
11. Classical conditioning

12. Operant conditioning
13. Social Learning
14. Self-efficacy
15. Continuous
16. Attitude
17. Personality
18. MBTI (Myers-Briggs Type Indicator) assessment
19. Perception
20. Motivation

Case Study

Two friends, Rohit and Veena work at a local super market to make ends meet and help pay for their college education. Veena works for Jeevan, who everyone admires for her friendly and relaxed management style. Veena enjoys her work arriving and leaving work each day with a smile, but Rohit often grumbles and complains about his work and his boss, Dharam.

Most employees want to work for Jeevan as he often assigns different duties, so workers do not get bored. Jeevan even encourages his employees to reorder items from vendors when stocks are running low. Rohit's supervisor Dharam prefers most of his employees to work in the same area, as he believes that is the best way to master a job. Rohit has to stock the same supply each day in the store's supply room. After a particularly boring morning, Rohit met Veena for lunch. He had a look of disgust on his face.

"Bad day again?" asked Veena.

Rohit retorted, "I stocked potatoes all day, what do you think?"

Veena inquired, "Why don't you tell your boss, Dharam that you want to do something else?"

Rohit frowned, "I don't even care anymore, what's the point?" "How's yours going?"

Veena replied "Pretty good, actually, Jeevan and I met earlier today, and we both set a goal for me for next week".

"Wow! That's great". Rohit said.

Veena replied, "It will be tough but I will do my best, as Jeevan has promised me a bonus of ₹ 5000."

Rohit said, "I would probably leave my job if I didn't have to pay my tuition fees."

"Look on the brighter side at least you make more money than Ritu" replied Veena.
"That's true", sighed Rohit, "but I hate my boss and I hate my job."

Questions:
1. Discuss Rohit and Veena in terms of each person's job attitude, that is, Job Satisfaction, Organisational Commitment.
2. Apply Motivation Theories, that is, Expectancy theory and Equity theory to the situations faced by Rohit and Veena.

Project / Activities

1. Do age, gender, race, reservation, and tenure affects performance at work?
2. Discuss advantages and disadvantages of using attitude surveys to measure Employee Job Satisfaction.
3. 'Heredity determines personality'. Build arguments for and against this statement.
4. What shortcuts do people frequently use in making judgements about others?
5. Can an individual be too motivated, so that performance declines as a result of excessive effort?

QUESTIONS FROM PREVIOUS PUNE UNIVERSITY EXAMINATIONS

1. Write short notes:
   (a) Development of Personality   **[MBA April 2007]**
   (b) Attitude   **[PGDBM April 2007]**
2. Explain various determinants of personality.   **[MBA April 2011]**
3. Explain the meaning of personality. What are the determinants of Personality?
                                                           [MBA April 2010]
4. Elaborate A. H. Maslow's Hierarchy Theory of Motivation, in detail.
5. Write Short Notes on:
   (a) Primary and Secondary Motives   **[M.B.A. April 2007]**
   (b) Herzberg's Theory of Motivation   **[P.G.D.B.M. April 2007]**
6. Discuss in detail Maslow's Theory of need hierarchy.   **[MBA April 2010]**
7. Discuss critically F. Herzberg and Maslow's need hierarchy theory of motivation.
                                                           [MBA Dec. 2010]
8. Write short notes on Maslow's Theory of Need Hierarchy. **[Dec. 2008, April 2009]**
9. Evaluate Maslow's Need of Hierarchy Theory. What are its main weaknesses.
                                                           [MBA Dec. 2011]

Weblinks / Books

1. Stephen P. Robbins, Timothy Judge, SeemaSanghi *"Organisational Behaviour"*, 13th **Edition**.

Chapter 3...

Interpersonal Processes and Behaviour, Team and Leadership Development

Contents ...

3.4.5   Contemporary Leadership

3.4.6   Contemporary Theories of Leadership

3.4.7   Common Contemporary Leadership Challenges

3.4.8   Success Stories of Today's Global and Indian Leaders

- Points to Remember
- Case Study
- Questions for Discussion
- Multiple Choice Questions (MCQ's)
- Activity
- Questions from Previous Pune University Examinations
- Web Links/Further Readings

Learning Objectives

After studying this chapter, you should be able to:

1.   Differentiate the working in Groups and Teams

2.   Describe the dynamics involved in the formation of Formal and Informal groups

3.   Identify the effects of Group Dynamics

4.   Enumerate the distinction between Types of Groups and Teams

5.   Illustrate the Five -Stage Model of Group Development

6.   Describe Work Teams

7.   Discuss the importance of Developing Work Teams

8.   Demonstrate Team Effectiveness

9.   Enumerate Team Building skills.

10.   Identify the nature of conflicts in Organisations

11.   Enumerate the causes of conflict in organisations

12.   Define the various methods of resolving conflict

13.   Identify cues and signals that causes conflicts

14.   List the advantages and disadvantages of conflicts

15.   Understand the significance of Leadership

16.   Identify the types of leaders required for different situations

17.   Distinguish between leaders and managers

18.   List the various leadership styles

19.   Highlight the importance of leadership in today's working times

3.1 Foundations of Group Behaviour

Introduction

Today, much of the work in organisations is undertaken by groups of individuals as employees. The work done by individuals, as employees alone has nowadays become quite rare.

Therefore there is a need to understand groups and the variables influencing its interrelationships between members in groups. All these are universally called 'Group Dynamics.'

Toothman I (2000) *Conducting the experiential group: An introduction to Group Dynamics, New York: John Wiley*, elaborates on Group Dynamics, *as the variables governing its formation and development, its structure and its interrelationships with individuals, other groups and the organisations, within which they exist.*

3.1.1 The Meaning of Group and Group Behaviour

Definition of a Group: A Group is defined as *"two or more individuals, interacting and interdependent, who have come together to achieve particular objectives."*

Group is also defined as, *"a social unit consisting of two or more interdependent, interactive people striving for common goods."*

A group has three characteristics:
- Interaction
- Dependence and
- Satisfaction

According to Schein, a group consists of:

Any number of people who,
I.   interact with each other,
I.   are psychologically aware of one another, and
III. perceive themselves to be a group."

Kurt Lewin introduced the term 'Group Dynamics' in 1930 for the first time.

> *A Group is defined as "two or more individuals, interacting and interdependent, who have come together to achieve particular objectives."*

This term 'Group Dynamics' carries the implication that, groups are to be considered as, entities characterised by change and on-going activity.

Special qualities of groups can be observed and measured in terms of the activity that takes place within their boundaries.

3.1.2 What is a Group?

Imagine three people waiting in line, at the bus stop for the bus and compare these to a group of people from different functions in an organisation, engaged in an important meeting. Quite obviously, the latter would be considered a group, although in everyday language even the former is considered a group.

Social scientists have defined a group as *"a collection of two or more individuals with a fixed pattern of relationship between them, who share common goals and who consider themselves to be a part of the group."*

From the above definition, the following are the features of Groups:

1. **Social Interaction:** One of the main characteristics of a group is an active social interaction between the members. This may take the form of verbal (in terms of discussing the plans, project outlines) or even nonverbal in terms of approval as a handshake, or a smile amongst the members.

    The parties must have an influence on one another to be considered to be a part of the group.

2. **Stability:** For members to be considered as a part of the group there must be some stability among the members for some time. For example, people waiting at the pizza outlet for collection of their orders for pizzas, are not stable at all.

    As a group, there must be some element of stability among the members to be thought of as a group.

3. **Common purpose or goals:** The members among a group must share a common interest or a goal. For example, in a club consisting of classical music lovers, the members share and discuss common changes related to classical or in a marketing group in a company, members share common plans for advertising or sales promotion of the products.

4. **Recognition as being in a group:** The members in a group share their membership with other members.

    In simple terms, each member knows that he or she is a part of a specific group. Like the music club members or the marketing group in an organisation know that they belong to that particular group. Whereas, for people waiting in a queue in a mall may make small conversation but, they do not recognise one another.

3.1.3 Group Behaviour

Group behaviour in sociology refers to the situations where people interact in large or small groups. The field of group dynamics deals with small groups that may reach consensus and act in a coordinated way.

Groups of a large number of people in a given area may act simultaneously to achieve a goal that differs from what individuals would do acting alone (herd behaviour).

A large group (a crowd or mob) is likely to show examples of group behaviour when people gathered in a given place and time act in a similar way—for example, joining a protest or march, participating in a fight or acting patriotically.

Special forms of large group behaviour are:

Crowd "hysteria"

Spectators - when a group of people gathered together on purpose to participate in an event like theatre play, cinema movie, football match, a concert, etc.

Public - exception to the rule is that the group must occupy the same physical place. People watching same channel on television may react in the similar way, as they are occupying the same type of place - in front of television - although they may physically be doing this all over the world.

Group behaviour differs from mass actions which refers to people behaving similarly on a more global scale (for example, shoppers in different shops), while group behaviour refers usually to people in one place. If the group behaviour is coordinated, then it is called group action.

Swarm intelligence is a special case of group behaviour, referring to the interaction between groups of agents in order to fulfil a given task. This type of group dynamics has received much attention by the soft computing community in the form of the particle swarm optimisation family of algorithms.

Measurement of Group Behaviour

How do we examine and understand the pattern of interactions in a group? Who likes and dislikes whom? Who is a centre of attention in the group? These types of questions are concerned with the study of the number of interactions of the individual in a group.

Socio-metrics is a technique for measuring this interaction pattern. This technique was developed by Jacob L. Moreno (1953). It collects the data on the choice of the rejections received by a given group members.

This technique consists of straight forward steps such as:

The group members are asked to make the choices from among members whom they would like to have as a friend.

The other variations of this could be the choice of members with whom they would like to share the dining table, go to the movie etc.

This gives quantitative data on the preferences of the group-members, with regard to associating with each other.

These choices are summarised such as –

1. The 'Stars' – the highly popular group members.
2. 'Isolates' – infrequently chosen members.
3. Pairs – two people having reciprocal choices.
4. Chains – clusters of the individuals whom can make clique.

3.1.4 Group Performance Factors

The performance of a group is affected by several factors other than reasons for formation and stages of its development. In case of high performance groups the groups' synergy efforts often develop in a way that the performance of the group is much ahead than the individual members.

The following are the group performance factors:

1.   Group Composition
2.   Group Size
3.   Group Norms
4.   Group Cohesiveness

1.   Group Composition

Group composition is understood in terms of the group's heterogeneity or the group's homogeneity.

In case of, projects or tasks which require cooperation, harmony among the group members and the group's tasks are simple. However, where the members share a common understanding and a common goal, then a homogenous group in terms of age, culture and background, technical expertise, work experience becomes important.

However, not all groups are homogenous.

Heterogeneous groups are groups which are varied in terms of age, size, technical expertise, culture, background, religion, experience, work orientation and so on.

Such types of groups are very useful when the work to be completed is of creative and an innovative nature and calls for differing perspectives and perceptions. Nowadays, with increasing competition and stiff rivalry among companies and their products and services, heterogeneous groups are becoming more acceptable in companies.

> *Today increasingly attention is being focused on how to deal with groups, which are made up of people from different cultures.*

Today with more and more joint ventures and collaborations among foreign companies with Indian ones, the need for becoming more flexible and adaptive is the need for success. Different countries have different languages, work styles, thought processes and methods of working. For example, when a Tata Company collaborated with a Company in Mexico, they had to change their lunch timings and make it more leisurely for about two to three hours, to suit the Mexican culture.

Such changes happen in a heterogeneous group. Today increasingly greater attention is being focused on how to deal with groups, which are made up of people with different cultures.

2.   Group Size

A group can have as few as two members or as many members as can interact and influence one another. Group size can have an important effect on its performance. A larger group has many members and so more resources available and so, is able to complete a large number of relatively independent tasks.

However, the disadvantage of a large group is a greater level of complexity of interaction and communication, which may make the group more difficult to function.

It is also brought out through research that large groups tend to concentrate on greater social interaction, or may concentrate on too many administrative duties. In other words, when the group is large, task orientation and meaningful work contributions can get affected. For example, a concept called **Social Loafing** can happen, which is the tendency of the group not to put too much effort in a group as compared to if he worked alone or independently.

Social loafers often assume that if some of the members do not work hard, then the other members in the group would pick up the slack. However much of the problem depends upon the nature of the task, the character of the people involved and the awareness of the group leader to be conscious of the problem and do something about it.

Hence, the ideal group size is determined by the group members' ability to interact and influence each other effectively.

3.   Group Norms

A norm is a measure or a standard against which an appropriateness of behaviour is judged. Thus, norms determine the expected levels of behaviour in situations. Group norms help to predict behaviour and enable people of a group to behave in a manner consistent with the norms and the requirements of the group for better performance. Lack of norms in a group results in or keeps the group in a chaotic condition.

Group norms should be enforced for actions, which are very important to the group. For example, if there is a group requirement for meeting or interacting with the clients, then the norm for "dress code" becomes important and everyone must follow it. However if the meeting with the clients is not necessary, then the dress code is not a part of the norm.

Norms serve certain purposes of the groups. They are as follows: they dictate a standard behaviour at work; they simplify and make the behaviour more predictable; norms help the group avoid embarrassing situations; members often want to avoid damaging other members' self-images and are therefore likely to avoid certain subjects that might hurt other members' feelings.

Norms express central values of the group and identify the group to others. Certain clothes, mannerisms, or behaviours in particular situations may signify to others about the membership of the Group.

4.   Group Cohesiveness

Group cohesiveness is the extent to which the group is committed to remaining together; it results from forces acting on the members to remain in the group. The forces that create cohesiveness are attraction to the group membership, resistance to leaving the group and the motivation to remain as the member of the group.

> *Group cohesiveness is related to many aspects of 'Group Dynamics' like: maturity, size, homogeneity, and frequency of interactions.*

Group cohesiveness is related to many aspects of Group Dynamics like maturity, size, homogeneity, and frequency of interactions. Research on group cohesiveness concentrates on factors related to the relationship between group performance and cohesiveness.

Highly cohesive groups appear to be more effective at achieving their goals than groups, which are low on cohesiveness.

Cohesiveness is also known to be a primary factor in the development of certain problems for some decision-making groups. An example is **Groupthink** which occurs when, a group's overriding concern is getting a majority or a consensus on issues rather than having an objective and analytical discussion of the same.

3.1.5 Group Dynamics

The term Group Dynamics refers to the complex of forces that determine group formation, its sizes and structure, conflict, change and cohesiveness, interaction and behaviour.

According to Fred Luthans, in *The Organisational Behaviour*, Group Dynamics is primarily concerned with *"The interaction of forces between group members in a social situation."*

Lewin's conception of Group Dynamics is centred around the internal character and compositions of groups, their structures and process and their impact on the individual members, inter-group interaction and organisation.

Group Dynamics are concerned with the interactions and forces among group members in a social situation. There is no agreement on what is meant by Group Dynamics.

Understanding Group Dynamics

Groups, like individuals have three basic interpersonal needs, namely: *inclusion, control and openness*. These needs determine how we treat other people in the group and how we want others to treat us.

Understanding and identifying behaviours that you observe in yourself and in your group members will help you communicate what is happening in the group, gain influence, and help the group become more effective and productive.

There are three views about Group Dynamics:

1. Group dynamics describe how a group should be organised and conducted. Having democratic leadership, member participation and cooperation are stressed in this view.

2. Another view states that Group Dynamics consists of a set of techniques such as role-playing, brain storming, leaderless groups, group therapy, sensitivity training, team building and transactional analysis and Johari Window technique.

3. Group Dynamics are viewed from the perspective of the internal nature of groups, how they form their structure and processes and how they function and affect individual members, other groups and the organisation.

This third view is the closest to Lewin's original conception.

Research on Group Dynamics

There are many studies on groups, which have implications for organisational behaviour and management. Hawthorne studies are widely known classic studies, which relate group dynamics to human performance in an organisational setting.

Other important studies include: Lippitt and White's leadership studies, Coach and French's study on overcoming resistance to change, Trist and Bamforth's study of British Coal mining and William F. Whyte's research on the restaurant industry.

In addition, there are a number of other research studies on Group Dynamics. Findings of these studies can be divided into two groups:

(i)   The impact of groups on organisational effectiveness.

(ii) The impact of groups on individual effectiveness.

(i)   The impact of groups on organisational effectiveness:

1. Accomplishing tasks that could not be done by employees themselves.
2. Bringing a number of skills and talents to accomplish complex and difficult tasks.
3. Providing a vehicle for decision-making.
4. Providing an efficient means for organisational control of employee behaviour.
5. Facilitating changes in organisational policies or procedures.
6. Increasing Organisational Stability by transmitting shared beliefs and values to new employees.

(ii) The impact of Groups on Individual Effectiveness:

1. Aiding in learning about the organisation and its environment.
2. Aiding in learning about self.
3. Providing help in gaining new skills.
4. Obtaining valued rewards that are not accessible by self.
5. Satisfying important personal needs like social acceptance and affiliation.

The Schechter Study on Group Dynamics:

Schechter's work seems important for the application of group dynamics research to human resources management.

Schechter tested that group cohesiveness and induction have effects on productivity under highly controlled conditions. Cohesiveness was defined as the average resultant force acting on members to remain in a group.

Women college students were used as subjects.

The researchers assumed that by making the group appearance attractive or non-attractive, the subjects would correspondingly feel high or low cohesiveness.

In this, experiment through manipulation of cohesiveness and induction the following experimental groups were created.

1. High Cohesive, positive induction (HiCO, + Ind)
2. Low Cohesive, positive induction (LoCO, + Ind)
3. High Cohesive, negative induction (HiCO, – Ind)
4. Low Cohesive, negative induction (LoCO – Ind)

The results of this study show that, highly cohesive groups have very powerful dynamics, both positive and negative for human resource management. The low cohesive groups are not so powerful.

Induction or influence is a more important variable. Performance depends largely on how the high or low cohesive group is induced. For example, a leadership may be substituted for induction. A highly cohesive group that is given positive leadership will have the highest possible productivity.

On the other hand, a highly cohesive group that is given poor leadership will have the lowest possible productivity. The implication is that, if management wishes to maximise productivity, it must build a cohesive group and handover it to a good leadership.

3.1.6 Types of Groups

There are many ways of classifying groups. The behaviour of group members will be affected by the types of groups in which they function. There are primary and secondary groups, formal and informal groups, membership and reference groups and in groups and out groups. Further, we can sub-classify the groups as command, task, interest and friendship groups. Each type of group has different characteristics and different effects on its member.

(a) Primary and Secondary Groups

C. H. Cooley defined and analysed a primary group. By primary groups, he means those characterised by intimate, face-to-face association and cooperation. Primary groups are those in which interpersonal relationship take place on a face-to-face basis and with great frequency. Primary groups are fundamental in forming the social nature and ideals of the individual.

Sometimes the terms small group and primary group are used interchangably. But technically speaking, all primary groups are small groups, but not all small groups are primary groups, because small group has to meet only the criterion of small size. But besides being small in size primary group must have a feeling of loyalty and togetherness. Families are the most obvious example of primary groups, but this category also includes peer groups, recreational groups and work groups, and indeed any type of group in which individuals have some depth of involvement.

OB scientists are keen about primary groups because Hawthrone studies revealed their special significance. Because of frequent face to face interactions and close associations work-group have qualities of primary group. The workers behaviour is influenced and determined by the group.

The Japanese style of management has developed this quality of work-group as a primary group in a significant and most effective manner. The concepts of Industrial Families and Quality Circles (also a primary group) have led them to tremendous organisational success. To a Japanese, employment in an organisation is always a life-long affair. Earlier the industries were owned by families but now Japan has industrial family.

Secondary groups are likely to be more impersonal and more characterized by formalized or contractual relationships among members. Money, goods, services, and information can be achieved through our involvement in secondary groups.

Love, disappointment, depression, rage and elation are more likely to express in primary groups, whereas expressions of emotion to members of secondary groups are more likely to be restrained or suppressed.

Hawthrone and many other studies pointed out the tremendous impact that the primary group has on individual behaviour.

(b) Membership and Reference Groups

Membership groups are formed informally and formally through membership cards or certificates. The Institute of Engineers is a membership group and is a secondary group.

Reference group is one in which individuals would like to belong or to identify themselves. The reference groups values and opinions are important to the individual. The reference group serves a normative function to the individual, it also serves as a source of individuals norms and attitudes.

(c) In and Out Groups

An "in–group represents a cluster of individual who hold the prevailing or powerful values in high esteem, thus 'in–group' represents 'power circle.'

The 'out–group' is one which does not have much influence on social thinking or powerful values.

(d) Open and Closed Groups

An open group is constantly adding and losing members whereas the membership is stable in closed groups.

In an open group, the frame of reference expands with the addition of the new members with new ideas and there by the activity also expands but it is stable in closed group.

Due to constant changes in an open group the perspective is limited to only near future whereas in closed group, because of its stability, it has longer time perspective.

(e) Formal and Informal Groups

A designed work group defined by the organisational structure is called Formal Group. A Group that is neither formally structured nor organisationally determined; appears in response to the need for social contact is called an informal group.

Formal groups are established by the organisation and have a public identity and goal to achieve. Informal groups are formal on the basis of common interest, proximity and friendships.

Primary groups are likely to be informal, whereas formality is more often a characteristic of secondary groups. Structure of formal group make a group more stable and enable it to resist drastic changes. The formal structures of religious organisations, work organisations and nations have enabled them to survive for centuries.

Different types of groups are relevant to the study of organisational behaviour, but the formal and informal types are most directly applicable. Formal and informal groups can be sub-classified as follows :

Forms of Formal Groups

1.   A Command Group: It is determined by the organisational chart. A command group consists of a superior and the immediate subordinates. The superior is granted formal authority over the other members of the group. The authority structure forms and determines the boundaries of division, departments and sections within the organisation and these departments or sections or divisions are known as command groups. The smallest command group consists of supervisor and his subordinates and the largest one consists of top management and the total personnel in the work force.

The chain of command as expressed by authority, responsibility, and accountability allocates the roles of each individual in the command group. It also spells out the member – authority relationship which exists between them. The superior of a particular group is the leader who performs important functions for his group. He sets goals for the group, suggests ways and means to get them and settles jurisdictional issues which arise between subordinates. The superior is an effective instrument for downward communication and an initiation for upward communication.

2.   Functional Group: Functional groups are those groups whose primary task is to carry on the operations. In many cases the functional groups may be congruent with the authority groups. Thus a single department in the organisation would probably be both command group and functional group. The department is a command group within the authority structure but the staff working in that department engaged in a particular activity and directed and coordinated by the same superior may form a functional group such as typist, clerks, salesman, etc. Thus a command group may have several functional groups.

The functional groups can be again classified into team, task and technological groups. The distinction between these groups involves the method, role allocation and role fulfillment.

(a) **Team Group:** Team group has no specified, fixed role to its individuals. The general role of the group is set and the members of the group are allocated the role according to the needs of the goal. Thus, roles of members in a team group are interchangeable without any clash.

(b) **Task Group:** Those groups working together to complete a job task is called a task group. The task group is formally designed to work on a specific project or a job. Its interaction and structure are formally designed to accomplish the task. Task groups boundaries are not limited to its immediate hierarchical superior. It can cross command relationships. Role of the members are not interchangeable and if superior does so there is personal resistance and friction between superior and the member.

(c) **Technological Group:** It is something different. Roles are assigned by the management. The position of the job is fixed and the methods are laid down and the speed of the work is fixed by some device. Thus members of the group have no choice over the method and the speed of the work.

(d) **Status Group:** Status group involves the members of the same status in an organisation. It includes a number of different ranking of positions. It makes distinction of a functional basis between manager and workers. In some cases status distinction is made on the basis of facilities or amenities to be enjoyed by the members.

3.   **Permanent and temporary formal groups:** Permanent formal groups are formed by the organisation on the permanent basis and exist so long as the organisation exist. Board of Directors, Departmental Units, Staff Groups, Standing Committees are examples of such groups.

Groups formed by the organisation, to carry the particular work or to perform the specific task are temporary formal groups. These groups come to an end as soon as the task assigned to them are over.

4.   **Committee Organisation:** Committee is the most important type of formally organised group. Committee is a group of people who function collectively. Committees maybe referred to as teams, commissions, boards, groups or task forces. Committees are found in all types of organisations. For example, Governmental, Educational, Religious and Business Organisations.

Committees may act in service, advisory, coordinating, informational or final decision-making capacity. Committees may reduce conflict and promote co-ordination between departments and specialized subunits. If individual is involved in the committee he will more readily accept and try to implement what has been decided. Thus, committee increases motivation and commitment. Committee also provides the opportunity for personal development.

Committees have certain disadvantages also:

1. They are time-consuming as well as costly.
2. Individuals may use the committee as a shield to avoid personal responsibility for bad decisions or mistakes.

Informal Groups: Formal groups have officially prescribed goals and relationships, but informal groups do not have such prescribed goals and relationships. We cannot separate formal and informal groups. Every formal organisation has informal groups and every informal organisation has formal group. Thus, these two types of groups co-exist and they are inseparable.

Mayo and Lambad have classified informal groups on the basis of the functions of the group in determining standards of conduct and internal structures into three categories, natural, family and organised. Thus informal groups may be grouped as on next page:

Forms of Informal Groups

1. Cliques: The number of members of this group tends to be smaller. The object is to provide recognition to each other and exchange information of mutual interest.

 Dalton has noted three types of cliques.

(a) **Vertical Cliques:** Such cliques consist of people working in the same department irrespective of their rank difference. Such groups develop because of earlier acquaintance of people or the dependence of superior upon his subordinates for some formal purposes.

(b) **Horizontal Cliques:** This groups consists of people of more or less same rank and working more or less in the same area. Such groups are formed cutting across organisational boundaries. Such members find some points of commoness and keeping the objectives in mind, come together. This is the most common form of informal group.

(c) **Random or Mixed Clique:** People from different ranks, departments and locations form such types of cliques. They have some common objective in mind. The member may be residing in the same locality, travelling by the same bus or train or may be member of the same club.

2. Sub-Cliques: The group consists of some member of a clique inside the organisation along with some other person outside the clique.

3.   Isolates: Actually it is not a group. An individual who is not the member of any group is called isolate. Such isolates do not participate in any social isolates do not participate in any social activity organized by the group. They avoid people and people avoid them.

4. Interest Group: Those working together to attain a specific objective with which each is concerned are interest groups. Interest groups may also be formally designed. They are established on an informal basis according to the common interests or attitudes in the manner described by Newcomb's balance theory. Common interest may be sports, hatred of management, to support a peer or to seek increased benefits.

5. Friendship Group: Those brought together because they share one or more common characteristics. These groups are extended outside the work situation having attended the same college, holding of similar political views, similar age are the examples of common characteristics.

Person joins this group in the manner of exchange theory, that means rewards of such groups outweigh the cost. These groups are formed in order to satisfy needs for affiliation. Thus, informal groups provide a very important service by satisfying their member's social needs.

Classification by Sayes

Sayes gave another classification of informal groups from the stand-point of pressure tactics.

(a) **Apathetic Group:** They always show indifferent attitude towards formal organisation. They are not sincere to their demand and members do not actively engage in union activity.

(b) **Erratic Group:** This group is very sensitive to their demand. Easily inflammed and easily pacified. Thus, they are marked by inconsistent behaviour and centralized autocratic leadership. Engage in union activity without working. Deep rooted grievances exist without any reaction from the group.

(c) **Strategic Group:** This group have high degree of internal unity and good production record in the long run. They have a well-planned strategy for fighting with the management for their grievances. Build continuous pressure.

(d) **Conservative Group:** These groups consists of members having critical or scarce skills. Though they have strong position by virtue of co-operation specific objectives and self assurance. They are least engaged in union activity.

Merits of Informal Group

Authority, Leadership and Communication are the three elements affecting and influencing human behaviour. These elements are very important in the working of informal organisation. Many virtues are attributed to informal groups. These may be listed as under:

1. Informal group works with the formal organisation group in parallel way to make a workable system for getting the work done.
2. Informal group lightness the work load of the manager and fills in some of the gaps in his abilities.
3. It gives satisfaction, support and stability to work groups. It inspires members to find solutions to mutual and personal problems. A concern for mutual help characterises informal groups.
4. It is a very useful channel of communication in the organisation. It provides members with information and knowledge much faster than formal communication channels. They are useful links in horizontal and upward communication among organisation members.
5. Keith Davis has observed that power in informal organisation is earned or given permissively by group members, rather than delegated. Therefore, it does not follow the official chain of command. Because of the subjective nature, informal organisation is not subject to management control. Thus, it is a source of protection for members against arbitrary and authoritarian tendencies inherent in some organisations.

People become a part of a Group for different reasons. For example: starting a hobby club for discussing classical music or collecting stamps or designing a sales programme for selling water purifiers.

Another classification of groups in given below.

All groups are formed with a specific purpose different from another and are classified accordingly as follows:
1. **Formal Groups**
2. **Informal Groups.**

1. **Formal Groups**

   Types of formal groups are described below:

   The most common way of distinguishing groups is Formal groups and Informal groups. Formal groups are generally created in organisations and are designed to direct members towards a specific organisational goal. One type of such a formal group could be termed as a **Task Group**.

   The members in such type of group are a part of task force to achieve a specific purpose. Like in the above example, members of the Sales Programme for selling water purifiers are members of the task group. They have been assigned a specific organisational task due to their special expertise or interest in the area.

   Leadership Groups or Command Groups are those who have been assigned a high sense of command or authority as supervisors or managers and who head a group consisting of subordinates, who have to report directly to them. Like, Vice President - Marketing, who, heads the entire operation of marketing for a particular product or service in an organisation. He designs the entire marketing programme and assigns specific roles and responsibilities to his subordinates, and also guides them if necessary.

Standing Committees are other types of Formal Group, whose members are more or less permanent and who has been formed to achieve a specific objective.

The members may be from different functional areas or different levels in an organisation. Like in Colleges, there could be Standing Committees as an Attendance Committee, whose members range from the Principal, Professor, Student Representative and an Office Superintendent.

At an organisational level, there may be Standing Committees such as a Vigilance Committee whose members are from Marketing, Production, Purchase and whose main objective is to oversee that all work is undertaken without any corruption or asking any favours from others.

An **Ad Hoc** committee is a temporary committee formed with a purpose of solving a temporary problem like a parking problem during a Conference, when there are many delegates coming from all over the country or a minor strike by the employees or workers due to a particular issue like Diwali bonus or wage revisions.

2.   **Informal Groups.**

> *In contrast to Formal groups, Informal groups are formed in an organisation without any direction from the top management or any specific organisation related purpose.*

Informal groups are purely voluntary and are related to a common interest among the members.

For example, **Interest Groups** is an Informal Group, where members of an organisation voluntarily form a group due to their common sense of culture in terms of a common language, a common hometown, a common love for trekking, or sharing a common sport like Cricket.

These members may be from different functions and levels in an organisation. The key factor is that membership to such groups are voluntary and are encouraged as an expression of common interests.

Friendship Groups are also formed in organisations. These arise out of formal connections. For example, employees working alongside the others in a factory or on the shop floor or in the office may develop bonding or attachment due to some interest or just to satisfy their social need.

Such Groups are called Friendship Groups and this forms an important component of an organisation's social structure. Today, many organisations like Barclays, McKenzie, have special bonding activities out of the workplace to facilitate social connections among the employees at all levels.

Research studies show the enhanced productivity emanating from such bonding at the workplace.

Classification of informal groups from the stand-point of pressure tactics:

(a) **Apathetic Group:** They always show indifferent attitude towards formal organisation. They are not sincere to their demands and members do not actively engage in union activity.

(b) **Erratic Group:** This group is very sensitive to their demand. Easily inflamed and easily pacified. Thus, they are marked by inconsistent behaviour and centralised autocratic leadership, engagement in union activity without working and deeply rooted grievances exist without any reaction from the group.

(c) **Strategic Group:** This group has a high degree of internal unity and good production record in the long run. They have a well-planned strategy for fighting with the management for their grievances and when required they build continuous pressure.

(d) **Conservative Group:** These groups consist of members having critical or scarce skills, though they have a strong position by virtue of co-operation for specific objectives and self-assurance. They are least engaged in union activity.

3.1.7 The Five-Stage Model of Group Development

The goal of most research on group development is to learn why and how small groups change over time. To do this, researchers examine patterns of change and continuity in groups over time.

Aspects of a group that might be studied include the quality of the output produced by a group, the type and frequency of its activities, its cohesiveness and the existence of group conflict. A number of theoretical models have been developed to explain how certain groups change over time.

In some cases, the type of group being considered influenced the model of group development proposed as in the case of therapy groups.

In general, some of these models view group change as regular movement through a series of "stages," while others view them as "phases" that groups may or may not go through and which might occur at different points of a group's history.

Attention to group development over time has been one of the differentiating factors between the study of ad hoc groups and the study of teams such as those commonly used in the workplace, the military, sports and many other contexts.

Bruce Tuckman reviewed about fifty studies of group development (including Bales' model) in the mid-sixties and synthesised their commonalities in one of the most frequently cited models of group development (Tuckman, 1965).

The model describes four linear stages (forming, storming, norming, and performing) that a group will go through in its unitary sequence of decision making.

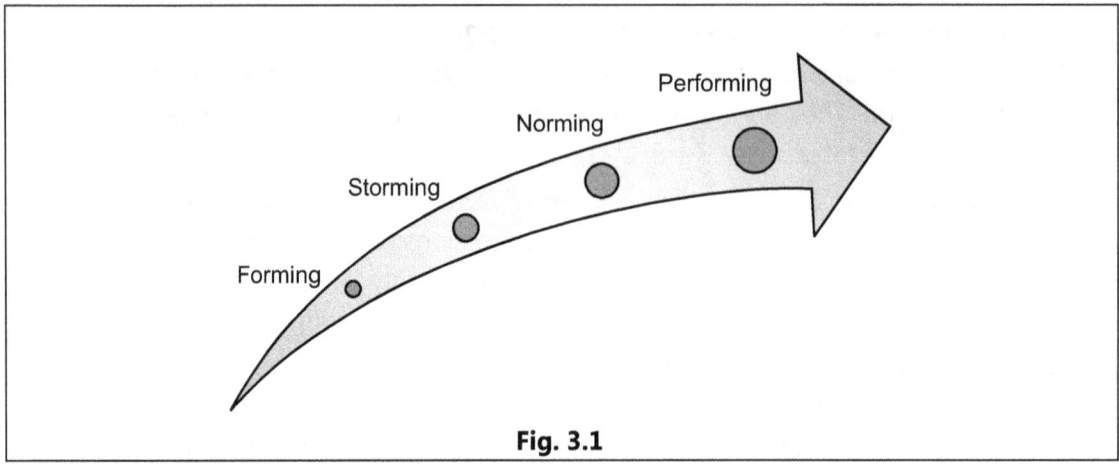

Fig. 3.1

A fifth stage, 'adjourning' was added in 1977 when a new set of studies were reviewed (Tuckman & Jensen, 1977).

Forming:	Group members learn about each other and the task at hand. Indicators of this stage might include: Unclear objectives, lack of involvement, Uncommitted members, Confusion, Low morale, Hidden feelings, Poor listening, etc.
Storming:	As group members continue to work, they will engage each other in arguments about the structure of the group which often are significantly emotional and illustrate a struggle for status in the group. These activities mark the storming phase: Lack of cohesion, Subjectivity, Hidden agendas, Conflicts, Confrontation, Volatility, Resentment, anger, Inconsistency and Failure.
Norming:	Group members establish implicit or explicit rules about how they will achieve their goal. They address the types of communication that will or will not help with the task. Indicators include: Questioning performance, Reviewing/clarifying objectives, Changing/confirming roles, Opening risky issues, Assertiveness, Listening, Testing new ground, Identifying strengths and weaknesses.
Performing:	Groups reach a conclusion and implement the solution to their issue. Indicators include: Creativity, Initiative, Flexibility, Open relationships, Pride, Concern for people, Learning, Confidence, High morale, Success, etc.
Adjourning:	As the group project ends, the group disbands in the adjournment phase. This phase was added when Tuckman and Jensen's updated their original review of the literature in 1977.

Each of the five stages in the Forming-storming-norming-performing-adjourning model proposed by Tuckman involves two aspects: *interpersonal relationships and task behaviours.*

Such a distinction is similar to Bales' (1950) equilibrium model which states that a group continuously divides its attention between instrumental (task-related) and expressive (socio-emotional) needs.

3.2 Managing Teams

Introduction

Team is a group of employees that works semi-autonomously on recurring tasks.

Work teams are most useful where job content changes frequently and employees with limited skills and a specific set of duties are unable to cope.

> *Teams definitely are forms of work groups, but not all work groups are teams.*

3.2.1 Why Work Teams?

Teams definitely are forms of work groups, but not all work groups are teams. In fact, plain work groups are much more numerous than teams.

Work groups function on three levels:

- **Dependent level**
- **Independent level**
- **Interdependent level**

• **Dependent-level work groups**

Dependent-level work groups are the traditional work unit or department groups with a supervisor who plays a strong role as the boss. Almost everyone has some experience with this work setup, especially in a first job.

Each person in a dependent-level work group has his or her own job and works under the close supervision of the boss. The boss is in charge and tells the employees the do's and don'ts in their jobs. In fact, most problem solving, work assignments, and other decisions affecting the group come from the supervisor.

A dependent-level work group can perform well in the short term. But for the long run, because group members operate separately and mostly at the direction of the supervisor, such work groups don't seem to go anywhere.

Maintaining the status quo and keeping operations under control are what they do best. Creating improvements, increasing productivity, and leveraging resources to support one another are quite uncommon with dependent-level work groups.

Independent-level work groups

Independent-level work groups are the most common form of work groups on the business scene. Like a dependent-level work group, each person is responsible for his or her own work area. But unlike the dependent level, the supervisor or manager tends not to function like the controlling boss. Instead, staff members work on their own assignments with general direction and minimal supervision.

Sales representatives, research scientists, accountants, lawyers, police officers, librarians, and teachers are amongst the professionals who tend to work in this fashion. People in these occupations come together in one department as they serve a common overall function, but almost everyone in the group works fairly independently.

If members of an independent-level work group receive the managerial guidance and required support they need on the job, such a work group can perform quite well.

Interdependent-level work groups

Members of an *interdependent-level* work group rely on each other to get the work done. Sometimes members have their own roles and at other times they share responsibilities. Yet, in either case, they coordinate with one another to produce an overall product or set of outcomes.

When this interdependence exists, you have a team by *capitalising* on interdependence.

> ***An independent work group can often be brought up to speed faster than an interdependent group.***

An *independent* work group can often be brought up to speed faster than an *interdependent* group. It simply takes more time to get a group of individuals to work as a team than to set a group of individuals off on their independent assignments. Yet when teams move into a high-functioning and high-producing state, where they capitalise on interdependence, they can outperform all other types of work groups.

To call a group a team does not make them a team: wishing for them to work as a team doesn't work either.

For a snapshot of the main differences between work groups and teams, take a look at Table 3.1. As you can see, work groups have a strong individual focus and teams have a strong collective focus.

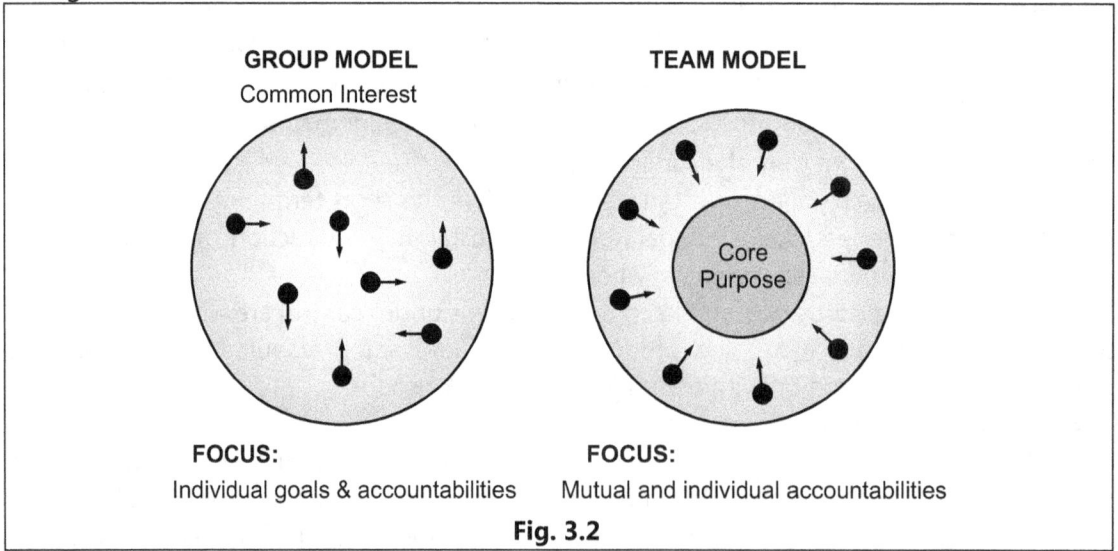

Fig. 3.2

Team concerns are much more focused on the outcomes of the overall unit rather than an individual's accomplishments.

3.2.2 Differences between Work Groups and Teams

Table 3.1

Work Groups	Teams
1. Individual accountability	1. Individual and mutual accountability
2. Come together to share information and perspectives	2. Frequently come together for discussion, decision making and problem solving, and planning.
3. Focus on individual goals	3. Focus on team goals
4. Produce individual work products	4. Produce collective work products
5. Define individual roles, responsibilities, and tasks	5. Define individual roles, responsibilities, and tasks to help team do its work; often share and rotate them
6. Concern with one's own outcome and challenges	6. Concern with outcomes of everyone and challenges the team faces
7. Purpose, goals, approach to work shaped by manager	7. Purpose, goals, approach to work shaped by team leader with team members

Table 3.1 also indicates that teams meet more often than traditional work groups. Work groups may meet periodically, based on the manager's style, primarily to hear and share information. Teams, by comparison, do much more than communicate when they meet. Team meetings are forums for planning work, solving work problems, making decisions about work, and reviewing progress. In short, meetings are vital to a team's existence.

The last item in Table 3.1 is crucial: Team leadership is participatory, in contrast to the primarily manager-driven nature of regular work groups.

On a team, the manager or team leader frequently involves team members in helping shape the goals and plans for getting the group's work done — may as well get them involved. But, in other kinds of work groups, managers more commonly work with staff individually to set goals and determine assignments.

Of course, in many cases, managers just assign work with little discussion or collaboration with the staff members and the staff is then left to figure out what's expected and how best to get it done.

3.2.3 Importance of Team-work in an Organisation

Teamwork is used across many different industries to increase performance, employee unity and company culture.

Companies that must frequently develop new ideas or products using a project-based approach assemble teams in order to diffuse responsibility.

Team members use teamwork to share ideas with each other before deciding on a development path for a project.

- **Problem Solving**

Teamwork is important due to the problem-solving synergy gained from multiple minds working on a solution. When one person works on a specific company problem, that person only has her personal experience and knowledge.

Using teamwork, team members pool their collective ideas together to generate unique ideas for dealing with problems. Problems in this case are not purely negative. The problem could be developing a product for a consumer to address a need that the consumer does not know that they have.

- **Communication**

Teamwork is the backbone of effective communication within a company. When employees work as individuals or independently on projects, they may not readily share knowledge or new information. This lack of communication increases the time it takes to complete projects, tasks or the development of solutions.

Teamwork promotes conversation between employees regarding the task at hand, possibly preventing employees from working in opposite directions.

For example, if one employee does not communicate that a particular method of addressing a problem is unsuccessful in solving it, another employee may still try to use the same method and productivity is lowered.

- **Cohesion**

Cohesion is an important byproduct of teamwork within a company. This cohesion could be the result of increased chemistry, trust or both from working on projects as a team.

Cohesive employees are less likely to be confrontational toward one another and more accepting of each others' decisions. Cohesion from teamwork can greatly increase the work-flow speed of a company.

- **Learning**

When employees work together as a team within a company, every employee learns from one another. This knowledge is not limited to the personal experiences of co-workers; employees from different departments may learn information from each other regarding the limitations and possibilities of those departments.

For example, if the marketing department consistently makes demands with unrealistic deadlines to another department, it may understand through teamwork why their requests are unreasonable.

3.2.4 Developing Work Teams

Teamwork originates with, and builds relationships amongst, a group of people who share a common interest or purpose. Working in teams allows individuals from different areas (e.g. programs, fund raising, marketing) with different roles (staff, volunteer, and client/ consumer/customer) and perhaps from different organisations to work together on issues of interest to team members.

A team focuses its work on common objectives and finding solutions to shared problems. It uses formal processes such as record keeping, facilitation and scheduled meetings to achieve its objectives.

Newly formed teams often move through a series of developmental stages when a number of individuals begin to work at interdependent jobs, they often pass through several stages as they learn to work together as a team. These stages are not rigidly followed but they do represent a broad pattern that may be observed and predicted in many settings.

The stages are the result of variety of questions and issues that the committee predictably faces, such as who should be included? Whom can I trust? Who will perform which functions and how do we resolve conflicts? In addition, members want to know which rules to follow and what each person should contribute?

As in group formation explained earlier in this chapter, there are four stages of a team's formation.

(1) **Forming:** Members share personal information, start to get to know and accept one another and begin turning their attention towards the group's tasks. An aura of courtesy prevails and interactions are often cautions.

(2) **Storming:** Members compete for status, jockey for positions of relative control and argue about appropriate directions for the group. External pressures interfere with the group and tensions rise between individuals as they assert themselves.

(3) **Norming:** The group begins moving together in a competitive fashion and a tentative balance among competing forces is struck. Group norms emerge to guide individual behaviour and co-operative feelings are increasingly evident.

(4) **Performing:** The group matures and learns to handle complex challenges. Functional roles are performed as needed and tasks are efficiently accomplished.

Not all teams may clearly experience all four stages. Some teams may be temporarily 'stuck' in a certain stage and others may find themselves reverting back to an earlier stage from time to time.

Advance awareness of these stages can be helpful to team members and their leaders. All team members can better understand what is happening to themselves and help each other work through the issues involved.

3.2.5 Team Effectiveness

Team effectiveness signifies the system of getting people in a company or institution to work together effectively. The thought behind it is that a group of people working together can achieve much more than if the individuals of the team were working on their own. The effectiveness of a team is determined by a number of factors.

How effective a team is depends in part on bringing together people who have different skills that somehow complement each other. This can comprise different technical abilities or communication skills. Teaming up people who share the exact matching characteristics can lead to disaster. Team effectiveness depends on people taking on diverse roles in a group setting. If there is no agreement on who does what in the group, it is unlikely that the team will do well. It is also important for a team to work towards a common goal. Working towards a specific goal enhances the effectiveness of a team significantly.

Research also indicates that the main reason why teams fail is that many employees are not prepared to make the change from individual contributor to team member. One of the basics to developing high performing and effective teams is to understand that successful teams do not simply happen. They take much effort and time. They take proper guidance and support from the team leader. They require an organisational culture which facilitates and fosters team work.

Intervention Strategies for Building a Winning and effective Team

- Goal Setting (Clarify Behavioural Expectations as to Desired Team Behaviours).
- Leadership — Modeling Desired Team Behaviours.
- Structural Changes — e.g., Reporting Relationships, Required Relationships, Required Interactions, Pairing, Task Enrichment.
- Empowering Group as a Whole — e.g. Allow for Group Decision Making and Problem Solving.
- Changes to the Performance Management System — Especially in the Area of Reward/Behaviour Links.
- Formal Training in Deficient Areas.
- Team Member Coaching by Team Leader or Peers.
- Behaviour Modification through Shaping.
- Constructive Feedback.
- Changing Membership {Transfers, Infusion of New Members, etc.).

An effective team will

- Retain valuable organisational knowledge that comes with the continuity of staff and sharing of information

- Enhance the power and feeling of satisfaction of individuals working on the team
- Establish trust relationships that lead to better sharing of knowledge and understanding
- Achieve objectives because individuals are working together
- Hold team members accountable to one another accountable
- Combine the talents of many individuals and therefore contribute more than the sum of its parts
- Create an environment where the input from people at all levels is valued
- Create new knowledge through working and learning with others
- Provide a process and place for multiple perspectives to be applied to complex problems and issues
- Generate new ideas and insights
- Turn knowledge into practical results that improve the organisation´s services
- Use a variety of communication processes (including technology) to support the sharing of information, knowledge and experience
- Create a climate where innovation and new ideas are supported and members listen to diverse points of view
- Multiply impacts while maintaining or reducing the resources needed to do the job
- Promote a culture that questions the status quo and looks for innovative ways to improve services and reach goals
- Empower individuals, the team and the organisations

3.2.6 Building Successful Work Teams

Success of work teams depends on the following:

- **Be clear about your objectives:** What do you want the team to achieve? Consider the potential roadblocks and opportunities and be realistic about how a team will help you find solutions. Make sure that all team members are aware of the objectives and how the team will reach them (and don´t forget to celebrate when the team achieves a milestone!). Identifying a team leader can help the group stay on task.

- **Determine who needs to be on the team:** Once you know your objectives you can decide who needs to be involved on the team. Consider whether you need to include staff members, board members, volunteers and/or clients/or other stakeholders.

  Choose people who have a good understanding of the issue. You may also want to include people who have limited knowledge because they will bring new perspectives and ideas and will learn from this process. Don't be afraid to add new members as the process continues.

- **Establish a time frame for completion of the team's work:** Remember that group work can often take longer than individual work.

- **Empower the team to work well together:** Be sure the team members have the skills and resources they need to work well together - for example, facilitation skills, finances, support staff, executive support, access to technology and the skills to use it.
- **Identify how the team will communicate:** You will need to establish a process for the team to report on its efforts and results. The team will have to establish how they will communicate among themselves and how they will communicate their work to others (for example, minutes of meetings, e-mail, web site and list-serves).

Other helpful tips

- Effective teams need to focus on both the group and the task
- All team members need a clear sense of their collective task
- Encourage team members to set and take ownership of goals
- Write down and regularly promote the group's task so everyone remains focused
- If individual conflicts arise, review and negotiate them in terms of the task that needs to be completed
- Encourage all team members to participate
- Keep a written record of group decisions to avoid returning to the same discussion
- Establish group norms that everyone feels comfortable with and hold group members accountable
- Handle feedback and debate fairly and look for alternative strategies that still fit with the group's task
- Recognise group effort instead of individual effort
- Focus on solutions - it's easy to identify the problem but more positive to focus on finding a solution
- Be mindful of verbal and non-verbal communication
- Affirm the importance of keeping commitments made to the group and by the group
- Have clear expectations and communicate them throughout the group
- Recognise positive contributions to the group
- Affirm that constructive conflict is ok but personal attacks are not
- Provide training in problem solving and conflict management to group members

Points to Remember for Groups and Teams

- *A Group is defined as two or more individuals, interacting and interdependent, who have come together to achieve particular objectives.*
- *Group is also defined as, "a social unit consisting of two or more interdependent, interactive people striving for common goods." A group has three characteristics: Interaction Dependence and Satisfaction.*

- *According to Schein, a group consists of "Any number of people who (i) Interact with each other (ii) Is psychologically aware of one another. (iii) Perceive themselves to be a group."*

- ***The following are the features of Groups:***

1. ***Social Interaction***.

2. ***Stability***

3. ***Common purpose or goals***

- ***There are a number of research studies on Group Dynamics, findings of these studies can be divided into two groups:***

    (i)   *The impact of groups on organisational effectiveness.*

    (ii) *The impact of groups on individual effectiveness.*

- *Formal groups are generally created in organisations and are designed to direct members towards a specific organisational goal.*

- ***Task Group***

- ***Interest Groups***

- *A five stage model of Group Formation has been developed and identified. Greenberg J (2001). The first stage is known as Forming, second is Storming, third is Norming and the fourth is Performing. The fifth stage is the state of Adjourning, which mentions how the groups may cease to exist because they may have been formed for a specific project or an assignment.*

- *A team may be defined as a group whose members have complementary skills and are committed to a common purpose or set of performance goals for which they hold themselves mutually accountable.*

- *In order to develop successful teams, it is necessary to adequately compensate team members, communicate the urgency of the team's mission and vision and train team members to be team members in terms of self-management, and learning to get along with people by promoting cooperation and harmony among them.*

Case Study: Teams

At Star Design Firm, which is engaged in Design Consultancy for advertising related functions including designing promos, there are distinct teams for each area of activity. For example, there is a Brochure Design team, Pamphlet Design team, Advertising design team and so on. All the team members of different teams have the requisite technical expertise. In spite of this qualitative manpower, teams are having a feeling of powerlessness and frustration because of the excessive interference from the top management. This has provoked many team leaders as well as members' to leave the organisation, resulted into high attrition rate in the organisation. Exit interviews have revealed this reason very strongly and even the managers are aware of this reason. Finally top management made an attempt to retrieve its star employees, by promising them total empowerment. This move helped them to stem attrition.

Question:

Q.   What are the benefits of empowering teams?

3.3 Managing Conflicts

Introduction

Conflicts are the result of Incompatible Interests. Conflict occurs quite commonly in organisations. Research has estimated that 20 per cent of the manager's time in any organisation is spent dealing with conflicts and its effects.

3.3.1 Meaning and Definition

In the context of organisations, conflict can be defined as *a process in which one party perceives that another party has taken or will take action that are incompatible with one's own interests.*

Other definitions are:

*   "*Conflict is a process in which an effort is purposefully made by one person or a unit to block another that results in frustrating the attainment of the other's goals or the furthering of his or her interests.*"
*   "*Conflict is a process that begins when, one party perceives that another party has negatively affected or is about to negatively affect something, the first party cares about.*"

This definition describes the point in any on-going activity, which makes an interaction cross over to become an inter-party conflict. It encompasses the wide range of conflicts that people experience in organisations – incompatibility of goals, differences over interpretations of facts, disagreements based on behavioural expectations and the like.

This definition is also flexible enough to cover the full range of conflict levels, from overt and violent acts to subtle forms of disagreement.

There are many definitions of conflict. All these definitions have several common themes. Conflict must be perceived by the parties in to it; whether or not conflict exists is a perception issue. If no one is aware of a conflict, then it is generally agreed that no conflict exists.

> *Sociologists and Researchers define conflict as, an interaction in which individuals and groups attempt to achieve their goals at the cost of others.*

Conflict has been and is studied by almost all the social sciences like sociology, anthropology, psychology, politics, law and behavioural sciences. All of them are in agreement about the essential qualities of conflict. 'A's success is always at the cost of 'B'. If 'A and B' both achieve their goals then it is not conflict.

Sociologists and Researchers define conflict as an interaction in which individuals and groups attempt to achieve their goals at the cost of others.

Sociologists who give more importance to interpersonal conflicts leading to neurosis and other mental illness define it as a situation in which a person is driven to engage in two or more mutually exclusive activities.

Behavioural scientists include both personal and social aspects in their definition. *"'Conflict' is a condition of objective incompatibility between values or goals, it is the behaviour of deliberately interfering with another's goal achievement; emotionally it is the cause of hostility."*

This definition states that –

1. Conflicts arise if values are discordant and
2. If goals are inconsistent.
3. Conflict is a deliberate action.
4. Conflict is interference in other person's achievement of goals.
5. Conflict is emotional enmity.

Conflict, competition and cooperation are three different types of social interactions sharing three common components.

1. Values of goals towards which actions are oriented.
2. Human groups related to each other in some degree for the achievement.
3. Pattern of action relating human groups to each other and to the achievement of goal values.

During conflict, interaction between relationship structures is direct and negative. Interaction towards the goal is reduced since eliminating the opposing group assures the goal.

In an organisation, conflict, competition and cooperation are usually inter-related. Members may cooperate with each other for achievement of work but they may be competing with each other to get to the senior's position. Simultaneously conflict may exist between members whose values differ vastly from each other.

> *It depends on the leader to use and convert conflict into a healthy organisational environment which leads to achievement of goals.*

Similarly, in an organisation conflict, competition and cooperation are also inter-changeable.

It is possible to change conflict into competition and cooperation and vice-versa. It depends on the leader to use and convert conflict into a healthy organisational environment which leads to achievement of goals.

The Conflict Process can be seen as comprising of five stages:
(i)   Potential Opposition or Incompatibility
(ii)   Cognition and Personalisation
(iii)   Intentions
(iv)   Behaviour
(v)   Outcomes

Stage I

Potential Opposition or Incompatibility

At this stage there is the presence of conditions that create opportunities for conflict to arise. They need not lead directly to conflict, but one of these conditions is necessary if conflict is to arise.

These conditions can be grouped into three general categories:
(a)   Communication
(b)   Structure
(c)   Personal Variables.

(a) Communication: A review of the research suggests that semantic difficulties (difficulties in understanding the meaning of words), insufficient exchange of information and noise in the communication channel are all barriers to communication and they are potential antecedent conditions to conflict.

Semantic difficulties arise as a result of differences in training, selective perception and inadequate information about others.

Research demonstrates that, the potential for conflict arises when either too little or too much communication takes place.

The channel chosen for communication can have an influence on stimulating conflict. The process of filtering information and making use of new channels rather than previously established channels also leads to conflict.

(b) Structure: The structure includes variables such as size, degree of specialisation in the tasks assigned to group members, jurisdictional, clarity, member goal compatibility, leadership styles, reward systems, and the degree of dependence between groups.

Research indicates that larger the group and the more specialised its activities, the greater the likelihood of conflict. Tenure and conflict have been found to be inversely related.

The potential for conflict tends to be greatest where group members are younger and where turnover is high. A lack of a precise definition of responsibility, leads to emergence of conflict. Jurisdictional ambiguities increase inter-group fighting for control of resources and territory.

Groups within an organisation have diverse goals this itself, is a major source of conflict.

Research tends to confirm that participation and conflict are highly correlated, because participation encourages the promotion of differences. Reward systems, are found to create conflict when one member's gain is at other's expense.

(c) Personal Variables: They include a person's individual value systems and the personality characteristics that account for individual idiosyncrasies and differences.

Certain personality types lead to potential conflict. For example, individuals who are highly authoritarian and dogmatic and who demonstrate low esteem lead to potential conflict. Prejudice, disagreements over one's contribution are diverse issues, which can best be explained with the help of value differences. Differences in value systems are important sources for creating the potential for conflict.

Stage II

Cognition and Personalisation

In this stage the potential for conflict or incompatibility becomes actualised. The antecedent conditions can only lead to conflict when one or more of the parties are affected by, and aware of the conflict.

Awareness by one or more parties of the existence of conditions that create opportunities for conflict to arise is a perceived conflict. Conflict results due to parties' misunderstanding of each other's true position.

> *Emotional involvement in a conflict creates anxiety, tension, frustration or hostility.*

Sometimes people perceive that there is a basis for conflict; however conflict will not arise unless the differences become personalised or internalised.

For example, X may be aware that Y and X are in serious disagreement over the interpretation of the policy, "Customer is the King" and are arguing for hours together. But if this episode does not make X tense or anxious and has no effect on X's relationship with Y then it can be concluded that the parties do not feel conflict.

Stage II is important because it is where conflict issues tend to be defined. At this stage parties decide what the conflict is about. This is a critical event because the way a conflict is defined goes a long way toward establishing the sort of outcomes that might settle it.

Emotions play a major role in shaping perceptions. Negative emotions have been found to produce oversimplification of issues, reduction in trust, and negative interpretations of the other parties' behaviour. In contrast positive feelings have been found to increase the tendency to see potential relationships among the elements of problems, to take a broader view of the situation, and to develop more innovative solutions.

Stage III

Intentions

Intentions are decisions to act in a given way in a conflict episode. Intentions intervene between people's perceptions and emotions and their overt behaviour. In order to respond to other's behaviour we have to infer the other's intent.

Using the two dimensions of cooperativeness and assertiveness five conflict handling intentions were identified by **Thompson.**

      (a) Competing   –   Assertive and Uncooperative

      (b) Collaborating   –   Assertive and Cooperative

      (c) Avoiding   –   Unassertive and Uncooperative

      (d) Accommodating   –   Unassertive and Cooperative

      (e) Compromising   –   Midrange on both assertiveness and cooperativeness

Cooperativeness means the degree to which one party attempts to satisfy the other party's concerns.

Assertiveness means the degree to which one party attempts to satisfy his or her own concerns.

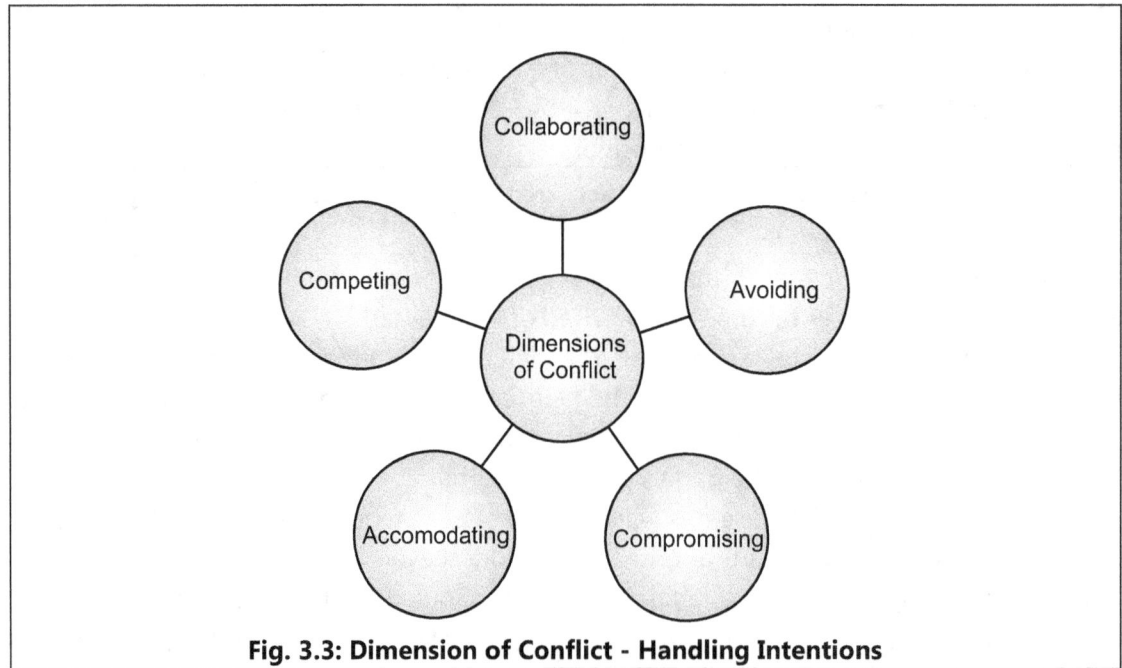

Fig. 3.3: Dimension of Conflict - Handling Intentions

Dimensions of Conflict - Handling Intentions

Source: S.P. Robbins, "Organisational Behaviour, Concepts, Controversies, applications" Prentice Hall of India, New Delhi 1997 Pg. 511.

(a) **Competing:** When one person seeks to satisfy his or her own interest, regardless of the impact on the other parties to the conflict, he or she is competing. For example, a person who convinces another person that his conclusion is correct and another person's is wrong i.e. a person achieves his goal at the sacrifice of the other's goal. Many times, in Indian organisations, the manager believes that he is always right and hence does not take the point of view of his subordinates, which then results in a common example of conflict.

(b) **Collaborating:** In collaborating, the intention of parties is to solve the problem by clarifying differences rather than by accommodating various points of view. Here the stance taken by all parties is to win and win rather than have an upper hand over another.

(c) **Avoiding:** It is the desire to withdraw from or suppress a conflict. Trying to ignore the conflict and avoiding others with whom you disagree are examples of avoiding. For example, many times during a performance appraisal the manager behaves as if there has been no difference between him and his subordinate.

(d) **Accommodating:** At times in order to maintain relationships, one party may be willing to place the opponent's interests above his or her own interest. such an intention is called accommodating. For example, a person supports a colleague's opinion despite his reservations about it.

(e) **Compromising:** In compromising, there is no clear winner or loser. Each party intends to give up something. The solution, which is accepted, provides incomplete satisfaction to both the parties concerned.

These intentions can be called *conflict resolution styles*. The choice and use of the five conflict handling styles is likely to depend upon both the nature of the individual and the situational factors.

Intentions provide general guidelines for parties in a conflict situation. During the course of a conflict people's intentions might change because of re-conceptualisation or because of an emotional reaction to the behaviour of the other party.

Research indicates that people have an underlying disposition to handle conflicts in certain ways. Individuals have preferences among the five conflict handling intentions. When confronting a conflict situation, some people want to win all at any cost, some want to find an optimum solution, some want to run away, others want to be obliging, and still others want to split the difference.

Stage IV
Behaviour

At this stage, conflict becomes visible. This stage includes the statements, actions and reactions made by the conflicting parties. Conflict behaviours are overt attempts to implement each party's intentions. At the same time these behaviours have a stimulus quality that is separate from intentions. As a result of miscalculations or unskilled enactments, overt behaviours sometimes deviate from original intentions.

Stage V
Outcomes

Outcomes may be functional or constructive and dysfunctional or destructive.

Features of Conflict as stated by experts:

1. Conflict occurs when two or more parties pursue mutually exclusive goals, values or events.
2. Conflict arises out of two different perceptions.
3. Conflict refers to deliberate behaviour. If interference is accidental there is no conflict.
4. Conflict can exist at the latent or overt level.
5. Conflict is different from competition. In competition both sides try to win, but neither side actively interferes with the other.

Indicators of Conflicts:

1. Frequency and unwarranted arguments among employees.
2. Communication problems.
3. Destructive competition between departments.
4. An inflexible and insensitive attitude towards other members of staff.
5. Unfair criticism of certain individuals.

3.3.2 Types of Conflicts

In order to understand conflict, we need to understand the various types of conflicts. **These are as follows:**

*   **Substantive Conflict:** This type of conflict is very common in organisations. It arises due to differences in perceptions and perspectives of people. Such a type of conflict is also beneficial as it forces people to think and discuss ideas openly and clearly.

    Such differences may allow innovation and also help the projects to be competitive. Substantive Conflicts are a common phenomenon and they are welcome as the members are encouraged to openly discuss differences.

- **Affective Conflict:** When people experience clashes of personalities, the resultant anger and frustration caused is called Affective Conflict. It is not unusual for people to experience affective conflict when team members of different projects come together or even similar projects come together and discuss common norms or behaviour.

  The clashes of personalities may be due to differences in ways of thinking, habits, work orientation and backgrounds. Affective Conflict is likely to affect the work performance and productivity.

- **Process Conflict:** Such type of conflict occurs as a result of differences in the ways of working or the processes or procedures adopted for working. For example, allocation of work, work responsibilities, job duties, and assignment of tasks area result of process conflicts. These conflicts also affect the performance of work in a group.

- **Intra Individual Conflict :** It is internal to the person and is probably the most difficult type of conflict to analyse. This conflict can be related to two things: conflict arising due to divergent goals, or conflict arising out of multiple roles to be played daily.

  (a) **Goal Conflict:** It occurs when a goal that an individual is attempting to achieve has both positive and negative features or when two or more competing goals exist. Approach – Approach conflict, Approach – Avoidance conflict and Avoidance – Avoidance conflict are the main types of goal conflicts. These types are explained in detail in chapter number 2.

  (b) **Role Conflict:** A role is a set of expectations people have about the behaviour of a person in a position. An individual occupies many different positions in a variety of organisations and performs multiple roles.

Role Conflict is the result of divergent role expectations. It exists when the expectations of a job are mutually different or opposite and the individual cannot meet one expectation without rejecting the other.

Role conflicts can have a markedly adverse impact on satisfaction and even on mental or physical health.

Roles such as of assembly line workers, clerks, supervisors, salespersons, engineer system analysts, departmental heads, vice-presidents and chairpersons of the board carry conflicting demands and expectations.

The first-line supervisor is often described as the person in the middle. One set of expectations of this role is that the supervisor is part of the management team and should have the corresponding values and attitudes.

A second set of expectations is that the supervisors come from the workers group and should have their values and attitudes.

Third set of expectations is that superiors are a separate link between management and the work force and should have their own unique set of values and attitudes. Conflict arises because supervisors do not know which set of expectations they should follow.

A Supervisor represents the extreme case of organisational role-conflict. Yet to the varying degrees depending on the individual and the situation, people in every other position in the organisation experience intra-role and inter-role conflict.

Research has found that role conflict is significantly related to areas such as participation in decision-making and organisation structure variables such as span of control span of subordination and formalization.

Filley and House conclude after an extensive review of the research literature on organisational role conflict that the extent of the undesirable effects from the role conflict depends upon four major variables.

1.   Awareness of the role conflict.
2.   Acceptance of conflicting job pressures.
3.   Ability to tolerate stress.
4.   General personality make-up.

Role conflict cannot be completely resolved. But management should recognize the existence of role conflict, attempt to understand its causes and then try to manage it as effectively as possible.

- **Interpersonal Conflict:** Conflict between two or more individuals is almost certain to occur in organisations. A frequent source of interpersonal conflict in organisations is the personality clashes when two people distrust each other's motives, and so simply cannot get along.

Joe Kelley says, "Conflict situations invariably are made up of at least two individuals who have polarised points of view, who are somewhat intolerant of ambiguities, who ignore delicate shades of grey (experience) and who are quick to jump to conclusions". This refers to conflict between members in-group. This type of conflict occurs especially when a new task or idea is being introduced.

Psychologists give reasons for inter-personal conflicts by examining different ways in which self and others may interact. One such attempt to understand dynamics of inter-personal conflict is known as the Johari window. It includes four points.

1.   A person knows about himself / herself and knows about the other - **Open self.**
2.   The person does not know about the other **(Hidden self).**
3.   The person does not know about him / herself. **(Blind self)**.
4.   The person does not know himself and others. (**Unknown self**).

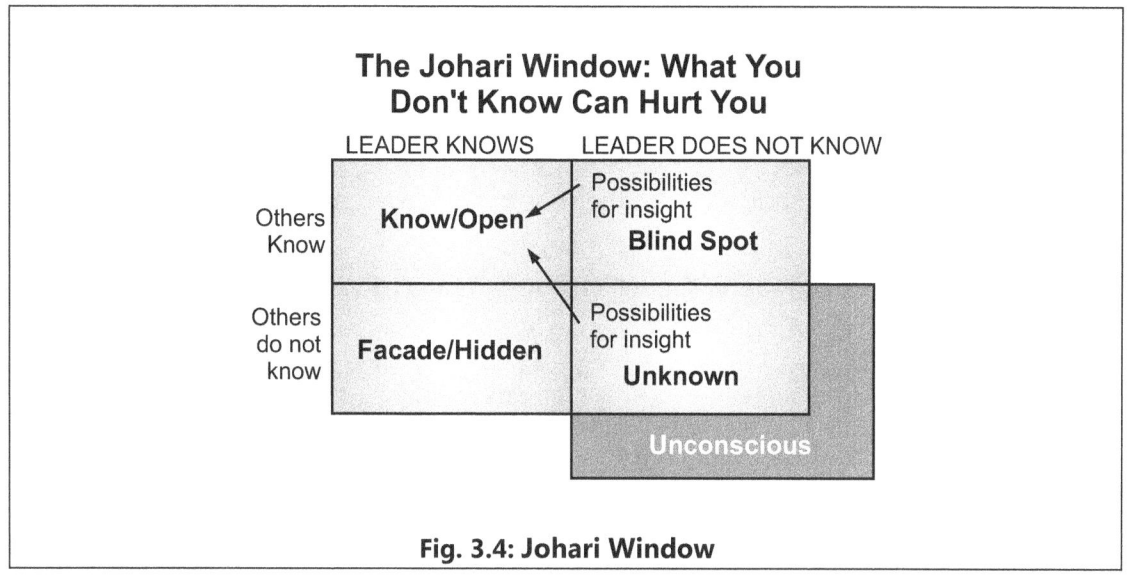

Fig. 3.4: Johari Window

These four points can help to understand and manage many interpersonal conflicts, within or without group setting.

> *The strategy to solve conflict is to increase the 'Open self' and decrease 'Hidden self'.*

According to the Johari Window, the strategy to solve conflict is to increase the **'Open self'** and decrease **'Hidden self'**. By disclosing information about oneself, the potential for conflict may be reduced, but individual risk is also involved in self-disclosure because the other party may use it for his/her advantage at the cost of the person who tries to reduce the 'hidden-self'.

Interpersonal conflict involves two or more individuals rather than one individual. Reasons for interpersonal conflicts are as follows:

1.   Personality differences
2.   Perceptions
3.   Clashes of values and interests
4.   Power and status differences
5.   Scarce resources.

* **Intragroup Conflict:** This type is known as 'hawks and doves'. When intragroup conflict becomes sufficiently strong, it may lead to formation of two new groups, which are in conflict with each other.

   Many times, a group of business partners breaks into independent groups. Groups usually come to conflict when one group can achieve its goal only at the cost of the other. In such a circumstance, members of one group become hostile to the other group.

This type of conflict can become hazardous to the development of the organisation, if it exists between two units of the same organisation.

- **Structural Conflict:** This type of conflict is caused because individuals working in an organisation are always under several cross-pressures.

  The boss wants more production but the subordinates want to relax. Customers demand faster delivery while suppliers want more time.

  These are four structural areas in which conflict may be caused:

  1. **Hierarchical Conflict:** Conflict among various levels of the organisation is called hierarchical conflict. For example, there may be conflict between management and subordinates or between peer members and the workers.

  2. **Functional Conflict:** This conflict is among various functional departments, for example, conflict between production and quality control departments.

  3. **Line-Staff Conflict:** This conflict results because employees do not possess formal authority over line personnel.

  4. **Formal informal conflict:** There may be conflict between formal and informal groups within the same organisation because there is a lag between their norms of performance.

- **Intergroup Conflicts**

This is a conflict between different project groups. It may be caused due to internal rivalry or competition over scarce resources or even poaching of members between groups and teams.

Groups of the same organisation fail to realise that they all are a part of the same organisation and the overall interests of the organisation are more important than their individual group interests.

Intergroup conflict is a part of the inherent nature of organisational life. Organisations are conceptualised as systems that consist of myriad pairs of opposing tendencies, for example, risk taking vs. risk avoiding and creativity vs. efficiency. Without conflict within these pairs one of the dimensions would become dominant in each case. As a result, the range of organisational skills and responses would become restricted, the organisation would lose its ability to adapt to a changing environment and it would run the risk of failure. Conflict is not only the functional part of organisations; it is also a critical determinant of their existence. Long term exposure to conflict situations can distort individual perceptions of other people.

- **Intra Personal Conflict**

This is a type of conflict, which lies within an individual. Many a times an individual is in conflict within his own ideas or perspectives. He or she is not able to decide which path to take and what choices to make, as his brain perhaps says something and his heart lies in something else. This is a case of an intrapersonal conflict. The JOHARI WINDOW reproduced above helps him to depict the forms of intrapersonal conflict and analyse them to find out the root causes of the same and think of ways of how to solve them and arrive at an acceptable solution.

It is internal to the person and is probably the most difficult type of conflict to analyse. This conflict can be related to two things: conflict arising due to divergent goals, or conflict arising out of multiple roles to be played daily.

(a) **Goal Conflict:** It occurs when a goal that an individual is attempting to achieve has both positive and negative features and when two or more competing goals exist. Approach – Approach conflict, Approach – Avoidance conflict and Avoidance – Avoidance conflict are the main types of goal conflicts.

(b) **Role Conflict:** A role is a set of expectations people have about the behaviour of a person in a position. An individual occupies many different positions in a variety of organisations and performs multiple roles.

Role Conflict is the result of divergent role expectations. It exists when the expectations of a job are mutually different or opposite and the individual cannot meet one expectation without rejecting the other.

Role conflicts can have a markedly adverse impact on satisfaction and even on mental or physical health.

Roles such as of assembly line workers, clerks, supervisors, salespersons, engineering system analysts, departmental heads, vice-presidents and chairpersons of the board carry conflicting demands and expectations.

The first-line supervisor is often described as the person in the middle. One set of expectations of this role is that the supervisor is a part of the management team and should have the corresponding values and attitudes.

A second set of expectations is that the supervisors come from the workers group and should have their values and attitudes.

Third set of expectations is that superiors are a separate link between management and the work force and should have their own unique set of values and attitudes. Conflict arises because supervisors do not know which set of expectations they should follow.

A Supervisor represents the extreme case of organisational role-conflict. Yet to the varying degrees depending on the individual and the situation, people in every other position in the organisation experience intra-role and inter-role conflict.

Research has found that role conflict is significantly related to areas such as participation in decision-making and organisation structure variables such as span of control span of subordination and formalisation.

Filley and House conclude after an extensive review of the research literature on organisational role conflict that the extent of the undesirable effects from the role conflict depends upon four major variables.

1. Awareness of the role conflict.
2. Acceptance of conflicting job pressures.
3. Ability to tolerate stress.
4. General personality make-up.

Role conflict cannot be completely resolved. However, management should recognise the existence of role conflict, attempt to understand its causes and then try to manage it as effectively as possible.

3.3.3 Causes of Conflicts within Organisations

Conflicts take different forms have different effects.

All organisational conflicts usually come under one of these categories;

- Conflicts of interest between functions, and
- Conflicts of authority involving manager and staff.

Let us now look at the underlying causes of Conflicts.

1. **Grudges:** Much of the conflict occurs when people who have lost their face in dealing with someone because of their fault but attempt to get even with that person by planning to take some sort of revenge. By building a grudge with someone, employees are trying to get even with others and so much of the valuable organisational time and energy is lost. Many times, in the name of difference of opinion, the employee takes the advantage and uses the opportunity to take revenge and get even with other members.

2. **Malevolent Attributions:** Why did the other person want to cause harm? What are the intentions of the other party for provoking such behaviour and causing harm? Many times it may be due to the malevolent activities of others or malevolent motives of others. Whenever we feel we have suffered some harm or malice because of the intentions of others, we call it the malevolent attribution. This causes much harm as the members have malice and it is likely to impact behaviour and lose energy of the members involved.

3. **Destructive Criticism:** Negative feedback and destructive criticism can cause unnecessary harm and untold destruction. Most of the times, during the performance appraisals, when the bosses give negative feedback, it is likely to cause a negative impact on the subordinates and so, the work performance is likely to suffer. Today, more and more supervisors are taught to remain positive and speak positively to the subordinates and help them to develop from their mistakes and faults.

4. **Distrust:** Lack of Trust is a very common cause of conflict. Many a times, when there is lack of trust and disbelief, superiors are likely to cause harm. Many bosses today are micromanaging, and do not give empowerment to the subordinates, due to the lack of trust between them. This is also, likely to cause a lot of damage and harm to them.

5. **Competition over scarce resources:** Because organisations do not have unlimited resources in terms of money, inputs, equipment, infrastructure, there is always a conflict in relation to the scarce resources. For example, the marketing department of organisations has rivalry with the production departments, for the limited resources. Each feels that its department deserves more than the other departments and this causes rivalry and differences between them.

Specific causes are:
-   Lack of coordination between employees from various departments; resulting in differing perceptions of objectives and roles.
-   Breakdown in communication lines and therefore barriers
-   Poor team engagement
-   Imprecise definition of goals.
-   Complex relationship between functions and sections.
-   Autocratic or dictatorial management style.
-   Personality difference among people.
-   Severe reductions in organisational resources.
-   Different perspectives and views.
-   Different perceptions
-   Competition among members to do better than the others

3.3.4 Consequences of Conflict

The negative consequences of conflicts are that it causes negative feedback. However, these emotional reactions are only a part of the chain reaction that can cause harmful effects in organisations.

Due to conflicts, there is a lack of coordination among the personnel or the team members and it is likely to cause harmful effects in organisations and also cause stress.

Recently, in an FMCG Company, when it was taken over by another company, the new organisation increased one layer in the organisation structure and so, as a result, the managers had to be report to one more level rather than the Vice President directly it caused ego problems between them. They considered themselves inferior in status and as a result, five managers from such managerial posts left the organisation.

> ***Organisational Conflict has costly effects on organisational performance.***

In short, Organisational Conflict has costly effects on organisational performance.

Conflict, especially when it goes out of hand, is stressful, unpleasant, distracting, interferes, with communication and can damage long term relationships. That's quite a list, and it suggests that that conflict is a serious issue, one that every manager and every organisation must takes seriously.

Overcoming Conflict

Conflict seems inevitable. It appears far easier to become irrational, not seeking common ground and not taking the others' perspective needed to find a win-win situation. In other circumstances, third parties can be useful to break the deadlock.

One widely used way of helping out of such situations is by turning to alternative dispute techniques or common grounds for discussion.

Tips on Negotiating Win-Win Situations and managing conflict effectively

1. **Avoid making unreasonable offers:** In order to minimise the occurrence of conflict, each party should bargain and negotiate reasonably with the others. For probability of Conflict to be minimised, the negotiation should be just. For example, in the case of the Maruti Suzuki strike at Manesar, in Gurgaon, the supervisors were not willing to budge and stuck to their stand on the workers' lunch timings. This only aggravated the conflict and so, resulted in acute loss to life and property.

2. **Seek the common ground:** Many times conflicts occur when one party believes that the other party is in opposition to its own interests. This is not always so. There could be many common grounds of interest between them and those should be explored in detail, so that the effects of the conflicts are minimised. As far as possible, it is necessary to find common areas of interest between parties.

3. **Broaden the scope of issues considered:** While discussing the reasons for conflict and seeking a redressal of the same, it is necessary that conflicting issues, be broadened to include bargaining powers. Like for an exchange of freezing the wages for the labour, the management can provide better canteen facilities, or a representation in the management for making decisions related to their areas of interest.

4. **Uncover the real issues:** Sometimes the real reason for the conflict may be hidden. It may show in some other way or in a superficial way. For example, a team member may show difference of opinion and so, there may be a reason for conflict or aggression, but however the real reason may be different, like getting even with the colleague or the peer. The process should help to clarify the real reason for the basis of the conflict and not the superficial one or the one that is really demonstrated.

Points to Remember

- *Conflict is a process in which an effort is purposefully made by one person or a unit to block another that results in frustrating the attainment of the other's goals or the furthering of his or her interests."*
- *"Conflict is a process that begins when one party perceives that another party has negatively affected, or is about to negatively affect something the first party cares about."*
- ***The Conflict Process can be seen as comprising of five stages:***
  - *(i)   Potential Opposition or Incompatibility*
  - *(ii) Cognition and Personalisation*
  - *(iii) Intentions*
  - *(iv) Behaviour*
  - *(v)   Outcomes*

a) **Five conflict handling intentions were identified by Thompson.**
  - *(a) Competing   –   Assertive and Uncooperative*
  - *(b) Collaborating   –   Assertive and Cooperative*
  - *(c) Avoiding   –   Unassertive and Uncooperative*
  - *(d) Accommodating   –   Unassertive and Cooperative*
  - *(e) Compromising   –   Midrange on both assertiveness and cooperativeness.*

Features of Conflict:

1. Conflict occurs when two or more parties pursue, mutually exclusive goals, values or events.
2. Conflict arises out of two different perceptions.
3. Conflict refers to deliberate behaviour. If interference is accidental there is no conflict.
4. Conflict can exist at the latent or at overt level.
5. Conflict is different from competition. In competition, both sides try to win, but neither side actively interferes with the other.

- **Causes of Conflict within Organisations:**
  - *Lack of coordination between people and departments; resulting in differing perceptions of objectives and roles.*
  - *Breakdown in communication.*
  - *Poor teamwork.*
  - *Imprecise definition of goals.*
  - *Complicated relationship between functions and sections.*

- *Autocratic management style.*
- *Personality difference among employees.*
- *Severe reductions in organisational resources.*
- *Different perspectives and views.*

In short, Organisational Conflict has costly effects on Organisational performance. Conflict, especially when it goes out of hand, is stressful, unpleasant, distracting, interferes, with communication and can damage long term relationships.

3.4 Leadership

Introduction

Leadership in an Organisation: In many senses, most people believe they can recognise it but find it difficult to define it.

Imagine you have recently joined an organisation and you have been assigned a team. How would you know who is the leader? Probably you have noticed the formal title of the member and you understand that he is the leader or the Project Head.

However, there is a member who with his technical expertise and skills is able to influence the other members of the team. Who would you consider as the leader? Sometimes, there are heads that have titles and are also influential in securing goals and alignment of the members towards the goals. Then in such cases the leader with the title and the power to influence are the same

3.4.1 Concept of Leadership

What is leadership? Who is a leader? How does he differ from a manager? What makes a good leader? We shall look at all these questions

Definition

All the above facts point out to the formal definition of leadership. According to Yukl G. (2006), Leadership in Organisations, 6th edition, *leadership is the process whereby one individual influences other group members towards the attainment of defined group or organisational goals.*

From the above definition, the following are the features or the characteristics of leadership. They are as follows:

1. **Leadership involves non coercive influence:** According to the above definition, leadership is a process involving non-coercive influence where the members are not forced to do anything but are influenced in a non-coercive way to change their attitudes and actions. The power of this influence is non-coercive and in no way are the members or the subordinates forced to do anything. They are influenced and willingly follow because of the admiration and respect that they have for the leader.

2. **Leadership Influence is goal directed:** The focus of the influence of the leader is towards the organisational goals and the goals of the team. He or she attempts to influence actions or attitudes of the subordinates or members to attain the goals or the purpose mentioned for the project or the organisation.

3. **Leadership requires followers:** The meaning of leadership exists only with the followers. It is reciprocal and assumes the similar type of influence by the followers too. In short, leadership is not a one-way direction in terms of influence or action, but a reciprocal arrangement between the subordinates and the leader.

Leadership versus Management

Although in everyday language these terms are used interchangeably, there are distinct differences between the two. Leadership in organisations is mainly concerned with establishing the dream or the vision, designing the mission or the reason for existence and establishing direction and bigger plans or strategies for the organisation.

Management on the other hand, is more focused towards implementing the goal, strategy or the vision and the mission and monitoring and supervising the execution of the policies, major strategies or plans and the overall mission and vision for the organisation.

There are however many areas where the functions of the two overlap. Still it is possible to make clear distinctions. It may be mentioned here that some managers are considered leaders but all managers are not leaders. For leaders too, all leaders do not take up managerial roles.

The distinction between the two is as follows:

Leadership	Management
Innovation	Administration
Asking What and Why	Asking How
Focus on People	Focus on Systems
Doing Right Things	Doing Things Right
Development	Maintenance
Inspire Trust	Rely on Control
Have a long term perspective	Have a short term perspective
Challenge the status quo	Accept the status quo
Eye on the Horizon	Eye on the bottom line
Originate	Imitate
Own person	Emulates or Follows

Not all managers or employees can become leaders. Few take up leadership positions and practically fewer make effective leaders.

3.4.2 Styles of Leadership

The following are the common types of leadership styles

- **Change Oriented Leadership:** Today organisations should be thriving and must be led by individuals, who have a strong commitment to change. As such, leaders must have a clear vision about what the future holds. According to a survey of CEO's of 20 different countries, having a "strong sense of vision" was identified as the single most important characteristic for a CEO to have. Hence, it is not a surprise that companies with the most visionary leaders tend to outperform the most.

- **Charismatic Leadership:** There are various examples to demonstrate how Charismatic leaders show their outstanding qualities through their words and action. Examples of the same are Nelson Mandela, Mahatma Gandhi and Steve Jobs. They have changed entire societies and have had powerful effects on the subordinates.

Qualities of Charismatic Leaders

1. **Self Confidence:** Charismatic leaders are highly confident of themselves and their technical expertise and abilities. Ratan Tata, Ex Chairman of Tata group of Companies, is an appropriate example of a charismatic leader.

2. **Vision:** He or she must have a vision that clearly challenges the status quo and helps to realise a dream. For example, Steve Jobs had a vision for Apple and the popularity and the transformation of apple is attributed to him.

3. **Extraordinary Behaviour:** Charismatic leaders show extraordinary behaviour in terms of ethics, earning respect or technical expertise. Narayan Murthy of Infosys shows extraordinary behaviour in dealing with challenges and projects.

4. **Recognised as Change Agents:** Charismatic leaders are treated as Change Agents and they are constantly looking for change. Like Azim Premjee initiated cloud computing as a measure of reducing costs, and this was a change, which other companies followed.

- **Laissez-faire**

  Laissez-faire leader lacks direct supervision of employees and fails to provide regular feedback to those under his supervision. Highly experienced and trained employees require little supervision, which comes under the laissez-faire leadership style. However, not all employees possess those characteristics. This leadership style hinders the production of employees needing supervision. The laissez-faire style produces no leadership or supervision efforts from managers, which can lead to poor production, lack of control and increasing costs.

- **Autocratic**

  The autocratic leadership style allows managers to make decisions alone without the input of others. Managers possess total authority and impose their will on employees. No one challenges the decisions of autocratic leaders. Countries such as Cuba and North Korea operate under the autocratic leadership style. This leadership style benefits employees who require close supervision. Creative employees who thrive in-group functions detest this leadership style.

- **Participative**

  Often called the democratic leadership style or participative leadership, it values the input of team members and peers, but the responsibility of making the final decision rests with the participative leader. Participative leadership boosts employee morale because employees make contributions to the decision-making process. It causes them to feel as if their opinions are taken into consideration. When a company needs to make changes within the organisation, the participative leadership style helps employees to accept changes easily because they play a role in the process. This style meets challenges, when companies need to make a decision in a short period.

- **Transactional**

  Managers using the transactional leadership style receive certain tasks to perform and provide rewards or punishments to team members based on performance results. Managers and team members set predetermined goals together, and employees agree to follow the direction and leadership of the manager to accomplish those goals. The manager possesses power to review results and train or correct employees, when team members fail to meet goals. Employees receive rewards, such as bonuses, when they accomplish goals.

- **Transformational**

  The transformational leadership style depends on high levels of communication from management to meet goals. Leaders motivate employees and enhance productivity and efficiency through communication and high visibility. This style of leadership requires the involvement of management to meet goals. Leaders focus on the big picture within an organisation and delegate smaller tasks to the team members.

  According to Bass and Avolio, transformational leadership is characterised by the following: idealised influence, inspirational motivation, intellectual stimulation, individualised consideration and servant leadership.

  Transformational leadership is that stage where leaders and followers raise one another to such high levels of values and motivation that it has a transforming effect in both of them. Transformational leaders are very relevant in today's work place.

  They can bring the organisations into futures not yet imagined. They fit the present organisational focus of revitalising and transforming organisations to meet competitive challenges.

Moreover, the model of transformational leadership places considerable emphasis on the importance of the direct reports, perceptions of leader effectiveness and the impact of the leader's behaviour on the direct reports.

This means that in order to a manager to be aware of how effective he or she is in adopting a transformational approach, he must obtain feedback from direct reports.

Clearly, it is also important that the manager obtains feedback from other work colleagues, including their line managers and their peers. Servant leadership has roots in both eastern and western thought, whereas the Taoist sages encouraged leaders to be humble. The basic premise of servant leadership is simple yet profound. Leaders should put the needs of followers before them. The followers judge leaders.

Basic Differences in Transformational and Transactional Styles

Transformational	Transactional
1. The transformational leader: Raises staff member's level of awareness and level of consciousness about the significance and value of designated outcomes.	1. The transactional leader: Recognises what it is that staff members want to get from work and tries to ensure that they get it (if their performance merits it).
2. Gets staff members to transcend their own self-interest for the sake of the team, department and organisation.	2. Exchanges rewards and promises for staff member's efforts.
3. Alters the need level (after Maslow) and expands the range of wants and needs of staff member's.	3. Is responsive to staff member's immediate self-interests.

- **Situational Leadership**

While the Transformation Leadership approach is often highly effective, there is no one right way to lead or manage that suits all situations. To choose the most effective approach a leader consider:

-   The skill levels and experience of the members of his team.
-   The work involved (routine or new and creative).
-   The organisational environment (stable or radically changing, conservative or adventurous).
-   His own preferred or natural style.

A good leader will find he/she switching instinctively between various styles according to the people and work, they are dealing with. This is often referred to as "situational leadership".

For example, the manager of a small factory trains new machine operatives using a bureaucratic style to ensure operatives should know the procedures that achieve the right standards of product quality and workplace safety. The same manager may adopt a more participative style of leadership when working on production line improvement with his or her team of supervisors.

3.4.3 Leadership Approaches

There are various approaches to becoming leaders. They are as follows:

A. The Trait Approach or the Trait Theory

Lincoln, Gandhi, Hitler, Ambedkar are all known as leaders. Early researchers believed that leaders were those who possessed some unique qualities and traits that distinguished them from their peers. These characteristics or traits were considered to be relatively stable over a period of time and enduring.

In this trait approach, these leaders possessed important traits like intelligence, dominance, self-confidence, energy, and technical and work expertise. These were possessed by leaders in varying levels of consistency and also there were innumerable traits that came to be listed over the years. This is however, also the criticism that this approach faced, because researchers were unable to enumerate the specific list of traits possessed by leaders to make them different from managers or management.

In recent years, though, the researchers have found renewed interest where they have been able to list out some specific traits common to leaders today. They are listed as emotional intelligence, drive, motivation, honesty, integrity, cognitive ability, self-confidence, technical expertise and charisma. So, this approach with these variations continues to hold in modern times of leadership.

B. The Great Person Theory

If you study the stories of the great leaders of this modern age like Bill Gates, Warren Buffet, Narayan Murthy, Azim Premjee, you will see that all of them possess extraordinary traits and an intense ambition and drive to succeed. It is the kind of orientation in this approach, which is known as Great Person Theory. According to this orientation, great leaders possess key traits that set them apart from other human beings.

It also suggests that all great leaders share these characteristics, which are as follows:

1. Leadership Motivation and the desire to lead
2. Flexibility
3. Focus on Morality

1. Leadership Motivation and the desire to lead

Such leaders are intensely motivated to lead. However even the motivation to lead can take a negative connotation like seeking power and the exertion of the same to be wielded by the leader. Such a power may be reflected by the leader to exert coercion and influence on the subordinates. The other kind of power is to seek influence and drive the subordinates and others and share expertise, ideas, innovation and drive to achieve shared goals and purposes. Such types of leaders seek networks, coalitions, and socialised power. They rely on motivation and cooperate with others, develop networks and generally work with subordinates rather than trying to dominate others. So, this type of leadership is far more adaptive for organisations rather than personalised leadership motivation.

2. Flexibility

Today the most effective leaders are the ones who are very flexible in their behaviour to situations and to their subordinates. They do not exhibit uniform behaviour but adapt to the situation and the needs of the subordinates and colleagues.

3. Focus on Morality

Authentic leadership is concerned with the focus on ethics or morally acceptable behaviour. Such leaders accept focus on morality and ethics in all their dealings and relationships. Authentic leadership is concerned with highly moral individuals with confident, hopeful, optimistic nature and who are aware of the contexts in which they operate. Their key role is in the development of the ethical and moral conduct and development of their peers and colleagues and not only themselves.

C. Contingency Leadership Approach

The Fiedler Contingency Model is a leadership theory of industrial and organisational psychology developed by Fred Fiedler (born 1922), one of the leading scientists who helped his field move from the research of traits and personal characteristics of leaders to leadership styles and behaviours.

The Two Factors of Fiedler's Contingency Model

Many scholars assumed that there was one best style of leadership. Fiedler's contingency model postulates that the leader's effectiveness is based on situational contingency, which is a result of interaction of two factors:

1. Least preferred co-worker (LPC)
2. Situational favourableness

More than 400 studies have since investigated this relationship.

1. Least Preferred Co-worker (LPC)

The leadership style of the leader, thus, fixed and measured by what he calls the least preferred co-worker (LPC) scale, an instrument for measuring an individual's leadership orientation. The LPC scale asks a leader to think of all the people with whom they have ever worked and then describe the person, with whom they have worked least well, using a series of bipolar scales of 1 to 8, such as the following.

Unfriendly 1 2 3 4 5 6 7 8 Friendly

Uncooperative 1 2 3 4 5 6 7 8 Cooperative

Hostile 1 2 3 4 5 6 7 8 Supportive

...........1 2 3 4 5 6 7 8.................

Guarded 1 2 3 4 5 6 7 8 Open

The responses to these scales (usually 18-25 in total) are summed and averaged: a high LPC score suggests that the leader has a human relations orientation, while a low LPC score indicates a task orientation.

Fiedler assumes that everybody's least preferred co-worker in fact is on average about equally unpleasant. But people who are indeed relationship motivated, tend to describe their least preferred co-workers in a more positive manner, e.g., more pleasant and more efficient. Therefore, they receive higher LPC scores.

People who are task motivated, on the other hand, tend to rate their least preferred co-workers in a more negative manner. Therefore, they receive lower LPC scores. So, the Least Preferred Co-worker (LPC) scale is actually not about the least preferred worker at all, instead, it is about the person who takes the test; it is about that person's motivation type. This is so, because, individuals who rate their least preferred co-worker in relatively favourable light on these scales derive satisfaction out of interpersonal relationship, and those who rate the co-worker in a relatively unfavourable light get satisfaction out of successful task performance.

This method reveals an individual's emotional reaction to people with whom he or she cannot work. Critics point out that this is not always an accurate measurement of leadership effectiveness.

2. Situational favourableness

According to Fiedler, there is no ideal leader. Both low-LPC (task-oriented) and high-LPC (relationship-oriented) leaders can be effective if their leadership orientation fits the situation. The contingency theory allows for predicting the characteristics of the appropriate situations for effectiveness.

Three situational components determine the favourableness or situational control:

1. **Leader-Member Relations**, referring to the degree of mutual trust, respect and confidence between the leader and the subordinates
2. **Task Structure**, referring to the extent to which group tasks are clear and structured.
3. **Leader Position Power**, referring to the power inherent in the leaders positions itself.

When there is a good leader-member relation, a highly structured task, and high leader position power, the situation is considered a "favourable situation." Fiedler found that low-LPC leaders are more effective in extremely favourable or unfavourable situations, whereas high-LPC leaders perform best in situations with intermediate favourability.

Leader-Situational Match and Mismatch

Since personality is relatively stable, the contingency model suggests that improving effectiveness requires changing the situation to fit the leader. This is called "job engineering." The organisation or the leader may increase or decrease task structure and position power, also training and group development may improve leader-member relations. In his 1976 book 'Improving Leadership Effectiveness: The Leader Match Concept', Fiedler (with Martin Chemers and Linda Mahar) offers a self-paced leadership training programme designed to help leaders alter the favourableness of the situation, or situational control.

Examples of Fiedler's Contingency Model

- Task-oriented leadership would be advisable in natural disaster, like a flood or fire. In an uncertain situation the leader-member relations are usually poor, the task is unstructured, and the position power is weak. The one who emerges as a leader to direct the group's activity usually does not know any of his or her subordinates personally. The task-oriented leader who gets things accomplished proves to be the most successful. If the leader is considerate (relationship-oriented), he or she may waste so much time in the disaster, which may lead things to get out of control and lives might get lost.

- Blue-collar workers generally want to know exactly what they are supposed to do. Therefore, their work environment is usually highly structured. The leader's position power is strong if management backs his or her decision.

  Finally, even though the leader may not be relationship-oriented, leader-member relations may be extremely strong if he or she is able to gain promotions and salary increases for subordinates. Under these situations the task-oriented style of leadership is preferred over the (considerate) relationship-oriented style.

- The considerate (relationship-oriented) style of leadership can be appropriate in an environment where the situation is moderately favourable or certain. For example, when

  (1) Leader-member relations are good,

  (2) The task is unstructured, and

  (3) Position power is weak.

Situations like this exist with research scientists, who do not like superiors to structure the task for them. They prefer to follow their own creative leads in order to solve problems. In a situation like this a considerate style of leadership is preferred over the task-oriented

Opposing views of Fiedler's Contingency Model

Researchers often find that Fiedler's Contingency Theory falls short on flexibility. They also noticed that LPC scores can fail to reflect the personality traits they are supposed to reflect.

Fiedler's Contingency Theory has drawn criticism because it implies that the only alternative for an unalterable mismatch leader orientation and an unfavourable situation is changing the leader.

The model's validity has also been disputed, despite many supportive tests (Bass 1990).

Other criticisms concern the methodology of measuring leadership style through the LPC inventory and the nature of the supporting evidence (Ashour 1973; Schriesheim and Kerr 1977a, 1977b; Vecchio 1977, 1983). Fiedler and his associates have provided decades of research to support and refine the contingency theory.

Cognitive Resource Theory (CRT) modifies Fiedler's basic contingency model by adding traits of the leader (Fiedler and Garcia 1987). CRT tries to identify the conditions under which leaders and group members will use their intellectual resources, skills and knowledge effectively. While it has been generally assumed that more intelligent and more experienced leaders will perform better than those with less intelligence and experience, this assumption is not supported by Fiedler's research.

Summary of Fiedler's Contingency Model

To Fiedler, stress is a key determinant of leader effectiveness (Fiedler and Garcia 1987; Fiedler et al. 1994), and a distinction is made between stress related to the leader's superior, and stress related to subordinates or the situation itself. In stressful situations, leaders dwell on the stressful relations with others and cannot focus their intellectual abilities on the job.

Thus, intelligence is more effective and used more often in stress-free situations. Fiedler has found that experience impairs performance in low-stress conditions but contributes to performance under high-stress conditions. As with other situational factors, for stressful situations Fiedler recommends altering or engineering the leadership situation to capitalise on the leader's strengths.

Despite all the criticism, Fiedler's contingency theory is an important theory because it established a brand new perspective for the study of leadership. Many approaches after Fiedler's theory have adopted the contingency perspective.

Fred Fiedler's situational contingency theory holds that group effectiveness depends on an appropriate match between a leader's style (essentially a trait measure) and the demands of the situation. Fiedler considers situational control, the extent to which a leader can determine what his or her group is going to do, to be the primary contingency factor in determining the effectiveness of leader behaviour.

Multiple Domains of Leadership

Scientists have acknowledged that today's leaders have to be smart and must be known to acquire multiple levels of intelligence which are as follows:

1. **Cognitive Intelligence –**

It is essential that leaders today are intellectually competent and are able to analyse and objectively evaluate large reams of data and information to a more credible picture or a pattern understood by all. This type of intelligence is essential for leaders today.

2.   Emotional Intelligence

As researched by experts, emotional intelligence refers to people's ability to be sensitive to one's own and others emotions and the skills to connect with others and empathise with them. Leaders need to develop and exhibit high levels of emotional intelligence in order to monitor and control their own emotions as well as those of others. In today's working environment, with the focus being on people orientation, and talent being scarce, the only differentiator is the leader's ability to connect with his team members as well as himself without losing his own sense of self-control.

3.   Cultural Intelligence

Today's leaders have to deal with technology, virtual teams from all over the world as well as people as employees spread across various borders and geographical boundaries. To cope with these requirements, leaders need to be educated on cultural differences in terms of language, work styles, habits, holidays, spiritual inclinations, religion, work orientation, and so on. The success of any leader is today very importantly influenced by their sensitivity to cultural needs and sensibilities of people.

Leadership Behaviour: What Do Leaders Do?

The leadership behaviour incorporates the feeling of doing the right things. This behavioural approach is appealing because it offers an optimistic view of the leadership process. The behavioural processes make them effective leaders.

- **Leadership Models**

Leadership models help us to understand what makes leaders act the way they do. The idea is not to lock in to a type of behaviour discussed in the model, but to realise that every situation calls for a different approach or behaviour to be taken. Two models will be discussed, ahead the *Four Framework Approach* and the *Managerial Grid*.

D.   Four Framework Approach

In the *Four Framework Approach*, Bolman and Deal (1991) suggest that leaders display leadership behaviours in one of four types of frame works.

Types of frame works:

- Structural
- Human Resource
- Political, or
- Symbolic.

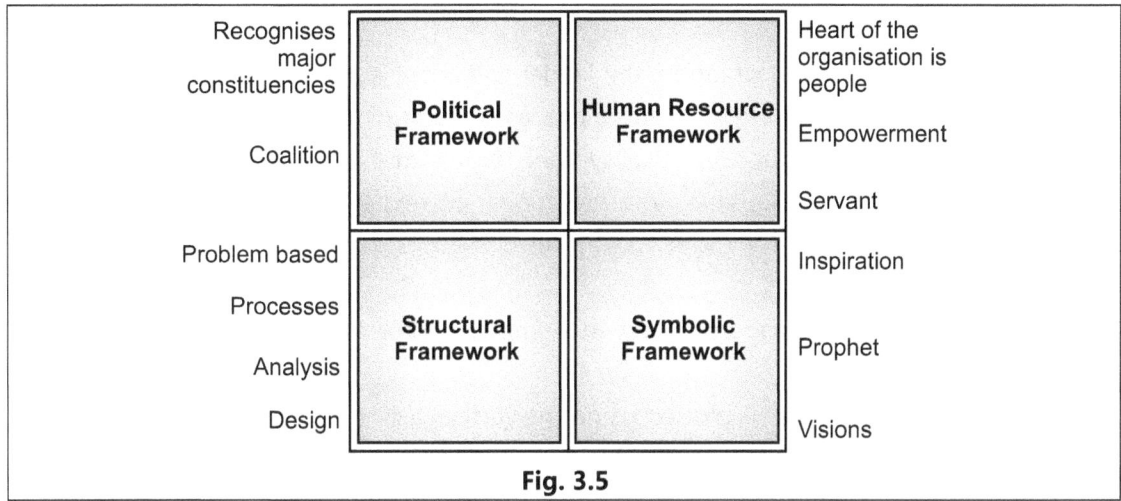

Fig. 3.5

This model suggests that leaders can be put into one of these four categories and there are times when one approach is appropriate and times when it would not be. That is, any style can be effective or ineffective, depending upon the situation.

Relying on only one of these approaches would be inadequate, thus we should strive to be conscious of all four approaches, and not just depend on one or two.

For example, during a major organisational change, a Structural Leadership style may be more effective than a Symbolic Leadership style; during a period when strong growth is needed, the Symbolic approach may be better.

We also need to understand ourselves, as each of us tends to have a preferred approach. We need to be conscious of these at all times and be aware of the limitations of just favouring one approach.

- **Structural Framework**

  In an effective leadership situation, the leader is a social architect whose leadership style is analytical and creative. Structural Leaders focus on structure, strategy, environment, implementation, experimentation, and adaptation.

- **Human Resource Framework**

  In an effective leadership situation, the leader is a catalyst whose leadership style is supporting, advocating, and empowering. Human Resource Leaders believe in people and communicate that belief; they are visible and accessible; they empower, increase participation, support, share information, and move decision-making down into the organisation.

- **Political Framework**

  In an effective leadership situation, the leader is an advocate whose leadership style, is coalition and building. Political leaders clarify what they want and what they can get; they assess the distribution of power and interests; they build linkages to other stakeholders, use persuasion first, and then use negotiation and coercion only if necessary.

- **Symbolic Framework**

In an effective leadership situation, the leader is a prophet, whose leadership style is an inspiration. Symbolic leaders view organisations as a stage or theatre to play certain roles and give impressions; these leaders use symbols to capture attention; they try to frame experience by providing plausible interpretations of experiences; they discover and communicate a vision.

Managerial Grid

The Blake and Mouton *Managerial Grid, also known as the* Leadership Grid (1985) uses two axes:

1. "Concern for people" is plotted using the vertical axis
2. "Concern for task or results" is plotted along the horizontal axis.

They both have a range of 0 to 9. The notion that just two dimensions can describe a managerial behaviour has the attraction of simplicity. These two dimensions can be drawn as a graph or grid:

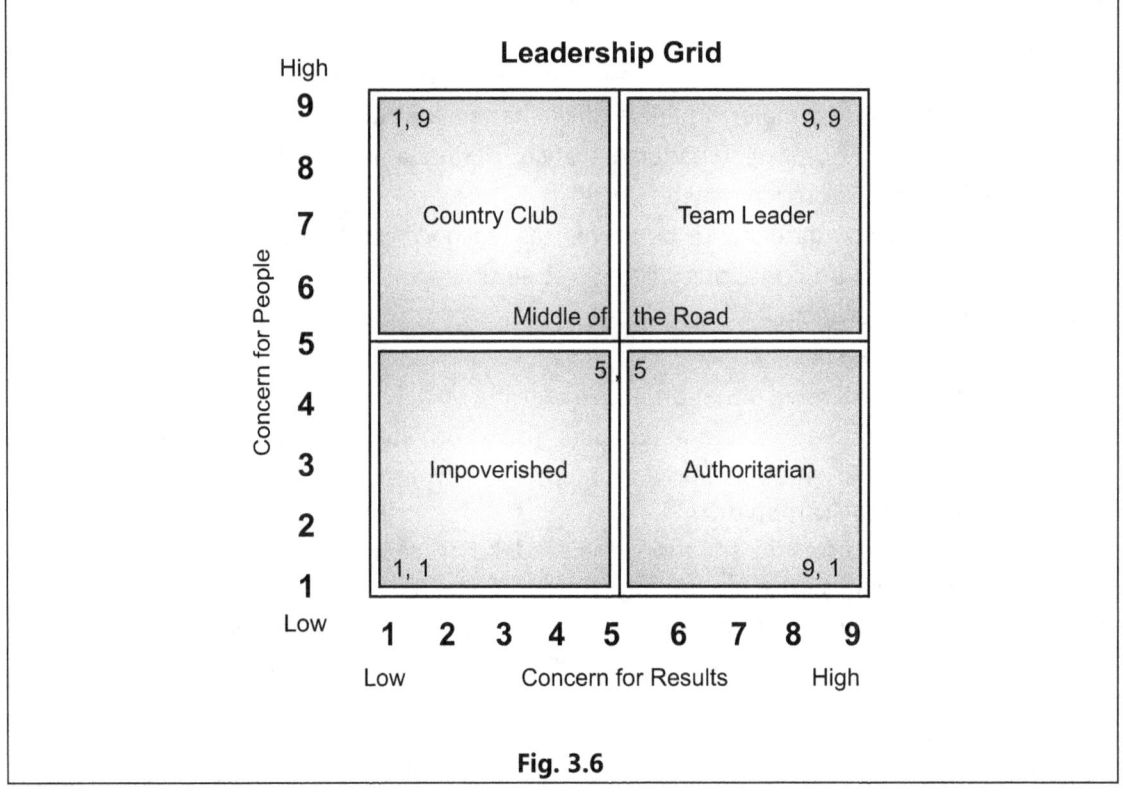

Fig. 3.6

Most of the people are covered somewhere near the middle of the two axis — Middle of the Road. But by going to the extremes, that is, people who score on the far end. They both have a range of 0 to 9. The notion that just two dimensions can describe a managerial behaviour has the attraction of simplicity. These two dimensions can be drawn as a graph or grid:

- **Authoritarian** — Strong on tasks, weak on people skills
- **Country Club** — Strong on people skills, weak on tasks
- **Impoverished** — Weak on tasks, weak on people skills
- **Team Leader** — Strong on tasks, strong on people skills

The goal is to be at least in the **Middle of the Road** but preferably a **Team Leader** — that is, to score at least between a 5, 5 to 9, 9. In addition, a good leader operates at the extreme ends of the two scales, depending upon the situation.

- **Authoritarian Leader (high task, low relationship)**

Leaders who get this rating are very much task oriented and are hard on their workers (autocratic). There is little or no allowance for cooperation or collaboration. Heavily task oriented people display these characteristics: they are very strong on schedules; they expect people to do what they are told without question or debate; when something goes wrong they tend to focus on who is to blame rather than concentrate on exactly what is wrong and how to prevent it; they are intolerant of what they see as dissent (it may just be someone's creativity), so it is difficult for their subordinates to contribute or develop.

- **Team Leader (high task, high relationship)**

These leaders lead by positive example and endeavour to foster a team environment, in that all team members can reach their highest potential, both as team members and as people. They encourage the team to reach team goals as effectively as possible, while also working tirelessly to strengthen the bonds among the various members. They normally form and lead some of the most productive teams.

- **Club Leader (low task, high relationship)**

These leaders predominantly use *reward power* to maintain discipline and to encourage the team to accomplish its goals. Conversely, they are almost incapable of employing the more punitive coercive and legitimate powers. This inability results from fear that using such powers could jeopardise relationships with the other team members.

- **Impoverished Leader (low task, low relationship)**

These leaders use a "delegate and disappear" management style. Since they are not committed for either task accomplishment or maintenance; they essentially allow their team to do whatever it wishes and prefer to detach themselves from the team process by allowing the team to suffer from a series of power struggles.

The most desirable place for a leader to be along the two axes at most times would be at 9 on task and at 9 on people — the Team Leader. However, do not entirely dismiss the other three. Certain situations might call for one of the other three to be used at times. For example, by playing the Impoverished Leader, you allow your team to gain self-reliance. Be an Authoritarian Leader to instil a sense of discipline in an unmotivated worker.

By carefully studying the situation and the forces affecting it, you will know at what points along the axes you need to be in order to achieve the desired result.

3.4.4 The Purpose of Business and Spiritual Leadership

This is a new concept associated with leadership and leaders are conscious of this holistic approach to managing people of all origins. The following is an extract from global dharma, which believes in the promotion of leadership.

In the rationalist, humanistic, and holistic contexts, if "spirituality" is considered at all, it is usually as one of many aspects of life along with work, family, leisure time, health, etc. If life is a pie, spirituality would be one slice of that pie. In this fourth context, spirituality is the pie itself. Work, family, leisure, and health are all "slices" of spirituality and gain their meaning from a spiritual context – including business.

The spiritual-based context transforms the nature of business itself – so that the primary purpose of business and leadership is the spiritual fulfilment and service to society, where both are derived from and motivated by a transcendent consciousness.

Wealth creation is no longer the goal; it becomes a means for enabling and sustaining this larger purpose. Business leaders promote the spiritual fulfilment of everyone touched by the business: employees, customers, suppliers, shareholders, and society. Likewise, business leaders develop selflessness in their service to society as they are aware of both the Transcendent and imminent spirituality in those whom they serve.

This new purpose for business and leadership is also a response to two major insights from the 1980's and 90's:

1.   Possessing material wealth doesn't really satisfy the inner yearning to access a deeper meaning and obtain fulfilment in work and life.

2.   What we've been doing with the earth's resources and with international relations (still based on "survival of the fittest") have been destructive, unjust, and unsustainable.

How does a purpose of "spiritual fulfilment and service to society," both derived from and motivated by a Transcendent consciousness look? An early example today would be Medtronic's chairman Bill George said that, they "lead by values" rather than "management by objectives."

Those values, in the order of priority, are:
1.   Restoring people to full health
2.   Serving customers with products and services of unsurpassed quality
3.   Recognising the personal worth of employees
4.   Making a fair profit and return for shareholders
5.   Maintaining good citizenship as a company

These values may seem similar to successful, customer-driven, holistic companies. But for Bill George, what's underneath these values is the consciousness that we are all spiritual beings. To unleash the whole capability of the individual – mind, body and spirit – gives enormous power to the organisation.

Furthermore, regarding this prioritisation of corporate goals, Bill George says: *"Medtronic is not in the business of 'maximizing shareholder value'; rather, our purpose is to 'maximise patient value.' The 'real bottom line' for Medtronic is the patients who were restored to full life and health last year by Medtronic products. At Medtronic, we believe that if we first serve our customers well, provide products and services of unsurpassed quality, and empower our employees to fulfil themselves and the company's mission, we will indeed provide an outstanding return for our shareholders."*

Notice that from a spiritual context, wealth creation for Medtronic is no longer the end goal for which everything else is the means. Instead, money is the means for the ultimate goal of enabling the organisation to sustain itself and grow in its ability to serve; wealth creation is implying a "natural result" of excellence in living and working from a spiritual context.

Leading and Managing People

From a spiritual point of view, the difference in motivation, jobs, and careers, can perhaps best be understood through the Sanskrit word "dharma," which means acting in accord with our essential nature and purpose. S.K. Chakraborty – founder of the Management Centre for Human Values at the Indian Institute of Management in Calcutta, India – writes that our most intrinsic motivation is to fulfil our essential nature and purpose – not to fill an ever-present set of "need-based" desires. By corollary, leading employees means evoking each person's sense of spiritual purpose in life. Jobs and career paths are based on having people follow and fulfil their dharma.

An early example of a business leader who is leading his employees from a spiritual-based context is Isaac Tigrett, founder of the wildly successful Hard Rock Café chain of restaurants, when he wasn't yet 20 years old. Isaac was raised in the Southern USA during the 1960's when his town was rigidly segregated, greatly offending his sense of fairness.

When the Civil Rights laws brought down segregation signs, he felt, "All of a sudden, all of us, not just Blacks, are more human." Soon after, living in London, he saw that, "The social classes were still completely separated. There was literally no place in London where a baker and a banker could meet to talk. I wanted to break that system."

He decided to open an "absolutely classless" restaurant, which became a smashing success from the very first day. Standing in line were those bakers and bankers, labourers and Labour politicians. Tirgrett's humanistic and holistic values were elevated to the level of spirituality when he travelled to India on a spiritual pilgrimage.

While there, he heard the teaching, "Love All, Serve All." He learned that "love" in that spiritual context meant unconditional, selfless, fearless positive in regard; the same unconditional love that Jesus spoke about coming from His Father. To Tigrett, "Love all, serve all" embodied the ultimate spiritual goal of life: becoming divine through love, and serving people from that place. It became the spiritual basis from which he began to lead his business. Being one of the Hard Rock Café families was therapy for people.

Even if they came from a violent home-life, here they were loved and they loved back in return and respect was the key. The same went for customers. He began putting "Love all, serve all" in the kitchens, on pay checks and menus, on T-shirts and Sweatshirts.

As the business exploded around the world, he continued his personal and business mission of fostering "classlessness" from this spiritual basis. For example, in Tokyo, he insisted that women, "who have non-entities there," be treated absolutely equally.

As Isaac noted, all that I did was put spirit and business together in that, big mixing bowl and add love. I didn't care about anything but people. Just cherish them, look after them, and be sensitive.

3.4.5 Contemporary Leadership

Meaning and Definition

A traditional definition – "Leadership is *an interpersonal influence directed toward the achievement of a goal or goals*". When broken down there are three key principles to this traditional definition which are:

- Interpersonal – meaning dealing with more than one person (thus a leader works with a group of people).
- Influence – the power to affect others.
- Goals – the end that one strives to attain.

This traditional definition of leadership can be re-worded to simply state *"a leader influences more than one person towards a goal"*.

A more contemporary definition – *"Leadership is a dynamic relationship (based on mutual influence and common purpose) between leaders and collaborators which leads both parties to higher levels of motivation and moral development as they evoke "real" change."*

When this definition is broken down there are also three key principles which are:

- Relationship – the connection between people.
- Mutual –sharing something in common.
- Collaborators – working together.

This more contemporary definition of leadership can be re-worded to simply state *"the leader is influenced by the collaborators while they work together to achieve real change"*.

Leadership is a recent term but what do we really know about it?

Early definitions were about the qualities or traits of the leader. These traits became so numerous that specific leadership characteristics were difficult to identify. The list spanned the traits of dictators like Hitler and Stalin to persons like Gandhi and Martin Luther King. Listing traits did little to really discriminate among leaders.

Research wasn't all that helpful either. When studies focused on behaviour with an emphasis on whether or not a leader's orientation was toward setting organisational goals or toward assisting people, the findings were inconsistent. So the best behaviour was obviously a balanced combination of both.

Next was a focus on leader and follower relationships under various situations. This model served us well until the variables were too numerous to generalise to anything resembling leadership. So what is the definition of leadership?

Contemporary definitions see leadership as a process.

"Leadership is a long-term, value-based process that encourages leaders and implementers to initiate actions that contribute to achieving a common purpose, and to willingly make significant contributions in meeting mutual objectives."

This definition encompasses several aspects of leadership from observation and contemporary research.

First, it is long-term even though the role of leader may pass to another person as soon as new circumstances and demands occur, however leadership continues.

Second, it is a relationship involving leaders and people who implement and make things happen. Often the qualities previously ascribed to leaders are now qualities of their "followers." People who implement well are competent and credible, tenacious and hardworking, trust worthy, team oriented, have good people skills, and are decisive.

Third, there is a unifying purpose with common objectives to meet. When people share a common goal they work hard to make significant contributions to achieving them. We now have a process for blending leader and follower competencies under common values.

Does this mean today's leaders exhibit different qualities than their predecessors when moving the process of leadership forward? Yes! Qualities of today's leaders emphasise what helps them keep ahead of and sharpens their relationship with their followers.

Leaders are: Conceptual thinkers and critical evaluators, consistent and articulate with their vision, humble and patient, persistent, humorous, resilient, emotionally mature, and collaborative with and respectful of others.

They keep ahead of their people with these qualities. When some people need a boost in performance, the contemporary leader accepts where they are and patiently coaches them to what's relevant for success.

A further contemporary and important dynamic is that leadership has no gender. As more women ascend in the hierarchy of business organisations and more significantly start and grow their own businesses, we are experiencing the unique contributions of women.

Some of their leader qualities include: Clearly focused on developing people, are more collaborative, focused on both the details and on the long term, willing to say what they know and don't know, focused on similarities more than differences, ask a lot of questions, and rely on their intuition to fill gaps.

The leadership styles of women are modifying the early qualities of leaders which were based primarily on men.

The contributions of men and women leaders are essential to fully understanding leadership. As their styles converge, businesses will be stronger in accomplishing their goals. Leaders will emerge at all levels of business organisations.

Here are four business and people development competencies where leadership convergence can make a positive difference in meeting today's challenges. They include: Technical/functional knowledge, interpersonal skills, strategy development, and organisational savvy. Technical or functional knowledge is knowledge of the functions of business that is used to meet company objectives. It includes finance, operations, marketing/sales, planning, information technology, and human resources.

Most people enter businesses from their educational preparation through one of these functions. Keeping pace with and sharing knowledge across business functions are contributing to more vibrant and successful businesses.

> ### *Interpersonal skills continue to be important to all business organisations.*

Listening well, articulating clearly, and recognising and respecting the diversity of talent and backgrounds available are critical especially when building a successful team. Collaboration in a global setting pushes leadership to new levels. Here social media are facilitating diverse groups in effectively implementing common goals across many boundaries.

Looking over the horizon is important. You can thrive on today's data but that may not be enough for the long term. The practice of looking ahead, reading the trends and analysing the current business results is a starting point. This focus permits the styles of men and women to converge and decide on strategies for future success.

Organisational savvy or knowing where key internal resources reside and how to mobilise them for action is another critical competency for convergence. It requires a strong internal network of resources to call on as needed. It crosses bureaucratic lines to meet common objectives. The benefits are better utilisation of resources, a more porous organisation, and higher talent retention rates.

These are exciting times for leaders and followers who understand that leadership is a dynamic process in which both participate. The old definitions are changing as men and women collaborate to lead their organisations forward.

The art of leadership is changing with our fluid and technology-driven times. Our insights into leadership will keep pace as we observe it happening around us.

3.4.6 Contemporary Theories of Leadership

The importance of understanding the models and techniques of leaderships are increasing due to the increase of complexity, diversity and rapid changes in today's organisations. Winston & Patterson (2006) presented an integrated definition for leadership as *"A leader is one or more people who selects, equips, trains, and influences one or more follower(s) who have diverse gifts, abilities, and skills and focuses the follower(s) to the organisation's mission and objectives causing the follower(s) to willingly and enthusiastically expend spiritual, emotional, and physical energy in a concerted coordinated effort to achieve the organisational mission and objectives."* (Winston & Patterson, 2006).

This emphasises the importance of leaders for organisations to achieve its goals and objectives. So it is important to understand, the different models of leadership styles since the leadership style which suits for one organisation might not suitable for another organisation.

Many people in the past have tried to come up with theories and techniques to understand the styles of leadership. Those leadership styles or models have changed from time to time. But at that time they were called emergent models for those models, which became more widespread and accepted within the last ten years time period.

For a clear understanding first we will review the literature of traditional leadership models. Secondly, we will explain the contemporary leadership models.

Finally, we will analyse the contribution of emergent models of leadership and justify how those emergent models of leadership have enhanced the contemporary leader in a world of rapidly changing technology.

Examples for traditional leadership models mainly include trait model of leadership and behavioural model of leadership. The main feature of a traditional leadership model is, one which "stresses on supervisory control over employees." (Schnake, Dumler, & Cochran, 1993).

The **trait leadership models** were determined by many theories such as "great man" theory where it tried to understand personal characteristics of great leaders who have lived in the past. Those personal characteristics include the "innate qualities and characteristics possessed by great social, political and military leaders such as Gandhi, Lincoln and Bonaparte." (Northhouse, 2010, p. 15) The fundamental principle of trait theory is that, a good leader was born as a leader and not made to be a leader.

These leadership traits mainly comprise individual's physical characteristics, intellectual qualities and personality features. (Slack & Parent, 2006, p. 293) Similarly, **Behavioural leadership model** emphasises the behaviours of the leaders or according to differences in the level of the authority given to their followers or subordinates.

Behavioural leadership have three styles called autocratic, democratic and laissez-faire.

> *Behavioural leadership have three styles called autocratic, democratic and laissez-faire.*

Autocratic style of leaders keeps all decision making and all other authorities to themselves and followers just do only what they were asked to do while democratic style of leaders encourage group participation and majority rule.

Laissez-faire style of leaders give maximum level of authority to their followers and less involved in their works. It is argued that the most effective behavioural style is democratic. The 'Leader behaviour description questionnaire' (LBDQ) was introduced by Ohio State University to assess how a leader's behaviour influenced on follower's performance (Manning & Curtis, 2003).

Moreover, **Situational leadership model** is another traditional leadership approach. In situational model "the style of leadership will be matched to the level of readiness of the followers." (Slocum & Hellriegel, 2007) Here, the readiness is the "follower's ability to set high but attainable task related goals and a willingness to accept responsibility for reaching them." (Slocum & Hellriegel, 2007)

The readiness depends on the task, which means the readiness of same group of people would vary depending on the level of training they have received, their previous experiences and their commitment to the organisation. (Slocum & Hellriegel, 2007).

On the other hand, the contemporary leadership models argue that the "effective leaders are those who have the cognitive and behavioural capacity to recognise and react to paradox, contradiction, and complexity in their environments." (Denison, Hooijberg, & Quinn, 1995).

Most common contemporary leadership models include charismatic, transformational and transactional leadership. "**Transactional leadership** style is based on an exchange of service for various kinds of rewards that the leader controls, at least in part." (Leithwood, 1992) Transactional leaders should be able to identify the rewards that would motivate their followers in orders to achieve their goals.

In contrast, **transformational leadership** is defined as "the collective action that transforming leadership generate empowers those who participate in the process." (Leithwood, 1992)

Transformational leaders are capable to bring up with a significant change. That is "it facilitates the redefinition of a people's mission and vision, a renewal of their commitments, and the restructuring of their systems for goal accomplishment." (Leithwood, 1992)

Charismatic leaders have supernatural powers over their followers. House & Baetz (cited in (Conger & Kanungo, 1987)) defined **charismatic leaders** as the leaders who "by the force of their personal abilities are capable of having profound and extraordinary effects on followers".

The followers of charismatic leaders are loyal and trust the charismatic leader's values, behaviours and vision. (Borkowski, 2005) Charismatic leaders use their own personal power instead of position power to influence followers in order to achieve their goals.

The emergent models of leadership turned up with the rapid increase of complexity, technological advancements and increasing demand for leaderful organisations and flexible firms.

The main difference between traditional models and modern leadership models would be all traditional models of leadership emphasise characteristics or behaviours of only one leader within a particular group whereas emergent models provide a space to have more than one leader at the same time.

According to emergent models a leader at one instance can be a follower in another instance. Traditional models do not tell the kind of skills that the leaders should have. But emergent models focus more on the special skills or talents that the leaders must have to practice to face challenging situations. For example Innovative thinking improves the decision making process of leaders by exposing better alternative options for current methods, techniques and solutions.

Emergent leadership approach argues the importance of '**systems thinking**' for more complex organisations, especially for flexible firms. 'Systems thinking' is defined as "an ability to think or analyse information and situations that leads to or causes effective or superior performance" (Palaima & Skaržauskienė, 2010).

"To engage in systems thinking means to start treating problems in an organisation as problems of a system and to start looking for system-integrated solutions." (Palaima & Skaržauskienė, 2010)

It helps to improve contemporary leader in many ways. The holistic approach of systems thinking enables to enhance the working system by innovative thinking. And it enables leaders to make more effective decisions by considering the organisation as an open system or considering the environmental influences to organisation and organisational influences to the environment. It also helps to understand the systematic forces for effective change management. (Palaima & Skaržauskienė, 2010)

Moreover, in the recent past the research investigators have found that **emotional intelligence** is very important for effective leadership rather than use of traditional leadership styles. *"Emotional Intelligence involves the ability to monitor one's own and others' feelings and emotions, to discriminate among them, and to use this information to guide ones' thinking and actions."* (Emmerling, Shanwal, & Mandal, 2008)

Transformational leaders can easily make the difference by taking decisions according to follower's emotions. "Inspirational, motivation and individualised consideration components of transformational leadership correlated with the ability to monitor emotions and the ability to manage emotions." (Rosete & Ciarrochi, 2005)

So it is important to improve emotional intelligence for an effective leadership. "Findings suggest that executives higher on 'EI' are more likely to achieve business outcomes and be considered as more effective leaders by their subordinates and direct manager." (Rosete & Ciarrochi, 2005)

Transactional leaders can also use their emotional intelligence to understand emotions of followers and give rewards according to their emotions. Furthermore, **boundary spanning** is also helpful in improving the effectiveness of contemporary leaders. "Boundaries are an unavoidable aspect of organisational life." (Christopher & Jeffrey, 2008) Organisations have boundaries for its functions or even boundaries can be created from its culture.

But the effect of globalisation, technological advancements, demographic changes and shifts of social structures enables people to work together without a limit, which creates "the need for leaders to bridge social identity boundaries among groups of people with very different histories, perspectives, values, and cultures." (Christopher & Jeffrey, 2008)

This might help transactional leaders to make a significant difference within the organisation easily. Also boundary spanning helps to spread the organisational experiences into local communities. "If people of different identity groups are provided with opportunities for positive cross-boundary contact in the workplace, then these experiences can spill over into local communities." (Christopher & Jeffrey, 2008)

Charismatic leaders might find this as an advantage to become a powerful leader not only to the company but also to outside communities. In addition, another very important and interesting approach of leadership is **leaderless organisation**.

This concept was introduced with the increased demand of organisations which have flattened structures where it is important to have self-managed teams. It directly challenges the traditional leadership model of being one leader for a group of people. Leaderless organisation emphasise the *"need to establish communities where everyone shares the experience of serving as a leader, not serially, but concurrently and collectively."* (Raelin, 2003, p. 5)

Unlike in traditional theories, here, the leadership is concurrent. That is there are a number of people acting as leaders on any one occasion. Moreover, it says that everyone is serving as a leader collectively. We know according to traditional models all the decisions are taken by one leader and he gives the authority or empower his followers to go beyond and do certain things if necessary.

But according to leaderless organisation, all the people have same type of authority or they were empowered equally to take necessary decisions to achieve their common objectives or goals.

As a final point it is very important to mention the importance of **expansive leadership**. *"Expansive leaders are people who are avid continuous learners."* (Diamante & London, 2002) Expansive leaders are always expanding their knowledge internally and externally. "Expansive leaders dive into the technology, thrive on their own development, and use their understanding of operations and linkages (connectivity) to push the organisation in new directions." (Diamante & London, 2002) Expansive leadership is vital to create expansive organisational cultures and expansive cultures promote learning organisations. The approach of learning organisation is essential for every modern organisation since those organisations are always facing into rapid technological advancements.

In conclusion, traditional leadership models which include trait model, behavioural model and situational model of leadership explain the personal and behavioural characteristics of a leader and the leader always has the control over followers.

Charismatic, **transformational** and **transactional leadership** models are the main **contemporary models** of leadership and those models argues that the effective leaders are the people who can manage followers and take effective decisions in complex, challenging and changing situations. Emerging models improve the effectiveness of contemporary leaders by enhancing their skills.

It have been identified that systems thinking, boundary spanning, emotional intelligent, leaderless organisation and expansive leadership approaches helps contemporary leaders to make effective decisions to cope with globalisation, rapid changes in technology and organisational structural changes such as flexible firms and virtual organisations.

Unlike traditional models, emergent models promote concurrent and collective leadership which helps transformational leaders to be more innovative and bring the significant change easily. Transactional leaders can use approaches like emotional intelligence to be more effective by understanding the emotions of followers to improve their effectiveness. Emergent approaches such as boundary spanning helps charismatic leaders to extend their leadership into outside communities.

3.4.7 Common Contemporary Leadership Challenges

- **Lack of a positive vision of the future**

Bibb and Kourdi (2004, p.155) suggested that one of the key reasons why people would need a leader is because they need to be inspired towards a positive vision of the future. And according to Kotter (1996), there are six elements of a successful vision: realism, power, communicability, desirability, focus and adaptability and lacking of these elements could make the effort of creating a positive vision of the future become obsolete. For example, the element of focus requests the vision to be specific enough to provide guidance to the decision making and business planning, but there are many leaders who only provide a positive vision of the future in a broad sense making the vision of little influence when it comes to the business practices.

- **Lack of an engaging and inclusive leadership**

The inclusive leadership is the acknowledgement of differences in term of culture, education background, gender, ethnic groups and other differences (Visser 2011, p.91). Engaging an inclusive leadership could act as a connection between different groups lacking which disputes and problems could be resulted. For example, when the decisions are made only by the male managers while the female managers' view of points are largely ignored, then leadership effectiveness could be largely reduced because female managers like the male counterparts could also offer very smart, sometimes the best solutions to the company and bypassing the women managers' idea would cause ineffectiveness in leadership and the failure to embrace other differences could result in similar consequences.

- **Lack of leadership courage**

"Courage is not about the absence of fear but rather it is to see oneself in a realistic perspective, considering options, and choosing to function in spite of risks" (Carter 2007, p.102).

There have been too many business failures caused by the lack of leadership courage as many leaders are not determined and decisive enough when faced by difficulties and fear of changes.

- **Lack of emotional intelligence competencies**

Emotional intelligence could be referred as a set of abilities to know and understand emotions and emotional processes in one's own self and others (Salovey & Mayer 1990). Emotional intelligence could be described by some key words such as self-control, capacity to communicate and co-operate (Jasper & Jumaa 2005, p.164)

The lack of emotional intelligence competencies also would bring impact to the leadership effectiveness. For example, Steve Jobs, the cofounder of Apple Inc, was known for his extreme personalities, when Jobs was focusing on the key projects, he tended to use an autocratic leadership style to fulfil his personal interest though it was also the interest of the company, but when the employees' requests were ignored many times, the successes that Jobs had achieved in developing new products had been brought down by his lack of emotional intelligence to deal with the interpersonal interactions.

- **Lack of inspiring core values**

When many leaders focus on making a vision of bright future for the followers and make them believe that they could achieve the vision, there are a smaller number of them who can inspire the core values along with the creation of the vision and insist on the core values persistently. For example, Toyota has been famous for producing quality cars but in 2009 according to an outside safety consulting firm, there had been about 2,000 documented accidents of unintended acceleration that have happened to the users of Toyota cars resulting in 16 deaths and 243 injuries and a lot of complaints and inquiries from the customers. (Maciariello & Linkletter 2011, p.12) .

But Toyota's very first response to the complaints regarding the sudden acceleration problem was to advise them to remove the floor mats from the cars before the later large scale recall of cars. Such a reaction had made the customers very angry when the "National Highway Traffic Safety Administration" (NHTSA) later found out that Toyota was aware of the problems before the issue of the recall (U.S. Department of Transportation, 2010).

The mishandling of the accelerator problem shows the fact that the Toyota management failed to exhibit the leadership effectiveness and integrity at many levels. And many other companies also fail to insist on their core values which they had tried to inspire and have posted in the official websites, especially when it came to the time of crisis.

3.4.8 Success Stories of Today's Global and Indian Leaders

A leader for a Global India Inc - Mukesh Ambani speaks

Economic prophets have billed India as an emerging global economic superpower. Economic reforms, high rates of economic growth, vibrant services and manufacturing sectors, rising exports, increasing foreign investments and global forays by Indian companies are factors that have contributed to such forecasts.

As a result, desires, as well as dreams, of being counted among the top three economies in the world, abound. However, in an environment of unbridled optimism, the aspect of evolving and implementing strategies to make India an economic superpower seems to have been glossed over.

We are at the doorsteps of an historical opportunity for India. We can bring about revolutionary changes in economy, society and human life. In the midst of these changes, we must not forget an important factor. In the final analysis, it is leadership that holds the key to our future.

My definition of leadership is not in a narrow political sense, but leadership in every walk of life—especially in business. The imperative of turning prophecies about India as an economic superpower to enable India perform and attain global economic superpower status is compelling. What then does India need to attain global leadership?

An enlightened, bold and purposeful leadership is critical to be able to successfully pursue the three pathways of economic, technological and social leadership to attain true global leadership. Without leadership, all talk of being a global economic leader will be just rhetoric.

India needs a clearly defined set of global leadership goals, defined pathways to attain these goals and an enlightened and bold national leadership that is passionate about realising India's true potential. Today businesses are firmly embedded in our social system.

Companies play a far deeper role in global affairs than they have ever done before. The revenues of certain large enterprises are greater than even the GDP of several countries in the world.

In 2006, global Official Development Assistance (ODA) totalled $103.9 billion. On the other hand, global Foreign Direct Investment (FDI) reached $1.3 trillion in 2006.

FDI, which is the key driver in the international economic system, outstripped ODA more than ten-fold! These figures show that companies, leveraging their investment dollars, have become key players in the process of global development.

Leaders in this century will need a completely different set of skills since their role will go well beyond the confines of their geography and also beyond the purview of business.

It is believed that the 21st century leader must remain in sync with dramatic changes sweeping the globe. However, a forceful leader must also be sensitive, caring and compassionate.

Consequently, business leaders will find their jobs extending into domains well beyond the scope of quarterly bottom line figures. Indian CEOs, as much as those anywhere else in the world, will have to take on the tsunami of global poverty, rooted in the deliberately inequitable distribution of wealth.

In the past, the involvement of the business sector in poverty alleviation has been overwhelmingly driven by a philanthropic rather than a business motives. Future leaders and managers, however, will have a far greater responsibility to the society in which they operate.

The leader must not only address the anxieties of his team and workforce, but also the problems and aspirations of society as a whole. I strongly believe that humility and not arrogance makes leadership most effective. And strong-minded focus is critical to success.

Global India Inc.'s new leaders will have to deal with a variety of issues in terms of changing economic patterns, demographics and migration, the pressures created by scarce essential resources like water and energy, their impact on the environment, religion and individual identity, the explosive impact of poverty and the governance issues that it throws up.

To the taxonomy of qualities that will be required to be a successful corporate chief in these conditions, the single most important feature— the ability to formulate a shared vision of the world over the next 50 years – must also be added.

That is and will always be the essence of leadership. The leaders for a global India Inc. will be prescient, rooted in the present but with an eye firmly fixed on the future on which they are willing to bet their careers and their fortunes.

They will see as part of their role, the need to create a sustainable business environment and to ensure gender diversity and equality of growth.

They will actively engage in social issues, recognising that business and society cannot operate in discrete silos, that the stakeholders in a company are no longer just the shareholders. They include the community and the world at large.

The global leader of tomorrow will have to handle far more ambiguity and uncertainty, and since no one can control all the vicissitudes of global business, there won't always be a guarantee on the results.

In the fast-changing landscape of business and politics, global Indian leaders will need to adapt, change and constantly think on their feet to keep pace with these differences.

The new age leaders must lead without any cultural bias and prejudice. They will need to recognise that there is no 'absolute culture'.

As they seek to cultivate new skills and abilities, India Inc.'s future global leaders will need to unlearn past assumptions and cultivate flexible thinking that allows them to handle incessant chaos and change, and evolve strategies that integrate different people, countries and cultures.

The language for the 21st century is global and India Inc.'s new leaders will have to master its vocabulary.

Dhirubhai Ambani, was a uniquely gifted leader of men, who had a strong emotional bonding with his colleagues and his shareholders.

He built a world-class business and yet it is doubted if any management book would ever have laid down the rules of leadership based on his style.

He always used to say: "If one focuses on goals, one will overcome obstacles. If one focuses only on obstacles, one will never reach the goals."

It is a leadership lesson that will always be relevant.

LAKSHMI MITTAL: ARCELORMITTAL

Also known as the 'Iron Man of Calcutta', Lakshmi Mittal is the Indian steel mogul who is the Chairman and Chief Executive Officer of ArcelorMittal, the biggest steel producing company of the world. In 2011, Mittal was ranked 6th amongst the world's richest people by Forbes. He is also number 47th on the Forbes list of 'most powerful individuals'.

Lakshmi Mittal was born on 15th June 1950 in the Churu district in Rajasthan, India to a business family. He studied in St. Xavier's College and graduated with a Bachelor of Commerce degree. After that he joined his father's steel business named 'Nippon Denro Ispat' where he was responsible of the international development. He founded his own company by the name of 'Mittal Steel' in 1976. Since then he has been in charge for the expansion of the business. In the early 90s the steel magnate bought failing or weakened companies and saved them. Mittal steel is currently a worldwide steel producer that operates in 14 countries. He also established the growth of incorporated mini-mills and use of DRI (direct integrated iron) as an ancillary for making steel. With shipments of 42.1 million tons steel and profits of more than 22 billion dollars (2004), Mittal Steel is by far the largest steelmaker of the world. Mittal has also been part of some controversies and allegations such as the Mittal Affair and slave labor, environmental damage and dubious safety records.

Mittal is a generous philanthropist and part of many trusts. He has the membership of the Foreign Investment Council (Kazakhstan), the International Investment Council of the World Economic Forum, the International Investment Council (South Africa) and the International Iron and Steel Institute Executive Committee. Along with this he holds the post of director of the ICICI Bank Limited and is also on the advisory board of the 'Kellogg School of Management' in the U.S. Lakshmi Mittal has received several awards and honors including the 'Forbes Lifetime Achievement Award' in 2008, the 'Padma Vibhushan' from the Government of India in 2008, the 'Grand Cross of Civil Merit' from the Government of Spain in 2007, the 'Dwight D. Eisenhower Global Leadership Award' from the Business Council for

International Understanding in 2007. He was Forbes 'European Businessman of the Year' in 2004. Wall Street Journal termed him 'Entrepreneur of the Year' in 2004 and the same year he was given the '8th Honorary Willy Korf Steel Vision Award' from the American Metal Market and World Steel Dynamics.

The Sunday Times 'Business Person of the Year' in 2006, Financial Time's 'Person of the Year' and Time magazine's International Newsmaker of the Year 2006' and one of the '100 most influential persons in the world', Lakshmi Mittal certainly has an exemplary life for those who wish to achieve success in their lives.

Indra Krishnamurthy Nooyi : Chairman and Chief Executive Officer of PepsiCo

Indra Nooyi is Chairman and Chief Executive Officer of PepsiCo. Mrs. Nooyi leads one of the world's largest convenient food and beverage companies, with 2008 annual revenues of more than $43 billion. The company's products are sold in approximately 200 countries, and it employs more than 198,000 people worldwide. Its principal businesses include Frito-Lay snacks, Pepsi-Cola beverages, Gatorade sports drinks, Tropicana juices and Quaker foods. In total, the PepsiCo portfolio includes 18 brands that generate $1 billion or more each in annual retail sales.

Mrs. Nooyi was named President and CEO on October 1, 2006 and assumed the role of Chairman on May 2, 2007. She has directed the company's global strategy for more than a decade and led PepsiCo's restructuring, including the divestiture of its restaurants into the successful YUM! Brands, Inc.; the spin-off and public offering of company-owned bottling operations into anchor bottler Pepsi Bottling Group (PBG); the acquisition of Tropicana and the merger with Quaker Oats that brought the vital Quaker and Gatorade businesses to PepsiCo.

Prior to becoming CEO, Mrs. Nooyi served as President and Chief Financial Officer beginning in 2001, when she was also named to PepsiCo's board of directors. In this position, she was responsible for PepsiCo's corporate functions, including finance, strategy, business process optimisation, corporate platforms and innovation, procurement, investor relations and information technology.

Between February 2000 and April 2001, Mrs. Nooyi was Senior Vice President and Chief Financial Officer of PepsiCo. Between 1996 and 1999, Mrs. Nooyi was Senior Vice President of Corporate Strategy and Development.

Before joining PepsiCo in 1994, Mrs. Nooyi spent four years as Senior Vice President of Strategy and Strategic Marketing for Asea Brown Boveri, a Zurich-based industrials company. She was part of the top management team responsible for the company's U.S. business as well as its worldwide industrial businesses, representing about $10 billion of ABB's $30 billion in global sales.

Between 1986 and 1990, Mrs. Nooyi worked for Motorola, where she was Vice President and Director of Corporate Strategy and Planning, having joined the company as the business development executive for its automotive and industrial electronic group. Prior to Motorola, she spent six years directing international corporate strategy projects at the Boston Consulting Group. Her clients ranged from textiles and consumer goods companies to retailers and specialty chemicals producers. Mrs. Nooyi began her career in India, where she held product manager positions at Johnson & Johnson and at Mettur Beardsell, Ltd., a textile firm.

In addition to being a member of the PepsiCo board of directors, Mrs. Nooyi serves as a member of the boards of the International Rescue Committee, Catalyst and Lincoln Center for the Performing Arts. She is a Successor Fellow of Yale Corporation and member of the Board of Trustees of Eisenhower Fellowships, and she currently serves as Chairman of the U.S.-India Business Council.

She holds a BS from Madras Christian College, an MBA from the Indian Institute of Management in Calcutta and a Master of Public and Private Management from Yale University. Mrs. Nooyi is married and has two daughters.

The social network: Kirthiga Reddy 40, Director Online Operations, Head, Facebook India

Because: She heads the India division of the world's largest social network with over 800 million active users. Because since Facebook set up an office in the country in 2010, the user base went up from eight million to over 40 million people in less than two years.

Because India is Facebook's third-largest market and has an average growth rate of more than one million people per month. Because Facebook users represent the youngest and most attractive market segment in the country.

Show stopper: Ekta Kapoor 36, Joint Managing Director, Balaji Telefims

Because: 2011 was a banner year with five film releases, the most successful of which was the critical and commercial success *"The Dirty Picture",* that grossed over Rs. 114 crore. Because despite having being written off in 2008 after the *Saas-Bahu* bubble burst, Kapoor came back with a bang with big screen releases like *"Love, Sex aur Dhokha", "Once Upon A Time in Mumbaai"* and *"Ragini MMS".*

Because her production house Balaji Telefilms had a sales turnover of ₹ 151 crore in 2011. Because from gifting her favourite writers money to buy a car, to throwing chairs at her staff in rage, she plays the role of a larger than life diva with élan.

Fresh start: Renuka Ramnath 50, CEO and Managing Director, Multiples Alternate Asset Management

Because: As the head of ICICI Ventures, she was dubbed the queen of private equity for managing funds of around ₹ 9,200 crore. Because she quit at the peak of her career in 2009 to start her own venture. Because her start-up is now a ₹ 2,025 crore private equity fund, backed by top Indian and global institutional investors.

Revolutionary road: Kiran Bedi 63, Social Activist

Because: She has stepped beyond the traditional role assigned to women and set a benchmark of courage for others. Her stand against corruption put her at the forefront of the neo-nationalist anti-corruption movement in 2011. Because her drive for social justice goes beyond her uniform. Because she was India's first female police officer.

Retail heaven: Ashni Biyani 26, Director, Future Group

Because: She is the heir apparent to the Future group that is leading the retail revolution in the country, with a group capitalisation of ₹ 5,900 crore. Because Big Bazaar now has 150 stores across 90 cities. Because she is managing the planned ₹ 300 crore investment to open 30 more Big Bazaar centres by June 2012. Because she is in-charge of Future Ideas that helps come up with strategies to boost sales.

The Powerhouse: Shikha Sharma 51, Managing Director and Chief Executive Office, Axis Bank

Because: She heads India's third largest private sector bank, and has recently been reappointed managing director for another three years. Because since she took charge in 2009, Axis Bank's performance has been admirable with a reported profit of ₹ 942 crore for the quarter ending June 2011, a 27 per cent increase year on year.

Because she revolutionised the private insurance sector as the head of ICICI Prudential, crossing 2,00,000 policies within two years and earning a premium income of ₹ 280 crore. Because after her exit from ICICI, Sharma bounced back twice as strong with Axis Bank, commanding a pay package of over ₹ 2 crore a year.

In equal measure: Naina Lal Kidwai 54, Executive Director and Country Head, HSBC

Because: She heads India's division of HSBC with deposits of close to $12,000 million. Because despite the sovereign credit crisis in the Eurozone, under her leadership, the pretax profit rose by 22 per cent to $813 million in 2011. Because she was the first woman to enter the world of investment banking.

Because she is the first woman vice president of the Federation of Indian Chambers of Commerce and Industry. Because she is a non-executive director on the board of Nestle and a member of the Audit Advisory Board of the Comptroller and Auditor General of India.

The frontrunner: Chanda Kochhar 51, Managing Director and Chief Executive Officer, ICICI Bank Limited

Because: She heads India's largest private bank with total assets of ₹ 4,062.34 billion and recorded a profit of ₹ 51.51 billion in 2011. Because this year the bank expects to maintain its net interest margin (a measure of lending profitablity) at 2.6 per cent, at a time when most lenders have reported a drop because of a hike in RBI interest rates.

Because besides being on the board of ICICI Bank, she is a member of the Prime Minister's Council on Trade & Industry, US-India CEO Forum and is a member of the Board of Governors of Indian Council for Research on International Economic Relations (ICRIER). Because she topped the Fortune India list of most powerful women in business in 2011.

Alok Kshirsagar

Alok Kshirsagar, is the Director (Senior Partner) McKinsey & Company, the global management consulting firm. He worked with many of the leading private and public institutions during his time at New York, London and Mumbai offices of the firm. He now heads the leads the McKinsey Asia Centre - a unique initiative to help Asian and Western companies capture the value of globalization. He has shown a great commitment to the society by offering his expertise to help the public policy in India as he co-leads relationships with the Ministry of Finance, the Economic Advisory Council to the PM, the planning commission and the Reserve Bank of India. He is also a member of the Next Gen Leaders Board at the Indian School of Business and is on the board of Parliamentary Research Services (PRS), the Governing Council and the National Association for the Blind. He has a bachelor's degree from St.Xavier's College, Mumbai where he was a National Merit Scholar and did his further studies at Oxford University where he was an Inlaks Scholar.

Points to Remember

- *Leadership is the process whereby one individual influences other group members towards the attainment of defined group or organisational goals.*
- *From the above definition, the following are the features or the characteristics of leadership. They are as follows:*
  - *Leadership involves non coercive influence*
  - *According to the above definition, leadership is a process involving non coercive influence where the members are not forced to do anything but are influenced in a non coercive way to change their attitudes and actions . The power of this influence is non coercive and in no way are the members or the subordinates forced to do anything. They are influenced and willingly follow because of the admiration and respect that they have for the leader.*
  - *Leadership Influence is goal directed*
  - *The focus of the influence of the leader is towards the organisational goals and the goals of the team. He or she attempts to influence actions or attitudes of the subordinates or members to attain the goals or the purpose mentioned for the project or the organisation.*
- *Leadership requires followers*
- *The meaning of leadership exists only with the followers. It is reciprocal and assumes the similar type of influence by the followers too. In short, leadership is not a one way direction in terms of influence or action, but a reciprocal arrangement between the subordinates and the leader.*

- *Leadership in organisations is mainly concerned with establishing the dream or the vision, designing the mission or the reason for existence and establishing direction and bigger plans or strategies for the organisation. Management on the other hand, is more focused towards implementing the goal, strategy or the vision and the mission and monitoring and supervising the execution of the polices, major strategies or plans and the overall mission and vision for the organisation. There are however many areas where the functions of the two overlap. Still it is possible to make clear distinctions. It may be mentioned here that some managers are considered leaders but all managers are not leaders. For leaders too, all leaders do not take up managerial roles.*

- *In this trait approach, these leaders possessed important traits like intelligence, dominance, self confidence, energy, and technical and work expertise.*

- **The Great Person Theory**
  - *If you study the stories of the great leaders of today like Bill Gates, Warren Buffet, Narayan Murthy, Azim Premjee, you will see that all of them possess extraordinary traits and an intense ambition and drive to succeed. It is this kind of orientation in this approach in the study of leadership which is known as The Great Person Theory. According to this orientation, great leaders possess key traits that set them apart from other human beings.*

- **Participative versus Autocratic Leadership behaviours**
  - *One type of behaviour is how much influence they have on their subordinates to have on the decisions that are made. There are two ways of describing their behaviour.*

  1. **Think of all the superiors or the bosses**, *who wanted to call all the shots at the office, make all the decisions and who would dictate to the subordinates what and how to do everything. Such leaders as bosses are called Autocrats and their style is autocratic. On the other hand, there are leaders as bosses who allow you or the subordinates or members to fully participate in the discussions before making decisions; they take their inputs and suggestions before making the final decisions. This is called the participative leadership style.*

  2. **Person oriented versus Production oriented Leaders**
     There are some bosses as leaders who are considered effective and some bosses as leaders are considered ineffective. The effective bosses are considered to be very helpful; they guide the subordinates, listen to them and answer their questions, whereas the ineffective leaders do not do this. Those at the high end of

the dimension are known as initiating structure or production oriented. These are concerned mainly with production and focus on getting the job done. They are involved in actions like getting the job done, by organising work, setting goals, making the roles and responsibilities clear of the subordinates and inducing the subordinates to follow goals.

- Leaders on the high end of the other spectrum, or the second dimension, are known as consideration or person centred and these are concerned primarily with establishing good relations with subordinates, doing favours for them, explaining things to them and ensuring their welfare.

- **Charismatic Leadership**

  There are various examples to demonstrate how Charismatic leaders show their outstanding qualities through their words and action. Examples of the same are Nelson Mandela, Mahatma Gandhi, and Bill Gates. They have changed entire societies and have had powerful effects on their subordinates.

- Laissez-faire leader lacks direct supervision of employees and fails to provide regular feedback to those under his supervision.

- **Autocratic:** The autocratic leadership style comprises managers who make decisions alone without the input of others. Managers possess total authority and impose their will on employees.

- **Participative:** Often called the democratic leadership style, participative leadership values the input of team members and peers, but the responsibility of making the final decision rests with the participative leader

- Leadership models help us to understand what makes leaders act the way they do. The ideal is not to lock yourself into a type of behaviour discussed in the model, but to realise that every situation calls for a different approach or behaviour to be taken. Two models were discussed, the Four Framework Approach and the Managerial Grid.

Case Study

At Gensoft, Software Company, there are several project groups working on varying projects. Each group is allocated projects depending upon the competencies of the members and their experience in the area most of the time, the project groups work independently and there is, barely any contact with the members across the groups.

The organisation realised this trend and set up a forum to attract an interaction and exchange of ideas among the group members. It was called Best Practices Forum, and every fortnight the members across groups met together and shared each one's mistakes and their learning, best practices in terms of culture adaptation, training experiences and client relationships.

These moves helped each group to bond with other group members and interact by sharing varied experiences. This apart, the overall productivity of the organisation was also enhanced as conflicts among members reduced and there was an easy exchange of members from one group to another which was not the case earlier.

Question:

Q.   In your view what are the benefits of Best Practices Forum?

Questions for Discussion

1.   Why groups are important in today's working organisations?
2.   Describe the various kinds of groups.
3.   Distinguish between groups and teams.
4.   How do informal groups facilitate better working?
5.   What are the distinct stages in Group Formation?
6.   What are the various types of Teams?
7.   Elaborate on the reasons for the failure of Teams.
8.   What is Social Loafing?
9.   What is Conflict? Why does it occur in organisations?
10. What are the various ways of resolving conflict?
11. What are the common or underlying causes of Conflict?
12. What are the various types of Conflict?
13. Elaborate on the Consequences of Conflict.
14. Why is leadership important in organisations today?
15. How would you distinguish between leaders and managers?
16. Elaborate on the various leadership styles.
17. Why is the Situational theory of leadership important? Explain the various Situational Theories.
18. Explain the Leadership Grid.
19. Explain the Framework Approaches to Leadership.

Multiple Choice Questions (MCQ's)

Qs. 1-10

State whether True or False

1.   Two or more individuals, interacting and interdependent, who have come together to achieve particular objectives is not a group.
2.   Today increasingly more attention is being focused on how to deal with groups, which are made up of people with different cultures.

3. Group cohesiveness is not related to aspects of Group Dynamics like maturity, size, homogeneity, and frequency of interactions.
4. Teams definitely are forms of work groups and all work groups are teams.
5. Teamwork promotes conversation between employees regarding the task at hand, possibly preventing employees from working in opposite directions.
6. Informal groups are formed in an organisation with direction from the top management or any specific organisation related purpose.
7. An *independent* work group can often be brought up to speed faster than an *interdependent* group.
8. Sociologists and Researchers define conflict as an interaction in which individuals and groups attempt to achieve their goals at the cost of others.
9. It does not depend on the leader to use and convert conflict into a healthy organisational environment which leads to achievement of goals.
10. Emotional involvement in a conflict creates anxiety, tension, frustration or hostility.

Qs. 11- 20
Fill in the blanks

11. The strategy to solve conflict is to increase the '......' and decrease 'Hidden self'.
12. Organisational Conflict has costly effects on ......
13. ...... skills continue to be important to all business organisations.
14. Behavioural leadership have three styles called autocratic, ... and laissez-faire.
15. Groups, like individuals have three basic interpersonal needs, namely: inclusion ......
16. ...... is the backbone of effective communication within a company
17. Teamwork originates with, and builds relationships among, a group of people who share a ...... interest or purpose.
18. "...... is a process that begins when one party perceives that another party has negatively affected, or is about to negatively affect, something the first party cares about."
19. Charismatic, transformational and ...... leadership models are the main contemporary models of leadership
20. Situational leadership model is another ...... leadership approach

Multiple Choice Questions (MCQ's)

1. False
2. True
3. False
4. False

5. True
6. False
7. True
8. True
9. False
10. True

Fill in the blanks

11. Open self
12. Organisational performance
13. Interpersonal
14. Democratic
15. Control and openness
16. Teamwork
17. Common
18. Conflict
19. Transactional
20. Traditional

Activity

1. Read and write about the success stories of today's global leaders.
2. Create a situation of conflict and discuss the causes and solutions of the conflict situation.
3. Develop teams and conduct an experiment on team effectiveness.

QUESTIONS FROM PREVIOUS PUNE UNIVERSITY EXAMINATIONS

1. "Both formal and informal groups are necessary for the group activity just as two blocks are essential to make a pair of scissor workable". Comment.

[PGDBM April 2007]

2. Explain theories of group formation and discuss the importance of group formation.

[PGDBM Dec. 2007]

3. Write short notes:
   (a) Team work   **[April 2007]**
   (b) Theories of Group formation   **[PGDBM April 2007]**
   (c) Group dynamics   **[Dec. 2008]**
   (d) Formal and Informal groups   **[April 2010]**

4. Define leadership. Explain the styles of leadership. **[April 2007]**

5. Explain the styles of leadership with justifying examples. **[PGDBM April 2007]**

6. Write short notes on:

    (a)   Role of a leader **[MBA Dec. 2007]**

    (b)   Nature of leadership **[MBA April 2009]**

    (c)   Qualities of a leader **[PGDBM April 2009]**

References / Further Readings

1. Borkowski, N. (2005). *Organisational behaviour in health care.* USA: Jones and Bartlett Publishers, Inc.

2. Christopher, E., & Jeffrey, Y. (2008). Bridging boundaries: Meeting the challenge of workplace diversity. *Leadership in Action* , 28 (1), pp.3-6.

3. Conger, J. A., & Kanungo, R. N. (1987). Toward a Behavioural Theory of Charismatic Leadership in Organisational Settings. *Academy of Management Review*, *12* (4), pp.637-647.

4. http://indiatoday.intoday.in/story/25-most-influential-women/1/177016.html

5. businesstoday.intoday.in/story/a_leader_for_a_global_inc.

Chapter **4**...

Organisation Systems

Contents ...

Learning Objectives

After studying this chapter, you should be able to:

1. Explain the concept of an organisation.
2. Define principles of organisational structuring.
3. Identify traditional and modern types of organisational structure.
4. List the considerations in choosing an organisational structure.
5. Explain the meaning and Importance of Culture.
6. Illustrate how culture impacts the working of an organisation, its systems and practices.
7. Identify changes in culture and its effects.
8. Define a positive organisational culture.
9. Identify characteristics of spiritual culture.

4.1 Foundations of Organisation Structure

Introduction

> *The organisational structure of an organisation tells you the character of an organisation and the values it believes in.*

Any operating organisation should have its own structure in order to operate efficiently. For an organisation, the organisational structure is a hierarchy of people and its functions.

Therefore, when a business man does business with an organisation, or getting into a new job in an organisation, it is always a great idea to get to know and understand their organisational structure.

4.1.1 Concept of an Organisation

Definition

"Organisations are social units (or human groupings) deliberately constructed and reconstructed to seek specific goals". **(Etsioni, 1964).**

In this definition organisations are seen as social units or a human grouping, which implies that the basic elements of organisations are individuals.

Thus the first key element of this definition is the fact that *organisations are groupings of individuals.*

Another basic element is deliberate construction, that is, *organisations are deliberately constructed for accomplishing specific objectives.*

The third element is of course the concept of goals; *organisations are established for the accomplishment of certain goals.*

In another definition organisations are defined as *"collectivities that have been established for the pursuit of relatively specific objectives on a more or less continuous basis."* (Scott, 1964). Again in this definition organisations are defined as social units composed of individuals, and they are specifically created for the pursuit of certain objectives.

According to Pfiffner and Presthus *"Organisation is the structuring of **individuals** and **functions** into **productive relationship**".* In this definition, organisation is not only a grouping of individuals, but also, a number of functions are brought together alongside individuals. The term, *"productive relationship",* simply implies that the individuals and functions are brought together for the objective of producing something, goods or services.

When the above definitions are evaluated carefully, it is obvious that there are certain common elements in the definitions of different scholars regarding the concept of organisation. These common elements are a grouping of individuals, deliberate establishment or construction, and the accomplishment of specific goals.

By referring to the above common elements, we will define organisations as *"Social units or human groupings deliberately established for the accomplishment of specific objectives."* Ministries, corporations, universities, hospitals, schools, political parties, prisons, associations etc. are organisations in this sense.

One of the major problems in discussing or thinking about organisations is that the very term is so similar to the broader term of "social organisation".

Social organisation refers to the ways in which human conduct becomes socially organised (Blau and Scott, 1962).

This statement simply indicates that the observed regularities in the behaviour of people are due to the social conditions in which they find themselves rather than to their physiological or psychological characteristics as individuals. That is, social conditions influence the conduct of people.

Social conditions which influence the behaviour of people can be divided into two main types:

(a) The structure of social relations in a group.

(b) The shared beliefs and orientations that unite the members of the group or collectively and guide their conduct.

These two main types of social conditions constitute the two basic aspects or characteristics of social organisations.

The conception of structure implies that in a social organisation, individuals stand in some relation to one another. Thus, there is a certain network of relations which is one of the dimensions of social organisation.

The second dimension of social organisation is the system of shared beliefs and orientations which serve as standards for human conduct.

In the course of social interaction, common notions arise as to how people should act that is, common expectations concerning how people ought to behave.

In short, social norms develop, and social sanctions are used to discourage the violations of these norms. By taking the above discussions into consideration, we can define social organisations as *"networks of social relations and shared orientations"*.

Society is a social organisation, of which municipalities, associations, ministries, political parties, corporations as organisations are parts. In this sense, the concept of social organisation indicates the broader set of relationships and processes.

Organisations, as we are using the term here, are parts of the more general concept of social organisation, being affected by it and, reciprocally, affecting it in turn. In this sense, society itself, ethnic groups, friendship groups, families, tribes etc, are social organisations.

When the term "Organisation" is used in this text, reference is made to what has been called by many as Formal Organisation. That is, the terms "Formal Organisation" and "Organisation" mean the very same set of relationship for our purposes. From now on, whenever the term "Organisation" is used in this text, we are referring to what has been called, "Formal Organisation".

Nature of Organisation

Organisation is one important element of the management process. It is next to planning. In management, organisation is both the process as well as the end-product of that process which is referred to as organisation structure. Such structure acts as the foundation on which the whole super-structure of management is built. Sound organisation structure is essential for the conduct of business activities in an efficient manner. It is within the framework of the organisation that the whole management process takes place. The success of the management process will be determined by the soundness of the organisation structure. Organising involves integration of resources in order to accomplish the objectives.

In an enterprise, many managers and employees work together for achieving common objectives. It is the organisation structure which binds them together and brings proper adjustment and coordination in their work. The division of work and authority and the establishment of relationship among individuals or groups are possible due to the organisation structure.

In simple words, organising means arranging the ways and means for the execution of business plan. It is the creation of administrative set-up for the execution of the plan. It suggests the framework within which the management functions. The term organisation suggests a functional group working together for achieving common purposes/objectives. Organisation provides mechanism for integrated and co-operative action by two or more persons with a view to implementing any plan. Organisation facilitates efficient administration, direction and control. It avoids wastage of raw materials and human efforts. Every management has to establish its own organisation structure for efficient conduct of business activities.

Organisation involves the following aspects:-

- Identifying the activities required to achieve organisational objectives.
- Grouping up of these activities into workable units (Departmentation).
- Assigning duties and responsibilities to subordinates in order to achieve the tasks assigned.
- Delegating authority necessary and useful for the accomplishment of tasks assigned.
- Establishing superior-subordinate relationship.
- Providing a system of co-ordination for integrating the activities of individuals and departments.

Importance of Organisation

1. Ensures optimum utilisation of human resources: Every enterprise appoints employees for the conduct of various business activities and operations. They are given the work according to their qualifications and experience. Organisation ensures that every individual. Is placed on the job for which he is best suited.

2. Facilitates coordination: It acts as a means of bringing coordination and integration among the activities of individuals and departments of the enterprise. It establishes clear-cut relationships between operating departments and brings proper balance in their activities.

3. Facilitates division of work: Different departments are created for division of work, specialisation and orderly working of the enterprise. Similarly, delegation relieves top level managers from routine duties.

4. Ensures growth, expansion and diversification: Sound Organisation structure facilitates expansion/diversification of an enterprise. Organisation structure has in-built capacity to absorb additional activities and also effective control on them. A business enterprise brings diversification in its activities within the framework of its Organisation.

5. Stimulates creativity: Organisation provides training and self-development facilities to managers and subordinates through delegation and departmentation. It also encourages initiative and creative thinking on the part of managers and others.

6. Facilitates administration: Effective administration of business will not be possible without the support of sound organisation structure. Delegation, departmentation and decentralisation are the tools for effective administration.

7. Determines optimum use of technology: Sound Organisation structure provides opportunities to make optimum use of technology. It facilitates proper maintenance of equipment and also meets high cost of installation.

8. Determines individual responsibility: Responsibility is an obligation to perform an assigned work. In a sound Organisation, the manager finds it easy to pinpoint individual responsibility when the work is spoilt.

4.1.2 Types of Organisations

The different types of organisations are:

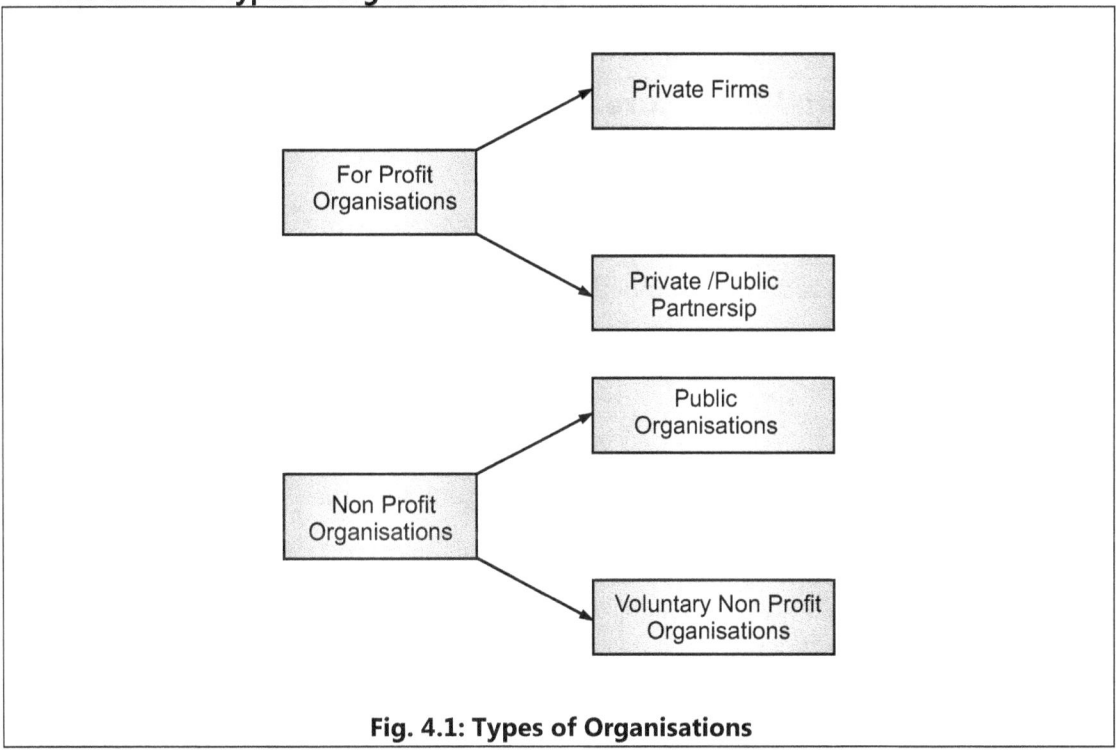

Fig. 4.1: Types of Organisations

Types of organisations based on profit or not for profit making:

1. **Private for profit**

    •   **Market sector organisations** includes business and corporation organised with the primary goal of making an economic profit.

    •   **Governmental** includes local, state, national, and international government organisations. (Examples are public health, education, and human service organisations)

2. **Private not for profit**
   - **Non-governmental organisations:** NGO's/Voluntary or service sector (Lions Club), provides civic and human services which are funded by private citisens (donations), fundraising organisations (example is united way), or privately funded foundations (example is Ford, Kellogg)
   - **Religious and Spiritual Organisations** includes churches, universities, hospitals, schools, political parties, etc.

On the basis of relationship between people in an organisation, organisations are of two types – formal and informal.

1. **Formal organisation** refers to the structure of well-defined jobs, each bearing a definite measure of authority, responsibility and accountability.
2. **Informal organisation** refers to the relationship between people in the organisation based on personal attitudes, emotions and prejudices, likes and dislikes.

4.1.3 Organisational Structure

What is organisational structure?

By structure, we mean the framework around which the group is organised, the underpinnings which keep the coalition functioning. It's the operating manual that tells members how the organisation is put together and how it works. More specifically, structure describes how members are accepted, how leadership is chosen, and how decisions are made.

Organisational structure pertains to the way in which companies arrange their departments. Smaller companies tend to have flatter organisational structures with few management levels. Larger companies use tall organisational structures with many levels of management and employees.

Organisational structure refers to the levels of management and division of responsibilities within a business, which could be presented in an organisational chart. For simpler businesses in which the owner employs only himself, there is no need for an organisational structure. However, if the business expands and employs other people, an organisational structure is needed. When employing people, everybody needs a job description. These are its main advantages:
- People who apply can see what they are expected to do.
- People who are already employed will know exactly what to do.

The typically hierarchical arrangement of lines of authority, communications, rights and duties of an organisation. Organisational structure determines how the roles, power and responsibilities are assigned, controlled, and coordinated, and how information flows between the different levels of management.

A structure depends on the organisation's objectives and strategy. In a centralised structure, the top layer of management has most of the decision making power and has tight control over departments and divisions. In a decentralised structure, the decision making power is distributed and the departments and divisions may have different degrees of independence. A company such as Proctor & Gamble that sells multiple products may organise their structure so that groups are divided according to each product and depending on geographical area as well.

An organisational chart illustrates the organisational structure.

Companies use several types of organisational structure for specific roles. For example, companies using a geographic organisational structure decentralise various functions like marketing because of varying regional needs.

An organisational structure consists of activities such as task allocation, coordination and supervision which are directed towards the achievement of organisational aims. It can also be considered as the viewing glass or perspective through which individuals see their organisation and its environment.

Organisations are a variant of clustered entities.

An organisation can be structured in many different ways, depending on their objectives. The structure of an organisation will determine the modes in which it operates and performs. Organisational structure allows the expressed allocation of responsibilities for different functions and processes to different entities such as the branch, department, workgroup and individual.

Designing an organisational structure requires consideration of an organisation's values, financial and business goals. It should allow for growth for the organisation and the ability to add additional jobs or departments.

Steps in developing organisational structure:
1. Define business units or departments.
2. Determine which type of organisational structure best fits one's business needs.
3. Define the executive and management teams.
4. Establish performance metrics and compensation.

Step 1: Define business units or departments.

Each business unit should have similar goals and responsibilities that can be overseen and directed by one or several managers. The business units or departments will then align to assist in creating an appropriate organisational structure.

Depending on which type of organisational structure is used, departments may align laterally with other departments or one may oversee another.

Step 2: Determine which type of organisational structure best fits one's business needs.

The several types of organisational structure ensure an organisation can successfully function with its reporting structure, expand if necessary and successfully meet its goals. For example, if an organisation is small, it may simply require the organisational structure be broken into departments, such as production, human resources and finance.

Organisational structure type that one chooses, determines the organisation's business type, units and how it operates.

Step 3: Define the executive and management teams.

Executives and managers are responsible for ensuring each business unit meets the organisation's goals. This may include one or several top executives to oversee the entire organisation and managers to direct each business unit within the organisational structure.

The organisation may require one supervisor to oversee all operations, or several supervisors to direct each business unit, ultimately reporting to a top executive or owner.

Step 4: Establish performance metrics and compensation.

When the organisational structure is determined, job descriptions can be clearly defined and where each job fits in the hierarchy. Each job description should reflect the competencies required to do the job and the expectations of each job to meet the organisation's goals. After each job within the structure is defined, compensation should be defined based on the responsibilities of each job.

Organisational structure affects organisational action in two big ways:

First, it provides the foundation on which standard operating procedures and routines rest.

Second, it determines which individuals get to participate in which decision-making processes, and thus to what extent their views shape the organisation's actions.

Why should you develop a structure for your organisation?

- **Structure gives members clear guidelines for how to proceed.** A clearly-established structure gives the group a means to maintain order and resolve disagreements.
- **Structure binds members together.** It gives meaning and identity to the people who join the group, as well as to the group itself.
- **Structure in any organisation is inevitable** -- an organisation, *by definition*, implies a structure. A group is going to have some structure whether it chooses to or not. It might as well be the structure which best matches up with what kind of organisation one has, what kind of people are in it, and what its goals are.

When should an organisation develop a structure?

It is important to deal with structure early in the organisation's development. Structural development can occur *in proportion* to other work the organisation is doing, so that it does not crowd out that work and it can occur *in parallel* with the organisation's growing accomplishments.

Principles of Organisational Structure

There are some principles which are common to all organisations that are established in a classical form i.e. the form where there is hierarchy of authority and responsibility and it flows downwards. The principles of Organisation offer guidance for the creation of a sound, efficient and effective Organisation structure. In other words, these principles are the sound criteria for efficient organising. They ensure smooth and orderly working of a business enterprise.

Principles of Organisation

The organisation of office is a continuous process. It should not be static, rigid or fixed. It should be flexible and adaptable to the changing objectives of an enterprise. Because of the great variety of organisations in existence, there can be no standard principles, which could be followed in all individual circumstances. However, there are certain principles, which have more or less universal application and which may be used as guidelines for organising an office. The task of the office manager in planning organisation becomes easier if he takes into consideration the following general principles of organisation:

(i) **Principle of Objective:** The objective of an enterprise should be clearly laid down. Within the enterprise, there should be unity and uniformity in the policies and objectives of different departments so that every part of the organisation, including the office, is geared to the attainment of these objectives. Not only should the objectives be stated in clear terms, the method of achieving them, too, should be indicated in detail and in precise terms so that the organisers may know the type of organisation that is needed.

(ii) **Principle of Inter-Related Function:** Because organisations no longer have a mutually exclusive function, but rather integrated functions, the functional area—for example, sales, production, finance, marketing and personnel—are interrelated. Because of the inter-relationships of the functions, the objectives of one function must be consistent with the objective of other functions. Further, similarities between various activities should be used as the basis for determining the function to where each activity belongs. Otherwise coordination between the activities will be seriously hampered.

(iii) **Principle of Definition:** The duties, responsibilities, authority and relations of everyone in the organisational structure should be clearly and completely defined, preferably in writing. An individual will accomplish a task in a given period when the responsibility for that task is fixed upon that individual.

(iv) **Principle of Work Assignment:** The work assignment for each individual in the organisation should take into consideration the special strength and talents of the individual. This means that an individual should be given an assignment commensurate with his or her ability and interests.

(v) **Principle of Span of Control:** The maximum number of employees or subordinates that can be supervised effectively by a person is known as the span of control. The span of control should be limited to a reasonable number according to circumstances. A span of control of 6 subordinates has been considered to be the most desirable.

(vi) **Principle of Unity of Command:** The core of this principle is that a man can serve only one boss. It means that instructions and directions to a subordinate must come from one person only. Each subordinate must have one superior, to whom he should be answerable. This helps in avoiding conflict in command and in fixing responsibility.

(vii) **Principle of Chain of Authority (The Scalar Principle):** The chain of authority or command refers to the formal specifications of 'who reports to whom' within organisation. The chain of authority must be clearly defined for sound organisational purposes. Every subordinate must know who his superior is and to whom policy matters beyond his own authority must be referred to for decisions.

(viii) **Principle of Commensurate Authority and Responsibility:** According to this principle, when an individual is responsible for a certain task, he should be given the authority to carry out that task. Without commensurate authority and responsibility, he cannot be held accountable for the unsuccessful completion of the tasks because he has very little control over the situation.

(ix) **Principle of Ultimate Responsibility:** The responsibility of a higher authority for the acts of his subordinates is absolute. The responsibility to his worker to do a given job, and when the worker commits a mistake, the supervisor is the one who is accountable to his superiors. He cannot escape from the responsibility by saying that the mistake was committed by a particular worker.

(x) **Principle of Flexibility:** The structure of an organisation must be flexible so that adjustments, necessitated by changed circumstances, may be planned and incorporated in it.

(xi) Principle of Division of Work: Specialisation in organisational functions is necessary for the most effective attainment of objectives. Specialisation depends on division of work. The total activities of an enterprise should be divided and grouped into departmental, sectional and individual activities to facilitate division of work.

(xii) Principle of Discipline: Discipline is vitally important in all types of organisations. In its absence, it is difficult to achieve success.

(xiii) Principle of Continuity of Operations: The form of an organisation should be such that it facilitates the continuous performance of all the activities necessary for the continuance and growth of the enterprise.

(xiv) Principle of Employee Participation: Employees should be encouraged to participate as much as possible in the decision-making process. By encouraging participation, employees are given recognition, and are motivated to work harder. But in spite of participation by employees in the decision-making process, the ultimate responsibility for the decision must rest with the manager or supervisor.

4.1.4 Role of Organisational Structure

Efficiency

One role of organisational structure is efficiency. Most companies need to make the most of various resources. Duplicating raw materials or job duties is wasteful and inefficient.

Consequently, a company will structure its organisation according to products and services it offers. A small software manufacturer may use a customer-oriented organisational structure because of its wide variety of customers. For example, the software company may sell to consumers, corporations, financial institutions, hospitals and health clubs.

In this case, organising departments by customers is efficient because of diversity. Product management duties may differ widely by customer type. Marketing to consumers is much different than targeting corporations.

Optimum use of available experience, skill and knowledge

Another role of organisational structure is to bring together and optimise the use of available experience, skill and knowledge. Companies may arrange their division by specific functions, such as marketing, accounting, finance and engineering.

The purpose of grouping departments by function is to use the experience of groups to accomplish tasks and projects. When skilled employees of similar talents work together as a whole, the output is higher than the sum total of the input. For example, marketing and advertising managers can better evaluate the potential success of a new product introduction as a group.

Decision Making

Organisational structure in a company also enhances decision making, according to *referenceforbusiness.com*. Companies will often structure their organisations to make the best decisions possible. For example, a company may decentralise its marketing to make quicker decisions locally. Consequently, the company may put marketing managers in one of the four different regions. It is much easier for regional marketing managers to make local decisions about consumer needs than a marketing manager in a distant corporate office.

Communication

Companies also use various organisational structures for communication purposes. Larger companies have many levels of management. Therefore, the most effective way to communicate is usually from the top of the organisation down.

Executives create certain operational procedures which they communicate to directors and managers. Managers, in turn, explain these operational procedures to subordinates or hourly employees.

Span of Control

Organisational structure is used for span of control. For example, a vice president of marketing may be in charge of four directors: One for marketing research, one for brand management, one for advertising and one for public relations. The directors may have three separate groups of managers reporting to them.

Span of control pertains to the number of employees an executive or manager oversees. This reporting structure is how companies establish accountability.

4.1.5 Models of Organisational Structure

Companies select models of organisational structure depending on their size, marketing strategy and industry. For example, extremely small companies often use flat organisational structures because they have fewer levels of management. Models of organisational structure can also be high, or composed of many management levels.

Companies often choose their model of organisational structure based on which one better helps facilitate communication and project completion.

The following types of organisational structures can be observed in the modern business organisations. The various Models of Organisational Structures are:

- Functions/Department Organisational Structure
- Divisional Organisational Structure
    1. Product Organisational Structure
    2. Regional Organisational Structure
- Matrix Organisational Structure

• **Functional Structure**

A department or functional organisational structure divides the company into departments or functional areas. For example, the CEO (chief executive officer) or president is usually at the top of the organisation, followed by multiple vice presidents of functional areas like marketing, advertising, finance and research and development.

The organisation is divided into segments based on the functions when managing. This allows the organisation to enhance the efficiencies of these functional groups. As an example, take a software company.

Software engineers will only staff the entire software development department. This way, management of this functional group becomes easy and effective.

Functional structures appear to be successful in large organisation that produces high volumes of products at low costs. The low cost can be achieved by such companies due to the efficiencies within functional groups.

In addition to such advantages, there can be disadvantage from an organisational perspective if the communication between the functional groups is not effective. In this case, organisation may find it difficult to achieve some organisational objectives at the end.

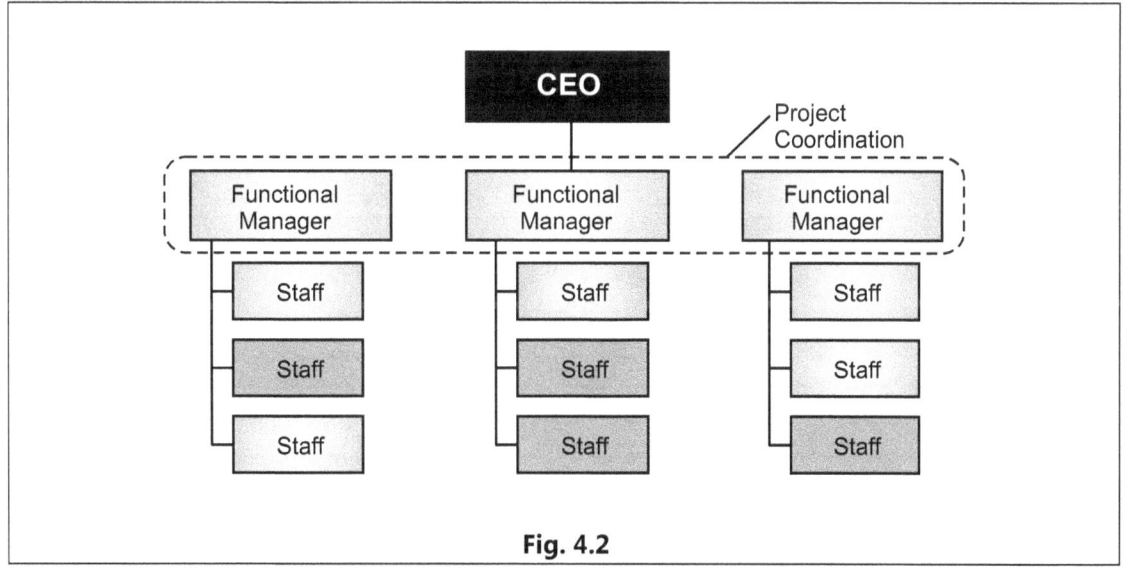

Fig. 4.2

Functional or Department Organisational Structure

Department directors usually report to specific vice presidents, and department managers report to these directors. Support people like clerical workers, clerks and coordinators, in turn, report to department managers.

The advantage of a department organisational structure is that it groups people by skills and knowledge, harnessing expertise where it is most useful. A disadvantage is that this structure can greatly narrow a worker's scope of responsibility. This narrower scope of responsibility can be detrimental to employees' motivation, especially those who are highly goal oriented.

- **Divisional Structure**

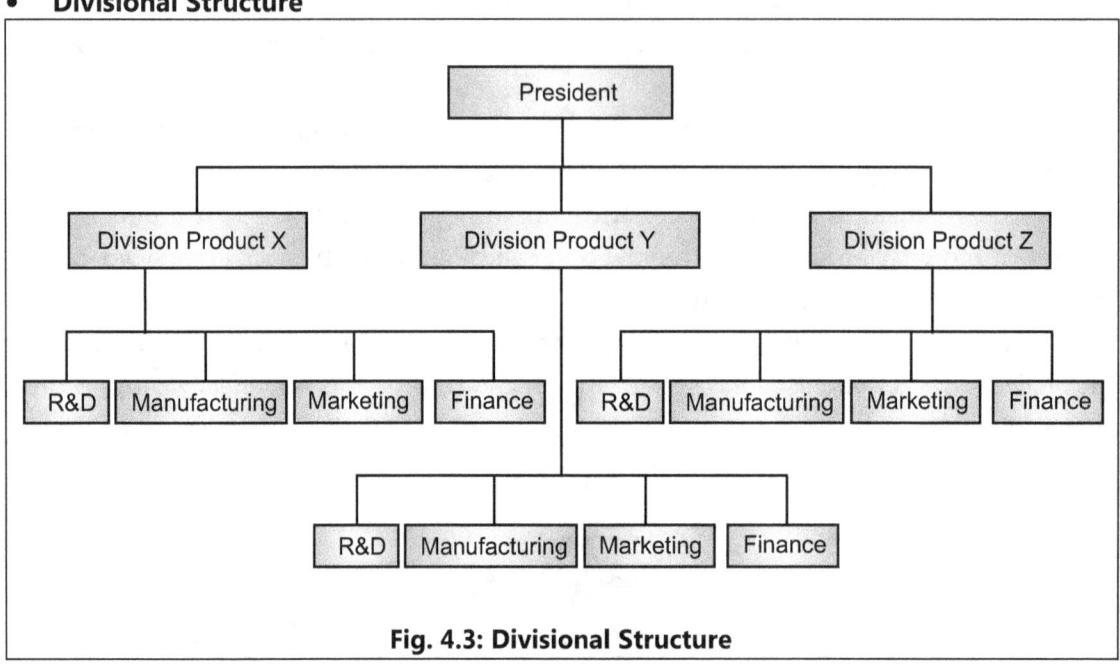

Fig. 4.3: Divisional Structure

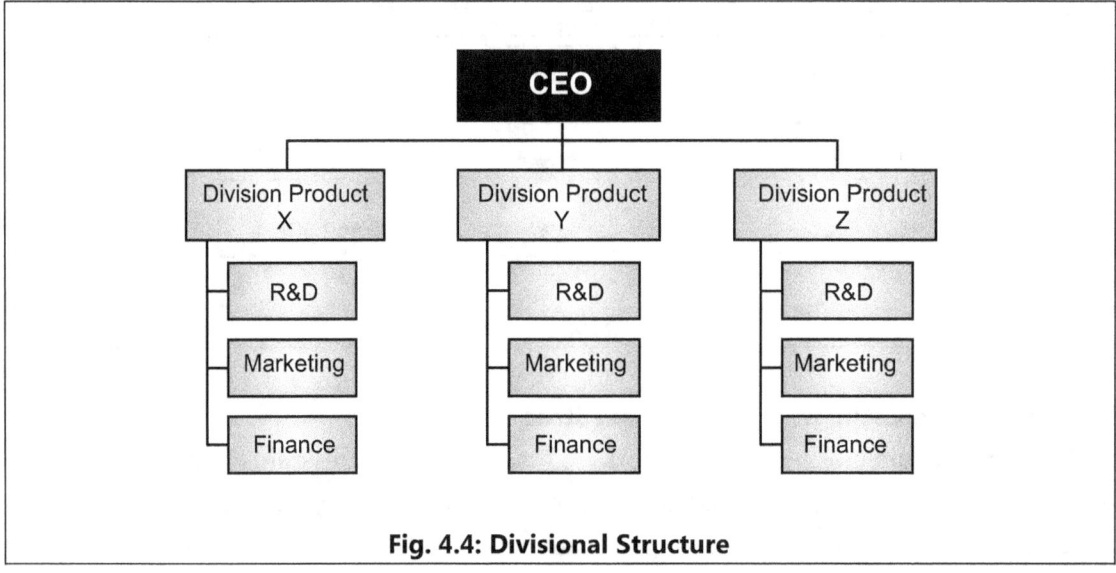

Fig. 4.4: Divisional Structure

These types of organisations divide the functional areas of the organisation to divisions. Each division is equipped with its own resources in order to function independently. There can be many bases to define divisions.

Divisions can be defined based on the geographical basis, products / services basis, or any other measurement.

As an example, take a company such as General Electric. It can have microwave division, turbine division, etc., and these divisions have their own marketing teams, finance teams etc. In that sense, each division can be considered as a micro-company with the main organisation.

1. Product organisational structure

Companies that use a product organisational structure model divide various tasks and responsibilities by product type. Retail or department stores often use this model. For example, a vice president may hold the title of vice president of house wares, with directors and managers of house wares lower down in the organisation.

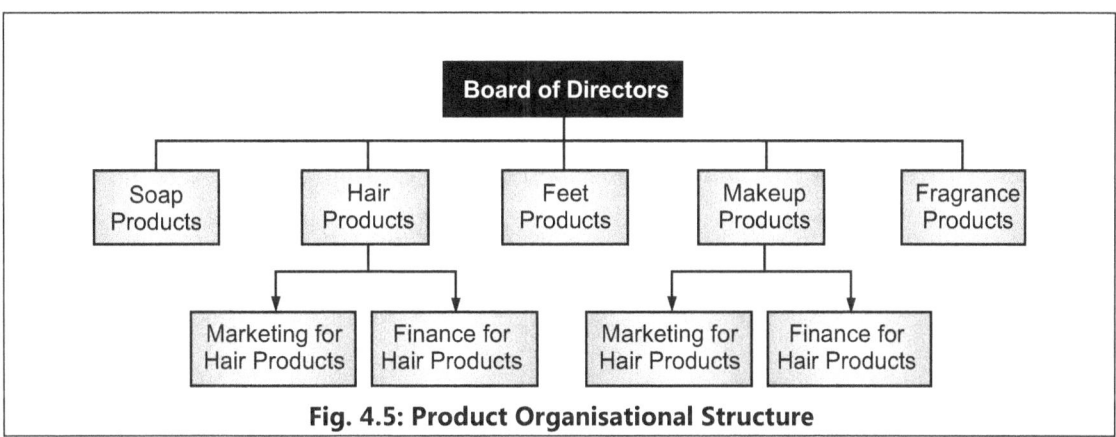

Fig. 4.5: Product Organisational Structure

One advantage of the product organisational structure is it greatly enhances product knowledge and expertise in a company. However, this structure can create a duplication of resources. For example, each product category will have a marketing or advertising manager. The responsibilities of these people may overlap, leading to confusion with regard to decision making.

2. Regional organisational structure

Some companies use a regional or geographical organisational structure, preferring to duplicate various departments or functional areas across regions. For example, a small consumer products company may employ marketing managers in the east, central, west and southern regions of the country.

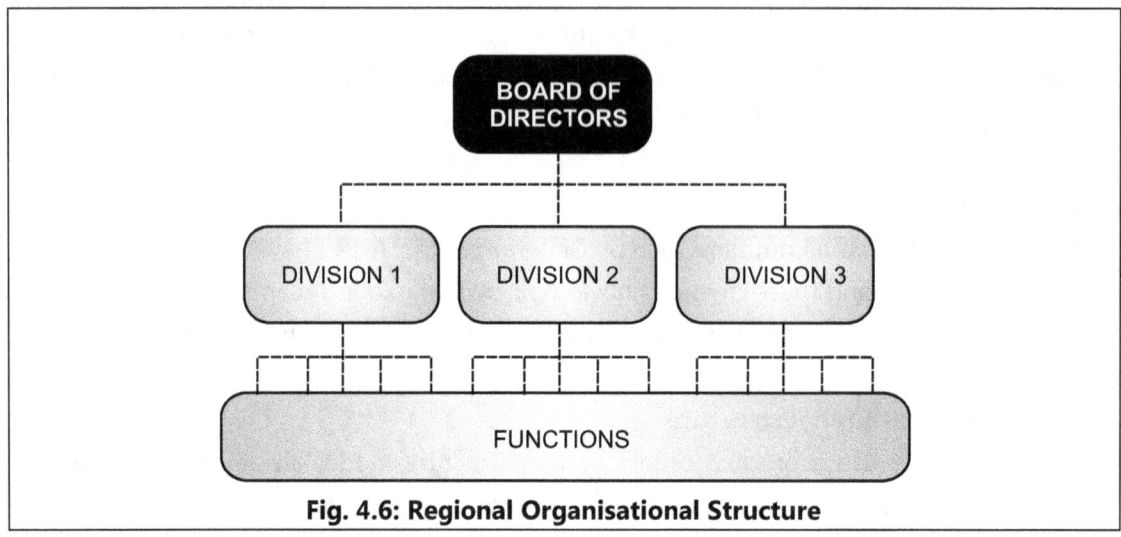

Fig. 4.6: Regional Organisational Structure

This model works best when a company needs to focus on more localised strategies. Competition may be unique in each region. Additionally, customer demands may vary, with people in various regions preferring different flavors or features.

*   **Matrix organisational structure**

The matrix organisation structure is a combination of at least two types of structure. Often these structures are combined for special projects. For example, a food company may combine a functional and product organisational structure to test the introduction of a new brand of soup.

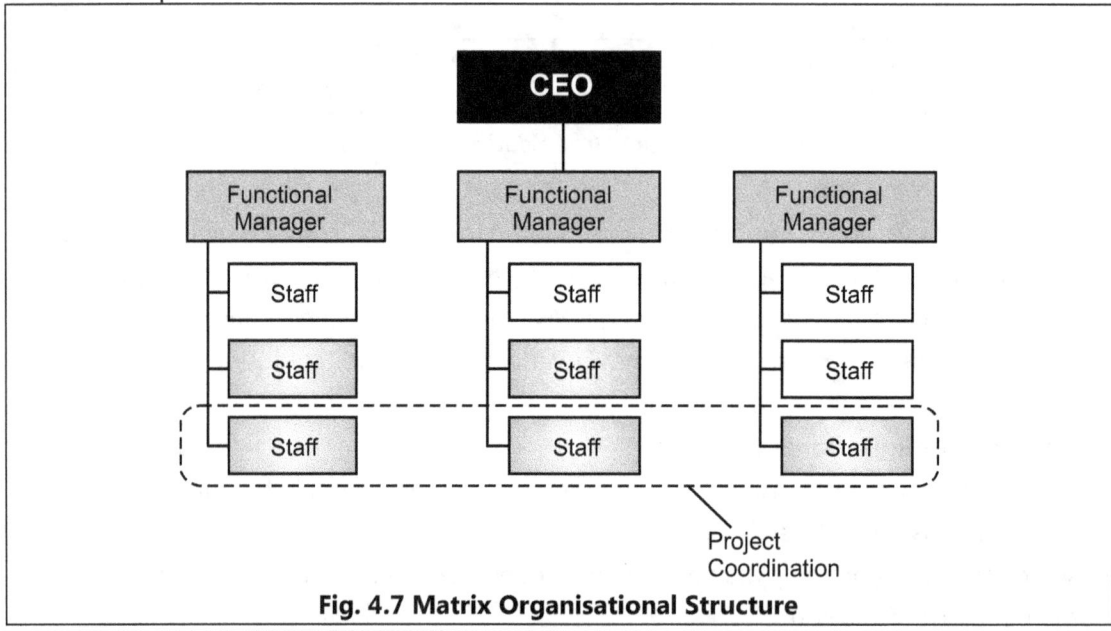

Fig. 4.7 Matrix Organisational Structure

The matrix structure may be used for several years and then dissolved after the product has been introduced and is selling. An advantage of the matrix structure is it places employees where they are needed the most. A disadvantage is it can create dual reporting, with employees having more than one manager.

When it comes to matrix structure, the organisation places the employees based on the function and the product.

The matrix structure gives the best of the both worlds of functional and divisional structures. In this type of an organisation, the company uses teams to complete tasks. The teams are formed based on the functions they belong to (ex: software engineers) and product they are involved in (ex: Project A).

In this manner, there are many teams in this organisation such as software engineers of project A, software engineers of project B, QA engineers of project A, etc.

4.1.6 Types of Organisation

There is no ideal organisation, which can produce the optimum result for all types of office. There are many types of organisation, each with its merits and demerits, and there may be variations in their application. Sometimes, a mixture of two or more types may produce the best result. The office manager should neither be guided by theories alone, nor he should be dogmatic about it. He should consider the needs of his office carefully and try to evolve the type of organisation, which will produce the best result and will fulfill the objectives more effectively. Above all, he must be ready to assess the changes in the requirement of the office from time to time and must be prepared to vary and adapt the organisational structure accordingly

Essentially, the problem of organisation involves combining and coordinating the efforts of a large number of staff in a useful and efficient manner to produce the desired result. In order to combine and coordinate the efforts of staff working at different levels of organisation, the proper relationship between their functions, authority and responsibility have to be set up through proper type of staff organisation.

Many types of organisational structures exist in the business environment. Many organisations choose an organisational type based on their operations and the number of employees in the business.

Centralised

A centralised organisational structure often relies on one individual to guide the business through various economic or operational decisions. Many small businesses use centralised organisational structures since the business owner is primarily responsible for the company. Many business owners attempt to maintain a centralised structure as their business continues to grow and expand. This organisational structure can quickly become difficult to manage when companies expand into multiple locations in different geographic areas.

Decentralised

Decentralised organisational structures may use a team of directors or executive-level managers to make business decisions. This structure works well with individuals who have specific expertise in different business functions. A decentralised structure also provides companies with multiple opinions about business expansion for selecting new business opportunities. Decentralised organisational structures can create difficulties if too many opinions exist about a business decision. Companies must often find ways to get all managers on the same page and agree on how to best approach business situations before making decisions.

There are four broad patterns of staff organisation, which may be considered for this purpose: (1) The Line Organisation or Military System; (2) The Functional Organisation; (3) The Line and Staff Organisation; and (4) The Committee Organisation.

Line Organisation: This is the oldest as well as the most common type of organisation. It is still used by many companies, especially the small one. It is also known as the 'Military System' as this type of organisation is usually found in the army. The characteristic feature of this type is the line of authority flows vertically from the topmost executive to the lowest subordinate throughout the entire organisational structure. The authority is greatest at the top and reduces through each successive level down the organisational scale. A variation of the pure line organisation is the departmental line organisation, under which the business enterprise is divided into several departments and the authority flows downward from the General Manager through the departmental managers to the lower subordinates. The departmental heads are independent of each other and enjoy equal status.

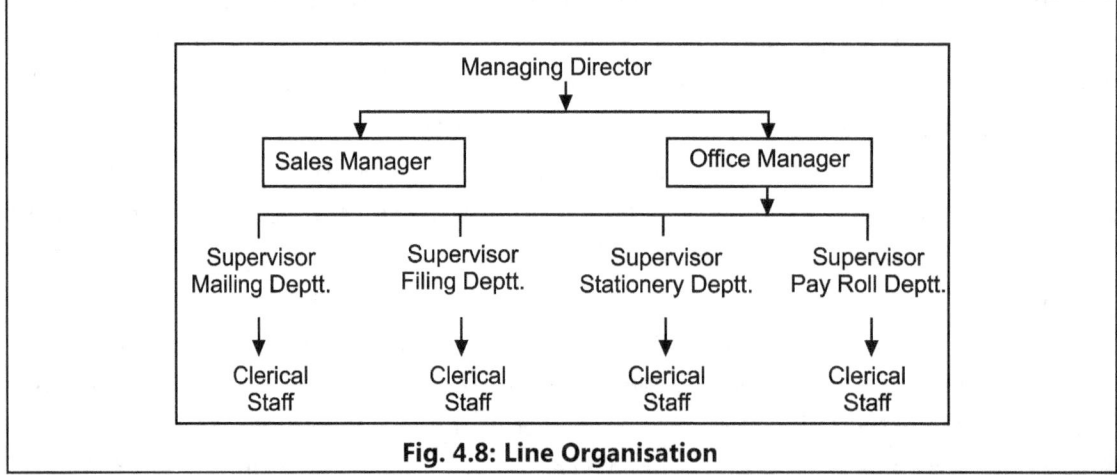

Fig. 4.8: Line Organisation

Merits

(i)   The greatest merit is its simplicity. It is easy to set up and the personnel can easily understand it.

(ii)   Fixing of responsibility is easier under this type of organisation. Each employee, at different levels of organisation, knows to whom he is responsible and who is responsible to him.

(iii)   It makes for unified control since the ultimate authority rests in the topmost executive.

(iv)   Since the authority and responsibility are fixed at every level it ensures prompt decision, which increases the effectiveness of the organisation.

(v)   Since every subordinate knows his immediate superior from whom alone he receives his instructions, *it fosters strict discipline* among the personnel.

Demerits

(i)   *Too much concentration of authority may lead to difficulties.* Since, at any particular level decision-making is done by one person alone, any error of judgment on his part hampers the efficiency of the department or section as a whole. Moreover, the load of responsibility may be heavier for any one executive to bear.

(ii)   Since each departmental head has sole charge of his department independent from others, it becomes *difficult to secure coordination* of the activities of different departments. This type of organisation *does not foster specialisation,* as one person has to think about and take decision on different types of work pertaining to his area of responsibility.

(iii)   The *lack of communication* from bottom to highest authority may often result in wrong judgment and decision-making on the part of higher executives. Experience gathered by subordinates during implementation of decisions and which is often helpful to higher executives in their decision-making cannot be utilised as it does not reach the higher executives due to lack of communication.

Functional Organisation: In this type of organisation, the personnel and their work are organised on the basis of the type of work or activities. All works of the same type are grouped together and brought under one department managed by an executive who is an expert. Thus there are separate functional departments for the major functions of the business *vis.,* engineering or production, purchase, sales, finance, personnel, etc. Each department performs its specialised function for the entire organisation. The research department or division handles research on behalf of all the departments, the purchase department deals with purchases on behalf of the entire organisation, and so on.

Nowadays, almost all business organisations usually follow some sort of functional plan to carry out the primary functions of business. However, it is rare to find a pure functional organisation and there is always an element of line organisation mixed with it. The following organisation chart will illustrate the type of organisation.

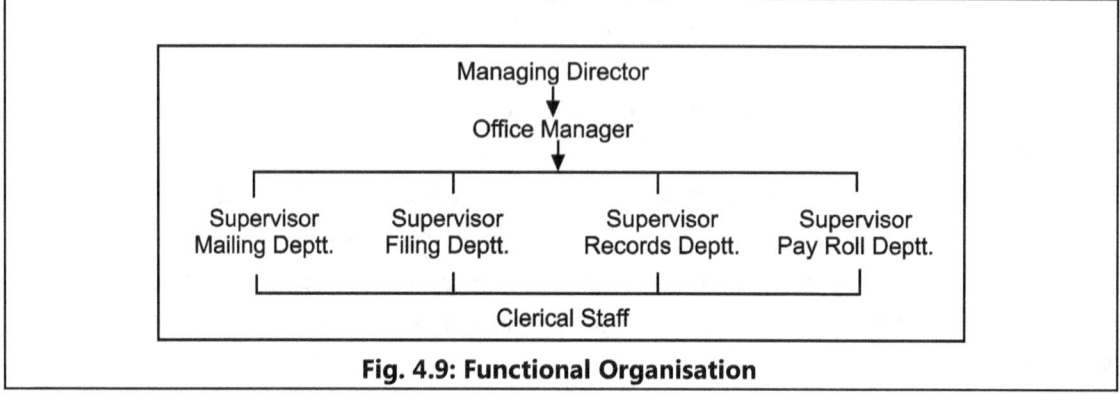

Fig. 4.9: Functional Organisation

Merits

(i)   This type of organisation makes the greatest use of the principle of *division of labour* resulting in a high degree of *specialisation*. Maximum benefit of specialised skills in the performance of each function is obtained without being restricted by arbitrary departmental boundaries.

(ii) Since the departmental executive and his subordinates have to perform a limited number of activities, it ensures *higher efficiency*.

(iii) Separation of mental and manual functions is possible under this type of organisation.

(iv) It facilitates *standardisation* of operations, methods and equipment.

Demerits

(i)   In a large organisation, the organisational structure becomes too elaborative. Too many experts and bosses *create confusion* among workers.

(ii) Its operation is too *complicated* to be understood by the subordinates.

(iii) *Fixing of responsibility* becomes difficult under this type.

(iv) Since authority and responsibility are not clearly demarcated, as in the line organisation, it leads to *conflict of authority* and *weakening of discipline*.

Line and Staff Organisation: In order to avoid the defects of the Line and Functional organisations, i.e. too much concentration of control in the Line and too much division in the Functional, the Line and Staff Organisation was evolved. It seeks to strike a balance between the first two types. Under this type, the organisational structure is based on the Line Organisation, but 'Staff officers are engaged to advise the line officers in the performance of their duties. 'Staff means something to lean on, and this is precisely the function of the Staff officers. Line officers are the executives, and the Staff officers are their advisers. Being an mixture of the Line and Functional organisations, it has the advantages of both and is admirably suited for large organisaitons. A large-sise business, with its multifarious functions of complicated nature, needs an organisation where should have an unbroken line of authority and responsibility so that responsibility can be fixed and discipline can be maintained whereas decision-making and execution will also be prompt. At the same time, it requires that a high degree of specialisation and coordination of functions be achieved without which efficiency is bound to suffer. The Line and Staff organisation caters to both these needs. The Line officers make the decisions and issue instructions to subordinates; the Staff officers have no authority to issue instructions. But in their decision-making the Line officers receive advice and guidance from the Staff officers.

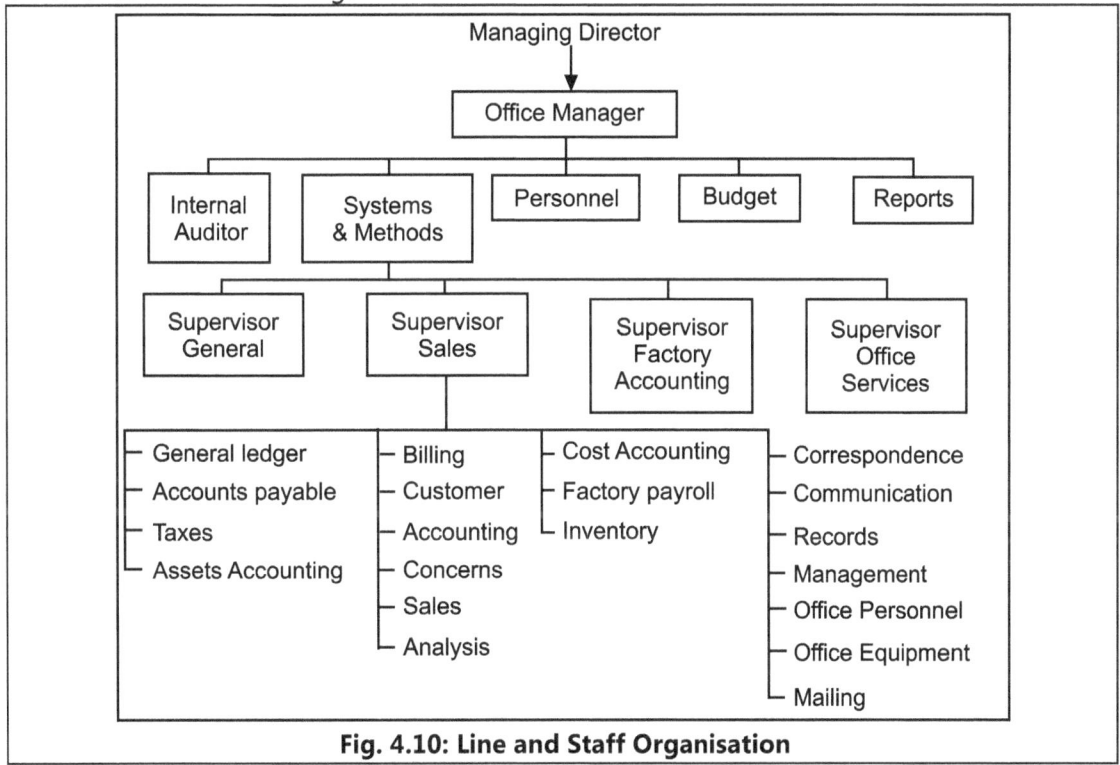

Fig. 4.10: Line and Staff Organisation

The merits of this type of organisation are outlined below:

Merits of Line and Staff Organisation

1. **Relief to line of executives:** In a line and staff organisation, the advice and counseling which is provided to the line executives divides the work between the two. The line executive can concentrate on the execution of plans and they get relieved of dividing their attention to many areas.

2. **Expert advice:** The line and staff organisation facilitates expert advice to the line executive at the time of need. The planning and investigation which is related to different matters can be done by the staff specialist and line officers can concentrate on execution of plans.

3. **Benefit of Specialisation:** Line and staff through division of whole concern into two types of authority divides the enterprise into parts and functional areas. This way every officer or official can concentrate in its own area.

4. **Better coordination:** Line and staff organisation through specialisation is able to provide better decision making and concentration remains in few hands. This feature helps in bringing coordination in work as every official is concentrating in their own area.

5. **Benefits of Research and Development:** Through the advice of specialised staff, the line executives, the line executives get time to execute plans by taking productive decisions which are helpful for a concern. This gives a wide scope to the line executive to bring innovations and go for research work in those areas. This is possible due to the presence of staff specialists.

6. **Training:** Due to the presence of staff specialists and their expert advice serves as ground for training to line officials. Line executives can give due concentration to their decision making. This in itself is a training ground for them.

7. **Balanced decisions:** The factor of specialisation which is achieved by line staff helps in bringing coordination. This relationship automatically ends up the line official to take better and balanced decision.

8. **Unity of action:** Unity of action is a result of unified control. Control and its effectivity take place when coordination is present in the concern. In the line and staff authority all the officials have got independence to make decisions. This serves as effective control in the whole enterprise.

However, it is not an unmixed blessing and has some *demerits,* which mainly concentrate round the understanding of the workers and the inter-relation of the role of the Line and Staff officers. For instance, the complicated nature of the organisational structure is not always understood by the workers and appears confusing to them. Again, if the Line and Staff officers fail to observe the respective roles assigned to them there may be chaos. The Line officers are not bound to accept the advice of the Staff officers, but if they persistently ignore the advice of the Staff officers or if the Staff officers start issuing instructions to the workers countermanding those of the Line officers, the very object of the organisation will be frustrated.

Demerits of Line and Staff Organisation

1. **Lack of understanding:** In a line and staff organisation, there are two authority flowing at one time. This results in the confusion between the two. As a result, the workers are not able to understand as to who is their commanding authority. Hence the problem of understanding can be a hurdle in effective running.

2. **Lack of sound advice:** The line official get used to the expertise advice of the staff. At times the staff specialist also provides wrong decisions which the line executive have to consider. This can affect the efficient running of the enterprise.

3. **Line and staff conflicts:** Line and staff are two authorities which are flowing at the same time. The factors of designations, status influence sentiments which are related to their relation, can pose a distress on the minds of the employees. This leads to minimising of coordination which hampers a concern's working.

4. **Costly:** In a line and staff organisations, the organisations have to maintain the high remuneration of staff specialists. This proves to be costly for an organisation with limited finance.

5. **Assumption of authority:** The power of the organisation is with the line official but the staff dislikes it.

6. **Staff steals the show:** In a line and staff concern, the higher returns are considered to be a product of staff advice and counseling. The line officials feel dissatisfied and a feeling of distress enters the organisation. The satisfaction of line officials is very important for effective results.

Committee Organisation: A committee means a body of persons entrusted with discharging some assigned functions collectively as a group. Committees may be permanent (standing) or temporary (*adhoc*) bodies. Normally committees are found to be at different levels of an organisational structure, it is even existent in both business and non-business institutions. However, a committee organisation is rarely found in its pure form; it is usually found in addition to a Line and Staff organisation. The committee itself may be organised with line or staff authority. If the committee is organised with line authority then it is usually vested with powers of decision-making and its execution. The committee assumes command and authority in the organisation and functions as a group of executives for achieving the common objectives of the organisation. Where it is organised on staff authority it has merely an advisory function. The example of a group executive is the Board of Directors of a business company, whereas the various committees of directors (both standing and ad hoc) as well as other committees at lower levels of organisation are staff or advisory committees. The successful operation of a committee organisation depends on several factors, vis., suitable subject matter, well-defined duties and authorities, chosen membership and a capable chairman. The committee form is best suitable for deciding broad issues like setting objectives and policies, review of activities, etc. Despite several limitations, the committee organisation has several distinct advantages. That is why it is widely used in all types of enterprises, though not in pure form.

The merits and demerits are discussed below:

Merits

(a) It helps in the *pooling of knowledge and experience* of several persons for the solution of many intricate problems. Sometimes collective advice, ideas and opinions are better than individual ones,

(b) It *also facilitates coordination* of activities of various departments. Departmental managers meeting in committees may discuss common problems, exchange experience and evolve solutions,

(c) It is an excellent medium for discussion and educating workers and also for informing the objectives and policies to workers,

(d) Group discussion in committees helps to inculcate a sense of participation among executives and workers. This secures the necessary motivation for better performances from subordinates.

Demerits

(a) Committees take much time in discussions to come for final decision. This slowed down process for decision-making often reduces the usefulness of the decisions,

(b) As decisions are taken by the committee are not fixed by any one person so those decisions taken in committee might not get accepted by management as reliable or final,

(c) Committee decisions are frequently found to be weak and indecisive, since it is invariably the product of a compromise between opposing opinions and viewpoints.

(d) Committee organisation is an expensive device both in terms of time and cost.

Selection of organisation

Choosing the right type of organisation for an enterprise is a difficult job. There are various factors to be considered in deciding whether any one of the above types of organisation or a variation of the same or an admixture of the two types will suit the particular requirements of the enterprise.

Some of the important factors to be considered are briefly discussed below.

(a) Size and nature of the business: The most important factor influencing the type of organisation is perhaps the size of the business. In a small-scale organisation, the problems of management are very less and simple, so a simple type of organisation like Line organisation may be successfully applied. Whereas a large-scale organisation with complexities of departments and varied types of functions will require a more complex type of organisation like Functional or Line and Staff Organisation.

(b) Continuity of business: The type of organisation suitable for an enterprise with steady flow of business throughout the year will be different from the type found suitable for an enterprise where flow of business fluctuates from season to season. A steady business organisation normally requires more permanent and complex type of organisation than any seasonal business.

(c) Geographical location: The geographical location of the various divisions or units of an enterprise is also an important factor in choosing the type of organisation. If the units or divisions like factory, sales, personnel, finance are located in the same premises or in close proximity to one another then a comprehensive but more complex type of organisation will be suitable. But if the units are located in separate buildings situated miles apart then separate organisations based on line and staff type may be more suitable.

(d) Staff ratio and degree of mechanisation: The degree of supervision needed and the placement of different functions at different levels will depend on the ratio of unskilled to supervisory staff. Again the degree of mechanisation (ratio of machines to operatives) is also an important factor. Both these factors will have to be taken into consideration in choosing the type of organisation.

4.1.7 Organisation Chart

Organisation structure of a company can be shown in a chart. Such chart indicates how different departments are interlinked on the basis of authority and responsibility. It is a simple diagrammatic method of describing an Organisation structure. It indicates how the departments are linked together on the basis of authority and responsibility. Such Organisation chart provides information of the Organisation structure at a glance. Organisation chart is like a blue print of a building. It indicates the number and types of departments, superior-subordinate relationship, chain of command and communication.

4.1.8 Basic Elements in Designing Organisational Structure

An organisation structure defines how job tasks are formally divided, grouped and coordinated. There are six elements that mangers need to address when they design their organisation's structure. These are :- a) Work specialisation. b) Departmentalisation. c) Chain of command. d) Span of control. e) Centralisation & Decentralisation. f) Formalisation

1. **Work Specialisation**: refers to the degree to which tasks in the organisation are subdivided into separate jobs. The essence of work specialisation is that, rather than an entire job being done by one individual, it is broken down into a number of steps, with each step being completed by a separate individual.

2. **Departmentalisation:** Once the jobs have been divided through work specialisation, these jobs have to be grouped together so that common tasks can be coordinated. The basis by which jobs are grouped together is called departmentalisation.

The activities can be grouped by functions performed. A manufacturing manager might organise his plant by separating engineering, accounting, manufacturing, personnel and supply specialists into common departments. Functional departmentalisation seeks to achieve economies of scale by placing people with common skills and orientations into common units.

Tasks can also be departmentalised by the type of product the organisation produces. Each major product is placed under the authority of an executive who has complete global responsibility for that product. The major advantage of this type of grouping is increased accountability for product performance, since all the activities related to a product are under the direction of a single manager.

Another way to departmentalise is on the basis of geography or territory. The sales function, for instance, may have western, southern, eastern region. Each of these regions is in effect, a department organised around geography. If an organisation's customers are scattered over a large geographic area and have similar needs based on their location, then this form of departmentalisation.

A final category of departmentalisation is to use the particular type of customer. An organisation can organise itself around customer groups like corporates, retail, government etc.

3. **Chain of Command** is an unbroken line of authority that extends from the top of the organisation to the lowest level and clarifies who reports to whom. It answers questions for employees such as" To whom do I go if I have a problem?" and ' To whom am I responsible?"

The unity of command principle helps preserve the concept of an unbroken line of authority. It states that a person should have one and only one superior to whom he or she is directly responsible. If the unity of command is broken, an employee might have to cope with conflicting demands or priorities from several superiors.

4. **Span of control** refers to the number of subordinates a manager can efficiently and effectively direct. Span of control is important because, to a large degree, it determines the number of levels and managers and organisation has all things being equal the wider or larger the span, the more efficient the organisation. Narrow span has three major drawbacks. First, they are expensive because they add to the levels of management. Second, they make vertical communication in the organisation more complex. The added levels of hierarchy slow down decision making and tend to isolate upper management. Third, narrow spans of control encourage overly tight supervision and discourage autonomy.

5. **Centralisation and Decentralisation:** Centralisation refers to the degree to which decision making is concentrated at a single point in the organisation. The concept includes only formal authority that is, the rights inherent to one's position. Typically,

it's said that if top management makes the organisation's key decision with little or no input from lower-level personnel, then the organisation is centralised. In contrast, the actually given the discretion to make decision, the more decentralisation there is. An organisation characterised by centralisation is an inherently different structural entity from one that is an inherently different structural entity from one that is decentralised. In a decentralised organisation, action can be taken more quickly to solve problem, more people provide input into decisions and employees are less likely to feel alienated from those who make the decisions that affect their work lives. Consistent with recent management efforts to make organisation more flexible and responsive, there has been a marked trend toward decentralising decision making. In large companies, lower-level managers are closer to "the action" and typically have more detailed knowledge about problems than do top management.

6. **Formalisation** refers to the degree to which job within the organisation are standardised. If a job is highly formalised then the job incumbent has a minimum amount of discretion over what is to be done, when it is to be done and how it is to be done. Employees can be expected always to handle the same input in exactly same way, resulting in a consistent and uniform output. There are explicitly job description lots of organisational rules, and dearly defined procedures covering work processes in organisations in which there is high formalisation. Where formalisation is low, job behaviors are relatively non-programmed and employees have a great deal of freedom to exercise discretion in their work. Because an individual's discretion on the job is inversely related to the amount of behavior in that job that is pre-programmed by the organisation, the greater the standardisation and the less input the employee has into how his or her work is to be done. Standardisation not his/her work is to be done. Standardisation not only eliminates the possibility of employees engaging in alternative behaviors, but it even removes the need for employees to consider alternatives.

4.2 Organisational Culture

Introduction

Forbes Marshall, a Boiler Manufacturing Company in Pune, has been ranked consistently as a 'Great Place to Work For'. One of the features in its working which has enhanced the satisfaction levels of its employees including the newly inducted ones, is that it is okay to make mistakes if it is done in the process of learning

The objective behind this message is that employees at all levels should experiment, innovate and try out new ways of doing things. In the course of this, employees may make mistakes and thereby, learn lessons from them.

It is this characteristic in Forbes Marshall that has made employees fearless, less anxious and open to creativity. This feature is called an aspect of organisational Culture.

Schein E R (1992), Organisational Culture and Leadership: A Dynamic View, San Francisco, Jossey Bass, defines Culture as *'a cognitive framework consisting of attitudes, values, behavioural norms and expectations shared by organisation members.'*

Hence it is often thought of as a set of basic assumptions shared by members of an organisation.

Many researchers compare the role played by organisational culture to the roots of trees. What roots do for the life of a tree, similarly, culture does for the life and performance of an organisation. Just as the roots provide nourishment to the trees, culture provides stability and nourishment to the organisations.

4.2.1 Meaning and Definition of Organisational Culture

Organisational Culture

- It is the shared experiences that organisational members hold in common, that merge into a whole pattern of beliefs, values, and rituals that become the "essence" of an organisation's culture.
- Organisational Culture can be defined as "the collective programming of the mind that distinguishes the members of one organisation from others".
- Organisational Culture can also be defined as the values and behaviours that contribute to the unique social and psychological environment of an organisation.

While not always easy to capture or define, culture is an observable, powerful force in any organisation. Made up of its members' shared values, beliefs, symbols, and behaviours, culture guides individual decisions and actions at the unconscious level. As a result, it can have a potent effect on a company's well being and success.

It is generally recognised that different organisations have distinguishing cultures. A commonly used definition of organisational culture is 'the way we see and do things around here'. Through tradition, history and structure, organisations build up their own culture. Culture as a result gives an organisation a sense of identity - 'who we are', 'what we stand for', 'what we do'. It determines, through the organisation's legends, rituals, beliefs, meanings, values, norms and language, the way in which 'things are done around here'. An organisations' culture encapsulates what it has been good at and what has worked in the past.

Organisational Climate

It reflects how organisation members communicate organisational culture in more visible or observable ways.

4 Key Climate Dimensions:
1. The nature of interpersonal relationships.
2. The nature of the hierarchy.
3. The nature of work.
4. The focus of support and rewards.

The Role of Culture and Climate

Some consider culture the glue that holds everyone together. Others compare it to a compass providing direction.

Operating largely outside of our awareness, culture creates a common ground for team members. It reduces uncertainty by offering a language for interpreting events and issues. It contributes to a sense of order so that all team members know what is expected. It provides a sense of continuity and unity. And it offers a vision around which a company can function.

At the observable level, culture is manifested in an organisation's climate — the behaviours and strategies that can be managed in support of organisational goals.

4.2.2 Creating and Sustaining Organisational Culture

The Importance of Culture in Organisations

Culture is intangible, but its impact and effect runs deep.

A strong culture in an organisation helps to achieve various roles in an organisation: They are as follows:

1. Culture provides a sense of identity

Employees in organisations with a strong sense of culture, identify themselves with the organisation. They feel proud and do not like to leave the organisation. For example, in Forbes Marshall, the rate of people leaving the organisation is minimal as people here are very homely and can strongly identify with its open and friendly culture.

2. Culture helps to create a commitment to the vision and the mission of the organisation

When there is a strong culture like an overriding mission and vision, people as employees believe they are a part of the larger canvas and the organisational interests for them take dominance than their own personal or individual interests.

3. Culture clarifies and reinforces standards of behaviour

Culture helps to guide employees' behaviour towards what is expected from them. They understand the priorities of the organisation and follow the expected behaviour. For example, if customer satisfaction is the most important, they will go out of the way to implement the demands of the customers and satisfy them.

How is Organisational Culture created?

There are various influences to organisational culture. It develops through all these influences and is shaped and revised by the same. The following are some of these influences:

1. Company Founders

Initially the company founders create the values and vision of the company. They are closely involved in the process of hiring initially and share these common values and dreams with them. This forms a culture and remains till the founders continue to take interest and head the organisation.

The founders form the initial systems, guidelines and way of working, which sustains for long. For example, in companies like Microsoft, the founder has set the culture of working long hours to complete the projects on time. This culture of long hour working continues even if the founder has diversified his interests.

2. Interaction with the Working Environment

The regular and constant interaction with the organisation's environment helps to alter the organisation's culture in response to these changes. This forms an important part of the organisation's memory and sets the trends of working. For example, in response to the external environment, individuals working alone stopped and many organisations formed teams and groups for people working together.

So, the culture of individuals not working alone and working now in teams and groups, even at the top level has become a norm.

4.2.3 Types of Culture

Just as there are many types of organisations, there are many types of cultures. Although each form of organisation may be unique in many ways, there would be underlying similarities.

Over the last few decades there have been numerous attempts made by researchers to identify predominant types of organisational culture. The idea of culture, as the discussion thus far shows, is extremely complex, but this has not deterred writers from offering their perspectives.

There are various types of Organisational Culture based on differences in values – in terms of flexibility and discretion as opposed to order, systems and control.

All these dimensions can be combined to form four types of Culture.

They are as follows:

1. Hierarchy Culture

Organisations having a hierarchy culture are more concerned with stability and order and with a formal level of systems, practices and policies. The managerial higher ups here believe in stability, order and following policies, systems and practices. They are excellent coordinators and handle projects with a lot of order and following systematic steps in order to execute them with a proper system and order.

Most government organisations follow such a hierarchical structure and culture. Even the traditional private organisations used to follow this hierarchical culture.

For example, even McDonald's has a 350 page manual designed with systems in mind. Such an organisation is overly concerned with internal systems and order and is quite immune to the demands of the external environment.

With today's volatile external environment, such culture will soon be out-dated and will have to replace by incorporating the volatility of the external markets and environments.

2. Market Culture

An organisation with such a culture is focused on stability and order but with an external orientation in mind. It realises that to survive in today's organisations, the focus should be on bottom lines, competitiveness and productivity. Such organisations realise the sensitivity to external markets and orientation and also the importance of order and systems. Hence they try to combine the effects of both.

Organisations like Hindustan Lever Limited (HUL) follow a market culture, where their Strategic Business Units or Divisions (SBU's) change their priorities and focus depending upon the market conditions.

3. Clan Culture

An organisation is said to have a clan culture which has a strong internal focus but with flexibility and discretion. Here the members as employees share the vision, mission and values of the organisation, and an atmosphere is created for fun and adventure with the spirit of work for the employees. Employees share the information and discretion for doing work efficiently and effectively.

Clan Culture is characterised by paying serious attention to meeting business objectives. For example, in companies like Nokia, the wellbeing of the employees is most important and they are motivated to put in their best. The internal systems and policies are conducive to allow flexibility and inputs for the employees to perform at their best.

Other organisations which put in their best and are employee centric having an internal focus and discretion and flexibility are American Express, Make My Trip, Forbes Marshall etc.

4. Adhocracy Culture

Organisations that have an adhocracy culture emphasise an orientation towards the external environment with an internal flexibility and discretion.

Adhocracy is defined as the opposite of hierarchy or bureaucracy. It is an example of modern organisations of today, which are prone to radical changes in response to the volatility of the external environment and the market and are considered to be very competitive.

The practices, principles, policies and values of an organisation form its culture.

The culture of an organisation decides the way employees behave amongst themselves as well as the people outside the organisation.

Handy's four types of organisational cultures

Another model of culture, popularised by Charles Handy (1999) – and following work by Harrison (1972) – also presents organisational cultures as classified into four major types: the power culture, the role culture, the task culture, and the person or support culture.

1. **A power culture** is one based on the dominance of one or a small number of individuals within an organisation. They make the key decisions for the organisation. This sort of power culture may exist in a small business or part of a larger business.

2. **A role culture** exists in large hierarchical organisations in which individuals have clear roles (jobs) to perform which are closely specified. Individuals tend to work closely to their job description, and tend to follow the rules rather than to operate in a creative way.

3. In contrast **task cultures** exist when teams are formed to complete particular tasks. A distinct team culture develops, and because the team is empowered to make decisions, task cultures can be creative.

4. **A person culture** is the most individualistic form of culture and exists when individuals are fully allowed to express themselves and make decisions for themselves. A person culture can only exist in a very loose form of organisation e.g. an overseas sales person working on their own for a company, allowed to make their own decisions. Culture change involves moving an organisation on from one form of culture to another, usually through a culture change programme.

Let us understand the various types of organisation culture according to dimensions of sports and character:

1. **Normative Culture:** In such a culture, the norms and procedures of the organisation are predefined and the rules and regulations are set as per the existing guidelines. The employees behave in an ideal way and strictly adhere to the policies of the organisation.

    No employee dares to break the rules and sticks to the already laid policies.

2. **Pragmatic Culture:** In a pragmatic culture, more emphasis is placed on the clients and the external parties. Customer satisfaction is the main motive of the employees in a pragmatic culture. Such organisations treat their clients as Gods and do not follow any set rules. Every employee strives hard to satisfy his clients to expect maximum business from their side.

3. **Academy Culture:** organisations following academy culture hire skilled individuals. The roles and responsibilities are delegated according to the back ground, educational qualification and work experience of the employees.

   Organisations following academy culture are very particular about training the existing employees. They ensure that various training programmes are being conducted at the workplace to hone the skills of the employees. The management makes sincere efforts to upgrade the knowledge of the employees to improve their professional competence.

   The employees in an academy culture stick to the organisation for a longer duration and also grow within it. Educational institutions, universities, hospitals practice such a culture.

4. **Baseball team Culture:** A baseball team culture considers the employees as the most treasured possession of the organisation. The employees are the true assets of the organisation who have a major role in its successful functioning. In such a culture, the individuals always have an upper edge and they do not bother much about their organisation.

   Advertising agencies, event management companies, financial institutions follow such a culture.

5. **Club Culture:** Organisations following a club culture are very particular about the employees they recruit. The individuals are hired as per their specialisation, educational qualification and interests. Each one does what he is best at.

   The high potential employees are promoted suitably and appraisals are a regular feature of such a culture.

6. **Fortress Culture:** There are certain organisations where the employees are not very sure about their career and longevity. Such organisations follow fortress culture. The employees are terminated, if the organisation is not performing well.

   Individuals suffer the most when the organisation is at a loss. Stock broking industries follow such a culture.

7. **Tough Guy Culture:** In a tough guy culture, feedbacks are essential. The performance of the employees is reviewed from time to time and their work is thoroughly monitored.

   Team managers are appointed to discuss queries with the team members and guide them whenever required. The employees are under constant watch in such a culture.

8. **Bet your company Culture:** Here the culture is one in which decisions are high risk but employees, may wait years before they know whether their actions actually paid off. Examples: Oil and gas, pharmaceutical companies.

The principles and policies of such an organisation are formulated to address sensitive issues and it takes time to get the results.

9. **Process Culture:** As the name suggests the employees in such a culture adhere to the processes and procedures of the organisation. Feedbacks and performance reviews do not matter much in such organisations.

   The employees abide by the rules and regulations and work according to the ideologies of the workplace. All government organisations follow such a culture.

Another very important classification is given below:

1. Strong vs. Weak Culture

Strong culture is said to exist where staff respond to stimulus because of their alignment to organisational values. In such environments, strong cultures help firms operate like well-oiled machines, engaging in outstanding execution with only minor adjustments to existing procedures as needed.

Conversely, there is weak culture where there is little alignment with organisational values, and control must be exercised through extensive procedures and bureaucracy.

Research shows that organisations that foster strong cultures have clear values that give employees a reason to embrace the culture.

> *A "strong" culture may be especially beneficial to firms operating in the service sector.*

A "strong" culture may be especially beneficial to firms operating in the service sector, since members of these organisations are responsible for delivering the service.

Research indicates that organisations may derive the following benefits from developing strong and productive cultures:

- Better aligning the company towards achieving its vision, mission, and goals
- High employee motivation and loyalty
- Increased team cohesiveness among the company's various departments and divisions
- Promoting consistency and encouraging coordination and control within the company
- Shaping employee behaviour at work, enabling the organisation to be more efficient

Where culture is strong, people do things because they believe it is the right thing to do.

2. Soft v/s Hard Culture

In a soft culture the employees pursue their own personal goals and give less importance to the organisational goals.

For example: In public sector enterprises in India productivity is low as employees focus more on pursuing their own individual personal goals.

3. Formal v/s Informal Culture

The concepts of formal and informal organisations relate to the nature of relationships and processes in the workplace.

A formal organisation is the literal structure of the organisation including its organisation chart, hierarchical reporting, relationships and work processes.

Factors influencing formal organisational culture:

- **Organisational Chart**

An organisational chart effectively outlines the structure of the formal organisation. It shows the hierarchy from the CEO and top management to mid-level management to front-line employees. It also shows the horizontal interrelationships of various functional divisions or departments.

The organisational chart provides a functional framework and is important in the workplace to establish stability, clarity in working relationships and reporting relationships between superiors and subordinates.

- **The Grapevine**

Though top management in some companies does not consider the reality of the informal organisation when trying to establish culture, it does have a significant influence on workplace dynamics.

Employees interact with each other at lunch, in the break room and in daily interactions . These encounters either positively or negatively impact each employee's sense of belonging within the workplace. If these encounters are generally negative, work morale is typically poor.

- **Office Politics**

In their February 2007 "Bloomberg Business week" article "Navigating the 'Informal' Organisation," Marshall Goldsmith and Jon Katsenbach explain that understanding the direct reporting relationships outlined in the organisational chart is often less important than knowing the "go-to people" in your company.

For ambitious employees, this may mean looking beyond immediate co-workers and managers and finding helpful mentors and internal coaches that want to help them succeed.

Information communication networks are also a useful means of learning how the company works beyond just what is conveyed from top management.

- **Balance**

Goldsmith and Katsenbach also point out that when front-line employees get promoted into management positions, they often forget the importance of balancing the formal structure and informal networks within organisations.

Disciplined structure and clear reporting relationships are important. However, managers also have a lot to gain by remembering that informal networks are real and useful.

Managers can often get the most insight on how employees feel and how departmental teams are functioning through informal, friendly conversations.

While formal relationships are a key to accomplishing organisational and departmental objectives, they are sometimes restrictive to open interaction.

The work culture of an organisation, to a large extent, is influenced by the formal components of organisational culture.

Roles, responsibilities, accountability, rules and regulations are components of formal culture. They set the expectations that the organisation has from every member and indicate the consequences if these expectations are not fulfilled.

4.2.4 Importance of Organisation Culture

> *Every organisation has its unique style of working, which often contributes to its culture.*

Every organisation has its unique style of working, which often contributes to its culture. The beliefs, ideologies, principles and values of an organisation form its culture.

The culture of the workplace controls the way employees behave amongst themselves as well as with people outside the organisation.

- **The culture decides the way employees interact at their workplace**. A healthy culture encourages the employees to stay motivated and loyal towards the management.

- **The culture of the workplace also goes a long way in promoting healthy competition at the workplace**. Employees try their level best to perform better than their fellow workers and earn recognition and appreciation of the superiors. It is the culture of the workplace, which actually motivates the employees to perform.

- Every organisation must have set guidelines for the employees to work accordingly. **The culture of an organisation represents certain predefined policies, which guide the employees and give them a sense of direction at the workplace**. Every individual is clear about his roles and responsibilities in the organisation and know how to accomplish the tasks ahead of the deadlines.

- No two organisations can have the same work culture. It is the culture of an organisation, which makes it distinct from others. **The work culture goes a long way in creating the brand image of the organisation**. The work culture gives an identity to the organisation. In other words, an organisation is known by its culture.

- **The organisation culture brings all the employees on a common platform**. The employees must be treated equally and no one should feel neglected or left out at the workplace. It is essential for the employees to adjust well in the organisation culture for them to deliver their level best.

- **The work culture unites the employees** who are otherwise from different backgrounds, families and have varied attitudes and mentalities. The culture gives the employees a sense of unity at the workplace.

  Certain organisations follow a culture where all the employees irrespective of their designations have to step into the office on time. Such a culture encourages the employees to be punctual which eventually benefits them in the long run.

  It is the culture of the organisation, which makes the individuals a successful professional.

- Every employee is clear with his roles and responsibilities and strives hard to accomplish the tasks within the desired time frame as per the set guidelines. Implementation of policies is never a problem in organisations where people follow a set culture. The new employees also try their level best to understand the work culture and make the organisation a better place to work.

- **The work culture promotes healthy relationship amongst the employees and where no one treats work as a burden and moulds himself according to the culture.**

- **It is the culture of the organisation, which extracts the best out of each team member**. In a culture where management is very particular about the reporting system, the employees however busy they are would send their reports by end of the day. No one has forced anyone to work. The culture develops a habit in the individuals, which makes them.

4.2.5 Features of Culture

1. Sensitivity to Others

The characteristic of culture includes an element of sensitivity to all. If the employees in the organisation do not like the leadership style of the superiors, which is more dictatorial, they may leave the organisation and so, the attrition rate or the rate of employees leaving the organisation may go up.

Hence, the organisation needs to be sensitive to this issue and it need to train its superiors to be more open and take inputs from their peers and subordinates before making any decision.

2. New ideas

The point is to bring in an element of newness or a different perspective to issues. Many companies attempt to introduce a constant change in their working by taking inputs and ideas from all levels of employees.

At Make My Trip organisation, employees have forums where they share their best practices and experiences, for others to follow. In short, there is a constant element of newness in the way things are done there.

3. Risk taking orientation

As mentioned in the above example of Forbes Marshall, one of the salient features of their culture is the ability to take risks by making mistakes. The objective is to do things differently and take risks in order to be innovative.

4. Value placed on people

Nowadays unlike earlier, organisations are realising the importance of people as employees and place a lot of value in them by inspiring them and motivating them to do their best. In earlier times, as far as the work was concerned, the employees were paid, and nothing more was to the relationship. Today, they are treated as individuals, having an individuality of their own, and the organisation works on inspiring them and driving them to do their best.

5. Openness to available communication options

In organisations today, the communication options are not rigid anymore and the lines are free and open. Employees can sometimes go and communicate with anyone including the top management to discuss and share ideas freely.

6. Friendliness and Warmth

The culture of many organisations is warm and friendly and congenial, where employees extend their friendships far beyond the working hours and meet informally outside.

Organisations with a strong culture are known to exhibit the following features:

1. Clear expectations about the business are mentioned
2. Lot of time is spent on communicating values and beliefs
3. A set of norms exists and are shared with all
4. New employees who join the organisation are screened to fit with the organisational culture.

4.2.6 Tools for Transmitting Culture

How do people in organisations understand the culture? How do they identify the same? There are various tools, symbols and stories that transmit about the culture. For example, In Godrej group of industries, the story goes about that whenever the peon was absent, the founder had personally cleaned his own cabin.

This was followed by all other members, who saw the humility of the chairman and also followed the same culture of cleaning their own cabins.

1. **Symbols and objects**

For examples, firms who have flowers, plants and decorations are known to promote a culture of friendliness, congeniality and warmth. Those who have medals, certificates and awards hung, promote the culture of performance related importance, where quality of performance matters most.

2. **Phrases, lingo and slogans**

The catchword in the organisations that are often reflected in the slogans and their promos, also convey messages of culture in organisations. Like Big Basaar says "Discounts and Free Gifts always", or Hyatt says 'feel the Hyatt touch".

3. **Stories**

This is also an effective way to convey culture. Many organisations transmit information by the stories they share with others. Such stories illustrate key aspects of the culture. For example, when Infosys was started, the story shared was whatever we do should be transparent and ethical, and so, if we earn money, others should also earn money. In short, the culture is of being fair and sharing equally,.

4. **Ceremonies, special programmes that reflect corporate values.**

There are special programmes that organisation's conduct, which reveal their values. For example, a special programme in Diwali for the family members of the employees, speak of the value of family relationship. Or special programmes to felicitate good performers, which speak of the value of meritocracy or performance based value.

4.2.7 Strength of an Organisation Culture

In many organisations, their culture has a deep impact on people as employees. Such organisations exhibit deep sharing of the features as discussed above in terms of innovation, openness to new ideas, free communication, risk taking ability and friendliness of people.

Such organisations are known to have a strong culture.

In contrast, there are organisations, where the impact of culture on people is very weak. Such organisations do not have too many new ideas or innovation or a risk taking capacity. Such organisations are known to have a weak culture.

Statements of Principle and Values

Some statements of principles and values are necessary to understand, to identify the culture of the organisation. Some examples of the same are:

1. **Quality:** Everyone's responsibility
2. **Innovation:** need of the hour to boost productivity

3. **Empowerment:** everybody has the freedom to do things their way and so, be creative.
4. **Trust:** Mutuality of respect and delegation to build trust

4.2.8 Changing Organisational Culture

A common set up where individuals from different back grounds, educational qualifications, interests and perception come together and use their skills to earn revenue is called an organisation.

The successful functioning of an organisation depends on the effort put by each employee. Each individual has to contribute his level best to accomplish the tasks within the desired time frame.

Every organisation has a unique style of working which is often called its culture. The beliefs, policies, principles, ideologies of an organisation form its culture.

The culture of the organisation is nothing but the outcome of the interaction among the employees working for quite some time.

The behaviour of the individual with his fellow workers as well as external parties forms the culture. The management style of dealing with the employees in its own way also contributes to the culture of the organisation.

Employees working for a considerable amount of time in any particular organisation tend to make certain rules and follow some policies as per their convenience and mutual understanding.

Culture often gives the employees a sense of direction at the workplace.

Such policies and procedures practised by the employees for a long time to make the workplace a happier place form the culture. The culture often gives the employees a sense of direction at the workplace.

Organisation culture however can never be constant. It changes with time. A change in the management changes the entire style of working.

Reasons for changes in work culture

*   **A new management, a new team leader, a new boss brings a change in the organisation culture.** A new employee but obvious would have new ideas, concepts and try his level best to implement them. He would want the employees to work according to him. His style of working, behaviour and ideologies would definitely bring a change in the work culture.
*   **Financial loss, bankruptcy, market fluctuations also lead to change in the work culture of the organisation.** When an organisation runs into losses, it fails to give rewards and appraisals to the employees as it used to give earlier.

- **Acquiring new clients might cause a change in the work culture**. The employees might have to bring about a change in their style of working to meet the expectations of the new clients.
- The employees on their own might realise that they need to bring a change in their attitude, perception and style of working to achieve the targets at a much faster rate. Such **self-realisation also changes the culture**

When and how does Culture Change?

It appears from the above features and examples that Cultures do not always change and they remain static for some time. However this is not true, although the essence of culture may remain stable for some time. Still with the change in the government policies, growth of technology, volatile changes in the market, transformation of the aspirations of the employees, (which is beyond money and power), cultures evolves and sometimes drastically changes.

Some of the factors that promote these changes are:

1. Composition of the Workforce

As the companies are getting more and more diverse, the composition of the workforce is constantly changing.

With workforce coming from diverse backgrounds and different exposures to culture, the new comers from diverse backgrounds may have different ideas about dress code, food served in the cafeteria, approaches to punctuality and time, differences in interpretations of behaviour like respect necessarily aligning with the ideas of the superior and so on.

Such a diverse workforce is likely to influence major changes in the culture or the way things have been done around in the organisation.

2. Joint ventures, Mergers and Acquisitions

When one company merges with another or is bought over by another, or amalgamates, there is likely to be a radical cultural difference. Companies earlier never considered the above differences, and only looked at profitability and material resources.

However there were major problems faced due to differences in norms, behavioural standards, and lifestyles. There are many such examples, of how these differences have caused conflicts and sometimes break ups of companies.

For instance, when Daimler Bens merged with Chrysler, there were major differences with each ones perceptions towards their way of working. Chrysler officials travelled economy class whereas the Daimler officials travelled only Business class and drove their lavish sedans and Mercedes cars. Such differences caused a lot of cultural conflicts. In India, when Daimler Chrysler set up operations, the Germans who were deputed found it difficult to adjust with the large variety of meals served in the canteen. Variations had to be made to accommodate their local tastes and preferences.

When the British head was deputed to Pune, with a joint venture of Atlas Copco, he found it vague, when his employees believed in large scales of hierarchies. He recalls an instance of a cricket match, which he organised at the company's branch and the workers were very hesitant and shy while playing with their superiors, as they were much higher in the hierarchy.

4.2.9 Strategic Cultural Change

Sometimes the management deliberately decides to transform culture and make changes in keeping with the changes in the market conditions and competition.

Some of these changes are:

1. Measuring performances

The purpose now is to objectively quantify all performance measures. Right from customer satisfaction surveys to employee satisfaction survey, the measures are being quantitatively rated. In companies like LG Electronics, a white goods manufacturing company, headquartered in Korea, all intangibles are being translated to some quantifiable measure.

These include, complaints sorted out, hindrances at work, employee engagements through celebrations and special events and so on.

2.   Integrating the new culture

Most companies today, develop and implement new methods of working to gain competitive advantage by regularly updating technology. For example, as a new culture norm, many company heads to take virtual meetings every week, where employees from all the branches take stock of the developments, share expectations from one another, create accountability for these expectations and thus work is more progressive.

3. Build support from culture change

More and more companies are holding training programmes to make people at all levels change oriented. They discuss in these forums how change can be built and the effects of change on performance and culture.

Training programmes on change are the norm in today's companies and they intend to acclimatise the need for people to foster and facilitate change for continuous progress and development.

4.2.10 Creating Positive Organisational Culture

A positive workplace culture leads to increased productivity, better employee morale and the ability to retain skilled workers.

> *A positive workplace culture leads to increased productivity, better employee morale and the ability to retain skilled workers.*

Negative attitudes in the workplace, particularly when they are displayed by the leadership, can have a dramatic impact on the entire organisation.

Taking the steps to ensure that a positive culture is present in the workplace will go a long way towards keeping your organisation running smoothly and keeping an engaged positive workforce.

Strategies for creating and maintaining a positive work culture

- **Open communication culture:** Organisations should encourage a culture where open communication between the employees is encouraged across its hierarchy.
- **Empowering employees:** Employees will have the power to make day to day routine decisions on their without having to consult their seniors.
- **Employees involvement in strategic decisions:** Employees feel valued when their suggestions are taken into consideration when important decisions affecting the organisation are being made.
- **Participative leadership style:** Establish an open-door policy and encourage interaction. Be honest and open. Ask people's opinions; listen to what they have to say.
- **Core Values:** Core values need to be communicated to employees on a regular basis.

4.2.11 Concept of Workplace Spirituality

Workplace Spirituality or Spirituality in the Workplace is a movement that began in the early 1920s. It emerged as a grassroots movement with individuals seeking to live their faith and/or spiritual values in the workplace.

One of the first publications to mention spirituality in the workplace was Business Week, June 5, 2005. The cover article was titled "Companies hit the road less travelled: Can spirituality enlighten the bottom line?"

A person's spirit is the vital principle or animating force traditionally believed to be the intangible, life-affirming force within all human beings. It is a state of intimate relationship with the inner self of higher values and morality as well as recognition of the truth of the inner nature of others. Today many individuals are struggling with what their spirituality means for their work since this is where they spend vast majority of their waking hours. The office is now where more and more people eat, exercise, date, drop their kids, and even nap. Many naturally look to their organisations as a communal center because they lack the continuity and connection found in other settings.

Because of this, a major change is taking place in the personal and professional lives of leaders as many of them more deeply integrate their spirituality and their work. Many agree that this integration is leading to very positive changes in their relationships and their effectiveness. There is also evidence that workplace spirituality programmes not only lead to beneficial personal outcomes such as increased job satisfaction, and commitment, but that they also deliver improved productivity and reduce absenteeism and turnover. Employees who work for organisations they consider to be spiritual are less fearful, more ethical, and more committed. And, there is mounting evidence that a more humane workplace is more productive, flexible and creative.

Most importantly for organisational effectiveness is the emerging research that that workplace spirituality could be the ultimate competitive advantage. Because of this, there is an emerging and accelerating call for spirituality in the workplace.

Workplace spirituality is not about religion or conversion, or about accepting a specific belief system. Spirituality at work is about leaders and followers who understand themselves as spiritual beings who have a sense of calling that provides meaning and purpose for their lives. It is also about membership where people experience a sense of belonging, connectedness to one another and their workplace community. It begins with the acknowledgement that people have both an inner and an outer life and that the nourishment of the inner life can produce a more meaningful and productive outer life that can have beneficial consequences for employee well-being, corporate responsibility and sustainability, as well as financial performance – The triple bottom line.

On the heels of big scams like Enron and Sarbanes-Oxley and the subsequent birth of the ethics consulting industry, conversations around the value and place of spirituality in the workplace have been further encouraged by the need for managers and leaders to behave more ethically in the world and to foster ethical decision making in their workforces. These events continue to impact the marketplace, yet decision makers are also struggling to understand the place of spirituality at work and its implications for character development while simultaneously handling a rise in requests by some employees to be able to express religious practices in the workplace.

Interest in workplace spirituality has increased steadily over the last decade of the twentieth century and into the new millennium (Giacalone & Jurkiewics, 2004). Spirituality, as defined by Mitroff and Denton (1999), is the basic feeling of being connected with one's complete self, others and the entire universe.

A growing number of companies are setting off on spiritual journeys. It's not about bringing religion into the office or requiring that employees chant mantras at their workstations. Rather the spirituality movement in the corporation is an attempt to create a sense of meaning and purpose at work and a connection between the company and its people.

Today, companies like Ford, Nike, Boeing, AT&T, and many others alike, have all begun incorporating spirituality into the workplace. There is the widespread belief that for companies to survive into the 21st century in the face of economical downturn and global competition, it would be helpful to seek inspiration from God and tap into employees' spiritual resources (Wong, 2003).

Workplace Spirituality is therefore defined as "A framework of organisational values evidenced in the culture that promote employees' experience of transcendence through the work process, facilitating their sense of being connected to others in a way that provides feelings of completeness and joy (Giacalone & Jurkiewics, 2004).

Key factors that have led to this trend include:

1. Mergers and acquisitions destroyed the psychological contract that workers had a job for life. This led some people to search for more of a sense of inner security rather than looking for external security from a corporation.

2. Baby Boomers hitting middle age resulting in a large demographic part of the population asking meaningful questions about life and purpose.

3. The millennium created an opportunity for people all over the world to reflect on where the human race has come from, where it is headed in the future, and what role business plays in the future of the human race.

Spirituality is shown in a workplace when the following activities are included:

- Bereavement programs.
- Wellness information displayed and distributed.
- Employee Assistance Programs.
- Programs that integrate work/family.
- Management systems that encourage personal and spiritual transformation.
- Servant leadership – the desire to serve others first in preference to self.
- Stewardship – leadership practices that support growth and well-being of others.
- Diversity programs that create inclusive cultures.
- Integration of core values and core business decisions and practices.
- Leadership practices that support the growth and development of all employees.

We share responsibility for creating the external world by projecting either a spirit of light or a spirit of shadow on that which is other than us.

> *A leader must take special responsibility for what's going on inside his/her own self, inside his/her consciousness, lest the act of leadership create more harm than good.*

We project either a spirit of hope or a spirit of despair...We have a choice about what we are going to project, and in that choice we help create the world that is.

A leader is a person who has an unusual degree of power to project on other people his/her shadow, or his/her light.

A leader must take special responsibility for what's going on inside his/her own self, inside his/her consciousness, lest the act of leadership create more harm than good.

Points to Remember

The organisational structure of an organisation tells you the character of an organisation and the values it believes in.

The various types of organisational structures are:

- Functions/Department Organisational Structure
- Divisional Organisational Structure
  1. Product Organisational Structure
  2. Regional Organisational Structure
- Matrix Organisational Structure.
- Every organisation has its unique style of working, which often contributes to its culture. The management must respect the employees to avoid a culture where the employees just work for money and nothing else. Culture often gives the employees a sense of direction at the workplace.
- The style and content of communication both have a strong impact on a company's culture. A positive workplace culture leads to increased productivity, better employee morale and the ability to keep skilled workers.
- A leader must take special responsibility for what's going on inside his/her own self, inside his/her consciousness, lest the act of leadership create more harm than good

Case Study

'Organisation A' was a well-known event management firm. Tom, Sandra, Peter and Jack represented the management. All the four were in their mid-thirties and thus emphasised on hiring young talent. No wonder this organisation followed a youth culture. The employees were aggressive, on their toes and eager to do something innovative always.

The organisation followed a macho culture where the employees performing exceptionally well were appreciated and rewarded suitably. Appraisals and promotions came in no time and feedbacks were quick. The management also encouraged informal get-togethers, dinners to bring the employees closer and increase the comfort level.

After proving their mettle for quite some years, Tom, Sandra and Peter decided to move on for better opportunities. Tim, Maria, Sara all in their fifties stepped into their shoes and took the charge along with Jack, the only member left from the previous team.

They did not somehow approve the previous style of working. They brought their own people from their previous organisations and thus caused problems for the existing employees. The management strongly supported punctuality and did not quite promote parties; get-togethers at workplace. There were no feedbacks or rewards. The employees lacked enthusiasm and never bothered to do something innovative.

Questions

Q. Explain how change in organisational culture impacts the motivation and work performance of the employees.

Questions for Discussion

1. What is an organisation? Describe its types.
2. Define principles of organisational structuring.
3. Describe in detail traditional and modern types of organisational structure.
4. What are the factors that need to be considered while choosing an organisational structure?
5. Explain the meaning and Importance of Culture.
6. Describe the common characteristics of organisational culture.
7. Describe how culture impacts the working of an organisation, its systems and practices.
8. What leads to changes in culture?
9. Define a positive organisational culture.
10. What are the characteristics of spiritual culture?

Multiple Choice Questions (MCQ's)

Q's 1-10 State Whether True or False

1. The organisational structure of an organisation tells you the character of an organisation and the values it believes in.
2. An organisational structure consists of activities such as task allocation, coordination and supervision, which are directed towards the achievement of organisational aims.
3. The structure of an organisation does not determine the modes in which it operates and performs.
4. Every organisation has its unique style of working, which often contributes to its culture.
5. The management must not respect the employees to avoid a culture where the employees just work for money and nothing else
6. A "strong" culture may be especially beneficial to firms operating in the service sector.
7. The style and content of communication do not have a strong impact on a company's culture.
8. A positive workplace culture leads to increased productivity, better employee morale and the ability to keep skilled workers.
9. A leader must take special responsibility for what's going on inside his/her own self, inside his/her consciousness, lest the act of leadership create more harm than good
10. Culture does not give the employees a sense of direction at the workplace.

Q's 11-20 Fill in the blanks

11. "Organisations are social units (or human groupings) deliberately constructed and reconstructed to seek ...... ".

12. Organisational structure pertains to the way in which companies arrange their ....

13. The ...... of an organisation decides the way employees behave amongst themselves as well as the people outside the organisation.

14. Fast paced industries like ...... companies expect the employees to be attentive, aggressive and hyper active.

15. Every organisation has a ...... of working which is often called its culture.

16. The beliefs, policies, principles, ideologies of ...... form its culture.

17. Organisation culture however can never be constant. It changes with time. A change in the ...... changes the entire style of working.

18. Strong cultures have ...... that give employees a reason to embrace the culture.

19. Soft work culture can emerge in an organisation where the organisation pursues ...... and ...... goals.

20. A ...... is a person who has an unusual degree of power to project on other people his/her shadow, or his/her light.

Answers to MCQ's

1. True
2. True
3. False
4. True
5. False
6. True
7. False
8. True
9. True
10. False

Answers to Fill in the blanks

11. Specific goals
12. Departments
13. Culture
14. Advertising, event management
15. Unique style
16. An organisation
17. Management
18. Clear values
19. Multiple, conflicting
20. Leader

Activity

Identify a set of characteristics that define your institution's culture.

Note: *Chapter 4 is newly introduced, so there are no Questions from Previous Pune University Examinations.*

References and Web Links

- http://ctb.ku.edu
- Berkowits, W. R, and Wolff, T. J. (1999). *The spirit of coalition building.* Washington, D.C.: American Public Health Association.
- Unterman, I. & Davis, R. H. (1984). *Strategic management of not-for-profit organisations: From survival to success.* New York, NY: Praeger.
- http://en.wikipedia.org/wiki/Workplace_spirituality.
- http://www.logosnoesis.com/create-positive-culture.

Managing Change

Contents ...

Learning Objectives

After studying this chapter you should be able:

1. To identify forces that act as stimulants to change.
2. To differentiate between Planned and Unplanned Change.
3. To list the sources for resistance to change.
4. To compare the various approaches to managing change.
5. To demonstrate different ways of creating a culture for change.
6. To define stress and identify its potential sources.
7. To identify the consequences of stress.
8. To compare and contrast the individual and organisational approaches to stress.

5.1 Organisational Change

5.1.1 Introduction

The real world is turbulent, requiring organisations and their members to undergo dynamic change if they are to perform at competitive levels.

If environments were perfectly static, if employees' skills and abilities were always up to date and incapable of deteriorating, and if tomorrows were exactly same as today, organisation change would have little or no importance for managers.

Managers are the primary change agents in most organisations and they shape the organisation's change culture through the decisions they make and by their role-modeling behaviour.

Management decisions related to structural designs, cultural factors, and human resource policies largely determine the level of innovation within the organisation. Management decisions, policies and practices will determine the degree to which the organisation learns and adapts to changing environmental factors.

5.1.2 Meaning of Organisational Change

In the modern business environment, organisations face rapid change like never before. Globalisation and the constant innovation of technology result in a constantly evolving business environment. Phenomena such as social media and mobile adaptability have revolutionised business and the effect of this, is an ever increasing, need for change and therefore change management.

Organisation change occurs when business strategies or major sections of an organisation are altered. Also, known as, reorganisation, restructuring and turnaround. Organisational change is a structured approach in an organisation for ensuring that changes are smoothly and successfully implemented to achieve lasting benefits.

> *The ability to manage and adapt to organisational change is an essential ability required in the workplace today.*

The growth in technology also has a secondary effect of increasing the availability and therefore accountability of knowledge. Easily accessible information has resulted in unprecedented scrutiny from stockholders and the media. Prying eyes and listening ears raise the stakes for failed business endeavours and increase the pressure on struggling executives. With the business environment experiencing so much change, organisations must then learn to become comfortable with change. Therefore, the ability to manage and adapt to organisational change is an essential ability required in the workplace today.

Due to the growth of technology, modern organisational change is largely motivated by exterior innovations rather than internal moves. When these developments occur, the organisations that adapt quickly will create a competitive advantage for themselves, while the companies that refuse to change are/get left behind. This can result in drastic profit and/or market share losses.

Organisational change directly affects all departments from the entry level employee to senior management. The entire company must learn how to handle changes in the organisation.

When determining which of the latest techniques or innovations to adopt, there are four major factors to be considered:

1. Levels, goals, and strategies.
2. Measurement system.
3. Sequence of steps.
4. Implementation and organisational change.

Regardless of the many types of organisational change, the critical aspect is a company's ability to win the support of their organisation's employees on the change.

Effectively managing organisational change is a four-step process:
1. Recognising the changes in the broader business environment.
2. Developing the necessary adjustments for their company's needs.
3. Training the employees on the appropriate changes.
4. Winning the support of the employees with the persuasiveness of the appropriate adjustments.

As a multidisciplinary practice that has evolved as a result of scholarly research, organisational change management should begin with a systematic diagnosis of the current situation, in order to determine both the need for change and the capability to change. The objectives, content, and process of change should all be specified as part of a change management plan.

Change management processes may include creative marketing to enable communication between changing audiences, as well as deep social understanding about leadership's styles and group dynamics. As a visible track on transformation projects, Organisational Change Management aligns groups' expectations, communicates, integrates teams and manages people training. It makes use of performance metrics, such as financial results, operational efficiency, leadership commitment, communication effectiveness, and the perceived need for change to design appropriate strategies, in order to avoid change failures or resolve troubled change projects.

Successful change management is more likely to occur if the following are included:
1. Benefits management and realisation to define measurable stakeholder aims, create a business case for their achievement (which should be continuously updated), and monitor assumptions, risks, dependencies, costs, return on investment, disadvantages and cultural issues affecting the progress of the associated work.
2. Effective communications that informs various stakeholders of the reasons for the change (why?), the benefits of successful implementation (what is in it for us, and you) as well as the details of the change (when? where? who is involved? how much will it cost? etc.).
3. Devise an effective education, training and/or skills upgrading scheme for the organisation.
4. Counter resistance from the employees of companies and align them to overall strategic direction of the organisation.
5. Provide personal counselling (if required) to alleviate any change-related fears.
6. Monitoring the implementation and fine-tuning as required.

Examples:
- Mission changes.
- Strategic changes.
- Operational changes (including structural changes).
- Technological changes.
- Changing the attitudes and behaviours of personnel.

5.1.3 Definition of Organisational Change

Organisational change is defined as the change that has an impact on the way that work is performed and has significant effects on staff.

This could include changes:
- In the structure of an organisation
- To organisational operation and size of a workforce
- To working hours or practices
- The way roles are carried out
- The scope of a role that results in a change to the working situation, structure, terms and conditions or environment.

5.1.4 Nature of Organisational Change

It is in human nature to resist change. ***"We resist change. We choose to keep our habits, rather the comfort of our habits"***. Change and the phenomenon of it, is fundamental to evolution; and yet it implies some sort of resistance.

Resistance to change can take various forms and the task of filtering out the cause of resistance can often be difficult. Examples include change in work processes where the needs, expectations, and concerns of individuals are ignored.

Change and resistance to it forms a knock-on-effect to both the construction and destruction of any organisation. Fear is one of the major forms of resistance to change and we shall discuss this in depth at a later stage. Alas resistance to change can be categorised to the organisational level and the individual level. It is these two separate levels which we shall discuss further exploring what steps may be taken to overcome resistance at both the organisational and individual level.

Organisational change takes place because of internal and external forces. The internal forces may create instant change, whereas the external forces may results in the gradual change. The effect of change in any one part of the organisation creates about the fundamental change in the entire organisation. The effect of change on various parts takes place in varying degree and rates. The means the effect of change will not be similar in every part of an organisation.

5.1.5 Major Types of Organisational Changes

Typically, the phrase "organisational change" is about a significant change in the organisation, such as re-organisation or adding a major new product or service. This is in contrast to smaller changes, such as adopting a new computer procedure.

> *Organisational change can have an impact irrespective of whether changes are viewed as large or small.*

Organisational change can seem like such a vague phenomena. It is helpful if you can think of change in terms of various dimensions as described below:

Organisation-wide Versus Subsystem Change

Organisation-wide change might be a major restructuring, collaboration or rightsizing. Usually, organisations must undertake organisation-wide change to evolve to a different level in their life cycle. For example, going from a highly reactive, entrepreneurial organisation to one that has a more stable and planned development. Experts assert that successful organisational change requires a change in culture; cultural change is an example of organisation-wide change.

Examples of a change in a subsystem might include addition or removal of a product or service, re-organisation of a certain department, or implementation of a new process to deliver products or services.

Transformational Versus Incremental Change

Transformational (or radical, fundamental) change might be changing an organisation's structure and culture from the traditional top-down, hierarchical structure to a large amount of self-directing teams. For example, Business Process Re-engineering, which tries to take apart (at least on paper, at first) the major parts and processes of the organisation and then put them back together in a more optimal fashion. Transformational change is sometimes referred to as quantum change.

Examples of incremental change might include continuous improvement as a quality management process or implementation of new computer system to increase efficiencies. Many times, organisations experience incremental change and its leaders do not recognise the change as such.

Remedial Versus Developmental Change

Change can be intended to remedy current situations, for example, to improve the poor performance of a product or the entire organisation, reduce burnout in the workplace, helps the organisation to become much more proactive and less reactive, or address large budget deficits.

Remedial projects often seem more focused and urgent because they are addressing a current, major problem. It is often easier to determine the success of these projects because the problem is solved or not. Change can also be developmental to make a successful situation even more successful, for example, expand the amount of customers served, or duplicate successful products or services. Developmental projects can seem more general and vague than remedial, depending on how specific goals are and how important it is for members of the organisation to achieve those goals. Some people might have different perceptions of what is a remedial change versus a developmental change.

They might see that if developmental changes are not made soon, there will be need for remedial changes. Also, organisations may recognise current remedial issues and then establish a developmental vision to address the issues. In those situations, projects are still remedial because they were conducted primarily to address current issues.

Unplanned Versus Planned Change

Unplanned change usually occurs because of a major, sudden surprise to the organisation, which causes its members to respond in a highly reactive and disorganized fashion. Unplanned change might occur when the Chief Executive Officer suddenly leaves the organisation, significant public relations problems occur, poor product performance quickly results in loss of customers, or other disruptive situations arise.

Planned change occurs when leaders in the organisation recognise the need for a major change and proactively organise/devise a plan to accomplish the change. Planned change occurs with successful implementation of a Strategic Plan, plan for re-organisation, or other implementation of a change of this magnitude.

> *The mantra of organisational success is proclaimed to be effective management of change as if "change" is inevitable.*

Note that planned change, even though based on a proactive and well-done plan, often does not occur in a highly organised fashion. Instead, planned change tends to occur in more of a chaotic and disruptive fashion than expected by participants.

Though people, structure, policies, practices and existing systems linked with an enterprise create forces to maintain continuity, continuously changing business "situation" (in particular due to globalisation) generates forces that direct organisations to strive for change.

The situational change forces could be both external and internal. The external change forces may emerge from changes on political, economic, social, and/or technological fronts. The internal change forces may be because of poor performance (low profitability, loss of market share), change in top management, and so on.

5.1.6 Forces that Act as Stimulants to Change

Stimulants to Change:

- Impetus for change is likely to come from outside change agents.
- Internal change agents are most threatened by their loss of status in the organisation.
- Long-time power holders tend to implement only incremental change.
- The outcomes of power struggles in the organisation will determine the speed and quality of change.
- Impetus for change is likely to come from outside change agents.
- Internal change agents are most threatened by their loss of status in the organisation.
- Long-time power holders tend to implement only incremental change.
- The outcomes of power struggles in the organisation will determine the speed and quality of change.

Forces that Acts as Stimulants to Change

Forces stimulating social change are stronger over time than barriers. So change is inevitable in the long term. Nonetheless most people resist change in the short term.

Forces for Change

1. **Organisations face a dynamic and changing environment:** This requires adaptation. Exhibit 19-1 summarises six specific forces that are acting as stimulants for change.

2. **The changing nature of the workforce:**
   - A multicultural environment.
   - Human resource policies and practices changed to attract and keep this more diverse workforce.
   - Large expenditure on training to upgrade reading, math, computer, and other skills of employees

3. **Technology is changing jobs and organisations:**
   - Sophisticated information technology is also making organisations more responsive. As organisations have had to become more adaptable, so too have their employees.
   - We live in an "age of discontinuity." Beginning in the early 1970s with the overnight quadrupling of world oil prices, economic shocks have continued to impose changes on organisations.

4.   **Competition is changing:**
   - The global economy means global competitors.
   - Established organisations need to defend themselves against both traditional competitors and small, entrepreneurial firms with innovative offerings.
   - Successful organisations will be the ones that can change in response to the competition.

5.   **Social trends during the past generation suggest changes that organisations have to adjust for:**
   - The expansion of the Internet, Baby Boomers retiring, and people moving from the suburbs back to cities.
   - A global context for OB is required. No one could have imagined how world politics would change in recent years.
   - September 11th has caused changes organisations have made in terms of practices concerning security, back-up systems, employee stereotyping, etc.

5.1.7 Barriers to Change

There are psychological, cultural, social, and developmental barriers to Change.

1. Psychological

The psychological impact of how change is introduced can be its own barrier. Perhaps there has been no explanation or information on why the change is required, or no consultation, negotiation and support. If members of the organisation were not involved in the decision-making process, they are likely to resist the change because of lack of trust, insecurity or poor employee relations.

2. Cultural

With change, resistance is expected throughout the organisation. If the current system is working well, employees might feel sceptical about changing existing processes, especially if in the past other initiatives did not work out. You'll need to demonstrate and convince your organisation how and why this approach is better. Show actual outcomes of success that the organisation can relate to. When necessary, seek outside experts to help employees understand the challenges and work through resistance to build a plan to break the barriers to change and reach your goals.

3. Social

Accepting change can be difficult. Strength is in numbers. Therefore, group participation encourages acceptance of the new enterprise. Changes that are incompatible with group norms might be resisted within a group, especially in a social system, resulting in confrontation of public opinion. By modifying a change, to show that you are compromising, you facilitate acceptance. Speaking to groups about possibilities for improvement and allowing each person to provide feedback and be involved in the decision-making process are possible solutions to social barriers to change.

4. Developmental Barriers

Inadequate training by management makes it uncomfortable for members of an organisation to change to new software and technology for fear of sabotaging a process, especially with increasingly specialized advances in applications. For example, a personal assistant who is computer-literate but confronted with challenging new accounting software, without adequate training, might not confidently apply his/her skills to operate the advanced software. As a result, he/she holds on to barriers of change.

Causes of resistance can be categorised in Individual resistance and Organisational resistance:

1.   **Individual Resistance:** Resistance is an economic factor (affect mostly workers and employees). It reflects both resistances. Resistance is because of:

- **Fear:** There is a fear of being Idle within the organisation. Hence, less importance will be given to them.
  There is a fear of Demotion among employees and worker which cause resistance.
  Fear among employee of not able to build up stets.
  Because of those three different fear, the entire worker community may fear technological unemployment.

- **Habits:** "Generally perused Trait". It leads to a general acceptability. If this acceptability is broken then the Resistance starts.
  Example: When the employee is transferred, his schedule is changed which includes shifting of goods, new school for children and movement to a new locality. Hence, this change of habits leads to resistance.

- **Insecurity:** Insecurity refers to uncertainty about the impact of change.
  Insecurity creates anxiety and apprehension.
  Anxiety is over worship for a particular work and apprehension is a negative apathy.

- **Lack of communication:** It is divided into interpersonal and interpersonal which is further of two part as participative and non-participative. If participation in communication leads to acceptance and if participation is reduced leads to resistance.

- **Extent of change:** It is of two types – Minor (acceptance) and Major (resistance.) The minor change is the change in daily routine of a person and major change is in the shifting network of the people.

- **Psychological factor:** Some factors are as fear of being criticised, fear of being idle, they feel that the new job will bring monotony and boredom. Hence due to some psychological factor they fear resistance.
- **Social factor:** some reasons are as:
  In the membership of informal group are effected, social needs are hurt.
  Breaking up of social relationship is also basic reason for the social needs to get hurt.
  A general dislike among a group of people for an individual member may also be the reason for the social need to be hurt.

2. **Organisational Resistance:**
   Some causes are:
   - **Threat to power:** Top level management has a threat to power and influences, which as middle level management has a threat that they will be throughout from the participative decision making and will not be in a position to function as self managed team.
   - **Group Inertia:**
     Group inertia depends upon two factors as:
     1. How loyal one individual member is to be group.
     2. How effectively the group resist the change.
     The members are influence by the patterns and the attitudes of the groups because they decide the group inertial.
   - **Organisational Structure:** Organisational structure is affected by the bureaucratic structure. The bureaucratic structure resists the organisation structure. It lead to resistance because of strict line of categorisation.
   - **Threat to specialisation:** An organisation may resist specialisation because it may threaten the expertise of the specialised groups.
   - **Resource constraints:** Resources are of two types adequate and inadequate. If it is a adequate there is a acceptance to change where as inadequate resources resist change.

Twelve Principles for Managing Change

These principles provide the cause and effect of managing change strategically:

1. Thought processes and relationship dynamics are fundamental if change is to be successful.
2. Change only happens when each person makes a decision to implement the change.
3. People fear change it "happens" to them.
4. Given the freedom to do so, people will build quality into their work as a matter of personal pride.
5. Traditional organisational systems treat people like children and expect them to act like adults.
6. "Truth" is more important during periods of change and uncertainty than "good news."

7. Trust is earned by those who demonstrate consistent behaviour and clearly defined values.
8. People who work are capable of doing much more than they are doing.
9. The intrinsic rewards of a project are often more important than the material rewards and recognition.
10. A clearly defined vision of the end result enables all the people to define the most efficient path for accomplishing the results.
11. The more input people have into defining the changes that will affect their work, the more they will take ownership for the results.
12. To change the individual, change the system.

5.2 Implementing Organisational Change

5.2.1 How to Overcome the Resistance to Change

In business, the one thing you can be assured of is change. As the economy ebbs and flows, so must the strategies employed by business. If your organisation experiences change it may also need to implement new business strategies, which can create resistance among employees.

As the economy ebbs and flows, so must the strategies employed by business.

While every organisation is different, there are some common best practices that can help to overcome resistance to new business strategies.

· **Step 1**

Create a way to communicate with employees about new initiatives and their progress. Instruct key management to provide employees with regular updates at team meetings.

· **Step 2**

Market the new business strategy to each group. Explain the new plan in terms (a common language) that help each group understand how the new strategy will make their own jobs better or easier. Everyone in the organisation must understand the goal of the new business strategy.

· **Step 3**

Invite a team member from each functional group to participate in meetings or provide seminars for each group to market the strategy.

· **Step 4**

Select a group of change agents from key positions to help manage planning and implementation. Find one person from each group who is vocal. Try to select those in non-management positions as well.

· **Step 5**

Develop key deliverables for each department, organisation and person involved in the new business strategy. A deliverable is a final report or the output from implementing the new business strategy. Each group head must tailor the deliverable to the goals of the group. For example, one deliverable can be to increase sales by 5 percent. Another can be lower costs by 5 percent.

• **Step 6**

Tie successful implementation to compensation. Create at least four key milestones and goals to measure success throughout the year. Report on performance regularly and publicly reward those people or groups that meet goals.

5.2.2 Kurt Lewin's Force Field Analysis Change Model

Kurt Lewin's force field analysis change model was designed to weigh the driving and restraining forces that affect change in organisations. The 'force field' can be described as two opposite forces working for and against change. In this illustration we'll learn how to analyse the force field.

Force Field Analysis Change Model

Have you ever had that conversation with colleagues about where to dine for lunch? You and a few others want to try the new Thai place, but your co-worker Jeanie and a few others want to go to the same old sandwich shop you've been going to for years. Well, Kurt Lewin's force field analysis change model describes a similar situation.

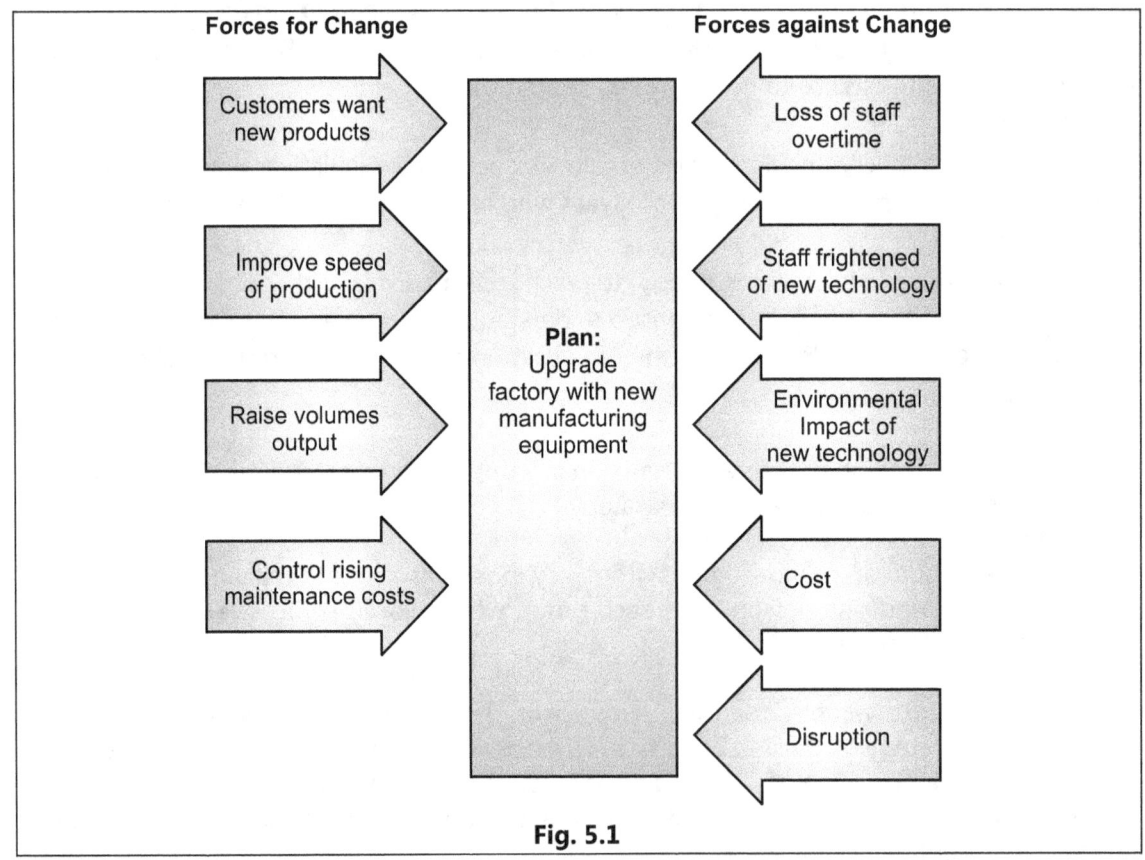

Fig. 5.1

The force field analysis is a method to:
- Investigate the balance of power.
- Identify the key players involved in decision-making.
- Identify who is for and who is against change.
- Identify ways to influence those against change.

In an organisation, change is a bit more complicated, but just like deciding where to go for lunch, there are driving and resisting forces at work. Driving forces are those seeking change. Resisting (restraining) forces are those seeking to maintain the status quo. The goal for the driving force is to gain equilibrium, or a balance of power. Resisting forces control the status quo, while driving forces seek change.

If driving forces exceed that of restraining forces, they will exact change. This will create equilibrium, or a balance of power.

Forces, whether driving or resisting, are a mix of:
- People
- Habits
- Customs
- Attitudes

How to Conduct a Force Field Analysis

The force field analysis involves:
- Stating the problem.
- Defining objectives.
- Determining resistant forces.
- Comparing strategy against organisational objectives.

In a Nutshell

Lewin's force field analysis change model works by investigating the balance of power, then determining the key players involved in decision-making and devising ways to influence them to accept change.

Driving forces are those seeking change, while *resisting forces* are those seeking to maintain the status quo.

The Force Field Analysis involves
- **Stating the problem** by determining the current situation in terms of the conflict at hand. This may also involve determining the desired state. Other things to consider are where the current situation will go if no action is taken.
- **Defining objectives** by listing the expectations or outcomes of change. If change occurs, equilibrium, or balance of power, has been achieved.
- **Determining resisting forces** to identify negative or resistant forces to change.
- **Comparing strategy against organisational objectives** to determine whether the strategies used are in line with the desired objectives.

A classic model of Organisational Development, commonly referred to as the 'force field' model, was proposed by Kurt Lewin in 1951. He described organisations as systems which are held in a constant state of 'equilibrium' by equal and opposing forces. The model suggests that a range of 'driving forces', which exert a pressure for change, are balanced by a number of opposing 'resisting forces'. Driving forces urging change might include the availability of new technology, economic pressure from competitors or even changes in local or national legislation. Conversely, resisting forces might include a firmly established organisational culture and climate or industry-specific customs. **Lewin** proposed that any process of organisational change can be thought of as implementing a move in the equilibrium position towards a desired or newly established position.

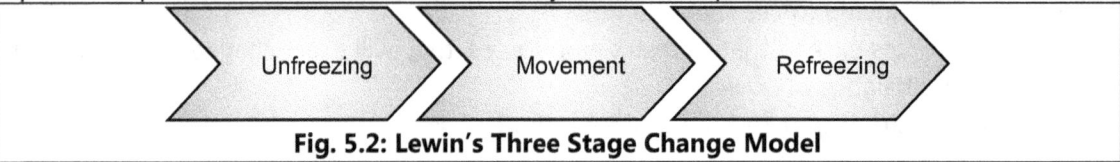

Fig. 5.2: Lewin's Three Stage Change Model

To elaborate on his model, **Lewin** also suggested a three-stage process of change implementation which is necessary for effective change within an organisation. Those three stages are:

- **Unfreezing:** Change efforts to overcome the pressures of both individual resistance and group conformity.
- **Driving Forces:** Forces that direct behaviour away from the status quo.
- **Restraining Forces:** Forces that hinder movement from the existing equilibrium.
- **Refreezing:** Stabilising a change intervention by balancing driving and restraining forces.

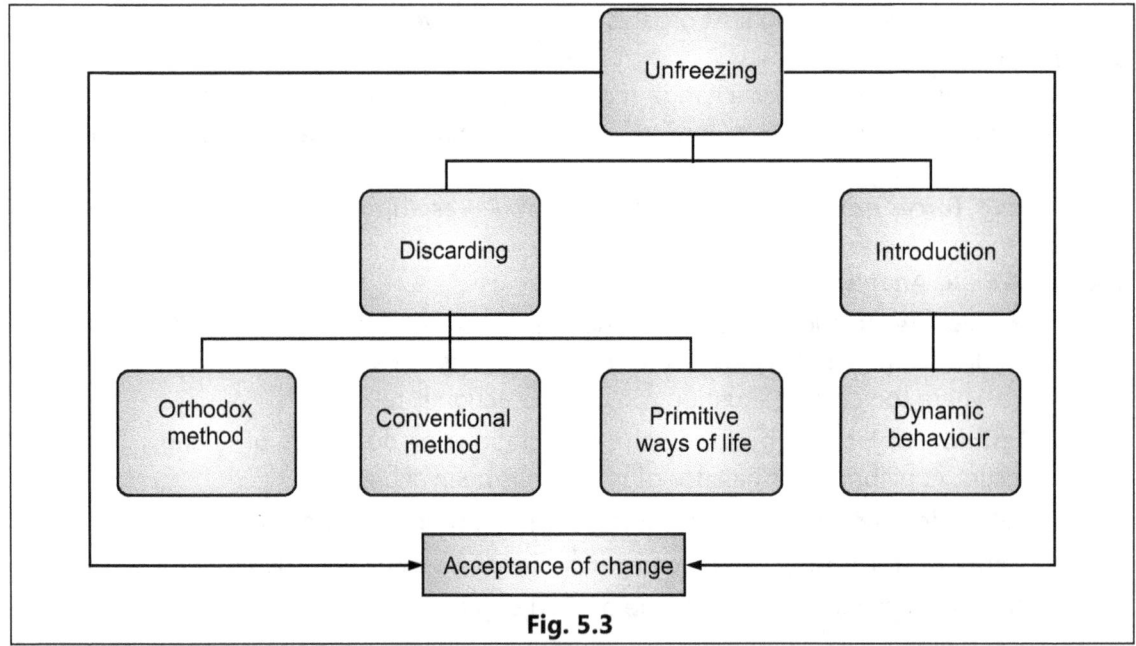

Fig. 5.3

An organisation must be prepared for any change which is about to occur. This process is known as 'unfreezing' and involves the investigation of resisting forces.

Any premature unilateral or authoritarian increase in driving forces for change will, according to the Lewin's model, be met by an equal and opposite increase in resisting forces.

No change will occur unless there is motivation within the organisation to do so. If there is no motivation, it must be induced. This is often the most difficult part of any change process.

Change not only involves learning, but unlearning something that is already present and well integrated into the personality and social relationships of the individuals. It is for this reason that an organisations culture can often act as a resisting force to change.

For a change to become routine and accepted into the day-to-day practices of an organisation, the organisation must go through the final stage of refreezing the organisational system. A variety of strategies may be adopted to achieve this, including new rules, regulations and reward schemes to reinforce the change process and maximise the desired behaviours of staff or employees.

5.2.3 The Seven Stage Model of Change

In 1980, **Edgar Huse** proposed a seven-stage OD model based upon the original three-stage model of **Lewin**.

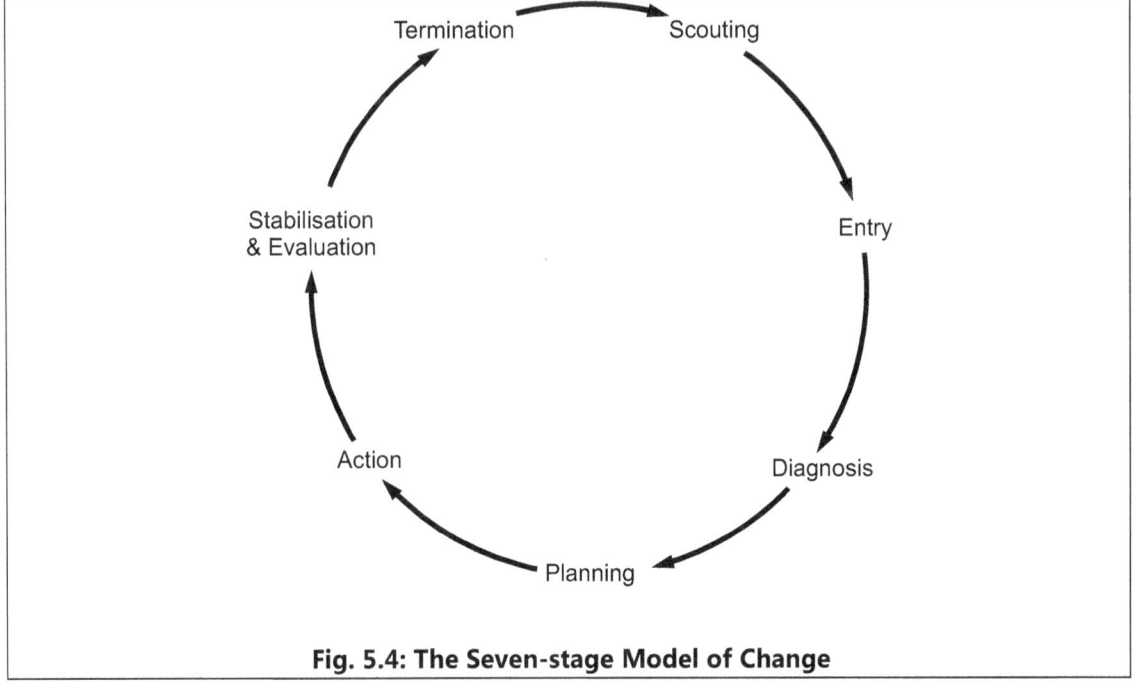

Fig. 5.4: The Seven-stage Model of Change

- **Scouting:** Where representatives from the organisation meet with the OD consultant to identify and discuss the need for change. The change agent and client jointly explore issues to elicit the problems in need of attention.
- **Entry:** This stage involves the development of, and mutual agreement upon, both business and psychological contracts. Expectations of the change process are also established.
- **Diagnosis:** Here, the consultant diagnoses the underlying organisational problems based upon their previous knowledge and training. This stage involves the identification of specific improvement goals and a planned intervention strategy.
- **Planning:** A detailed series of intervention techniques and actions are brought together into a timetable or project plan for the change process. This step also involves the identification of areas of resistance from employees and steps possible to counteract it.
- **Action:** The intervention is carried out according to the agreed plans. Previously established action steps are implemented.
- **Stabilisation and Evaluation:** The stage of 'refreezing' the system. Newly implemented codes of action, practices and systems are absorbed into everyday routines. Evaluation is conducted to determine the success of the change process and any need for further action is established.
- **Termination:** The OD consultant or change agent leaves the organisation and moves on to another client or begins an entirely different project within the same organisation.

Practice: The 7-stage model is a useful heuristic to illustrate the complex nature of organisational change. However, such neat linear models are prone to oversimplify situations. The pace of organisational change in today's rapidly developing economic climate can result in the 'refreezing' stage never being reached or completed. This means that organisational systems often undergo a continuous series of change interventions and rarely revert to a stabilised state of equilibrium. In other words, change is often so rapid and recurrent that the system fails to re-stabilise itself before the next change initiative is conducted. Organisations prone to fashion and fads in managerial practice particularly suffer from this effect.

5.2.4 Eight Step Change Process

There are many theories about how to "do" change. Many originate with leadership and change management guru, **John Kotter**. A professor at Harvard Business School and world-renowned change expert, Kotter introduced his eight-step change process in his 1995 book, **"Leading Change"**.

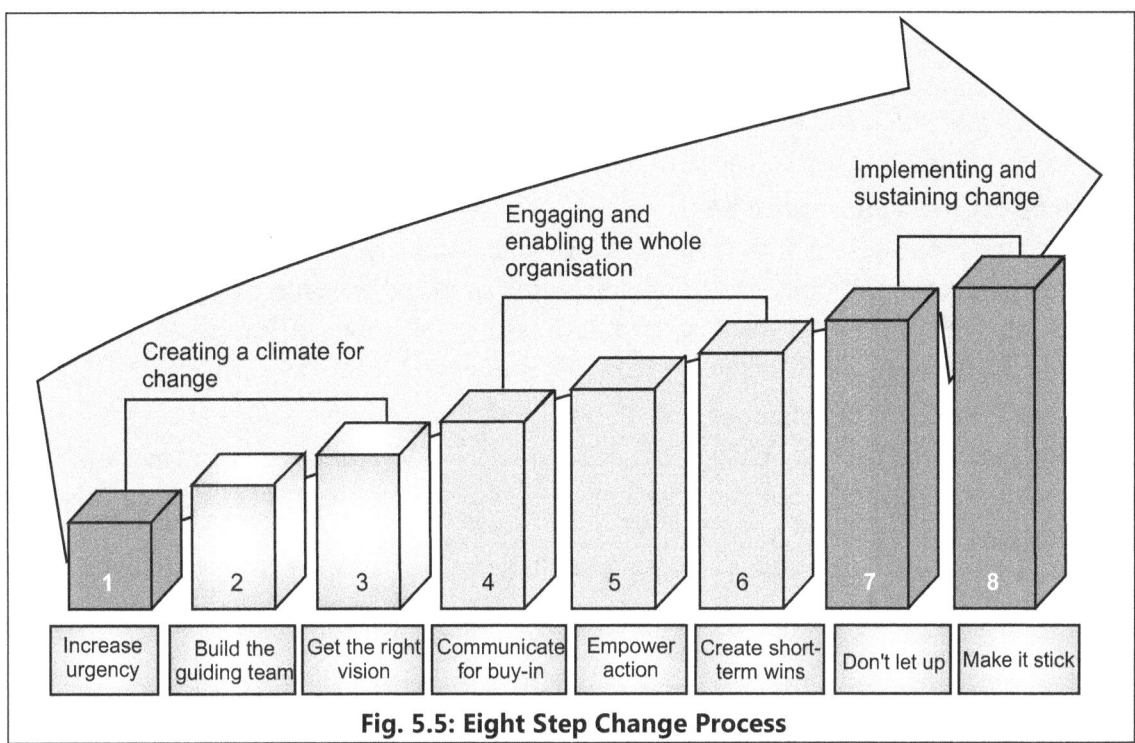

1	Increase urgency
2	Build the guiding team
3	Get the right vision
4	Communicate for buy-in
5	Empower action
6	Create short-term wins
7	Don't let up
8	Make it stick

Creating a climate for change

Engaging and enabling the whole organisation

Implementing and sustaining change

Fig. 5.5: Eight Step Change Process

We look at his eight steps for leading change below.

- **Step 1: Create Urgency**

  For change to happen, it helps if the whole company really wants it. Develop a sense of urgency around the need for change. This may help you spark the initial motivation to get things moving.

- **Step 2: Form a Powerful Coalition**

  Convince people that change is necessary. This often takes strong leadership and visible support from key people within your organisation. Managing change isn't enough – you have to lead it.

- **Step 3: Create a Vision for Change**

  When you first start thinking about change, there will probably be many great ideas and solutions floating around. Link these concepts to an overall vision that people can grasp easily and remember.

- **Step 4: Demonstrate the kind of behaviour that you want from others.**

  What you do with your vision after you create it will determine your success. Your message will probably have strong competition from other day-to-day communications within the company, so you need to communicate it frequently and powerfully, and embed it within everything that you do.

- **Step 5: Remove Obstacles**

  If you follow these steps and reach this point in the change process, you've been talking about your vision and building buy-in from all levels of the organisation. Hopefully, your staffs want to get busy and achieve the benefits that you've been promoting.

- **Step 6: Create Short-term Wins**

  Nothing motivates more than success. Give your company a taste of victory early in the change process. Within a short time frame (this could be a month or a year, depending on the type of change), you'll want to have results that your staff can see. Without this, critics and negative thinkers might hurt your progress.

- **Step 7: Build on the Change**

  Kotter argues that many change projects fail because victory is declared too early. Real change runs deep. Quick wins are only the beginning of what needs to be done to achieve long-term change.

  Launching one new product using a new system is great. But if you can launch 10 products, that means the new system is working. To reach that 10th success, you need to keep looking for improvements.

- **Step 8: Anchor the Changes in Corporate Culture**

  Finally, to make any change stick, it should become part of the core of your organisation. Your corporate culture often determines what gets done, so the values behind your vision must show in day-to-day work.

  Make continuous efforts to ensure that the change is seen in every aspect of your organisation. This will help give that change a solid place in your organisation's culture.

Key Points

You have to work hard to change an organisation successfully. When you plan carefully and build the proper foundation, implementing change can be much easier, and you'll improve the chances of success. If you're too impatient, and if you expect too many results too soon, your plans for change are more likely to fail.

Create a sense of urgency, recruit powerful change leaders, build a vision and effectively communicate it, remove obstacles, create quick wins, and build on your momentum. If you do these things, you can help make the change part of your organisational culture. That's when you can declare a true victory then sit back and enjoy the change that you envisioned so long ago.

5.2.5 Popular Change Management Interventions

- **Survey Feedback:** A complex and skilled set of procedures involving the design, administration, analysis and feedback of a series of questionnaires to tap staff attitudes and opinions. Feedback meetings are also held with staff to change attitudes and modify behaviour.

- **Quality Circles (QCs):** Where small groups of employees who work in a similar field meet regularly to identify, analyse, and solve product-quality and production problems and to improve general operations. It helps to motivate change by increasing perceptions of employee participation, communication and job satisfaction. Although QCs have been shown to influence staff attitudes, this impact may not necessarily translate into higher levels of production.

- **Process Consultation (PC):** A client-centred approach to help the client organisation to help itself. PC has the underlying objective of facilitating and developing the capacity of the client organisation to self-rejuvenate over the longer term. The process of PC is a set of activities conducted by the OD consultant that helps the client to perceive, understand, and act upon the process events that occur in the client's environment in order to improve the situation. PC may be compared to the 'purchase of expertise' concept and the 'doctor-patient' analogy.

- **Team Building:** Groups of workers are formed into 'T-groups' (or 'encounter groups') and examine intra-group processes and their own interpersonal styles and impacts upon others. However, there is weak evidence of success as T-groups are often poorly facilitated and are commonly left purposefully unstructured by the 'trainers'.

5.2.6 The Focus of Change Management Agents

- **Technician:** The client organisation diagnoses their own problems and formulates their own solutions. The OD consultant merely comes in to implement their plans. In this situation the organisation is in complete control.

- **Expert:** The client organisation diagnoses their problems and the consultant is hired to propose solutions. In this case there is a joint ownership of the solution.

- **Coach:** In this case the organisation is aware of a problem and can see symptoms but is not certain what exactly the problem is, or how to go about finding a solution. Here, the consultant helps the organisation to understand their problems. In this scenario there is a joint ownership of both the problem and solution between the consultant and the organisation.

- **Mentor/Counsellor:** Relationship based on support and partnership enables organisation to help itself. Consultant operates at very senior level, sets up future success, as the organisation solves its own problems.

5.2.7 Managing Organisational Change

Organisational change occurs when a company makes a transition from its current state to some desired future state.

Organisational change occurs when a company makes a transition from its current state to some desired future state. Managing organisational change is the process of planning and implementing change in organisations in such a way, as to minimise employee resistance and cost to the organisation while simultaneously maximising the effectiveness of the change effort.

Today's business environment requires companies to undergo changes almost constantly if they are to remain competitive. Factors such as globalisation of markets and rapidly evolving technology force businesses to respond in order to survive. Such changes may be relatively minor—as in the case of installing a new software programme—or quite major—as in the case of refocusing an overall marketing strategy, fighting off a hostile takeover, or transforming a company in the face of persistent foreign competition.

Organisational change initiatives often arise out of problems faced by a company. In some cases, however, companies change under the impetus of enlightened leaders who first recognise and then exploit new potentials dormant in the organisation or its circumstances. Some observers, more soberly, label this a "performance gap" which able management is inspired to close. But organisational change is also resisted and—in the opinion of its promoters—fails. The failure may be due to the manner in which change has been visualised, announced, and implemented or because internal resistance to it builds.

Employees, in other words, sabotage those changes they view as antithetical to their own interests.

Areas of Organisational Change

The first area, strategic change, can take place on a large scale—for example, when a company shifts its resources to enter a new line of business—or on a small scale—for example, when a company makes productivity improvements in order to reduce costs.

There are three basic stages for a company making a strategic change:

(1) Realising that the current strategy is no longer suitable for the company's situation;

(2) Establishing a vision for the company's future direction; and

(3) Implementing the change and setting up new systems to support it.

Technological changes are often introduced as components of larger strategic changes, although they sometimes take place on their own.

An important aspect of changing technology is determining who in the organisation will be threatened by the change. To be successful, a technology change must be incorporated into the company's overall systems, and a management structure must be created to support it.

Structural changes can also occur due to strategic changes—as in the case where a company decides to acquire another business and must integrate it—as well as due to operational changes or changes in managerial style. For example, a company that wished to implement more participative decision making might need to change its hierarchical structure.

> *Almost, always people changes are the most difficult and important part of the overall change process.*

People changes can become necessary due to other changes, or sometimes companies simply seek to change workers' attitudes and behaviours in order to increase their effectiveness or to stimulate individual or team creativeness.

Almost always people changes are the most difficult and important part of the overall change process. The science of organisation development was created to deal with changing people on the job through techniques such as education and training, team building, and career planning.

5.2.8 Resistance to Change

Resistance to change is normal; people cling to habits and to the status quo.

A manager trying to implement a change, no matter how small, should expect to encounter some resistance from within the organisation.

Resistance to change is normal; people cling to habits and to the status quo. To be sure, managerial actions can minimize or arouse resistance. People must be motivated to shake off old habits. This must take place in stages rather than abruptly so that "managed change" takes on the character of "natural change." In addition to normal inertia, organisation change introduces anxieties about the future. If the future after the change comes to be perceived positively, resistance will be less.

Education and communication are therefore key ingredients in minimizing negative reactions.

Employees can be informed about both the nature of the change and the logic behind it before it takes place through reports, memos, group presentations, or individual discussions. Another important component of overcoming resistance is inviting employee participation and involvement in both the design and implementation phases of the change effort. Organised forms of facilitation and support can be deployed. Managers can ensure that employees will have the resources to bring the change about; managers can make themselves available to provide explanations and to minimize stress arising in many scores of situations.

Some companies manage to overcome resistance to change through negotiation and rewards.

- Some companies manage to overcome resistance to change through negotiation and rewards. They offer employees concrete incentives to ensure their cooperation.
- Other companies resort to manipulation, or using subtle tactics such as giving a resistance leader a prominent position in the change effort.

- A final option is coercion, which involves punishing people who resist or using force to ensure their cooperation. Although this method can be useful when speed is of the essence, it can have lingering negative effects on the company.
- Of course, no method is appropriate to every situation, and a number of different methods may be combined as needed.

Change is a continuous and natural process. Change is essential for the survival and growth of a business enterprise. In order to be successful, an enterprise has to forecast change so that the advantage of the opportunities offered can be taken. The employees resist change. It should be an objective of the management to analyse the sources and causes for resistance to change, to overcome the resistance, to build in its organization an awareness of change and to develop an ability in itself to forecast it and also to form favourable attitude towards change.

Why people resist change? / Reasons of resistance to change by people?

The basic problem in the management of change is the study of reasons of resistance to change. Change is a persistent phenomenon but people resist change in the context of their pattern of life or in the context of their situations in the organization. Change of any type demands readjustment while it is not simple, possible and favourable to all. Hence, resistance to change is also very usual as the change itself.

I. Resistance by employees

(A) Economic Causes

1. **Fear of losing job or reduction in employment:** Due to the change in technology, methods of work, use of automatic machines, quantity or quality of work, people think that there will be a reduction in their employment opportunities as they will not be able to cope up with the machines. This fear leads to resistance to change on the part of the workers.

2. **Insecurity of job:** Generally, change in technology, is expected to result in technical unemployment as old employees may not be able to handle new machines. Hence, the fear of unemployment leads to resistance to change. Such resistance is individual as well as collective. (See chart given above).

3. **Doubt about future or fear of obsolescence:** The employees may fear that they may be demoted, if they do not possess the new skills required for their jobs after the introduction of change. There is uncertainty of adjustment, separation of group, etc. Hence, they prefer statusquo positions.

4. **Fear and increased work load:** Change in work technology and methods may results in the fear that work-load will be increased while there will be no corresponding increase in their remuneration. This feeling results in resistance to change.

(B) Personal Causes

1. **Requirement of training:** If due to changes in technology and work, the organisation requires training and relearning for employees, it may lead to resistance as all persons may not like to undergo refreshers and training courses.

2. **Boredom and monotony:** If the proposed change is expected to lead to greater specialisation resulting in boredom and monotony, it may also be resisted by people.

3. **Non-involvement in decision-making:** If employees are not allowed to take part in the decision-making process for change, then they may resist any change. When they do not understand fully the implications of change, they resist it. Some employees resist change as it implies a criticism of the present methods as inadequate or unsuitable for which they may not agree.

(C) Social causes

1. **Need for new social adjustment:** Any organizational change requires new social adjustments with the group, work situation and new employer. All individuals are not ready to accept this challenge. Some people even refuse promotions on this ground as they may have to break their present social contacts.

2. **Taking change as pressure of outside power:** Some employees take any change as imposed from outside, power upon them. This happens particularly when change is brought about abruptly. If employees are consulted and given due participation in the process of introducing change then their objection and resistance can be minimised.

3. **Orthodox mentally:** Some employees consider that every change is for the benefit of the management and enterprise itself, rather than the benefits of employees or even the general public. Hence, they resist change.

II. Resistance by management

The management opposes changes because of the following reasons:

1. **Increase in responsibility:** Due to changes in the methods of working, the management also finds it difficult in adjustments with the workers. Management has to train the workers to new atmospheres and changes in process and production. It has to assign new responsibilities to them which imposes new tensions, stresses and strains on them.

2. **Changes on experimental basis:** Many a times, changes are made on an experimental basis. If the changes are appropriate and adjust to circumstances, they will be accepted otherwise rejected. Because of this feeling of uncertainty to handle new circumstances, they oppose.

3. **Indifference of the top management:** The behavior and attitudes of the top management are critical in the implementation of change. If the top management does not show much enthusiasm or interest in the change, the people at lower levels will have increased resistance to change.

4. **Changes introduced by labour union or government:** Management opposes because the changes suggested by labour unions or government sometimes may not be favourable to certain industries. They may feel disgraced and hence oppose.

5. **Increase in costs:** The management feels that change is necessary but due to cost involvement, resists the change.

5.2.9 Techniques For Managing Change Effectively

Managing change effectively requires moving the organisation from its current state to a future desired state at minimal cost to the organisation. Key steps in that process are:

1. **Understanding the current state of the organisation:** This involves identifying problems the company faces, assigning a level of importance to each one, and assessing the kinds of changes needed to solve the problems.

2. **Competently envisioning and laying out the desired future state of the organisation:** This involves picturing the ideal situation for the company after the change is implemented, conveying this vision clearly to everyone involved in the change effort, and designing a means of transition to the new state.

    An important part of the transition should be maintaining some sort of stability; some things—such as the company's overall mission or key personnel—should remain constant in the midst of turmoil to help reduce people's anxiety.

3. **Implementing the change in an orderly manner:** This involves managing the transition effectively. It might be helpful to draw up a plan, allocate resources, and appoint a key person to take charge of the change process.

    The company's leaders should try to generate enthusiasm for the change by sharing their goals and vision and acting as role models. In some cases, it may be useful to try for small victories first in order to pave the way for later successes.

Change is natural, of course. Proactive management of change to optimise future adaptability is invariably a more creative way of dealing with the dynamisms of industrial transformation than letting them happen willy-nilly. That process will succeed better with the help of the company's human resources than without.

5.2.10 Techniques for Implementing Change in an Organisation

As an organisation grows and evolves, it will experience change. Implementing change can be a challenge if improper techniques are used. Developing efficient ways to introduce and implement change can ease the stress your staffs feels when change is introduced, and it can also help your vendors, customers and business partners adjust to any changes in the way you do business.

- **Ownership**

When your employees are on board with organisational change, they can then make the internal transition smoother and help clients and vendors adjust as well.

A technique that can get employees personally involved in change is to encourage them to look at the business as though they were running it.

Virgin International CEO Richard Branson, writing on the Entrepreneur website, says that having employees think like entrepreneurs by letting each employee know how their impact on implementing change can improve profitability makes change a personal responsibility.

- **Map it out**

If you leave too much to the staff's imagination when it comes to change, that can create misinformation and make change management difficult.

In the Kotter 8-Step Change Model, it is recommended that employees be given the details of what the change is and how it will affect the company. Trying to make drastic changes without informing employees of the nature of the changes can create confusion. Tell employees exactly what is going on and create understanding from the beginning.

- **Go in stages**

Change should be implemented in stages. Create the sense of urgency that gathers support for change. Then develop a solution that should be rolled out on a trial basis. Do not go live with the change immediately. Have a small group of employees try the change first to work out any errors and make any changes. Then slowly integrate the change into your organisation. This gives employees a chance to become familiar with the changes being made and adjust to them gradually.

- **Get everyone involved**

For change to take hold, the entire management and executive teams need to get involved and create enthusiasm among the staff. Even if a manager or executive is not directly involved in the change, his/her support for the new plan can help the staff feel more at ease. When the management team shows unified support for an initiative, it is easier for employees to accept.

Technology is introducing a lot of change in the business world. Companies are struggling with security and cost strategies for BYOD (bring your own device) and mobile applications, deciding which applications and processes to move to the cloud, ensuring effectiveness in business intelligence and Big Data solutions, incorporating social media data for a holistic customer view and implementing a collaborative environment.

Whatever the change, there is one question on every executive's mind: "How do I ensure that this change gets the return that I need?"

If your change programme does not deliver the intended return, there are three possible causal factors:

- Your employees weren't engaged in implementing or accepting the change introduced by your business strategy.
- Your leaders weren't successful in connecting employees to the change.
- Your business system didn't adequately support the change.

5.2.11 Steps to be taken by Management to Overcome the Resistance to Change

Management is responsible for bringing various changes. Hence, it acts as an agent for the changes. If the management has to introduce change slowly and successfully in the organiSation, it has to overcome the resistance and make it a successful venture. An atmosphere for change is to be created. The management must realise that resistance to change is basically a human problem, though on surface, it may appear to be related to technical aspects of change. So, it must be tackled in a human and social manner. In short, the following steps can be taken by management to facilitate change acceptance.

1. **Discussion about the changes with workers/employees:** Before introducing any change, the employees should be fully consulted and they must be made a party to any such decision. The meaning and purpose of the change must be fully communicated to those who will be affected by it. Sufficient time should be allowed for discussion and for inviting their suggestions.

2. **Proper planning for change:** Changes should not be forced at once. They should be planned. People should get an opportunity to participate both in planning the change and installing it. This will help the group of the affected people to recognise the need for change and thus prepare themselves for receiving it without any fear. The time, place and quantum of change should be determined and the mode of introduction of change should also be planned.

3. **Protection of the interest of employees:** Management should ensure that employees will be protected from economic loss in status or personal dignity. If these things are protected, the degree of resistance to change will be very low.

4. **Group dynamics:** Group dynamics refers to the everchanging interactions and adjustments in the mutual perceptions and relationships among members of the groups. Such group interactions are the most powerful instruments which facilitate or inhibit adaptation to change. Adaptation is a team activity which requires conformity to the new group norms, criterion, traditions and work patterns and styles. If these could be positively introduced by the management and group-based techniques for introduction of change are adopted, the results are likely to be more successful and durable.

5. **Changes should be slow in parts:** The management should not introduce any change at once and abruptly. The management must create awareness of change and develop an ability to be introduced in parts. If possible, the results must be reviewed and if required, adjustments must be made in it. This will not overload the management with responsibility and the whole system of change can be introduced with tested results at each stage.

6. **Proper training:** In order to bring firmness in the changed order, the concerned employees should be properly trained. They should be able to know new techniques and knowledge. The concerned employees should be given orientation training. The policy of positive motivation should be used.

7. **Sharing of income:** The extra income desired from changes should not be taken away by the management only, but should be shared with all the employees.

5.2.12 Forms of Resistance to Change

- Overt and immediate,
- Voicing complaints, engaging in job actions,
- Implicit and deferred.
    - Loss of employee loyalty and motivation, increased errors or mistakes, increased absenteeism.

Tactics for Dealing with Resistance to Change
- Education and communication
- Participation
- Facilitation and support
- Negotiation
- Manipulation and cooptation
- Coercion

5.2.13 How to Recognise Whether Employees are Engaged in Implementing Change

An Employee Engagement Report published by Blessing White in 2011 found that globally only 31 percentage of employees were engaged and 17 percentage were disengaged at their company. You need employees to engage in the implementation of your business strategy and to accept the subsequent change. How do you know if employees are engaged? One way is to recognise employee behaviour patterns.

The following behaviours describe employees who are not engaged:
- **Passive behaviours:** They do the bare minimum to implement your strategy and barely use what has changed after implementation.

- **Passive-aggressive behaviours:** They support the change in front of you, then undermine the change behind your back.
- **Dominant behaviours:** They are openly defiant about the change.
- **Independent behaviours:** They continue to do things their own way regardless of what the change requires.

> ***Knowing that your employees are not engaged is the first step to getting their support for your change programme.***

The desired behaviour from employees is interdependent behaviour — where they collaborate with each other and their managers on how to best implement the change and how to continually improve results after the change.

5.2.14 Overcoming Resistance at Organisational and Individual Level

Organisational Level:

Overcoming resistance at organisational level are as follows:

- **Overcoming Undefined Goals and Objectives:** Goals and Objectives should be frequently redefined and relayed to all employees. This shall aid towards clearing up any misunderstanding and possible conflicts.

- **Overcoming Financial and Environmental Issues:** Organisations should have a contingency fund to cater for changes in demand or develop a very good relationship with their bank manager in case you need to borrow money at hard times. At the other end of the scale if demand sores suppliers must be able to satisfy demand. Benchmarking suppliers shall help determine your best suppliers.

  A good supplier may be one that allows you to have a 30 day or more credit account, which leave you with more working capital. Essentially corporate business strategies should have a degree of flexibility to act as a defence to sudden changes.

- **Overcoming Structural Problems and Insufficient Communication:** In a large organisation, employees may wish to elect a spokes person who can act as a collective voice to air potential barriers directly to management. Surveys can be conducted and results analysed. In a small organisation employees should be encouraged to speak up if they feel that change is causing a conflict.

- **Overcoming Lack of or Bad Leadership:** It is a natural human instinct to follow leadership as children we look up to our parents and as adults we look up towards our superiors. Leaders must lead the way and be an example for others to follow. In leading and setting an example to others leaders must take an active role a "hands on approach" side by side with the employees in order to motivate and encourage.

- **Overcoming Lack of Preparation for New Roles:** The importance of planning must be emphasised and reflected. The new roles should be concisely explained to the respective employees prior to implementing change, to stifle out any doubts, fears or resistance.
- **Overcoming Cultural Issues:** The cultural characteristics once identified need to be overcome and evolved into a non-blame culture. By doing so the employees shall have the freedom to evolve and try innovative ways of doing their jobs without the fear of being penalised for mistakes.

Individual Level:

Employees should be directly involved in the change process, which shall motivate and reduce resistance. Extra incentives should be made available to further encourage and reward compliance. Support networks should be established as a means to reinforce the change theory. Maslow's Hierarchy of Needs depicts the theory of psychological needs, values of authority, hierarchy and rationality, security needs.

The model consists of many levels. Maslow argues that once the basic level of air, food, water and sex are met the next "hierarchical" or "rational" need is for safety. An organisation must concentrate on invoking a sense of "Belonging" to the organisation by keeping them informed, involved and sharing the success.

"Esteem by others" should be achieved by promoting teamwork and the occasional appraisals by management.

5.2.15 Facilitating Change

How the Business System and Culture Impacts the Success of Change

Business systems are another reason that change efforts fail or aren't as successful as they could be. Your business system comprises your organisational structure, management systems, processes and information technology. Change programmes often address only some of the business system components, but success requires addressing all of them. For example, a company may acquire another company and only focus on how the acquired company fits into its organisational structure.

Its acquisition business strategy does not consider needed changes to management systems, processes and information systems. The acquired company may be brought in as a separate business unit and, for the most part, allowed to operate autonomously. And then the executives wonder why the synergies that they hoped to gain were not achieved.

Executives need to look at the whole business system to ensure that all needed changes are implemented to support the business strategy. With any system, if three things are broken, the system won't run properly if you only fix one or two of the problems.

Additionally, business systems have certain characteristics built into them that don't encourage the right behaviours from employees and leaders, thereby negatively impacting change programmes. For example, hierarchical organisation structures with strict chains of command and bureaucratic processes that require frequent management approvals encourage leaders to use more authoritarian behaviours and employees to use more passive behaviours.

These business system characteristics usually don't support change programmes well since they don't provide the flexibility necessary for successful implementation.

Other examples of business system characteristics that don't encourage the right employee and leadership behaviours are decentralised management plans, unclear roles and responsibilities and flexible and unenforced processes. These characteristics encourage a laissez-faire/independent culture. This makes it difficult for employees to meet business objectives and leverage the teamwork that is often required to successfully implement today's business change programme.

Business systems that include characteristics such as supportive organisation structures, aligned management plans, shared data and end-to-end processes encourage leaders to use more connective behaviours and employees to use more interdependent behaviours.

These characteristics provide employees the freedom and support to complete change implementation tasks and to solve problems in a timely and accurate manner. These characteristics also provide a collaborative environment for employees to work together and to see how their efforts impact others.

5.2.16 Factors that benefit Change Programmes

Most change programmes would benefit from the following three critical success factors:

1. **Engaged employees**: Encouraging employees to use interdependent behaviours will help them get engaged in your change effort.
2. **Effective leadership**: Coaching and mentoring your leaders on connective behaviours will help them encourage interdependent behaviours from employees.
3. **Business system characteristics that are right for the change**: Improving your business system characteristics to encourage the right leadership and employee behaviours will give your change programme a higher chance of succeeding.

Together, these three critical success factors are a holistic approach to creating business success through change and, at the same time, improving happiness among employees and managers.

5.2.17 Developing a Learning Organisation

The Learning Organisation Model:

Definition: *A learning organisation is the term given to a company that facilitates the learning of its members and continuously transforms itself.*

Learning organisations develop as a result of the pressures facing modern organisations and enables them to remain competitive in the business environment. The Learning organisation concept was coined through the work and research of **Peter Senge** and his colleagues. It encourages organisations to shift to a more interconnected way of thinking. Organisations should become more like communities that employees can feel a commitment to. They will work harder for an organisation they are committed to.

Features:

A learning organisation has five main features:
- Systems Thinking
- Personal Mastery
- Mental Models
- Shared Vision and
- Team Learning.

• **Systems thinking**

The idea of the learning organisation developed from a body of work called systems thinking. This is a conceptual framework that allows people to study businesses as bounded objects. Learning organisations use this method of thinking when assessing their company and have information systems that measure the performance of the organisation as a whole and of its various components. Systems' thinking states that all the characteristics must be apparent at once in an organisation for it to be a learning organisation. If some of these characteristics are missing, then the organisation will fall short of its goal. However it is believed that the characteristics of a learning organisation are factors that are gradually acquired, rather than developed simultaneously.

• **Personal Mastery**

The commitment by an individual to the process of learning is known as personal mastery. There is a competitive advantage for an organisation whose workforce can learn more quickly than the workforce of other organisations. Individual learning is acquired through staff training and development; however learning cannot be forced upon an individual who is not receptive to learning. Research shows that most learning in the workplace is incidental, rather than the product of formal training; therefore it is important to develop a culture where personal mastery is practiced in daily life. A learning organisation has been described as the sum of individual learning, but there must be mechanisms for individual learning to be transferred into organisational learning.

- **Mental Model**

    The assumptions held by individuals and organisations are called mental models. To become a learning organisation, these models must be challenged. Individuals tend to espouse theories, which are what they intend to follow, and theories-in-use, which are what they actually do. Similarly, organisations tend to have 'memories' which preserve certain behaviours, norms and values. In creating a learning environment it is important to replace confrontational attitudes with an open culture that promotes inquiry and trust. To achieve this, the learning organisation needs mechanisms for locating and assessing organisational theories of action. Unwanted values need to be discarded in a process called 'unlearning'. **Wang and Ahmed** refer to this as 'triple loop learning.'

- **Shared Vision**

    The development of a shared vision is important in motivating the staff to learn, as it creates a common identity that provides focus and energy for learning. The most successful visions build on the individual visions of the employees at all levels of the organisation, thus the creation of a shared vision can be hindered by traditional structures where the company vision is imposed from above. Therefore, learning organisations tend to have flat, decentralised organisational structures. The shared vision is often to succeed against a competitor, however **Senge** states that these are transitory goals and suggests that there should also be long term goals that are intrinsic within the company.

- **Team Learning**

    The accumulation of individual learning constitutes Team learning. The benefit of team or shared learning is that staffs grow more quickly and the problem solving capacity of the organisation is improved through better access to knowledge and expertise. Learning organisations have structures that facilitate team learning with features such as boundary crossing and openness. Team learning requires individuals to engage in dialogue and discussion; therefore team members must develop open communication, shared meaning, and shared understanding. Learning organisations typically have excellent knowledge management structures, allowing creation, acquisition, dissemination, and implementation of this knowledge in the organisation.

Development

    Organisations do not organically develop into learning organisations; there are factors prompting their change.

- As organisations grow, they lose their capacity to learn as company structures and individual thinking becomes rigid.
- When problems arise, the proposed solutions often turn out to be only short term (single loop learning) and re-emerge in the future.

- To remain competitive, many organisations have restructured, with fewer people in the company. This means those who remain need to work more effectively.

- To create a competitive advantage, companies need to learn faster than their competitors and to develop a customer responsive culture.

- Argyris, identified that organisations need to maintain knowledge about new products and processes, understand what is happening in the outside environment and produce creative solutions using the knowledge and skills of all within the organisation.

- This requires co-operation between individuals and groups, free and reliable communication, and a culture of trust.

Characteristics

There is a multitude of definitions of a learning organisation as well as their typologies.

Benefits

The main benefits are:

- Maintaining levels of innovation and remaining competitive.
- Being better placed to respond to external pressures.
- Having the knowledge to better link resources to customer needs.
- Improving quality of outputs at all levels.
- Improving Corporate image by becoming more people oriented.
- Increasing the pace of change within the organisation.

Barriers

Even within or without learning organisation, problems can stall the process of learning or cause it to regress. Most of them arise from an organisation not fully embracing all the necessary facets. Once these problems can be identified, work can begin on improving them.

In addition, organisational size may become the barrier to internal knowledge sharing. When the number of employees exceeds 150, internal knowledge sharing dramatically decreases because of higher complexity in the formal organisational structure, weaker inter-employee relationships, lower trust, reduced connective efficacy/efficiency, and less effective communication.

As such, as the size of an organisational unit increases, the effectiveness of internal knowledge flows dramatically diminishes and the degree of intra-organisational knowledge sharing decreases.

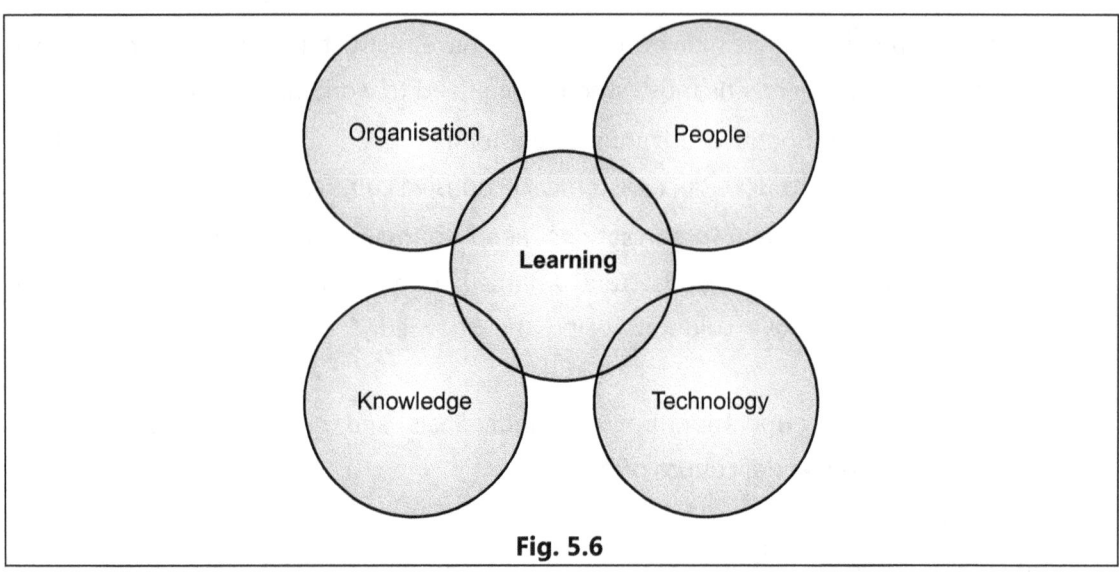

Fig. 5.6

The Learning Organisation Model

The subsystems of a learning organisation:

- Organisation,
- People,
- Knowledge,
- Technology.

Each subsystem supports the others in magnifying the learning as it permeates across/flows throughout the system.

- **Organisation**
- There is an inspiring vision for learning and an organisational learning strategy that clearly communicates that learning is critical to organisational success.
- Leaders take an exemplary leading role in creating and sustaining a supportive learning culture.
- The formal organisational structure facilitates learning, adaptation, and change.
- Sanctioned informal organisational structures enable and encourage learning across formal structural boundaries.
- Good use is made of communication systems to facilitate the lateral transfer of information and knowledge and to minimise the development of "silos."
- Adequate resources are allocated for learning in terms of time allocation, specialist support staff, budgets for knowledge management infrastructure, formal and informal communities of practice and other value networks, and learning and development programmes.

- A balanced approach to learning that recognises the importance of both planned and emergent learning is taken.
- Planned learning is addressed through the careful design of strategy, structure, systems, procedures, and plans.
- Emergent learning is encouraged by creating opportunities for informal sharing of knowledge and experience.
- Failures and unintended outcomes are the focus of constructive discussions leading to new approaches. When such incidents involve clients, care is taken to protect their reputation.

- **People**
- Staff members are required to be reflective practitioners to reflect on their experience, develop experience-based theories of change, continuously test these in practice with colleagues, and use their understanding and initiative to contribute to knowledge development.
- All staff members make frequent use of a range of tools, methods, and approaches for learning and collaborating with others.
- Staff members experience a high level of psychological safety and trust; they can rely on colleagues and are not exposed to unfair negative criticism.
- Teams operate as learning communities in which success and unexpected outcomes are analysed and in which sensitively expressed dissent, conflict, and debate are encouraged as positive sources of learning.
- Staff members are encouraged to look outside the organisation for new ideas, trends, and practices and to share what they learn with colleagues.
- Equal attention is paid to developing and retaining staff members at all levels.
- Staff members successfully use a wide range of opportunities for individual and team-based learning and development.
- Time and effort spent by staff members on learning and knowledge development are recognised as core activities in the organisation's time and performance management systems.
- A wide range of formal and informal rewards and incentives for contributing to organisational learning and knowledge development is used (e.g., career advancement, increased income, informal peer status, additional time provided for study, and public acknowledgment for innovative contributions made).
- Leadership (based on the possession of expertise and knowledge) is expected from staff members at all levels in the organisational hierarchy.

- **Knowledge**
- There is a widespread recognition that while knowledge is created in the minds of individuals, knowledge development thrives in a rich web of professional networks among individuals.
- Important knowledge is easily accessible to people who need and use it.
- There are creative opportunities for knowledge to be developed and shared with others by facilitating networks between individuals.
- The design and delivery of products and services demonstrate how effective the organisation is at applying what it has learned about the nature of good practice.
- The necessary systems and infrastructure for knowledge management are in place, understood, and working effectively.
- Evaluations are carefully designed with learning (as well as accountability) in mind. Systems ensure that the outputs of internal and independent evaluations are made widely available; carefully examined; and used to influence decision making and planning, question orthodox thinking, and trigger creativity and innovation.
- Peer assists, drawing on individuals' expertise and documented lessons learned, are used in planning new initiatives to reduce the likelihood of repeated and unintended negative outcomes.
- The organisation has a resilient organisational memory and is not vulnerable to the loss of important knowledge when staff members move to other jobs in the organisation or leave.
- Individuals and teams successfully use a range of methods for surfacing their tacit knowledge and making it available to others, for example, by using carefully targeted documentation and collaborative working practices.
- Adoption of after-action reviews and retrospect to learn from experience has been successful.
- The use of a six-point scale from Strongly Agree to Strongly Disagree is recommended.
- **Technology**
- There is a thorough and shared understanding of the value of information and communication technologies for knowledge management and learning.
- Information and communication technologies facilitate but do not drive or constrain knowledge management and learning in the organisation.
- Information and communication technologies are successfully used to create and sustain learning communities.

- Information and communication technologies are successfully used to keep people informed and aware of corporate developments.
- Information and communication technologies are successfully used to create unexpected, helpful connections between people and to provide access to their knowledge and ideas.
- Information and communication technologies are successfully used to encourage innovation and creativity.
- Information and communication technologies are successfully used to enable people to share and learn from good practices and unintended outcomes.
- Information and communication technologies are successfully used to enable people to identify internal sources of expertise.
- Creative use of information and communication technologies is high. At least five of the following have been successfully adopted: shared document drives, intranet pages, online communities and networks, wikis and other means of collaborative document production, blogging, online storytelling, lessons learned databases, staff profile pages, online webinars, podcasts, and social network mapping.
- Sufficient opportunities are provided for staff members to learn how to make use of available information and communication technologies for learning and knowledge sharing.

5.3 Stress

5.3.1 Introduction

Greater work load and having to work longer hours because of downsizing at their companies has resulted in greater employee stress.

BPO's invest heavily in theme days, after work treats and many other tricks to keep employees going and reduce work related stress. The call centre employee's job has been rated as the most stressful job in the world – the physical and mental demands of dedicated and interactive work at night force many of them to quit their jobs. The work is highly pressurised, closely monitored, and monstrously routine. Employees suffer from mental strain, physical illness, sleep disorders, digestive trouble and eye sight problems.

Definition: *A dynamic condition in which an individual is confronted with an opportunity, constraint, or demand related to what he or she desires and for which the outcome is perceived to be both uncertain and important.*

Stress is not necessarily bad in and of, itself. It can also have a positive value. It is an opportunity when it offers potential gain. Many professionals see the pressures of heavy workloads and deadlines as positive challenges that enhance the quality of their work and satisfaction they get from their jobs.

5.3.2 Causes of Stress

There are three categories of potential stressors:

Environmental, Organisational, and Personal.

- **Environmental** uncertainty is the biggest reason people have trouble coping with organisational troubles.
- Pressures to avoid errors and complete tasks in a limited time, work overload, demanding and insensitive boss, and unpleasant co-workers, are a few examples of **organisational** factors that cause stress.
- The experiences and problems that people encounter in the non-working hours can spill over to the job and are **personal** factors that cause stress.

Stress builds up and each new and persistent stressor adds to an individual stress level.

A.   Environmental Factors

- Economic uncertainties of the business cycle.
- Political uncertainties of political systems.
- Technological uncertainties of technical innovations.
- Terrorism in threats to physical safety and security.

B.   Organisational Factors

- Task demands related to the job.
- Role demands of functioning in an organisation.
- Interpersonal demands created by other employees.
- Organisational structure (rules and regulations).
- Organisational leadership (managerial style).
- Organisation's life stage (growth, stability, or decline).

C.   Individual Factors

- Family and personal relationships.
- Economic problems from exceeding earning capacity.
- Personality problems arising for basic disposition.

Individual differences in term to their ability to handle stress play an important role in causing stress. Some people thrive on stressful situations, while others are overwhelmed by them.

Individual Differences

- Perceptual variations of how reality will affect the individual's future.
- Greater job experience moderates stress effects.
- Social support buffers job stress.
- Internal locus of control lowers perceived job stress.
- Strong feelings of self-efficacy reduce reactions to job stress.

5.3.3 Consequences of Stress

An individual who is experiencing high level of stress may develop high blood pressure, ulcers, irritability, difficulty making routine decisions, loss of appetite and accident proneness.

Managing Stress

Management may not be concerned when employees experience low to moderate levels of stress. As they may, lead to higher employee performance.

But high levels of stress or even low level sustained over long periods can lead to reduced employee performance requiring actions by management.

A. Individual Approaches

- Implementing time management.
- Increasing physical exercise.
- Relaxation training.
- Expanding social support network.

B. Organisational Approaches

- Improved personnel selection and job placement.
- Training.
- Use of realistic goal setting.
- Redesigning of jobs.
- Increased employee involvement.
- Improved organisational communication.
- Offering employee sabbaticals.
- Establishment of corporate wellness programmes.

Stress can be either positive or negative influence on employee performance. For many people, low to moderate levels of stress enable them to perform their jobs better by increasing their work intensity, alertness, and ability to react.

Job related tension, tends to decrease job satisfaction and employees find stress dissatisfying.

Important Definitions

Organisational change is defined as change that has an impact on the way that work is performed and has significant effects on staff.

A learning organisation is the term given to a company that facilitates the learning of its members and continuously transforms itself.

Stress is a dynamic condition in which an individual is confronted with an opportunity, constraint, or demand related to what he or she desires and for which the outcome is perceived to be both uncertain and important.

Points to Remember

- **Change:** Making things different.
- **Planned Change:** Activities that are intentional and goal oriented.
- **Change Agents:** Persons who act as catalysts and assume the responsibility for managing change activities.
- **Goals of Planned Change:** Improving the ability of the organisation to adapt to changes in its environment. Changing the behaviour of individuals and groups in the organisation.

Forms of Resistance to Change

- Overt and immediate.
- Voicing complaints, engaging in job actions.
- Implicit and deferred.
    - Loss of employee loyalty and motivation, increased errors or mistakes, increased absenteeism.

Tactics for dealing with resistance to change:

- Education and communication
- Participation
- Facilitation and support
- Negotiation
- Manipulation and cooptation
- Coercion

Stimulants to Change:

- Impetus for change is likely to come from outside change agents.
- Internal change agents are most threatened by their loss of status in the organisation.
- Long-time power holders tend to implement only incremental change.
- The outcomes of power struggles in the organisation will determine the speed and quality of change.
- Impetus for change is likely to come from outside change agents.
- Internal change agents are most threatened by their loss of status in the organisation.
- Long-time power holders tend to implement only incremental change.
- The outcomes of power struggles in the organisation will determine the speed and quality of change.

Lewin's 3–Step Change Process:

- **Unfreezing:** Change efforts to overcome the pressures of both individual resistance and group conformity.

- **Driving Forces:** Forces that direct behaviour away from the status quo.

- **Restraining Forces:** Forces that hinder movement from the existing equilibrium.

- **Refreezing:** Stabilising a change intervention by balancing driving and restraining forces.

Creating a Learning Organisation

- **Single-Loop Learning:** Errors are corrected using past routines and present policies.

- **Double-Loop Learning:** Errors are corrected by modifying the organisation's objectives, policies, and standard routines.

- **Fundamental Problems in Traditional Organisations:**

    - Fragmentation based on specialisation.

    - Overemphasis on competition.

    - Re-activeness that misdirects attention to problem-solving rather than creation.

Managing a Learning Organisation:

Managing Learning

1. Establish a strategy

2. Reshape the organisation's culture

3. Redesign the organisation's structure

Stress

A dynamic condition in which an individual is confronted with an opportunity, constraint, or demand related to what he or she desires and for which the outcome is perceived to be both uncertain and important.

Questions for Discussion

1. What are the forces that act as stimulants to change?

2. What is Planned Change? How is it different from Unplanned Change?

3. What are the sources for resistance to change?

4. What are the different approaches to managing change?

5. How would you create a culture for change in the organisation?

6. What is stress? What are its potential sources?

7. What are the consequences of stress?

8. What are the individual and organisational approaches to managing stress?

Multiple Choice Questions (MCQ's)

Qs. 1-6:

State Whether True or False:

1. Planned Change is not activities that are intentional and goal oriented.

2. Change Agents are persons who act as catalysts and assume the responsibility for managing change activities.

3. The Goals of Planned Change are not improving the ability of the organisation to adapt to changes in its environment.

4. The goals of planned change are changing the behaviour of individuals and groups in the organisation.

5. Single-Loop Learning errors are not corrected using past routines and present policies.

6. Double-Loop Learning is errors are corrected by modifying the organisation's objectives, policies, and standard routines.

Qs. 7-10

Tick the most appropriate answers:

7. Forms of Resistance to Change are as follows:
   (a) Overt and immediate
   (b) Voicing complaints, engaging in job actions
   (c) Implicit and deferred loss of employee loyalty and motivation, increased errors or mistakes, increased absenteeism
   (d) all of the above

8. The following are the tactics for dealing with resistance to change:
   (a) Education and communication
   (b) Participation
   (c) Facilitation and support
   (d) Negotiation
   (e) Manipulation and cooptation
   (f) Coercion
   (g) All of the above

9. Lewin's 3–Step Change Process comprises of the following:
   (a) Unfreezing: Change efforts to overcome the pressures of both individual resistance and group conformity.
   (b) Movement takes place when:
       (i) Driving Forces: Forces that direct behaviour away from the status quo Overcome the

    (ii) Restraining Forces: Forces that hinder movement from the existing equilibrium.

    (c) Refreezing: Stabilizing a change intervention by balancing driving and restraining forces.

    (d) All of the above.

10. The following are Fundamental Problems in Traditional Organisations:

    (a) Fragmentation based on specialization.

    (b) Overemphasis on competition.

    (c) Re-activeness that misdirects attention to problem-solving rather than creation.

    (d) All of the above.

Qs. 11 to 20

Fill in the Blanks:

11. For a change to become routine and accepted into the day-to-day practices of an organisation, the organisation must go through the final stage of …… the organisational system.

12. Today's business environment requires companies to undergo …… almost constantly if they are to remain competitive.

13. Companies change under the impetus of enlightened …… who first recognise and then exploit new potentials dormant in the organisation or its circumstances.

14. To be successful, a technology change must be incorporated into the company's overall …… and a management structure must be created to support it.

15. Sometimes companies simply seek to change workers' attitudes and behaviours in order to …… their effectiveness or to stimulate individual or team creativeness.

16. Almost always …… changes are the most difficult and important part of the overall change process.

17. If the future after the change comes to be perceived positively, resistance will be …….

18. …… involves punishing people who resist or using force to ensure their cooperation.

19. Managing change effectively requires …… the organisation from its current state to a future desired state at minimal cost to the organisation.

20. Developing efficient ways to introduce and implement change can ease the …… your staffs feels when change is introduced, and it can also help your vendors, customers and business partners adjust to any changes in the way you do business.

Answers to MCQs:

1. False
2. True
3. False
4. True
5. False
6. True
7. d
8. g
9. d
10. d
11. Refreezing
12. Changes
13. Leaders
14. Systems
15. Increase
16. People
17. Less
18. Coercion
19. Moving
20. Stress

Case Study

Habits, customs and attitudes affect change as well. The marketing executives at Faircell were used to a fairly relaxed environment. Most have been with the company for several years and consider they are pretty secure in their positions. Since they are a tightly knit group of executives, they have habits, customs and attitudes that contribute to their arrogance.

They want to maintain the status quo. Management feels differently. Change means more profitability, and that is written into Faircell's corporate objectives.

Faircell's lacked systems to remain competitive. Marketing executives must endure extensive training and certification to continue working on their accounts. If no action is taken - well, no systems training and certification - there will be no jobs.

If change occurs, Faircell's gains a competitive edge against other leading marketing firms. Profits increase, and the execs experience job security.

Marketing executives resist change for many reasons. The executives just don't want to change the way things are done.

Faircel's management team identified their strategy of training and certifying marketing execs. It is the edge they need to compete in a marketing industry.

Eventually, marketing executives did get on board with training. Management strengthened the driving forces, like remaining competitive, and weakened the resistance to the inconvenience of training and studying. After much deliberation, management won. However, the training schedule was modified to allow execs to train during work hours and earn extra time off for hours spent studying and testing.

Question:

1. How did management convince this resistant group of marketing execs to go with the change?

Projects/Activities

1. Conduct a survey on how changes in the work force has affected organisational policies.
2. Conduct a survey on what steps organisations are taking to reduce employee stress.

QUESTIONS FROM PREVIOUS PUNE UNIVERSITY EXAMINATIONS

1. How do employees resist change? Illustrate your answer giving suitable examples.

[MBA April 2010]

Weblinks/Books

1. Stephen P. Robbins, Timothy Judge, Seema Sanghi *"Organisational Behaviour"*, 13th Edition.

DECEMBER 2013
M.B.A. (Semester I)
105: Organisational Behaviour
(2013 Pattern)

Time: 2 ¹/₂ Hours   Max. Marks: 50

Instructions to the candidates:
1. All questions are compulsory.
2. Each question has an internal option.
3. Each question carries 10 marks.
4. Figures to the right indicate marks for that question/sub question.
5. Your answers should be specific and to the point.
6. Support your answers with suitable live examples.
7. Draw neat diagrams and illustrations supportive to your answer.

Q. 1 (a) Explain the following statement "People influence organisations, and organisation influence people". **[10]**

OR

(b) Differentiate between cognitive, behaviouristic and social cognitive framework and support them with relevant example.

Q. 2 (a) Using Vroom's Expectancy Model Analyze following activity: **[10]**
   (i) Individual Efforts at workplace
   (ii) Performance Appraisals

OR

(b) Explain the Big-Five Model of personality with reference to Ms. Indra Nooyi CEO of PepsiCo as an example.

Q. 3 (a) Explain the Five-Stage model of group development and relate it with following groups.
   (i) Study Groups **[5]**
   (ii) Picnic Groups **[5]**

OR

(b) Explain the Leadership Theory with reference to following leaders
   (i) Mr. J. R. D. Tata – Transformational Leadership **[5]**
   (ii) Mr. Mahatma Gandhi – Charismatic Leadership **[5]**

Q. 4 (a) Explain what factors create and sustain an organisation's culture? **[10]**

OR

(b) Critically examine the concept of Organisational Spirituality.

Q. 5 (a) Using Kurt Lewin's three steps model explain how change is managed in organisations with example. **[10]**

OR

(b) Discuss what are the forces acts which as stimulator to change?

***

APRIL 2014
M.B.A. (Semester I)
105: Organisational Behaviour
(2013 Pattern)

Time: 2 $^1/_2$ Hours   Max. Marks: 50

Q. 1   (a)   "Organisational behaviour is a misnomer because it is not the study of how organisations behave but rather the study of individual behaviour in an organisation". Discuss briefly the three levels of analysis of organisational behaviour.   **[10]**

       (b)   "Organisational behaviour is relatively young field of study that borrows many concepts and methods from behaviour and social sciences". Comment. Also explain the challenges of OB in the content of present day environment.

Q. 2   (a)   "Most people believe that biological factors are important in determining the personality of a person", comment on this statement by taking various biological factors relevant for personality and their impact.   **[10]**

OR

       (b)   "Non-financial incentives are as strong as financial ones". Critically examine this statement in the light of Maslow's need hierarchy".

Q. 3   (a)   "High cohesiveness in a group leads to higher group productivity". Discuss. **[10]**

OR

       (b)   "Team building activities among company employees like mountain climbing increase productivity". Elaborate on this statement.

Q. 4   (a)   "The basic factor which determines human behaviour in an organisation is related to the quality of human relations". Discuss.   **[10]**

OR

       (b)   What are the main features of Indian Socio-Cultural factors? How do these features affect the behaviour of people in an organisation?

Q. 5   (a)   "Employee resistance is a symptom, not a problem in the change process". Explain and Discuss the methods of overcoming resistance to organisational change.   **[10]**

OR

       (b)   "The secret to real success is effective management of the emotional vulnerability that accompanies organisational change". Comment with relevant examples.

***

APRIL 2015
M.B.A. (Semester I)
105: Organisational Behaviour
(2013 Pattern)

Time: 2 $^1/_2$ Hours   Max. Marks: 50

Q. 1 (a) Why organisational Behaviour is needed to study in the modern era? Explain.

[10]

OR

(b) There are always limitations to study the field of social science. Discuss the limitations of an organisational Behaviour with examples.

Q. 2 (a) Financial or non financial motivation is a need human being in day to day work environment in the organisation. Explain with the help of A.H. Maslow's hierarchy theory of motivation.   **[10]**

OR

(b) Motivation helps to achieve the organisational goals-Discuss it with any one motivational theory.

Q. 3 (a) People in the organisation can't live alone, they join the group-Discuss Explain-How group efforts are important to achieve the organisational productivity.   **[10]**

OR

(b) An individual can't achieve the target but a team can do it more effectively - Discuss.

Q. 4 (a) Do you agree that organisational culture determine human behaviour in an organisation. It further helps to create healthy human relations - Explain.   **[10]**

OR

(b) Discuss the main feature of Indian culture and it's impact on sustaining the multi National companies business.

Q. 5 (a) Resistance to change is natural attitude of human being-Discuss with few examples.   **[10]**

OR

(b) Change always lead the business in this modern era-Explain and Discuss with examples.

***

APRIL 2015
M.P.M. (Semester I)
105: Organisational Behaviour
(2013 Pattern)

Time: 2 $^1/_2$ Hours   **Max. Marks: 50**

N.B.:

  (i)   All questions are compulsory.

  (ii)   Each question has an internal option.

  (iii)   Each question carries 10 marks.

1. (A)   Define Organization Behaviour. Explain relationship between OB and the Individual.

                                                                              [10]

                                          OR

    (B)   Explain the organizations perspectives of organizational effectiveness. Also explain role of people in organizational performance.   **[10]**

2. (A)   What is an 'Attitude' ? Explain the relationship between the Attitude and Behaviour.

                                                                              [10]

                                          OR

    (B)   Explain the meaning of Personality ? Enumerate the Big Five Personality Model with suitable examples.   **[10]**

3. (A)   Explain the meaning of "Conflict". Also explain the various types of conflict.   **[10]**

                                          OR

    (B)   What is contemporary leadership ? Explain the various issues involved in contemporary leadership.   **[10]**

4. (A)   Explain the meaning of "Organizational Culture". Also explain the importance of work place spirituality in organizational culture.   **[10]**

                                          OR

    (B)   What is "Organization Structure" ? Explain it with suitable example.   **[10]**

5. (A)   Explain the meaning of organizational change. Also explain the various types of organizational change.   **[10]**

                                          OR

    (B)   "Employees in the organization don't like to change in their routine work" Justify. Also suggest suitable steps to overcome the employee resistance to change.   **[10]**

                                          ✱✱✱

Appendix (For Chapter 4)

4.2 Stress Management

Work Stress: Meaning of Stress, Stressors, Sources of Stress, Types of Stress, Burnout, Stress Management - Individual and Organisational Strategies.

(A) Meaning and Definition of Stress

Stress, is an integral part of human existence. It has been with us in the past and most probably, will remain with us in future also. It is both an external and internal phenomenon. Over the years man has learnt to manage its external sources to a large extent but still has to learn to manage its internal sources – the sources which lie within the human nature. Many a times, stress is our own creation a manifestation of our anxiety and fear.

To understand stress as a managerial phenomenon, it can be defined as 'as fairly predictable arousal of phycho-biological (mind-body) system which is prolonged, can fatigue or damage the system to the point of malfunction or disease'.

Definition:

Stress is a general term to define tense situations and reactions to them, usually with a strong emotional content (**Gilmer**, **1984**).

Stress is the response to events that are threatening or challenging (**Feldman**, **2004**).

Nature of Stress:

Stress can occur in situations like: an examination, facing an interview, a surgery, hockey finals, a presentation, a family problem, a natural calamity or a communal riot. Despite its negative connotations, many experts believe that some level of stress is essential for well-being and mental health.

Spielberger defined stress as 'an interaction between the coping skills of the individual and the demands of his/her environment.

Stressors are circumstances and events that produce threats to our well-being. Stressors range from daily hassles like traffic jams to serious dangers like nuclear holocausts. The Life Events Scale lists these events as top ten stressors: death of spouse, divorce, marital separation, jail in term, death of close family members, personal injury or illness, marriage, being fired, marital reconciliation and retirement.

It is obvious from this list that even good things like marriage, retirement, marital reconciliation can cause substantial stress. Therefore, let us look at four types of stress: distress, eustress, hyperstress and hypostress.

(a) Eustress:

Eustress is positive stress or stress that creates a positive feeling. Exciting, challenging, joyous events, that we look forward to create eustress. For e.g. sports, competitions, festivals, celebrations, parties, marriage ceremony, foreign travel, a new job, winning a lottery, etc.

In fact, some people cannot sleep the day before a picnic or travel due to excitement. This stress is not harmful, and we find it exhilarating and refreshing.

Eustress is short-term. It strengthens people for immediate physical activity, creativity and enthusiasm. It arises in motivating and inspiring situations.

(b) Distress:

Distress is negative stress or a negative feeling associated with stress. We experience more distress and less eustress in our day-to-day life. Distress leads to anxiety, worry, anger, helplessness and depression. Lack of money, resources, sudden responsibilities, overwork, an examination can all lead to distress.

Disasters, bomb blasts, communal riots also cause a lot of distress.

In fact, the victims of major catastrophes experience **post-traumatic stress disorder** or PTSD, in which they re-experience the original stress event and associated feelings in vivid flashbacks or dreams.

Distress is negative and harmful stress that causes us to constantly readjust or readapt.

It can be divided into two types: **acute stress** or superficial, intense stress that can disappear quickly and **chronic stress** or prolonged stress that can linger for non-specific period.

(c) Hyperstress:

Hyperstress is also called 'overload'. This occurs when events pile up and stretch the limits of what people can deal with. It is excessive amounts of stress. For example, a housewife who has to cook, clean, look after guests, do shopping and other household chores will undergo this stress periodically.

(d) Hypostress:

Hypostress occurs when people are bored or unchallenged. It is an insufficient amount of stress. For e.g. a software engineer, who is benched, has no work, keeps waiting for work, feels hypostress. An old person, who is still energetic, physically and mentally healthy feels 'useless', has no routine or assigned work, may undergo hypostress.

The phenomenon of stress has different connotations for different people. Some people do very well under stress while some may buckle down to pressures. For every individual there is an 'optimum level of stress' for performance.

(B) The Phenomenon of Stress and Causes of Stress

Stress experienced by an individual is the product of two factors: Environmental Stimuli and Basic Anxiety. Environmental stimuli of a job related stress experienced by an individual could be the new job, inexperienced subordinates, bully type of boss, dark, dingy or congested work place etc. But the phenomenon of Basic Anxiety is rather complex. It is a legacy of man's early developmental period, and is related to his Birth Trauma and Dependency Syndrome. These two factors are discussed below:

(a) Birth Trauma: In the pre-natal stage of development when the child is in the mother's womb, it is in a blissful state. All its requirements of food, oxygen, comfort, are met without asking. But when it is born, its contact with that blissful state is broken, and it feels many pressures like those of gravity, noise, light, need for oxygen, etc. It is stunned by the change and is brought out of that stupor by the nurse's slap. It adjusts to, the new circumstances gradually, but it appears that certain amount of feelings related to birth trauma never leave the man and are varied by him to the years of adulthood also. Therefore, four fears — fear of darkness, fear of falling, fear of getting suffocated (in congested places), and fear of the unknown, are a part of human nature. However, depending upon the process of development in later years, different individuals would have these fears in different degrees.

(b) Dependency Syndrome: During the first five to seven years of its development, a child is entirely dependent upon others for survival. Not 'only its requirements of food, clothing and shelter, etc. are met by them, but they are also responsible for building up its confidence to combat the above mentioned four fears. This prolonged dependency upon others during the formative years instills a sense of inadequacy and inferiority in man. There is nothing wrong about it so long as it remains within limits. In fact, it is this sense of inadequacy which makes man a social and religious being. But when in excess, this sense of inadequacy makes mar, prone to stress. It creates a tendency in him to exaggerate the intensity and gravity of environmental few years of their retirement than in later years. Deprivation of meaningful stimuli, therefore, serves as the basis of stress of its own type.

(c) Frustration: Man lives in, a competitive world. In the pursuit of his objectives, he faces many obstalces both social and physical type. They may take the form of delays, losses or failures. They may prove unsurmountable causing intense frustration. Also, after achieving an objective through great effort and struggle a man may be struck by the ultimate meaninglessness of his pursuit. These frustrations too become the basis of stress in one form or the other.

(d) Adaptation: Certain situations force man to stretch, and summon up extra energy from his physiological system to meet their challenges. He may be required to run fast to catch an enemy, may have to pull a heavy weight over the precipice of a hill, may have to keep awake during the night for performing the night duty. The human physiological system is quite capable to cope with such contingencies but later it must rest to make good the chemicals expended for generating that extra energy. In other words, the system must attain its 'homeostasis'. If the extra energy is called up too often, the 'homeostasis' would suffer. That would adversely affect the health of the person.

Biological Factors:

The following constituents related to this factor are important:

(i) Biological Rhythm: Each individual has his own biological rhythm. It also gets modified, to a certain extent, by the environment in which he happens to live for long.

Individuals must give time to their biological rhythm to adjust to the changed surroundings. Otherwise, the quality of their judgement and decision likely to prove erroneous.

(ii) Nutrition: Diet which is deficient of protein, iron, calcium, salt, etc. can aggravate the stress proneness of an individual. Certain observations of medical experts in this regard are worth noting, especially for those who have crossed the age of forty since cell decay starts at about that time and keeps doubling every year thereafter:

- Restrict the intake of refined carbohydrates such as sugar, sweets, white starches etc.
- Take meals cooked in unsaturated fats like sunflower oil, corn oil etc.
- Avoid excessive intake of caffeineated beverages like coffee, tea, colas, chocolates etc.
- Reduce the intake of additives and preservatives which are used to soften, colour or flavour foods and drinks.
- Eat raw vegetables and fruits.
- Increase the quality of protein in your eats.
- Supplement your diet with vitamins B, C and E.
- Have large breakfast, medium lunch and light supper.

(iii) Noise: Both types of noise, biological and psychological, are distressful. However, grating type of noise and sudden bursts of high intensity noise, are stressful and injurious to human system than continuous noise.

Personality Factors:

This includes the dynamics of an individual's perceptions and attitudes which make him relatively more prone to the experience of stress. The important among these are:

(i) Self Concept: Carl Rogers has defined 'self' as a composite of all the ideas, perceptions, and values which formulate the 'I' and 'Me' of a man. It also includes the awareness of 'what I am and 'what I can do'. The self Concept, according to Rogers, influences mans perception of things and events, and his reactions to them. A man with a poor self-concept, therefore, is likely to magnify a situation of stress, while one with rich/high self-concept would weigh it realistically and face it boldly.

(ii) Type "A" Personality: This is also called coronary prone behavior of an individual, and is identified by a particular type of action-emotion-response pattern. A, man having this, type of personality is likely to reveal the following characteristics:

(aa) An intense sense of time urgency.

(ab) A high order achievement motivation which, however, may be lacking in clarity of goal.

(ac) An aggressiveness in interpersonal behavior which may make the individual incapable of 'playing for fun'. In fact, his 'gate-crashing type of behavior may arouse annoyance and jealousy of his colleagues, and may generate hostility in his surroundings; and

(ad) A tendency to get involved in multiple and diverse type of tasks at the same time, revealing lack of single-mindedness of purpose.

All the above mentioned factors can cause stress leading to the malfunctioning of human system in one manner or the other.

Causes/Sources of Stress:

Job stress or stress related to the workplace is "a condition arising from the interaction of people and their jobs, characterized by changes within people that force them to deviate from their normal functioning".   **– (Beehr and Newman)**

Job stress has become an important topic for the study of organizational behavior according to *Steers*. Stress at the workplace can originate from:

(a) The nature of the job.

(b) Job insecurity.

(c) Interpersonal conflicts.

(d) Workplace or Group culture.

(e) Performance demands.

(f) Structural factors at the workplace.

(g) Role related factors.

(h) Stress from other non-work areas such as technology.

(a) Nature of the job:

Pressures at the workplace involving job demands, time pressures, monotony of the job, frequent transfers, travel, moral conflicts can be casual factors of stress. Lack of organization and ill planned work environments can also lead to work related stress. The nature of the job itself, for example, jobs such as of those of the bomb squad, fire fighters, police etc. induce stress in an individual.

(b) Job insecurity:

Organized workplaces go through changes all the time due to economic constraints and consequent pressures. Reorganizations, takeovers, mergers, downsizing and other changes have become major stressors for employees as companies try to live up to the competition to survive.

(c) Interpersonal Conflicts:

Factors such as poor communication, interpersonal conflicts, unpleasant relationships, lack of group cohesion and many others can be sources of stress. Misunderstandings, colleagues or superiors who are difficult to work with, open conflict situations can lead to stressful situations.

(d) Workplace Culture/Group Culture:

Every organization has a workplace culture. Adjusting to this workplace culture, can be intensely stressful. Adapting oneself to the various aspects of an organization, such as communication patterns, hierarchy, dress code if any, workspace, and the most important of all, the working and behavioral patterns of the superiors and colleagues is very crucial to avoid stress. Maladjustment to the culture at the workplace can cause conflicts. Office politics or gossiping can also be major stress inducers.

(e) Performance Demands:

Unrealistic expectations in the form of increased workload, extremely long work hours, intense pressure to perform at peak levels all the time with no increase in salaries puts unhealthy and unreasonable pressures on employees. Excessive time away from family and the above given factors can leave employees physically and emotionally drained.

(f) Workplace Structural Factors:

Structural factors at the workplace include environmental factors such as noise, heat, poor ventilation, space, lighting, insufficient resources are sources of stress. Stress and strain are bound to take place when employees have to produce and perform with poor resources on a continuous basis.

These factors also include lack of a proper organizational structure, rules and regulations, reward systems, lack of career progress. They can lead to constant stress in the form of tension, fear of failure and many more.

(g) Role related factors:

An employee who does not get a clearly defined role to perform at the workplace and is confused about what is expected of him can feel stressed. This is also called *Role ambiguity*.

When an employee is asked to do different things by two or more superiors in the organization, *role conflict* occurs. The employee is given conflicting directions which act as stressors.

(h) Stress from non-work Areas:

Employees with personal or family problems have a tendency to carry their worries and anxieties to the workplace. Other stressors include unexpected changes in the market place, financial market, outside party demands, red-tape procedures etc.

(i) Technology:

The constant pressure to keep up with technological breakthroughs and improvisations, forcing employees to learn about computers, new software, machines etc. can lead to stress. The expansion of technology has resulted in increased expectations for productivity, speed and efficiency.

(j) Job Stress and Women:

Apart from common job stressors, employees especially women may suffer from mental and physical harassment at workplaces. A major source of worry for women has been sexual harassment. They may suffer from tremendous stress in the form of 'hostile work environment harassment' which is 'offensive or intimidating behavior in the worikplace'. Subtle discriminations at the workplace, family pressures and societal demands add to these stress factors.

(C) Types/Classification of Stress

Stress can be classified according to different criteria

1. According to effect:

❖   Positive Stress – Eustress

❖   Negative Stress – Distress

❖   Indifference to Stressor neutral stress – Neustress

2. According to Availability:

- ❖ Avoidable Stress – For e.g. responsibility
- ❖ Non-Avoidable Stress – For e.g. an accident

3. According to Intensity:

- ❖ Life - threatening Stress – For e.g. death
- ❖ Non-life threatening Stress – For e.g. school examination.

4. According to Levels:

- ❖ Extrinsic Stress at the Organizational level.
- ❖ Intrinsic Stress at the individual level.

5. According to emergence – Source of Stress.

- ❖ Adjustment Stress
- ❖ Adaptability Stress
- ❖ Confusion Stress
- ❖ Conviction Stress
- ❖ Ego Stress
- ❖ Situational Stress
- ❖ Frustration Stress

(D) Stress Management - Individual and Organisation Strategies

Major remedies used to alleviate and overcome stress are simple and straight forward. Normal individuals can restore balance without specialist consultation.

As people grow and mature they learn new ways of predicting and controlling most aspects of their everyday life. Adaptation is a continuous process and strategies for adaptation differ from one individual to other. Studies show that the ability to cope is largely inborn, but environment, training and practice can improve this ability.

Coping strategies for stress can be divided into three types.

(i) **Direct Coping:** It involves self-awareness in order to avoid the harmful and far-reaching consequences of stress. Activities in this strategy are intended to improve environmental accommodation or to change it. It deals with how to change the stress response from distress, from distress to eustress by getting to the root of the problem. Creating positive attitudes and regular physical exercise are two ways of using direct coping.

(ii)   **Defensive Coping:** It involves mental or physical escape from the stressful situation by automatic mental processes. The ego - defense mechanism is useful in preserving self-esteem, averting personality disorganization. Some of the more common defense mechanisms are Projection, Repression, Regression, Rationalization, Day-dreaming, and Displacement.

(iii)   **Dysfunctional Coping:** It involves maladaptive stress coping behaviors as a result of which individuals might become alcoholics, overweight, chain smokers or drug addicts. They become accident-prone, have suicidal tendencies, a tendency towards divorce with an increase in business breaks-ups and a low job performance.

Both organizations and individuals are highly concerned about stress and its effects. There are two types of deliberate coping strategies for dealing with job stress.

(a) Individual Strategies which tend to be reactive in nature. They include implementing time management techniques, increasing physical exercise, relaxation training and expanding a social support network. These strategies tend to be ways of coping with the stress that has already occurred.

(b) Organizational Strategies: These are proactive strategies, that act as preventive medicines by preventing the onset of stress for employees. The main idea behind these strategies is to remove existing or potential stressors.

A discussion on these individual and organizational approaches for stress management is given below in detail.

(a) Individual Strategies: According to this approach an employee can take personal responsibility for reducing his or her stress level. There are specific techniques that individuals can use to eliminate inevitable or prolonged stress. They are as follows:

(i)   **Time Management:** The well organized employee, accomplishes twice as much as the person who is poorly organized. If the employee can understand and utilize the basic time management principles, he can cope better with tensions caused by job demands. These basic time management principles are:

*　　Making list of activities to be accomplished.

*　　Prioritizing activities by importance and urgency.

*　　Scheduling activities according to the priorities set.

*　　Knowing your daily cycle and handling the most demanding parts of your job during the high part of your cycle when you are most alert and productive.

(ii) **Physical Exercise:** People of all ages can cope better with stress by doing physical exercises such as aerobics, walking, jogging, swimming or rigid exercises as a way to deal with excessive stress levels. Exercising increases heart capacity and provides mental diversion from work pressures, offering a means to let off steam.

(iii) **Relaxation Techniques:** Meditation, hypnosis and biofeedback are some of the main relaxation techniques. The intention of these techniques is to eliminate the immediately stressful situation, and reach a state of deep relaxation.

Meditation involves quiet, concentrated inner thought in order to rest the body physically and emotionally. The person slowly repeats a peaceful phrase or word or concentrates on a mental picture in a quiet location. A few organizations have established meditation rooms for employees with employees who meditate reporting favorable results.

Through biofeedback, in which a person gets feedback about internal body processes, an individual can control his heart beat, oxygen consumption and brain waves. Biofeedback is found to be helpful in reducing undesirable effects of stress.

Through these relaxation techniques one can detach himself/herself from the immediate environment, and from his/her body sensations. Fifteen to twenty minutes a day of deep relaxation releases tension and provides a person with a pronounced sense of peacefulness.

(iv) **Social Support:** Some people experience stress because they are detached from the world around them and lack warm interpersonal relationships. Individuals who have high ambition and a strong need for independence find it difficult to develop close attachments to friends and colleagues. This may result in anger, anxiety, and loneliness leading to stress.

Social support is a network of activities, interactions and relationships that provide an employee with the satisfaction of important needs. There are four types of support in a network:

Instrumental (task assistance); informational,; evaluative and emotional.

Social support may come from supervisors, co-workers, friends or family. Social support may take the form of games, jokes or teasing. Researchers suggest that when employees have at least one person from whom they can receive social and emotional support, they will experience lower stress. Social support provides you with someone to hear your problems and a more objective perspective on the situation.

(v) Behavioral Self-control: This strategy involves the individual controlling the situation instead of letting the situation control them. In this technique people deliberately manage the antecedents and consequences of their own behavior. For example, rewarding themselves when they remain calm and collective is part of the strategy. People can also become more aware of their limits and learn to avoid people or situations that they know will put them under stress.

(vi) Cognitive Therapy: Techniques such as Ellis's Rational Emotive model and Meichenbaum's Cognitive behavior modification strategy have been successfully used as individual strategies for reducing job stress. These strategies teach us to remain positive and avoid negative, self-defeating thoughts. This treatment consists of off-line lectures and interactive discussions.

(b) Organizational Strategies: In order to reduce job stress for individual employees, management designs coping strategies which either eliminate or control the organizational level stressors. These strategies include improved personnel selection and job placement use of realistic goal setting, redesigning of jobs, increased employee involvement, improved organizational communication and establishment of corporate wellness programs.

(i) Improved personnel selection and job placement: While selecting an individual for a particular job, management should consider that individuals differ in their response to stress situations. For example, experienced individuals with an internal locus of control may adapt better to high stress jobs and perform those jobs more effectively.

(ii) Use of realistic goal setting: Researchers have found out that individuals perform better when they have specific and challenging goals and receive feedback on how well they are progressing towards these goals. It has been proved that goal setting can reduce stress and also provide motivation. If an employee sets attainable goals role ambiguity and frustrations will be reduced.

(iii) Redesigning of jobs: Careful managing of task designs may be an effective way to cope with job stress. This is also called as enriching the job. This can be done in two ways,

1. By improving content factors such as responsibility, recognition and opportunities for achievement, advancement and growth.

2. By improving core job characteristics such as skill variety, task identity, task significance, autonomy and feedback.

Enriched tasks will eliminate the stressors found in routine, structured jobs. Thus redesigning of jobs can reduce stress because these factors give the employee greater control over work activities and lessen the dependence on others.

However, not all people respond favorably to enriched job designs, for example, individuals with low growth needs experience increased stress in an enriched job.

(iv) **Increased employee involvement:** When an employee feels uncertain about goals, expectations and how he will be evaluated, then there will be a large extent of role stress. In order to reduce this stress organizations should make the structure more decentralized and organic. Management should create a supportive organizational climate with participative decision making and upward communication flows.

Employees should give voice to those decisions that directly affect their job performances. Thus by increasing employee involvement in decision making, management can increase employee control and reduce role stress.

(v) **Improved organizational communication:** If management increases formal communication with employees, it will reduce role ambiguity and role conflict. Role conflict and ambiguity are the major individual stressors. In order to clarify specific roles, employees should be given a list of management's expectations. This list should be compared with an employee's expectation about his job. The differences should be openly discussed to clarify ambiguities and negotiations should be made to resolve conflict.

Management can also use effective communication as a means to shape employee perceptions. Interpretation of any event as demands, threats or opportunities can be affected by the symbol and actions communicated by management.

(vi) **Establishment of corporate wellness programs:** The assumption underlying wellness programs is that employees need to take personal responsibility for their physical and mental health. Through these programs, organizations provide workshops on how to quit smoking, how to control alcohol, how to lose weight, eat better and develop a regular exercise program. Most organizations who have introduced wellness programs have found that these programs are beneficial for employees who participate in them thus claiming less health expenses, and asking for fewer sick leaves.

Phases of Stress Management:

Stress management can be divided into **two phases**; the first is **coping with stress** and the second is **counteracting the stress** response with the help of relaxation response. There are **five methods for coping with stress:**

1. **Avoidance:** In this method particular stressors are never met and are avoided.

2. **Evasion:** In this method stressors are side - stepped so as to postpone stress reactions.

3. **Diversion:** One's mind is distracted from potential stressors by developing hobbies like drawing, gardening, photography, reading. Diversion can be made by frequent visits to movies, hotels, and shopping malls, participating in sports, picnics or by visiting religious places.

4. **Preparations:** In this method, an individual prepares himself mentally, nutritionally and physically to cope up with stress.

5. **Eustress response:** In this method an individual tries to change his response of distress to eustress with the help of a positive and optimistic mental attitude and regular physical exercise.

The second phase of stress management is counteracting stress response. In this method the individual tries to elicit relaxation response by indulging in a restful sleep or taking a nap. There are various techniques to elicit a relaxation response, for example, self-hypnosis, meditation, and biofeedback. Proper use of massage, heat and cold are also refreshing and relaxing.

Beyond all these measures, the individual has to develop a stress management philosophy to serve him as a guide.

Skills for effective Stress Management:

* Earning one's neighbor's love and respect.

* Developing a positive attitude with an optimistic outlook

* Developing a sense of humor.

* Proper management of time.

* Learning to be assertive: This includes the ability to say no, ability to make requests and ask for favors, ability to express positive and negative feelings.

    The ability to generate, continue and terminate discussions is also a part of being assertive.

*   Learning to understand ones own emotions.

*   Recognizing the inevitable and learning to accept it.

Effective Stress Management advice us to remember to points, "Treat Stress as your friend not Foe" and "Anticipate Stress and Be prepared."

Remedial Measures

"We is another name of a long sequence of stresses," said Mirza Galib, the great Urdu poet. For a living man there is no escape from difficulties, problems and stresses, added the great poet.

However, they must remain within controllable limits to make life positive and productive. There are a number of steps which can be taken to exercise this control. These steps which relate both to improving OSL as well as recovering from the adverse effects of stresses faced, are described below in the succeeding paragraphs.

Reducing Overload:

(a)   Define the parameters of your job to avoid role conflict.

(b)   Learn to divide your task into stages and phases.

(c)   Develop the technique of saying a polite but firm NO where necessary.

(d)   Learn to delegate and develop interdependence in the performance of task-related activities.

(e)   Save yourself from self-imposed pressures like working for promotion and MBA examination simultaneously.

(f)   Set your professional and non-professional goals realistically.

Avoiding Frustration:

(a)   Determine your OSL and set your objectives taking that into account. The OSL can be determined by taking tests of Anxiety, Tolerance for Ambiguity, Self-Concept, etc. which are available with behavioral scientists.

(b)   Have an alternative goal to pursue. Let that be a part of your original planning process.

(c)   Accept vulnerability to deprivations. No one can get everything he desires.

(d)   Accept fallability. No one is perfect. Each one of us would have one fault or the other. Knowing it and accepting it as a part of life lessens the intensity of pain caused by the imperfect aspect of the personality.

Improving Adaptation:

    (a)   Plan your activities using foresight to meet the future, critical events.

    (b)   Set apart time for different types of activities like meeting, visitors attending meetings, handling important files, taking critical decisions, etc.

    (c)   Make minimum changes in your work situation, and where necessary, make these changes after deliberation and discussion with the concerned staff.

    (d)   Balance your life with work, social and recreational activities.

    (e)   Learn to relax through the pursuit of a non-ego involving activity like fishing.

Develop Positive Personality:

    (a)   Verbalise your positive qualities. It is a part of auto-suggestion technique.

    (b)   Accept compliments. Generally, we Indians are too modest to accept compliments paid to us for the positive efforts and achievements made by us. That amounts to negating one's personality. Compliments earned through efforts must be accepted to become a part of our self-concept.

    (c)   Practice assertiveness. There is no use compromising your status and position to earn cheap popularity. In fact, you can enhance the effectiveness of your position by letting others know that you are quite capable of taking hard actions and firm decisions'.

    (d)   Engage thought stopping. Retrospection and reflection must become a part of your work routine. Give a few minutes to go over the activities of last few hours. Consider if all the hectic activities performed by you during the last week were necessary. Re-adjust - your work schedule, if required.

Going through stress leaves behind certain toxic matters in the body system; they must be made good and homeostasis achieved before the system is made to face another bout of stress. The following steps, can be taken in this regard:

    (a)   Certain amount of physical exercises especially proper yoga exercises, can help in 'burning off' toxic matters and preparing the system to meet the next challenge.

    (b)   Certain amount of energy loss can be made good through dietary control. Otherwise also a nutritive and balanced diet can keep the system in good gear.

    (c)   Spending, some time with the members of your family just chit-chatting and listening to their stories of achievements and failures, can help a person a lot in acquiring emotional balance and mental peace.

(d) For acquiring a balanced attitude towards life and its vagaries, taking recourse to meditation has been recommended by all religions. Hinduism calls it shay asana, Christianity calls it the prayer of the Heart, Jain Buddism calls it zazen, Judaism has named it as Rabbi Abulafia, Mystics of Islam call it Dhikr, and so on. Even medical examinations have revealed that meditation helps in bringing down blood pressure and its associate concomitants. There are various methods of meditation but the essence of all is controlling major muscle groups, one by one, for a short period, and then relaxing, which the individual focusses on breathing deeply and with regularity. However, it is advised that this practice must be learnt from a master or a Guru.

Balance Sheet of Stress:

Human personality develops through facing difficulties, solving problems and going through stresses. The more varied the problems the better. Relevance of the old saying, "Failures are the pillars to success", can also be seen in this light. Stress, therefore, is the spice, nay tonic for the development of a healthy and mature personality. After passing through a period of stress, a new, a better man emerges. The following points are worth noting in this regard:

(a) Through his experience of a difficult situation, a person may get a clearer picture of his assets, liabilities, and adaptive potential. He may acquire a new understanding of his self.

(b) After failing in a test, a person may start putting in more effort and may devise more effective methods of studying and learning. That may increase his competence.

(c) What we call innovativeness is nothing but finding a new way to solve the old nutty problem.

(d) Each failure gives a man an idea about the difference between his capabilities and his aspirations. It makes him more realistic and practical.

(e) By living through difficulties and stresses, a man can develop greater confidence in his abilities to face similar situations in future. In other, words, facing, stress increases a person's 05L. Stress therefore, chastens life. It purifies life. It is the fire of life. However, we must learn to manage it to serve as OSL.

***